~10 years earlier

"It's just the four of us now guys," she whispered, holding her teen-aged children close as they lowered her husband of twenty years into the ground.

His heart attack had been something the cardiologist had called a "widow-maker" and true to form, it was. On Monday, she'd played a round of golf with Jared, and here she was on Saturday, burying him. The doctor had said that he'd died instantly and most likely, simply dropped in his tracks, without experiencing any pain; a fact, whether true or not, that she'd hold on to. As she looked into the expressionless face of her son, she saw her beloved Jared's profile and posture. Joshua, her oldest, reminded her so much of what Jared had looked like when they'd met their freshman year at Utica College.

After playing Junior B hockey for a few years following high school, he was attending on an academic scholarship, and although she knew nothing about the sport, she quickly learned to love it, and the captain of the team. Knowing there'd be no academic or sports scholarship for her, Elizabeth had decided to work a few years before applying to various colleges that offered Nursing degrees. Not because she necessarily needed to attend a private school, but because Utica College had the first available opening. When accepted into their fall semester of nursing, Elizabeth jumped on the chance and scraped

1

together every cent she could to avoid hefty student loans. Within a month of starting school that fall of 1984, Jared and Elizabeth became inseparable. They were engaged immediately upon graduation, married that same fall and had spent the last two decades completing each other sentences, sharing parenting responsibilities and simply enjoying their time together. His death hadn't even begun to sink in, despite being the one who had to make all the funeral arrangements for a man that wasn't supposed to die for at least another four decades. She'd been forced to make the unbearable calls to family and friends to deliver the news. Though it would have been so much easier and mentally less taxing to simply post his death on Facebook, or as a group text, she felt that each person, whether family or close friend, deserved to be notified personally. Standing here now, as the hoists lowering her husband into his last permanent home on this earth stopped, the finality of his death hit. Elizabeth found herself feeling faint and if not for the loud sob that her youngest tried hard to suppress, she knew that she too, might have ended up on the cold, rain-soaked ground. But hearing her daughter Deidre's wail snapped Elizabeth back to the here and now. Squeezing her tighter, she whispered into her ear. Through her tears, Deidre allowed a smile to form on her face, and nodded in silent solidarity with her mother. Margaret, or Maggie May, her middle child didn't know what her mother had said but was thankful that her little sister was finally done losing it. Always the analytical one, she never understood the value in crying, because in her eyes, it wouldn't solve a thing and all it did was ruin your makeup, make your eyes puffy and if prolonged enough, give you a splitting headache. She was also breaking inside at the loss of her father, her role model and the only male she'd ever loved, beside her brother of course; but she refused to break down in front of all of the people standing beside and behind her. Some things were meant to be done in private, and Maggie would mourn in her own way and in her own time. For now, she'd be the pillar that her mom and sister would need and knew that it was up to she and Josh to step up and help their mom keep the family unified, the way their father would have wanted. The spring of 2006 was when everything changed.

~Chapter 1~

"Mom, momma, are you in pain?" Deidre whispered, holding back tears, as she held her mother's hand. Joshua and Maggie stood behind their younger sister, staring down at what had become of their strong, vibrant mother. After their father's sudden death, Elizabeth, though forced to do so, had taken on the role of both father and mother to her three children with zest and vigor and had never let them see her down, depressed, or pitying herself. Sure, they'd seen her sad on occasions; especially when Jared's birthday rolled around, or during the Christmas season; but despite it all, Elizabeth was always there for her three children and defeat was not an option or part of her vocabulary. Now here she was, a shell of the woman they'd all looked up to, withering away hour by hour as Morphine pumped into her veins as the rapidly growing cancer aggressively tried to take their mother. Elizabeth faded in and out of consciousness as the medicine served its' intended purpose. Her disease might have taken her strength, her hair, and withered her weight down to near emaciation level, but it had not stolen her courage, and desire to live. She knew, whether while conscious or in her subconscious, that she'd fight her battle until the very end. For the grace of God, when she woke from the dreams that seemed to be lasting longer and longer, and coming more frequently, she woke lucid. When awake, she spoke to her children as if the end was approaching but promising them that everything was going to be alright. She'd raised Joshua, Maggie and Deidre to be fiercely independent, ambitious and motivated. She prayed that she'd done right by her three precious children, the culmination of her undying love for her Jared; and knew in her heart that although she'd be reunited with her true love soon, her heart ached for the ones she'd leave behind. She also realized that her time was running short and it was time to tell them about Michelle Marie, before it was too late.

Over the years she'd rehearsed it repeatedly, when and how she'd tell them, and a few times had come so close to telling them about their sister. She'd even used her best friend as a trial run so to speak, but Brenda's shocked expression revealed her worst fear; and the thought of telling her children that she'd had a child before she'd met their father terrified her.

When she'd fallen for Jared, actually before she'd admitted to herself or to him that she'd fallen in love with him, she'd been upfront and brutally honest with him. She wanted their relationship to be built on trust, love, honesty and respect, and knew that in order to do that, she'd have to tell him the truth. He'd listened silently as she told him about Daniel and the child they'd conceived. She told him about the home for unwed mothers that her parents had insisted she reside in until after she'd given birth. Elizabeth explained to Jared, through tears about how heartbreaking it had been to go through labor alone, to name their daughter, care for her, and then, with the stroke of a pen, sign away all of her rights to the daughter she'd come to love. She knew that she was doing the right thing for her daughter and knew that she and Daniel couldn't take care of an infant, with their minimum wage, after school jobs, but the truth hadn't made it any less painful for her when it came time to relinquish her rights. They'd been only eighteen and both had their lives planned out before them, and having a baby wasn't part of the plan. She'd tried to convince herself that doing the selfless thing was the only answer to guarantee her daughter a better future. But when Daniel came to pick her up in Buffalo and bring her back home, one week after she'd given birth to their daughter; she knew that she'd sold her soul for the sake of convenience and her good name. As they rode in virtual silence along the thruway, she knew that giving up their daughter for adoption, had been the beginning of the end of their relationship.

It had taken less than two months for Daniel to forever change their relationship. She'd never forgotten the night that her entire world came crashing down. The date was Saturday, October 9th, when Daniel picked her up just before seven. She'd checked her hair one last night before rushing out to meet him. He'd rang her doorbell but hadn't entered her parent's home, the way he always had during the two years they'd been together. She known before she'd even climbed up in the cab of his truck that something was horribly wrong.

Within an hour, she was back home, sobbing in her room. He'd told her that he still loved her but couldn't continue living his life like it was make believe. He tried the best he could to describe his feelings, stating that it wasn't right that they'd given up their child, and that in a sense, she'd given up on him. He admitted that he'd been terrified when she'd told him that she was pregnant and had been silently relieved when she said that she was giving it up for adoption. Through tears of his own, he told her that it wasn't fair that he'd never even gotten to hold his own child. Daniel explained to her that maybe their relationship wasn't as strong as they thought it was, because if it had been, they both would have fought harder to come up with a way to keep their daughter. As he listened to the words leaving his mouth, he knew that it sounded like he was blaming her for making the decision; but deep down, he knew that he was blaming himself for not asking her to marry him and keep their family together.

He reassured her that he wanted to stay together and promised her that maybe someday when they were older and more ready to be parents, they could find their daughter, and let her get to know her first set of parents. Those words were what finally broke Elizabeth's heart for she knew that their one chance to be Michelle Marie's parents had come and gone, and now and forever she would simply be her daughter's biological incubator, not her mother. Daniel had wanted to tell her that he'd dropped out of school to take a job at his father's insurance company so they could be together, but she didn't seem to understand how disappointed he was in her lack of empathy towards his feelings. When he couldn't get through to her, he simply brought her back home.

When Elizabeth wouldn't pick up the phone when he called, nor return his call despite his begging, he knew that the baby that filled each of his waking moments was the reason. He, with his parent's blessings, tried to contact Catholic Charities to gain custody of his daughter and legally adopt her. Elizabeth had never named who the father was, but Daniel knew that he was, and after numerous discussions with his parents, told them that he wanted to remove her from foster care and raise his daughter with or without Elizabeth's help. His parents hired a lawyer and filed a formal petition to legally adopt Michelle Marie, but it was too late. He and his parents were notified, through their lawyer that his infant daughter had already been adopted by a childless couple earlier that month, and was already settled in their home. It was only then that Daniel realized how his Elizabeth must have felt surrendering their daughter.

He, like Elizabeth, sulked in his bedroom as day turned to night and back to day again. He had never experienced such pain and knew that until he was reunited with his little girl someday, his heart would never be whole again. He'd lost the love of his life when Elizabeth had been coerced into giving away their daughter, and lost his soul when Michelle Marie became someone else's child.

Knowing he couldn't go back to college, wouldn't be able to face the familiar faces of all the employees at his father's insurance company, and still unable to convince Elizabeth to see him; Daniel felt like he'd suddenly slipped into a void with no way out. He'd never known that at age eighteen, when everyone said that your teenage years are the best years of your life, he could experience such complete and utter despair. His entire existence had lost meaning and with no direction that meant anything to him anymore, he felt more lost than he ever had in his life. All of that changed when he stopped to put a few dollars of gas into his hand me down truck.

"You need help with that sir," he asked.

At first the old man hadn't heard Daniel's question. Hunched over, fighting with a sticking gas cap, he didn't know anyone was speaking to him until he saw a weathered Columbia hiking boot step up next to his own boot. He stopped fussing with the rust on his gas cap and looked up into the eyes of a stranger and was greeted by a smile.

Daniel didn't ask, as he could clearly see the old man's frustration in his eyes, he just acted.

"Here sir, let me give you a hand with that." Daniel gave the slightly rusty Camaro a hard knock where the gas cap met the side panel, and then twisted firmly and steadily until it loosened.

"Wow, that sucker was on there pretty tight! When's the last time you put gas in her sir?" Daniel asked, eyeing the old man, who now seemed to stand a little taller and straighter after watching the youngster struggle with the same cap that he'd just been fighting with.

"I reckon, the last time old Betsy here had a fill up was June 1st, 1969. That's the day before my boy left for Basic Training on a fast track for Vietnam," he answered in a tone that reveled in pride and sadness. "I promised him I wouldn't drive her until he came home. He didn't come home," he said flatly, as if there was no more emotion left in him.

"She's sat in my garage for years now and I'm getting too old to drive such a hot rod, so I figured I'd take her for one last spin before I sell her."

"She sure is beautiful," Daniel said, as he made small talk with the stranger as he pumped the gas. He wanted to ask what happened to the man's son but already knew. He'd known other families who'd lost their son's to the Viet-Cong and jungles of Vietnam, and seen others who'd made it home, but not in one piece.   As he finished pumping the old man's gas and replacing the nozzle, he looked down at the blue eyes that he now noticed were analyzing him.

"You look a lot like my Johnny you know. He was tall and strong and had just enough meat on his bones and muscle to fill out a shirt much the way you do. I wanted him to be an electrician like me, but he wanted to serve his country. He told me once when I tried to talk him out of it "That it was something he had to do and that he wanted to give back. "He thought he could make a difference in people's lives and I guess that he really did," he said proudly, "well that is until they shot the chopper down that he was in," he finished softly, with one lone tear running down his cheek. "Anyways," he said, casually trying to wipe the tear away. "Thank you for filling her up. Now time for her bath and styling at the car wash, and she'll be ready to sell," he smiled, extending his hand out to shake Daniel's as he stood there.

"You're welcome," Daniel replied as he took the man's arthritic hand. His hands looked weathered, but his grip remained firm as he shook the teen's hand. It was at that moment that Daniel had two epiphanies, one was what career path he could pursue that might actually make a difference in his now shattered life, and the second was simply a gut reaction to the old man's story.

"What are you asking for your Camaro sir," Daniel asked, knowing that he could never afford it, but felt with every ounce of his being that he was supposed to have it.

"Not sure yet," he answered honestly, and then with a twinkle in his eye, he knew what was the correct asking price. "What do you think it's worth?" he asked noncommittedly.

"I don't honestly know sir. Even with the rust, she sure is a sweet looking car. Not sure what she's worth but I know the $2200 I have in my savings isn't enough to have her," he answered honestly.

The old man paused for less than five seconds before he answered. "Tell you what son," he said with a tone of authority that gained Daniel's immediate attention, "You promise me that you'll take good care of Betsy, and promise me that you'll make a difference, a real difference in this world of ours, and she's yours for $1800. How does that sound? But I want your word, man to man, that you'll never abuse her, never race her, and cherish her the way my boy did. You give me your word, and she's yours."

Not quite sure what to say, and having a hard time believing that this stranger standing before him, would sell his Camaro just like that. Also, not sure what his parents would say, despite the fact that the money in the bank was savings that he'd earned himself, and less than a week ago had been more than willing to spend it on attorney's fees to get his daughter back, he hesitated just briefly. Seeing his reluctance, the elderly gentleman asked him to speak his mind.

"Well sir, I have the savings and would gladly give you every cent of it, but I feel that I need to speak with my parents before making such a huge decision. Can you give me a day to discuss it with them?"

"I have a better idea son. Are your parents' home right now?" he asked, wanting to seize the moment.

"Yes sir, they are."

"Good, how about you lead the way and I'll follow you over to your place, so they can check her out for themselves and then you can take her for a test drive."

Smiling, Daniel could hardly contain his excitement. For the first time in days, he felt like a weight was lifted off his shoulders. He'd hopefully buy this man's pride and joy, and if all went well, he'd ask his dad to keep it in storage until he came home from serving his country. He didn't know what branch the old man's son had served in but looking at the wings clipped to his tattered cap, he assumed either father or son must have been a pilot. And upon looking at that simple symbol affixed to his cap, knew that he would be as well.

He drove the few miles out of town toward his home. As he drove, he continuously checked his rear-view mirror, making sure he wasn't going too fast. It was then that he realized that he didn't even know the old man's name. Luckily for him, he was greeted by his father in the drive.

"Hey Joe!" he shouted warmly to his long-time friend.

"What brings you out to our neck of the woods," he asked as he walked over to shake his hand. "Say, isn't that your boy Johnny's ride? She sure is a beauty," he remarked as he peered in the window, admiring the cream colored leather interior. Daniel stood silently watching the exchange.

"Good memory my friend. She sure is. And if it's alright with you and the misses, she's about to become your boy's new toy." Before Daniel's father could even respond, Joe Murray squelched any possibility of an argument.

"Your boy and I have already worked out the amount, but you sure did raise him right Hank. He insisted that we bring old Betsy here for you to inspect yourself before he said yes to me. I know a responsible lad when I see one, and if it's alright me saying so, you raised a fine son Hank.

And I know my Johnny would be tickled pink to know that his baby is going to someone who will love her like he did. It's been a long time since she's been driven the way my Johnny used to enjoy her. So, what do you say, is it okay that I sell her to your son?" he asked, extending out his hand to seal the deal.

Not quite ready to give in yet, Joe looked at his son, who remained silent, and then back at his friend.

"So you say you've agreed on a price?"

"That's right Hank. It's a fair deal and one that I know you'd approve of. Your boy says he's got the money saved up in the bank, and" winking at Daniel, who remained silent listening to the exchange, and praying his father would say yes, "he knows that he'll be responsible for the insurance premium as well."

Joe took his friends hand and shook it. "It sounds like you two have got it all figured out then. I'd say you have a deal, under one condition," Joe responded, turning toward his son.

Trying to contain his excitement, Daniel stepped to attention in front of his father. "Sure dad, anything..."

A huge grin appeared across his father's face. " I always wanted a hot rod like this baby, so I want two things; one, I want to ride with you when you take her for a test drive, and two, I want to be able to drive her someday."

Instead of shaking his father's hand like he would typically do; instead, he pulled him into a huge bear hug.

"Yes sir. Of course, sir!" he nearly shouted.

"Well if you would be so kind as to give me a ride back to town, I'll let you gentleman get to know Johnny's "Betsy" here. She'll give you years of pleasure and as long as you don't abuse her, she'll be a fun, dependable ride for as long as you own her."

Looking at his watch, Daniel felt the bottom drop out from under him when he realized the time. It was already after four and the bank would already be closed for the day, and he knew that the ATM wouldn't allow him to withdraw enough to cover the cost of the car.

"Sir, I can't get the money out of the bank until the morning," he announced, sounding defeated.

"Son," the old man chuckled. "We shook, didn't we? And a deal's a deal. I know where you live, and I've known your father all my life, so your word is good with me. You can bring me the money anytime this week, there's no rush."

With that, he tossed the keys towards Daniel and shook his long-time friend's hand before leaving.

"Support whatever he tells you Hank. He's got a good head on his shoulders, and he's going to make a difference in this world, you just wait and see. And my friend, when he tells you his plans, don't react the way our parents did; just encourage and support him. He's had to deal with a lot recently and he needs direction."

Having no clue what his friend was talking about and knowing that there was no way he could have known about Elizabeth's baby, the child she and Daniel had given up, he shook the extended hand of his oldest brother's best friend and mouthed "Thank You."

It took Daniel only a few minutes to drive the old man home, turning as directed. He kept his new car well below the speed limit, as both he and the car got to know one another. She practically purred as he accelerated, and he could feel the slight vibrations from the steering wheel that she was dying to hit the highway and show him what she was made of. But that would have to wait for another day. As he pulled into the long drive as Hank directed, he came to a halt in front of a tiny Cape Cod. The driveway hid the home from the road and it was only then that Daniel could see the chipping paint, and broken shutters. He looked around, making a mental list of what the house needed to look more rejuvenated. And then he had an idea.

He turned toward his passenger and offered nonchalantly, "Sir, I would like to bring you the money on Saturday if that's alright with you. And since you gave me more than a fair deal, would you let me help you spruce up your home just a little? I'm not much with a paintbrush, but if you'd like, I'd come by on Saturday morning and scrape those few spots you've got chipping and touch up the paint on the shutters for you. Sort of like an additional payment for selling me Betsy."

Knowing from the tone of his voice and the gleam in his eye, that the teen sitting beside him, where his own boy used to sit, had something up his sleeve. But as he had nothing to lose, he played along with him.

"I suppose that would be alright. It's hard for me to balance myself on a ladder and living alone, I don't want to fall off and break my neck," he laughed. "They might not find me for quite some time and that isn't part of the plan!" he laughed. "So how about I pick up some scapers, paint, and a few brushes between now and Saturday and when you come, I'll let you help me tidy this place up a bit. You do a good job and I'll order us a pizza; how does that sound?"

"Yes sir Mr. Murray, I'll be here, and I'll take you up on that pizza," he answered, watching the old man climb out of the car and start towards his run-down home.

It took a second to sink in that he was presently sitting in his new Camaro, a car he'd dreamt of all his teenage years. Its' candy apple red paint was still as showroom bright as the day it'd left the dealership, but currently had several years of dust dulling its' sheen. He didn't turn the radio on during the ride back into town. Instead he listened to the sound of the engine and let his mind wander. He made a mental note to ask his father what had happened to Mr. Murray's son, and also came up with a list of friends that he could elicit help from, with the bribe of pizza and maybe a few cold beers.

He thought about Elizabeth and how much he still loved her and wanted to show her his new ride. He started to turn onto the road leading towards her home, but pulled over as soon as he made the turn. Sitting there, ecstatic about his new car, but still crushed over losing his daughter and ultimately her mother, Daniel felt like he was at a crossroads in life. Going to Elizabeth's now to show off his new car, made it feel like nothing had changed between them, when in fact, everything was different. Admitting to himself for the first time since surrendering their daughter, he allowed himself to acknowledge how furious and disappointed he was in her. He admitted to himself that he resented her for discarding their child like Michelle was a piece of trash. Yes, he knew that if they'd kept Michelle Marie, his life plan would have to change; but damn it, who was she to make that decision for him? She never gave him the option of keeping his daughter, instead, she took it upon herself to make the decision for the two of them and signed away his rights with the stroke of her pen. For the first time in a week, he finally admitted to himself how pissed he was at her and that what had been such a great relationship, would never be the same. She had treated their daughter like an inconvenience and sitting there now, realized that he'd never feel the same way about her again. He'd always thought that they'd be together forever but realized now, that she was not the same person that he'd thought she was, and if she could make decisions without his consent, so could he. Putting his new toy in gear, he turned around and away from Elizabeth, and headed toward a new chapter in his life, which would start when he announced to his parents that he was joining the military.

~Chapter 2~

Joe Murray rose at 0600, the same way he had all his life. He shuffled his way from his tiny bedroom to his kitchen. Before starting his percolator, he bent down to pet Fritz, the orange tabby cat who'd marched himself into his home nearly three years before and had never left. Fritz was ornery and headstrong, and that suited Joe just fine. The two of them had their morning routine, and just because it was Saturday, Fritz made it very clear that he still needed his Friskies and warm bowl of milk before anything delayed his breakfast. Once Fritz was fed, and given a little attention, Joe set about making his own breakfast. Two slices of bacon, one fried egg, two slices of toast and a donut. He'd had the exact same breakfast for the last three decades. The day he was honorably discharged from the Air Force was the last day he'd leave the table still hungry he'd promised himself, and to this day, he'd make sure that his breakfast was substantial enough to carry him over until lunch. Joe liked to eat and despite a frame that was hunched due to too many years of hard work, and arthritis; he still packed away more in a meal than most men twice his size.

Breakfast came and went, dishes followed afterward, and then finally it was time for round two of his freshly perked coffee. Filling his cup to the brim, he sat down in his favorite leather chair to read the newspaper. Joe had never understood, how anyone could drink instant coffee. He took pride in trying new brands of coffee but would never settle for tearing open a packet and adding hot water and calling it a "cup of Joe". It was preposterous to him to think that in a world where everyone wanted extravagance, that someone wouldn't take the time to perfect the most important staple of the morning. His coffee was his lifeline to the world and if he didn't have his two cups of freshly brewed coffee each morning, the world would have to wait!

It took a moment to hear the approaching vehicles. He got out of his chair after gently nudging Fritz off his lap and made his way to his front porch. He couldn't help but grin as he watched the parade of pickups, cars and one oversized station wagon make their way down his gravel drive. He could tell from the music blasting from their speakers, Zeppelin, Skynyrd, and what he thought might be Hendrix, that Hank's son had been true to his word, and was not only reporting for duty as promised, but was obviously bringing in reinforcements. His heart nearly burst at the greetings as he counted seven lanky, but strong looking teens climb out of their respective vehicles.

"Good morning Mr. Murray. Hope you don't mind that I brought some extra hands to get your home spruced up," Daniel smiled. "I figured the more help we have, the faster we can get everything done. And you don't need to feed us sir, I'll take care of the extra pizzas," he added, seeing a look on the old man's face that he didn't know how to decipher. "They're here because they wanted to say thank you to you for your service and for your son's service and sacrifice," he stated matter of factly, but very sincerely.

Joe stood as tall as his body would allow and willed the emotion that he was feeling away. The sight of the group of teens had caught him temporarily by surprise and given him flashbacks of Johnny and his gang of friends who would invade his little homestead all the time. The clothing styles might have changed a bit, but teenagers were still teenagers, with their beat-up trucks and loud music. He saw the group watching him and he stood silently on his weathered porch. Oh, how he missed his boy and the times like this; but those days were long gone, and he'd enjoy today as if his boy were still with him and these were his friends.

"Think I'm gonna need a few more pizzas," he announced, letting a big smile form on his face. "Time's a wasting, so what do you say, we get this place spruced up a bit, and then we'll eat," he offered, making his way down to meet the young men approaching him. "Let's get going and maybe I'll join you boys down at the river later this afternoon. Don't think I don't see those rods in the back of your truck boy," he chuckled. "I might be old, but I'm not blind," he laughed.

He started giving directives to the teens, with each of them jumping into action, grabbing paint brushes, scrapers, and buckets. They paired off and before Joe knew it, his house started transforming right in front of his eyes. Within a few hours, they'd pressure washed the entire house and painted his shutters. No longer were there patches of wood showing through the white paint on the exterior of his home. Two of the boys were trimming his hedges, while Daniel and his friend Patrick were raking the piles of grass that mowing the very overgrown lawn had created. Joe himself had been given the assignment of applying a fresh coat of black paint to his front lights and railing leading to his porch. Daniel had insisted that he sit while finishing up on the rail, to which Joe reluctantly agreed. And that was how Hank found his long-time friend as he pulled down his drive with lunch in tow. Daniel's mother had insisted that Hank bring a batch of her cookies over to the boys who had all very graciously agreed to help the old war veteran out. Of course, it didn't hurt that her son had very ingeniously called in a few favors and bribed a few others with the promise of food and probably a little booze. She'd made sure that her husband picked up enough soda and pizza to fill several teenage stomachs, especially because she suspected that they'd down a few beers after they were finished. She knew that kids would be kids, but also wanted to make sure that if they were drinking later, they at least had full stomachs before they started.

Hank saw the difference in his friend's home as soon as he pulled up and put his truck in park. Gone were the overgrown branches that had appeared to be swallowing his tiny Cape Cod home, and the hedges in front were now shaped and neatly manicured. He saw that not only had they pressure washed years of crud from the siding but had changed the color of his shutters to a bright evergreen color which complimented the manicured landscape nicely. He couldn't help but fill with pride when he saw what his son and friends had done to help a stranger. Sure, Joe had given his son one hell of a deal on the car, but the kids standing in front of him were there because his boy had asked his buddies to help; that simple. He lifted the pizzas out of his truck and the aroma immediately caught everyone's attention.

"Well I'd say that you gentlemen definitely have earned these pizzas and wings? And I guess it's a good thing that Mrs. O'Malley likes all of you enough to have made you a tray of her famous Italian sugar cookies!"

Rushing over to help carry the food and soda to the porch to eat, the boys eagerly awaited their turns at grabbing the still warm slices.

They made small talk while inhaling the pizza and wings. Hank insisted on helping the boys finish up with the remaining trim work and then cleaning everything up. He personally thanked each of them as they loaded up their respective vehicles, getting ready to head to the river. Hank lingered behind after Joe offered to pay each of the six teens for their hard work, with each refusing, shaking his hand and thanking him again for his service. And then, as quickly as they arrived, they sped off toward the beer and ladies, waiting for them a few miles away. After the dust settled and the air was quiet once again, Joe spoke.

"They did a fine job here today Hank. I never expected they'd do so much to make my place look so pretty. I can't believe how much better it looks and if this damn arthritis doesn't keep acting up so much, I'll keep her looking this good."

Hank remained silent for a moment before commenting.

"It looks real good Joe. And I know you won't ask, but I'm telling you; you need help, you ask me. I've got nothing but time now…"

His friend picked up on the hesitancy in his voice. "Now? Anything you want to talk about Hank," he asked, looking straight ahead as they sat on his porch.

Hank hadn't shared the news with anyone except his immediate family but needed to speak candidly to an old friend.

"My boy told the misses and me last night that he met with a recruiter and signed on with the Air Force. We were shocked, but he told us that due to some circumstances out of his control, he wanted to take control of his life again, and the see the world, and hopefully make a difference in it. Told us that he wanted to someday get his wings and become a fighter pilot. I tried to talk him out of it, God knows I tried; but he is set on making a difference and says that he wants to serve his country. I'm so proud of him, but I'm also terrified of losing him. You know as well as I do Joe, how hard it can be, being enlisted. I hope that he's not making a knee-jerk decision that he'll come to regret."

He absorbed everything that his friend had said and took a moment to respond. He'd served, his brothers had all served and their daddy and granddad before him. In his generation, it was almost expected. He knew that Hank had been in the Marines like his brother Earl, and though he never spoke of it, Joe was sure that he'd seen some things that he'd rather forget. He knew all too well how war could change a man, but also knew that regret could be a life sentence. He chose his words carefully when he finally answered his friend.

"Signing on for four years is a huge decision, and I would have to bet one that your boy took some time to come to. I don't know what things he's had going on at his age that put him at such a crossroads in his life, but Daniel is a very smart young lad with a good head on his shoulders. He's got two parents who raised him right, and raised him to be independent, and responsible and accountable for his actions. I know how scary it is, thinking that your only son just signed up for four years of potentially putting himself in harm's way; but I have to believe that he knows what he's doing and is mature enough to have thought it through before he signed on. My only word of advice for you Hank, would be, to make sure Daniel knows that you both support him."

"I do Joe. I honestly do. It's just hard letting go you know," he sighed. "He made me promise that I'd keep his new car, your boy's car, in the garage for safe keeping until he's home on leave."

The flashback of his son having the very same conversation came crashing back to him. The quick twinge of heartache came and went as it so frequently did, but he never regretted his son's decision to join the military, despite how it turned out.

"You tell Daniel that I'm very proud of him and I expect a ride, each and every time he comes home on leave!" he chuckled, slowly making his way to his feet. He extended his hand to his longtime friend.

"Thank you for giving me a hand around here. I appreciate beyond words what you and those boys did for me today. Don't be a stranger Hank. Once Daniel's gone, and your home feels a little bit too quiet, you stop by and we'll talk. Okay?"

"Fair enough Joe; I just might be doing that." He shook his friend's hand and headed toward home, where he knew his wife was waiting.

~Chapter 3~

In the three weeks leading up to his departure date for Basic training, Daniel attempted to reach Elizabeth at least a half dozen more times. Her mother ran interference for her, stating she wasn't feeling up to talking, or wasn't home, and even had nerve enough to tell him face to face that she was out with friends when he'd stopped by her house. Her friends were his friends and he knew Elizabeth's mother was lying but didn't want to cause a commotion. He knew through their mutual friends that she hadn't told anyone about their baby and when pressed, she had used the excuse that he'd smothered her and that she just needed some time and space. Well if she wanted space, she'd certainly get it when he left for Lackland Air Force Base in forty-eight hours.

He spent the night before he left at home instead of going out partying with his friends. He had told all of them a few days before that he was heading out of town for awhile but hadn't told them his exact plans. He didn't want it getting back to Elizabeth until he was gone. He longed to see her but since he was shipping out in the morning, he didn't see any sense of it at this point in his life. She'd made her decisions and in turn, he'd made his.

He relaxed in his parent's living room, making small talk and found himself hugging his mother frequently, every time she sniffled or openly cried. When it got late, he promised to eat breakfast with them in the morning before departing. Once he turned in for the night, he locked himself in his bedroom, and penned one last letter to Elizabeth. He would mail it in the morning, knowing that she wouldn't receive it until after he was out of her life for good. Maybe it was the coward's way of telling her, but he'd tried every other avenue and she'd rejected him at every juncture. He had things that he needed to say to her, and if he was forced to do it via letter, then so be it, and that was on her. He'd tried and tried to reach out to her, but after coming home from Buffalo, she'd become a person he hardly knew and by refusing to talk to him, she'd forced his hand. As he finished saying what needed to be said, he sealed the letter and tucked it inside his bag.

He woke early, and despite seeing the letter to Elizabeth tucked just inside his duffel bag, he felt great, and surprisingly ready to start the next chapter of his life. He took one last look around his room, trying to absorb it and made his way toward the kitchen. He knew as soon as he walked down the hall, that his mother was already up. The aroma of bacon accosted his senses as he made his way down the stairs leading to the first floor. He was greeted by both his mother and father when he entered and was relieved to find his mother composed and not tearful. They ate a huge meal together and laughed, reminiscing about anything and everything they could come up with. As the meal finished up, he stood side by side with his mother, helping her with dishes. She knew it was time, and when her husband took his keys off their hook, and said they needed to get going, she turned toward her son and hugged him tight. She would not cry today, and kissed her son gently on the cheek, wishing him well, promising she'd write him often. He grabbed his duffle bag, put his letter in the mail and headed off to his new life in the Air Force.

~Chapter 4~

Elizabeth woke early after an unsettling dream. She didn't know why but knew that something was very wrong. She had felt so incredibly guilty not taking Daniel's calls and refusing to see him, but how could she face him, knowing that she'd let him down. How could she face the man who professed to love her more than life itself and tell him that she felt relieved to have given up their daughter. How could she explain to him that she felt so unworthy of him since she'd abandoned the product of their love. Yes, her mother had been the driving factor behind her decision, but none the less, she had only herself to blame for taking the easy way out and giving up her child as if she'd meant nothing. She'd spent the last several weeks trying to convince herself that it had been the right decision for everyone involved. Lying in her bed as the sun started to rise, she knew it was all a lie. She and

Danny should have fought to keep their child, and she should have believed in the power of their love, their bond and the family that they'd created. She showered and dressed in record speed, racing out the door and to her car. She drove the four miles from her home to Daniel's as fast as she dared, pulling into his drive seven minutes later. She shut the car door before running up the steps to his parent's home, knocking and ringing the doorbell simultaneously, barely containing her excitement. She'd apologize to her Danny, explaining that she'd been confused and lost since they'd given up Michelle Marie, and had needed time to figure out what to do with her life. She'd kiss him, and explain to him that she'd been wrong, so incredibly wrong, and that maybe it wasn't too late to get her back. They'd marry and find a place to live in town and she'd put off college until Michelle was older, and he could work for his father as they'd discussed, and everything would be alright. She'd rehearsed what she'd say and knew that he'd understand once she explained to him why she had been so distant these last weeks.

It was Daniel's mother who greeted her at the door, and not with her usual smile. "Hi, sorry for disturbing you so early, but I really need to talk to Danny," she exclaimed, trying to contain her enthusiasm.

"Well, I'm sorry Elizabeth, but that's not going to happen for several weeks. And you would know that if you'd bothered to return my son's calls," she added, slightly standoffishly.

Very confused with her verbiage and her slightly rude tone, Elizabeth looked back at Daniel's mother, silently, not quite sure what to say. From the look on the girl's face, she knew that she had no clue that her son was gone for good.

"Um, Mrs. O'Malley, what's going on? I really need to speak to Danny," she insisted, standing her ground on the senior woman's front porch.

"Elizabeth, you broke his heart when you gave his daughter up without even asking him what he wanted. Do you know, that a few days after he brought you home from having her, my son hired a lawyer and tried to legally adopt his daughter?" Seeing the shock come over her, Mrs. O'Malley continued. "My son was willing to give up college, and work his ass off to provide for his child, only it was too late. Our granddaughter, our little Michelle had already been adopted and there was nothing the courts or our lawyer could do about it. You're now to blame for my son leaving and I don't know if I'll ever forgive you for that! You took my son and my granddaughter away from me," she sobbed. "And now, I would like you to please leave my property, and never come back here. You're no longer welcome here Elizabeth. You made your decisions and I'm making mine." She turned to walk back into her home as Elizabeth felt herself starting to shake. She had no idea what was going on, especially since Mrs. O'Malley had always been so kind and gracious to her during the two years that she'd dated her son. She still had no idea what the woman had been talking about, and now was more confused that ever. The door shut swiftly behind her, and she heard the click of the deadbolt from inside. She knew that she wasn't going to get any answers there, so she raced to her car and sped over to Gil, Daniel's best friend's house. Luckily for her, he was an early riser and was already outside, working under the hood of his forever braking down truck. Hearing her pull in and come to a screeching halt less than a foot from where he was working, he stood up, eyeing her over the hood of his truck.

"Jesus Liz! You could have killed me!" he shouted at her as she jumped out of her car and stormed toward him.

"Where is he Gil and what the hell is going on? Mrs. O'Malley just snapped at me and told me Danny's gone. What is she talking about and don't bull shit me Gil, I'm warning you!"

Wiping his hands on a rag, he could tell that she was furious, and obviously had no idea that his buddy had walked out of her life. And it wasn't his job to tell her.

"Wow, hey," he said putting his hands in the air, "I'm not sure what happened between you two, he started.

"Nothing happened between us Gil. Where's Danny?"

"Well you could have fooled me. He's been moping around town now for weeks, you two haven't been out with any of us in forever, he quit his job at his father's insurance company and then up and tells me he's joining the military. So, don't tell me that nothing happened between you two Lizzie. I might be slow, but I ain't stupid!"

His words hit her like a sledgehammer to her chest. It took a few seconds to process what he'd just told her and could barely choke out the next question. "When did he say he was leaving Gil? Please," she pleaded, "I need to know."

"Well shit Liz, I'm sorry. I just assumed you knew. He left this morning to catch a flight to Texas. His father brought him to the airport before sunrise this morning. Hey, I'm sorry. I thought you knew." He caught her as she collapsed in his arms.

While Gil was holding Elizabeth, Daniel was hugging his father one last time, before saluting him, picking up his duffel bag and walking through security at the Syracuse Airport, to start his new life.

~Chapter 5~

Elizabeth opened her eyes despite the drug induced cloud that always seemed to envelope her. She knew the time was nearing, and despite the fact that she knew she was actively dying, she didn't feel afraid. Her only concern was for her children, who were barely adults in her eyes. Sure, they weren't teens anymore and were very close despite their very different and distinct personalities, but they were about to lose their lone parent and she knew that she'd worry about them until her last breath, and probably after that, if possible. She relied on her faith to give her strength and comfort. She wasn't completely sure what she believed about the afterlife, but she knew that if she had any say in the matter, she'd come back in one form or another to watch over her children. But until then, there were so many things that she needed to do and say to the three of them before she passed.

She'd met with her attorney on several occasions when she'd first been diagnosed, and again as her disease progressed and she realized her prognosis was grim. She went through the stages of grieving like anyone else who was handed down a death sentence due to a terminal disease would but refused to allow Cancer to define her. Right up until coming into the hospital less than a month prior, she was still doing her thing, going to the gym and working out as best she could, still going out to lunch with her co-workers, and behaving like anyone else, despite living with Metastatic Cancer throughout her petite frame.

As she looked at her three children standing vigil by her bedside, she knew how blessed she'd been in her life. Jared had given her his undying love until the day he died and had given her a wonderful life and three beautiful children. She looked at their faces and saw Jared in each of them; with each having different characteristics from both their father and her. Joshua was so much like his father, always the rock, steady and level headed. Her Maggie May was probably the most like she was, hot headed, a fighter, but loyal to a fault. Then there was her Deidre, whose kindness was overly abundant in everything that she did. Deidre was the sweetest little girl as a child, who grew into an even kinder woman. She was her charity worker so to speak, the one who was always saving the world, or at least trying to. She reminded Elizabeth of someone else she'd once known and loved, who set out to do the very same thing years before.

"Hi guys," she smiled, forcing her grin to appear genuine, despite the continuous throbbing in her back. There was no time to waste and she had so much that she wanted to tell them and knew that her attorney would take care of the rest.

Asking Joshua to lift the head of her bed up, she repositioned herself in bed, careful not to dislodge any of the tubes. An IV for fluids and Morphine streaming in, and a catheter for urine going out, she hated being the patient instead of the nurse that had been her profession for years.

She'd attended college to become a registered nurse and found her calling in Labor & Delivery. She'd lost count years ago as to how many babies she'd assisted in bringing into the world, and despite the occasional very sad delivery of a stillborn or severely deformed child, she had loved being able to help woman deliver their children. Her co-workers always called her the backbone of the unit, a name she wore proudly. She'd worked the night shift when her children were young, and despite the fact that they had been old enough to be left alone at night for years, she remained on the night shift after Jared passed and the kids left the house for college. She preferred the solitude of the 3rd shift and had always found something cathartic about being awake to see the sun rise day in and day out. As a nurse, she knew all too well what the monthly full moon did to people in labor; but thought of it as a challenge, not a dreaded curse. Yes, full moons and babies were definitely Elizabeth's thing and she knew she'd miss them both.

After Joshua lifted her into a sitting position, she took a sip of Diet Coke and looked from one of her children to the next. She wasn't sure how to start, so she just took a deep breath and started talking.

"Joshua, Maggie, Deidre; there's something I've put off telling you, something that I should have told you a long time ago, but it never seemed like the right time."

She gasped for air as she spoke, signally her son to again, hand her the glass of Coke, which he did, helping her bring it to her lips to sip. She knew that she was so weak, and the time was getting so near, but felt that she had to get the truth out; felt that her children needed to hear it from her, so that she could explain. Her eyes filled with tears when she thought of Danny, the boy she'd given her heart, soul and virginity to. She wanted, and needed, to tell her children about him, make them understand that everything about her marriage to their father had been genuine and true, but that she'd in fact, loved before she'd met Jared. She'd loved with all her heart and through that love, had conceived a child. Maybe she was delusional in what she was going to ask of her children, but if she knew her kids the way she thought she did and had raised them to be the kind of adults that she knew they were, she knew that eventually they'd come around and understand her request.

"First of all, let me start by telling you how very proud I am of the three of you." That was all it took to have Deidre's tears start to flow. Maggie leaned in to appear to console her kid sister, whispering for her to put a lid on it, an order that didn't go unheard by Elizabeth. Always the warrior, Elizabeth chuckled to herself as she pretended not to hear Maggie's not so subtle warning to her overly sensitive little sister. Joshua cleared his throat in an attempt to silence them both.

"Your father would be so proud of the people that you've become, and I need the three of you to know that I couldn't have loved you anymore than I do right now. Your father and I raised you to be independent and believe in yourselves and whatever you set your mind to do. All three of you followed not only your heads, but also your hearts and are doing exactly what you want, and I couldn't be prouder. If he doesn't already know, I give you all my word that when I reach heaven and am finally reunited with your dad, I'll make sure he's caught up to speed on how much you've accomplished since he left us. With that said, there's a few things that I know your father would say to you if he were here." She took another sip of her Coke and continued, as she'd rehearsed in her mind.

"Joshua, you're my oldest and only son. Your father and I used to comment when you were little how serious you always were, even as a little kid. It's like you need to prove to the world that you need to be taken seriously. My wish for you is twofold; one, that you stop putting off asking Jena to be your wife. You are perfect together and I would hate to have her slip through your fingers because she got sick of waiting. Trust me, sometimes you need to just jump in with two feet and take a chance; otherwise you might miss out on something that's meant to be. That girl has waited long enough, if you love her like I know you do, then ask her to be your wife! Secondly, stop coming up with excuses as to why you can't submit the manuscript of your screenplay. How will you know if it's any good if you don't take a chance? Promise me that you'll follow through with at least talking to someone about your play. Deal?" she asked, squeezing her son's hand.

Reaching into his jacket pocket, he smiled. "I promise momma, I will look into submitting it. What's the worst that can happen right?" he chuckled. "And I wanted to show you first," he said, opening the box and handing it to his mother. Peering into the box, she smiled in approval at the beautiful Chocolate Diamond. Its' emerald cut and platinum band sparkled, much the way her son's face was as he looked at it. His sister's gasped as they realized what the ring meant; and were thrilled to be gaining a sister. Jena had been part of their family for as long as they could remember, so their brother making it official was a wildly anticipated surprise.

"It suits her," Elizabeth commented. "Elegant and classy, just like our Jena. So now you have the girl and the ring," she continued, not quite ready to let him off the hot seat yet. "So, when are you going to ask her Josh? No time like the present," she kidded.

"Mom, it can wait. Being here with you is more important right now, don't you think?"

"No, actually I don't. The three of you have sat vigil around my bed day in and day out for a week now. I'm not going anywhere yet, and I know that you three are going home to sleep in your own beds tonight and I'm not leaving that topic open for discussion," she added, knowing that her children would object. "And I expect you to go home, wash up, and take your beautiful future fiancée out for a nice dinner this evening and pop the question. You can tell me all about it in the morning. Deal?"

Knowing that there was no sense in arguing with her, he leaned in to hug his mother, his best friend and his rock.

"Deal."

Next, she turned her attention to her middle child. Serious like her brother, but much more untrusting of people, her Maggie May protected her heart like a fiercely guarded jewel. She'd dated here and there but whenever a relationship appeared to be getting serious, she'd end it, swiftly and abruptly, and usually without a valid reason. Elizabeth wouldn't call her daughter a loner, but she also knew that someday her middle child would need more in her life than her career and her dog. Her Maggie was as analytical as they came, and had chosen a career in cyber security, long before it was in vogue. She'd worked her way up from a tiny desk in a windowless room searching software for money laundering for the banking industry, to a high security classified job on the base nearby, working as a civilian with the military. She loved her job, especially since it allowed her minimal contacts with humans, and the only people she had to be concerned with were in the form of faceless names on her computer screen.

"You Maggie have always been like a Minnie me in the sense that you're fiercely independent, loyal to a fault, and don't take shit from anybody, and for that I love you with all of my heart. But if nothing else, you should have learned from growing up in a household full of love and respect for one another, that it's okay to count on and rely on someone else. Being married to your father never diminished my independence, if anything, it allowed me to grow. My wish for you is that you open your mind to the possibility of loving someone. I want you to join more clubs, teams, or places where you can expose yourself to more people. If you can't think of any options to start with, I already have one place where you can go to meet new people." Before Maggie could interject or argue, her mother continued. "Your sister desperately needs help down at the soup kitchen, and I expect you to go there on Tuesday evenings and at least one Saturday a month to help her out. And when Deidre tells you that she doesn't need the help, you will ignore her and go anyways," she said, trying to smile. "That is my only request of you Maggie, and I don't expect you to let me down..." Knowing it was futile to argue with her mother, Maggie leaned in and kissed her mother on the cheek. "As long as I don't have to cook, I'll do it momma," she laughed. "But don't expect miracles either mom. I like things the way they are."

"Maggie May," their mother addressed her oldest daughter again. "I also want you to promise me that you'll sign up for a CrossFit, or Zumba class at that gym that you hardly go to anymore, and yes, I know that you can never find the time," she added, when she saw her daughter's mouth about to open in argument. "I want you to promise me that one night per week is for you, not your client's or your siblings, or friends; for Maggie. If it's not the gym, then sign up at Munson Williams or The View in Old Forge and take a class on making pottery, stained glass, basket weaving, whatever suits your fancy. Just promise me you'll do it. You're in survival mode, and not living; and its' about time that you start living. And don't shake your head at me in disagreement. I know you work all your crazy hours to hide from living. And I expect you to start enjoying what life has to offer because sooner or later, you'll realize just how short life actually is."

Elizabeth smiled and squeezed her daughter's hand.

"That's the funny thing about life Maggie; sometimes when things seem the most structured and calm, is when God decides to shake things up a little. And it just might be your time. If it is, don't fight it, and don't rebel against it; just let it be."

Lastly, she looked at her baby, her youngest child who definitely had an old soul. Her Deidre was so very different from her other children. Her strawberry blonde hair had just a hint of curl to it, and she was the only of her three children who had freckles pop out during the lazy days of summer. Jared had always told her that their baby was the spitting image of his grandmother who'd come from Ireland, and as Deidre had grown into the young woman that she was today, Elizabeth could see more and more of her husband's side of the family in her daughter. She had such a soft side, and gentle way about her. She was the dreamer of the family, the one who saw only good in everything and everyone around her. She didn't have a mean bone in her body and took everyone for their word, which had been her downfall in a few business transactions. Luckily, her son, the analytical math whiz had saved her baby girl from financial disaster, and from then on, Deidre had allowed her big brother to keep an eye on her finances as she continued doing what she did best; taking care of people in need.

Jared would have been so proud to see what his little girl had accomplished on her own. She had been just a child when she'd been exposed to a homeless person asking for a few quarters and a hot meal. Jared had obliged and given the man enough money to buy himself a meal. Instead of heading into the local fast food joint in front of him, she'd watched the man with the baggy clothes and dirty hair go into the store and come back out again with his bag of food in tow. He proceeded to sit down next to a woman who was just as filthy as he was and share the meal with her. Deidre knew that she shouldn't be staring but couldn't help but watch as the two street people said a quick prayer, and rejoiced in the warm meal in front of them. That simple act of kindness set the stage for the rest of Deidre's formative years. She's majored in marketing in school, minoring in business. When she wasn't studying, she could be found at one not for profit organization or another, rescuing kittens, building homes for veterans or immigrants, or serving nightly meals. Even as a child, she'd asked for simple things for her birthday like hats, scarves, and socks in order to give them away to people she'd see living on the street. She'd learned to knit and crochet as a child and could be found with yarn and a hook in her hand on any given day, making a pair of mittens or a scarf for the next person she saw in need. She'd dreamt of opening a soup kitchen while in college and had been able to see her dream to fruition when her girlfriend mentioned she'd like to be part of the start up. They'd been in business for less than two years but luckily, they had sponsors and support from their city, and frequent donations from various businesses to help them keep out of debt. They'd taken their dream one step further by starting a small business in the back of the warehouse, and to date, had been able to hire eight homeless men and women to work part time for them. They made coats that turned into sleeping bags at night and were pleasantly surprised and shocked when two local stores in town had asked to pick up the line. Nearly every cent that Deidre made, went back into her soup kitchen and her dream. She patted the side of her bed, inviting her baby girl to sit beside her.

"My beautiful Deidre, you have always been my dreamer," Elizabeth started. "You reached for the stars and not only imagined holding them, but making them shine just a little bit brighter and that's what you do to everything you touch. You have such a kind heart, and an old soul and my wish for you is simple. When you find your business expanding larger and faster than you ever predicted, I want you to let others help you, the way you've always helped others. I want you to promise me that you'll never lose yourself in the shuffle and chaos of trying to save the world. Lastly, if your business keeps growing the way that I know it will, and if by chance, you pitch my idea," she winked, "and get a corporate sponsor behind you, then I want you to branch out a little. I know that your plate is full enough honey, but I think there's one thing missing."

"What momma? What haven't I done that you want me to do," she pleaded, always trying to meet everyone's approval. "Tell me and I'll get started on it today. I have some money saved up, so I can do whatever you need or want me to do; just tell me and consider it done."

"I have some great ideas, but those dreams can wait for another day. When I tell you about them, I know that you'll implement them and you'll give back to so many people in our city. I know you will and just thinking about it makes me so happy and proud of you."

Tears streaming down her eyes, she nodded yes. "Of course momma, yes, I'll do it. But tell me, tell us of your dream. We would like to know what wish you'd like us to fulfill for you in a year or two."

"I have a couple wishes and dreams that I have set in motion for you and your sister and brother, but we can talk about them another time." Josh looked at this ever-suspicious sister, and from the look in her eyes, she also had no idea what their mother could be talking about.

"Tell us anyway momma, what is your dream?"

"My sweet Deidre," she started, squeezing her daughter's hand. "When I pass, the three of you are going to inherit a very substantial amount of money. You may all spend your shares however you see fit. But if the idea intrigues you, I've set aside a small amount of money to see my dream come alive; that is, if you're interested in pursuing it."

Joshua and Maggie pulled their chairs closer and leaned in toward their mother, whose voice had become barely a whisper. Obviously fatigued from talking more than she had in days, they encouraged Deidre to let her drift off to sleep again. Elizabeth willed herself to stay awake, knowing that she wanted to get the words out before it was too late.

"I know that it sounds silly, but after watching HGTV time after time, I have been completely enthralled in the concept of tiny living. Now I know that a family of four living in a home 200 square feet or less, is a little on the crazy side, but what about developing a program to help the homeless population that have been working for you in the kitchen? What if you developed a community of tiny houses for the homeless to utilize? What I envisioned, was purchasing some of the land on the outskirts of town, but still on the bus line, and building twenty or so tiny homes for the homeless. Each dwelling would sleep at least two individuals and would be a place that they could call home. Obviously, my dream is still in the infancy stage, but I thought it would be nice to help the ones that are in fact, trying to help themselves. With the right sponsorship, you'd be surprised how much money the state might grant to subsidize such an idea. The individual living in the tiny home would rent the home and could stay as long as they were working and paying rent, which of course would be nominal. Don't kid yourself when you look at the people living on the streets. Many are educated, former veterans, parents, and simply people who have had multiple bad breaks in their lives. If asked, most would tell you that they want to work, and are willing to work; and just need to be given a chance. In the perfect world," Elizabeth sighed, "and if I could have made my dream come true, I would have helped you expand your company and saw my tiny house community come to fruition. But it was only a dream and concept that I'd dreamt up, and probably would have been squashed by too much red tape anyways," she stated, letting the words linger, and knowing her daughter was always up for a challenge.

It was Maggie who spoke first. "Well I can see where Deidre gets her bleeding heart from. Those people wouldn't be on the street if they didn't want to be."

"You're full of crap and don't know shit about those people," her sister pounced. "If you ever bothered to talk to anyone of them, you'd know that they are good people, people like you and me, except that they've been served raw deal after raw deal," Deidre exclaimed, near tears. Turning back at her mother, she smiled. "I think it's a wonderful idea mom, and I will start looking into options right away. But I need you to stay with us a little longer and help me get your dream off the ground. And when it's completed," she laughed to herself, how about we call it "Elizabeth's Estates?"

Her mother smiled through the pain. "It sounds wonderful Deidre. If you, Maggie and Joshua ever decide to pursue my tiny house community, please do it together, and as a family. Also promise me, that you'll take help when it's offered to you."

"We will," her three children answered in unison.

"Guys," their mom whispered, "I'm getting pretty tired and need to sleep soon. I need you to know how much I love each of you and love your individual personalities. I see your father in all of you, and I see myself. I know you know how much I loved your father, and I couldn't have asked for a better person to raise you kids with. But you need to understand," she whispered, eyes closing, "that there was another man, boy actually, that stole my heart before I met your father. He was my childhood sweetheart and the man I thought I'd be with forever. After I'm gone, I want you to find him and deliver a package to him, either in person or by mail, I'll leave that decision up to you. His name is Daniel O'Malley, and the last correspondence I had with him was when we were eighteen and he'd left for the Air Force. When the time comes, I'll provide you with more information, but it's imperative that he gets the package that Mr. Phelps, my attorney, is holding for him. He will explain the rest. I need you three to promise me, that with all the modern technology of today, that you'll find Danny and deliver the package. And before I sleep, know that he was my first love, but your father was my forever love, and when I join him soon, it'll be one of the happiest days of my life. I love you all so much and I promise you all, I will always be here for you."

As the last words escaped her lips, their mother drifted off to sleep as her children sat silent, trying to absorb what she'd asked of them.

Joshua motioned for his sisters to join him outside of their mother's hospital room. Each bent down and kissed her gently on the cheek, taking one last look at their mother, who appeared so peaceful in sleep. Cancer had robbed her of her strength but not of her beauty. Her face was thinner than they'd ever seen it, but as she lay in the bed, she looked almost regal, with her hands clasped together on her chest, and a smile on her lips. Little did they know that the request that their mother had just asked of them, was truly her dying wish.

Once outside their room, Joshua ushered his sisters toward the coffee machine in the family lounge. Each had consumed more than their share of hospital coffee, but it was convenient and free, so they each poured themselves a cup and sat at a table off to the side. It was Maggie, always the suspicious one, who spoke first.

"What the hell do you think that was all about?" she asked, taking a large gulp of mediocre coffee.

"I'm sure it's nothing important Mags, probably just wants to return his letterman sweater, or class ring or something from their high school days that she'd held on to. It's not a big deal, I'll track him down sometime next week, mail the package out to him and tell mom that it's all taken care of. She'll be happy, and he'll have his stuff back, or whatever it is she wants him to have, and he'll be gone out of our lives as quickly as he was brought into them. Case closed," he smiled, already strategizing how he would find a person with such a generically Irish name. He assumed that they'd gone to high school together, so he'd start with her yearbook and expand from there, realizing that there were far too many Daniel O'Malley's listed on Facebook, he knew because he'd already checked while sitting in his mother's hospital room.

"There's more to it than just returning some 40-year-old crap Josh. I could feel it in her tone; there's more to it than what she said," Maggie stated, matter of factly. Up until then, Deidre had kept her thoughts to herself, but now wanted to weigh in with her opinion.

"I think she has some kind of unsettled business with this Daniel O'Malley guy and she needs us to finish it for her," she offered, sipping on her coffee. "I think either she had something she needs us to do for him, or something she needs him to do; either way, looks like we're going to be tracking down our mother's first love."

"You think they were lovers," she asked innocently, afraid to make eye contact with her siblings.

"Ew, how the hell would I know. But either way, I say we just track down the guy and mail him his shit and like Josh said, good bye and good riddance Mr. O'Malley."

Unfortunately for her sister and brother, Deidre wasn't quite ready to let it go. "What if they were secret lovers and were supposed to marry and their parents wouldn't let them, so out of despair, he joined the Air Force and mom went away to college and their paths never crossed again. That would be really sad you know."

"What if," Josh added, to tease his baby sister, "They did get married, had a couple kids and then their parents found out and separated them and put the kids in Foster Care? Now that would be tragic," he added, winking at Maggie. "Deidre, you're a sap for a good love story you know. Please don't read more into it than what's actually there. She asked us to find her old high school friend, and that's what we're going to do; nothing more, nothing less."

As her children sat feet away in the lounge, Elizabeth had company of her own. She wasn't sure if he came to her in a dream, or if she was awake but fuzzy because of the Morphine filling her veins, but one thing was for certain, her beloved Jared was at her side.

"Hello my love," he smiled. "You've certainly been busy this morning, setting all of your plans in motion."

"Jared, my Jared," she whispered, "Is it really you?" She could see and feel her husband standing beside her and could feel his lips as he bent down, kissing her gently on the lips.

"Are you in pain my love," he asked, praying that she wasn't suffering too much. He'd been blessed actually and hadn't felt any pain except for the one quick stab of pain when his aorta blew out and he dropped where he stood.

"No Jared, it isn't so bad. But I'm tired, so tired honey. And I think it's almost time for me to rest," she acknowledged. And then it dawned on her. "Jared, did God send you down for me?" she asked, already knowing the answer.

"Yes, my love, your job here on earth is nearly done, and I asked if I could come down and escort you home," he smiled. "I've waited so long to be reunited with you again and asked to be the one to accompany you during your final journey. And I must say," he chuckled, "You certainly know how to exit a party. Good Lord you riled our kids up and certainly have them speculating about your relationship with Daniel," he laughed. "Our Maggie May is right outside your door, already figuring out how she can kick the guy's ass if he asks about you," he announced, laughing as he spoke. "And our Deidre is already planning out her tiny home community as we speak. Joshua, analytical as always, is formulating a list of search engines to use to narrow down the search in finding your Danny, and between the three of them, I know they'll accomplish the journey that you've sent them on. But the one thing I don't understand my love, is why didn't you tell them about Michelle? Our children deserve to know that they have a half-sister out there, don't you think?"

"Oh Jared, you have such a kind heart and for that I love you more than words could ever express. Yes, yes, I want them to know about their sister, but I couldn't bare the thought of them judging me, or rejecting me for telling them about the daughter that I conceived with Danny. Maybe it's the easy way out, actually I know that it's the coward's way out, but I was terrified of seeing them disappointed in me, so I am leaving it up to Mr. Phelps to provide them with that information. I know that they'll be hurt and disappointed in me for not telling them the whole truth when I told them about Danny, but when it was the right moment, I simply chickened out. Do you think they'll forgive me?" she asked, fighting back tears.

"My love, you're human. Of course they'll not only forgive you, but understand completely. They love you."

Jared took his beloved Elizabeth into his arms, felt her take her last breath, and welcomed her home.

~Chapter 6~

Joshua found it hard to concentrate as he sat looking out the window of his corner office. It had been less than two weeks since they'd buried their mother and reunited her with their dad at the Greensville Cemetery. The days following her death, leading up to her calling hours and Christian funeral service were a blur, with Joshua, Maggie and Deidre going through the motions as best they could. They'd received calls day and night, flowers from so many people that were sent to the funeral home for her service, and all three had been overwhelmed by the number of friends and colleagues who attended her calling hours. They'd heard story after story, and too many antidotes to count; and it was only after the formalities were complete and their mom was settled in beside their father, that they truly understood what a pillar their mother had been in not only her neighborhood, but in her job at the hospital as well. Elizabeth had been loved by so many and surely would be sorely missed.

Joshua thought back to his mother's last coherent conversation with him, and despite the sorrow he still felt, smiled as he recalled her last requests. Looking outside, he caught himself staring into the eyes of a cardinal and knew that his mother, barely in heaven, was already sending him messages.

"Alright, alright mom. I was picking up the phone to call her anyways. Relax, I'll ask her tonight," he chuckled, dialing his long-time girlfriend's number.

After explaining to her that he'd like to talk to her about something his mother had asked of him, he asked Jena if it was alright to go out to dinner that evening, despite their crazy work schedule, to which she happily said yes. She explained that she'd just juggle a few appointments around and be home by six, change and be ready to go out by 6:15, 6:30 at the latest. He smiled as he hung up the phone, knowing that if everything went as planned, he would be calling Jena his fiancée by this time tomorrow. Looking back out the window, he eyed the cardinal once again.

"Okay mom," he whispered, "You can go harass Dee or Maggie now. I'm going to propose to her tonight." He looked back at his computer screen after the cardinal flew away and found himself in a much better mood than he'd been in just moments earlier.

~Chapter 7~

Maggie returned to work less than twenty-four hours after burying her mother, citing that returning to her job didn't change the outcome, her mother was still dead. She locked herself in her office after hearing the fourth or fifth co-worker's condolence. She knew they were only being sincere and kind, but what she needed at that moment wasn't their pity, it was her mother. She was pissed that she wasn't given more time and opportunity to tell her mom just what she had meant to her, and only hoped that her mother knew how much she had looked up to her all those years that she'd raised she and her siblings as a single parent. She knew that her mother was in a better place and no longer suffering, but damn it, she missed her already. As she turned back toward her computer screen, her cell rang. Not recognizing the number, she allowed it to ring a few more times, almost declining the call and letting it go to coverage, but at the last second, decided to answer it. The call was from Mr. Phelps, her mother's attorney, and once he was on the line, he had her undivided attention.

The call only took a few minutes and left her with more questions than answers. Mr. Phelps had informed her that it was their mother's request that her three children be present for not only the reading of her will, but also her final request. As soon as she hung up, she called her sister first and told her about the call, and that they needed to go to Mr. Phelps office on Genesee Street, on

Friday at 4pm sharp. She explained that she didn't know anything other than that the three of them had to be together and would be meeting with their mother's attorney at that time. When Deidre kept asking questions that she couldn't answer, she found herself getting agitated, but took a deep breath and politely ended the call. Next, she called her brother. He picked up on the second ring.

"Hey, it's me. I just got off the phone with mom's attorney."

"Okay, what did he have to say?" he asked, hesitantly.

"Nothing really. He said that as per the request of his client, our mother, blah, blah, blah, that he was authorized to read and execute her will only if the three of us were present. She specifically instructed him that we must all be in attendance at the time of the reading. Mom was always so incredibly laid back about everything, and it seems so odd that she had such specific requests from us before she died, and now has all these contingencies about her estate."

"I agree, but it is what it is, and after Friday, we'll know what all her secrecy and planning was about. It'll be alright Mags. You and I don't need whatever money she's giving us as part of our inheritance, and I'm asking Jena to marry me this evening so I'm already fulfilling my part of the deal. So, say," he laughed on his end of the phone," have you signed up for your basket weaving class yet," he asked, knowing he'd get a rise out of her.

"Bite me!" she responded, laughing as he teased her. "Actually, as promised, I signed up for a CrossFit class that is held at my gym on Saturdays, so I too, have met my part of mom's request."

"Gold star to you, you signed up. But you haven't fulfilled mom's request until you've actually started taking the class," he teased again.

"Touché, but you haven't fulfilled your part of her bargain either then. You're going to ask Jena to marry you but that doesn't mean she's going to say yes, and that my dear brother, was part of mom's request."

"Oh fuck me, you're right." Suddenly nervous at the thought, he felt his palms start to sweat, just a little.

"You don't think she'll say no do you? I mean, we've been together for awhile now, and we've lived together for over six months. Jesus Mags, you don't think she'll say no? I guess I just always assumed that we'd get around to getting married. Jesus, I hadn't thought of the possibility that she'd say no."

"Would you stop Josh. Of course she's going to say yes. She's head over heels in love with you, and I can't remember when you weren't with her, so of course she'll say yes you knucklehead. She's been waiting for you to pop the question and it's about time you did!"

Thinking that his sister's revelation probably cost him a few year's off his life, he decided that he would up his game just a little to ensure she would said yes. He concluded his call with his sister and immediately started googling florists.

Once she'd hung up with her brother, Maggie found her mind wandering, trying to figure out why the attorney had insisted that she and her siblings all be present for the reading of the will. Her mother had been a nurse and knew that after her father passed away, money had been a little tight. Sure, they had the cabin at the lake, but that had been built by her mother's parents, and paid for years ago. Maybe she wasn't dividing everything in thirds she thought or maybe she was donating everything to the church or her sister's soup kitchen. Maggie wasn't concerned about it either way because material possessions had never meant a thing to her. She had squirreled away nearly every penny that she had made and already had a very sizable nest egg saved. She'd donate every penny that she was about to inherit if she could have her mother back, but since that wasn't possible, she would accept what was offered, and like her paycheck, deposit it into her savings. She didn't need anything more than what she already had, to live her minimalist lifestyle. Her Jeep might have over 70,000 miles, but it was paid for and ran just fine, so she saw no sense in trading it in. Her condo was tiny but had all the room that she and her beloved lab needed. Sinjin was her two year old yellow lab, and they got along just fine in the small living space that she called home.

Her gut told her that there was more to the story than simply the reading of the will, but Mr. Phelps had been very evasive in his answers to any of her questions. She had resolved herself to the fact that she'd just have to wait until Friday to find out what was truly going on.

She returned to her computer screen and tried to think about the numerous case files neatly stacked on her desk. Looking out the window, she watched a few stray leaves blowing in the wind and let her mind wander to the lake, and all of the wonderful vacations that she'd spent there not only as a child, but as a teen and adult. Her parent's rules had been simple: the door was always open to friends, but they had to pick up after themselves, bring their own beach towel and toothbrush, and once old enough to drink, leave their car keys in a basket by the front door until the next day if they intended to drink while visiting. And lastly, if drinking, the hot tub and lake were off limits.

Her family had kept a book on their hutch and it was a family tradition that when someone joined their family at the lake, whether for an afternoon, weekend or longer, that the guest had to make an entry in their lake house journal. The tradition had been started by her mother's parents and still held true today, and something that she and her siblings would continue.

Maggie had no idea what made her think of their cabin by the lake but watching the leaves swirl around on the ground outside her window, she had already made up her mind that she should pack up Sinjin and head for the mountains for the weekend since she didn't have anything else planned. After the reading of her mom's will on Friday, she'd confirm that neither of her siblings had called dibs on it, and if not, she'd head up right after their meeting with the attorney while there was still some daylight left. Maybe she'd take Sinjin for a hike, or maybe she'd kayak, or simply curl up with her dog, a glass or bottle of wine, and a good book. That was one of the things that she loved about the lake, she was never forced to be on a schedule. Schedules, she hated them; and here she had just signed up to take a weekly class at her mother's insistence, which meant following a schedule.

The Crossfit class that she'd signed up for was held on Saturdays, at the butt crack of dawn, and again on Wednesdays. She considered herself in relatively good shape but knew that if she didn't hit the gym a few times before the class started, she'd die during the first few sessions. She'd packed her change of clothes, and since her head wasn't into chasing cyber criminals today, she cut out of work a little earlier than her usual departure time. She thought that she'd just hit the Treadmill and Stairstepper a bit, and maybe do a few circuits on the machines, and then she'd be in a little better condition for the class that she was already starting to dread.

The gym was on her way home and from the looks of the parking lot, wasn't very crowded from outward appearances. "Good," she thought, "I'll just scoot in and out in under an hour and get it over with."

She was correct in her assumption she noted as she walked briskly toward the women's changing room, eyeing the machine that she'd like to grab first. It only took her a few minutes to get out of her work attire and into yoga pants and a tank top, and sneaks. She pulled her shoulder length, auburn colored hair back in a headband that made her eyes look a few shades greener than they already were. Gone was her summer tan, and as she walked out of the locker room, she felt pale in comparison to the women who obviously used the tanning beds that were included in their gym membership. Her complexion was fair enough she thought to herself; she certainly didn't need to go looking for skin cancer in the form of high-powered UV lights in some tanning bed.

She made her way to the closest open Treadmill and climbed on, not paying attention to anyone in her immediate surroundings. She was there to work out and wasn't interested in the who's who of the gym. She hit the quick start button and started walking on the track and she increased the vertical height to ten, as high as it would go.

"Wow, that's one way to get your heart pumping," he laughed, and he ran on the treadmill beside her. She turned to see a smiling face, attached to a Neanderthal looking man currently running and sweating profusely next to her. It wasn't that he looked like a Neanderthal, she surmised quickly; it was just that the guy had to be at least six two or six three, and despite the vertical incline she was presently on, he looked enormous compared to her five-foot two stature. Instead of being irritated by the intrusion of her workout, she laughed.

"Isn't that calling the kettle black?" she laughed. "You've got that thing going at near mock speed and appear to be running like your life depended on it," she kidded back.

"I am. My big sister signed us both up for a half marathon in Disney that's in less than two months, and I'm not a runner! But I'll be damned if I'm gonna let her show me up," he answered, jokingly. "Oh, and my name's Garrett, and I apologize in advance for any swearing or sweating that comes your way. I just hate running inside and would prefer to be climbing a mountain, anything other than killing myself on this contraption! But a bet's a bet," he smiled, with the slightest of just one dimple showing.

She knew she should just smile, put her ear buds in and pay attention to her own treadmill, but something about the goofy looking man caught her attention. She wasn't sure if it was his attire, that obviously his wife or girlfriend had NOT picked out for him, the way he'd spoke about his older sister, hinted of pure love and admiration for her, or his smile. He was by no means gorgeous, and certainly didn't smell all that wonderful at the moment; and had obviously been running on his treadmill for quite some time before she arrived. But still, there was something about the guy that intrigued her for some reason, and that, made him interesting.

"I'm sure you'll do fine at your marathon in Disney. I've heard about that race and know that they give out really cool medallions when you complete it. Oh, and my name's Maggie, nice to meet you Garrett. And Garrett, I prefer climbing mountains over running marathons as well," she added, as she put her earbuds in and started climbing her stationary mountain.

She tried ignoring him as he finished up his run and slowed it down, eventually concluding his workout. She refused to acknowledge that he was leaving as he wiped down the machine and picked up his water bottle, trying to catch her attention. She purposely turned her head as if watching the television screen hanging from the ceiling, until he was out of sight.

"Phew," she thought to herself, "Crisis averted, he's gone." She had to admit, she had enjoyed the small talk, and he did have great legs. Thinking about it as she continued climbing her imaginary high peak, the man had looked rather cute in his sweaty t-shirt and shorts. But as quickly as she'd given him any more thought, Maggie silently chastised herself, thinking she needed a man in her life, like a hole in the head. "Besides, he's gone now and nothing more to think about." She cranked the speed up on her treadmill, and started running up the vertical incline, hoping to sweat Garrett out of her mind. It was working, until she felt a slight touch on her arm.

Startled, she heard herself shriek and nearly fall off the steep incline she'd been concentrating on. Seeing her losing her balance, Garrett immediately hit the emergency stop button on the machine and reached out to catch her. She found herself nearly falling and as quickly as she had lost her balance, strong arms picked her upright again. Her head started spinning from the sudden stop in motion and she saw stars in front of her eyes for just a brief second. He saw the change in her and tightened the grip on her arms.

"Easy now Maggie, take a deep breath, in through your nose and out through your mouth. That's it, do it again Maggie," he said, speaking calmly and softly to the woman presently in his arms. She did as instructed because her head couldn't process anything else. After the fourth or fifth breath, her head started clearing and the room stopped spinning. She looked up into bright blue eyes that showed a distinct look of concern.

He could tell from the color returning to her face and her pupils going back to a normal size that she was starting to feel better. Always conscious of boundaries, he took a step back, but maintained his firm grip on her arms, just in case. He saw her looking up at him and realized that although she wore minimal makeup, and tried to blend in with the crowd, she was genuinely beautiful and definitely stood out from the rest of the gym crowd. He could also feel her tense up where his hands were touching her skin, and now that she had her balance, immediately let go and took another step back.

"If I want a woman to fall for me Maggie, I usually take a different approach than this," he said innocently. "I'm really sorry for startling you. I just wanted to say goodbye and that it was very nice meeting you today, and maybe I'll see you on the trails sometime."

She'd been prepared for some pick up line and not for his honesty. He hadn't tried to hit on her, but instead, was simply saying goodbye and see you around so to speak. It took her a moment to respond, and the sharp rejection phrases that had been on the tip of her tongue needed to be tucked away before she responded.

"You just scared the crap out of me," she laughed. "It was nice meeting you as well Garrett, and maybe I'll see you on the trails, or maybe I'll see you here again someday."

She thought about saying more but left it at that. She didn't want to give him the wrong impression or any false hope. He seemed nice enough, but she didn't need any complications in her life. And men were definitely complications.

She could tell that he wanted to say something more or possibly ask her out or for coffee, but didn't.

He smiled, and turned to walk out, gym bag in hand. "See you around Maggie."

She waved, but he had already turned and was walking toward the door. From where she was standing, he looked even better in his street clothes than he had in his gym attire. She found herself staring until he'd opened the door and stepped outside. Feeling the need to drink, she took a big swallow of water, and decided that she needed to put her tongue back into her mouth and continue her workout, forgetting about a man she'd spoken with for all of five minutes. She cranked up the speed on her treadmill, turned up the volume on her music and set about finishing her work out.

~Chapter 8~

Friday morning Josh woke early with his now fiancée by his side. Jena had been blown away by his proposal and as everyone had speculated, had said yes. No date had been set, but Josh didn't care; the love of his life had said that she'd be his bride, and that was all that mattered. He slid out of bed silently, showered and made his way toward their kitchen.

He found that he'd tossed and turned all night and knew that his unease was due to the meeting that he had with his sisters, and their mother's attorney later that afternoon. It wasn't about the money, because between he and Jena, who was one of the city's highest ranked defense attorneys, made more than enough money to be comfortable. He had no clue what his mother's net worth was and like Maggie, would gladly give away every cent if they could have their mother back. But the world didn't work like that, and she was gone. After their meeting with the attorney, the three of them would have to decide what they were going to do with their mother's home, possessions, lake house and so much more. He'd already decided that they should set up a trust fund for the lake house. It had been in his mother's family for generations and needed to be a legacy to the woman that had been their role model, mother, and best friend. It was paid for, and yearly maintenance was minimal, and though on the Fulton Chain of Lakes in the Adirondack Mountains, the taxes weren't insanely high compared to other waterfront properties. He and his sisters didn't have children yet to pass it down to, but knew that his mother and his mother's parents would want it kept in the family.

As he sat at his kitchen table, enjoying his first cup of coffee, both his sisters were doing the same thing in their respective homes. Maggie was online, checking the forecast for the weekend in Old Forge, trying to decide how many layers she'd need to pack for late October in the mountains, while Deidre was presently spread out on her living room floor stretching after completing her yoga video and second cup of chamomile tea. She made it a point to practice yoga every day before she headed down to the soup kitchen. As she stretched, and sipped her tea, her mind kept wandering to what her mother had talked about, that last day before she'd lost consciousness and subsequently passed away. Her mind was cluttered with so many ideas as to how she could incorporate her mother's wishes and dreams about providing the homeless population with a roof over their heads.

The more she thought about it, the more she was convinced that maybe she should take her sister up on her offer to join her at camp. Sasha, her beloved Persian cat could stay behind for the weekend, or maybe she'd just cart her along to liven up the place a little bit. Sinjin, Maggie's dog and Sasha, her cat had shared living quarters in the past, with no bloodshed, so she'd decide by the end of the day whether she would join her sister and bring the cat or stay home and relax. As she stood to shower, she watched her cat roll over, absorbing the ray of sunshine on the floor. She watched Sasha, realizing that cats had pretty good lives, with their biggest concerns being where they should curl up and sleep next, and when should they clean their paws. Deidre noted that her body was still a little tense, even after her yoga session and knew it was because she was nervous about meeting with the attorney later in the afternoon. She had no idea why she was worried but knew that something was in the air and that her life was about to change.

~Chapter 9~

Despite their individual apprehensions and anxiety, the day flew by quickly for all three of Elizabeth's children with each arriving a few minutes before their scheduled appointment time. Elizabeth had instilled in them the importance of always being punctual, and to always fulfill any obligation expected of them. That particular expectation was about to be put to the test for her three children to decide for themselves what they wanted to do.

They were escorted into Elizabeth's attorney's conference room. Tall black leather chairs lined a massive table, that appeared to accommodate 12 to 14 people. They felt dwarfed sitting at one end, waiting for Mr. Phelps to start their meeting, read their mother's will and let them get on with their weekend.

Within a minute or two of them sitting down, Mr. Phelps shuffled in. He had been their mother's attorney since the time of their father's death, and had been invaluable to her, helping with all the legal complications of a spouse dying without a will. They'd only met him once before, but knew that if their mom trusted him, then they would trust that he did right by her, in preparing her will the way she wanted things distributed. As they stood to greet her attorney, it became real again, the reason for them all being together. This was the final time that they'd be discussing anything legal with this man and the finality of their mother's death hit them all again as they were greeted by the somber looking man in front of them. In his arms, he carried two binders, and a cup of coffee. Setting down his coffee, he greeted each one with a stiff handshake, and eventual smile. He asked them to be seated and make themselves comfortable, as he took another sip of his coffee, and proceeded to slide a DVD into the blue ray player in the corner of the room. The three of them watched him precariously but remained silent. When he didn't turn the TV on, they all assumed that he'd brought it for a meeting following theirs and had simply wanted to set it down.

"Thank you all for coming today. Let me start by saying, that I'm very sorry for your loss. Liz was a wonderful person and I'm sure that she'll be missed by everyone whose lives she touched."

Deidre willed back tears, as her sister reached under the table and squeezed her hand. Always the emotional one, Maggie knew that she had to help her sister stay in control or the meeting would become a fiasco for everyone in the room.

Joshua addressed the attorney standing before him.

"Thank you Mr. Phelps. Our mother was an incredible lady and we were blessed to have had her as our mother, and father figure after the passing of our dad. Coming here today has been very emotionally draining for all of us so I know that your time is very valuable, so maybe we should just jump into this and get started."

Mr. Phelps chuckled. "You're a lot like your father Joshua," he smiled. "Yes, I knew him. We all attended college together, and your dad was one of my best friends at school. I lost a part of myself when he passed. I can say with great sincerity that he'd be so proud of everything the three of you have accomplished."

He let the realization that he was not only their mother's attorney but obviously also her friend, sink in. Before he said another word, he sat down next to Elizabeth's children to be eye level with them before he proceeded.

"Let me begin by telling you that your mother had already put her will in place, shortly after she lost your father, so everything in it, she did with a sound mind, and before the cancer was present. With that said, she wanted me to stress to you all how much she truly loved you and that not only were you three her world, but your father was as well."

Always the romantic, Deidre interrupted the attorney in between sentences.

"What were they like in college Mr. Phelps? If you knew them back then, tell us what mom and dad were like? That is, if you have time before your next client arrives," she added softly.

He smiled, remembering back to years ago, when life was carefree and less stressful. "Of course I have time Deidre," he answered.

"Let me first start by saying that your father and I were inseparable that first semester of college. We met the first week there and had many classes together and were actually housed in the same dorm, but on different floors. We partied and studied together and simply hit it off from the day we met. And then Elizabeth came along," he smiled, reminiscing.

"Your father saw her in the cafeteria that first day, and we both commented on how gorgeous she was. Your mother was a looker back then, and we both wanted a chance to get to know her; but the instant she made eye contact with your dad, I knew that I didn't stand a chance," he chuckled. "One thing about your momma," he laughed, "Was when she set her sights on something, she made it happen. Your mother knew that we were both watching her, and after she got her meal, she walked right up to the table where your dad and I were sitting and asked if she could join us. Your father damn near spit his coke out, he was that flabbergasted that someone that looked like her would be actually speaking to us. Elizabeth was so self-assured, she simply smiled and sat down next to your dad before either of us could formulate any words to respond to her. We ate our lunch together that day, and almost every day forward from then on. She told us where she was from, and that she'd worked a few years out of school to save up some money to attend, and that she was a nursing major. Your father hung on every word she spoke, and within a week, I knew that I was a third wheel," he laughed, caught up in his own memories of a time so long ago. "Bet you kids didn't know that your dad stood up for me in my own wedding? Your dad got the girl from Utica, but I was fortunate enough to find my Betty about a month later when we all attended a frat party down on Rutger Street. Back then, all of the frats and sororities were located on Rutger. Luckily for me, my Betty was more into nerdy looking guys who studied all the time, and she became my bride one month before your dad married your mother."

"But enough about the past," he said, suddenly turning very serious. "I know that we're here for the reading of your mother's will and testament, which we will be doing shortly. I will read to you what she asked me to execute, followed by a short DVD your mother compiled prior to her death. One explains the other, so please bear with me, and reframe from any questions until after we've finished both. At that time, I'll answer your questions to the best of my knowledge," he said somberly.

He looked around the room at the two women and Elizabeth's son and without further delay, put his reading glasses on and proceeded to read their mother's will. As they'd expected, she'd divided her assets in thirds, leaving them all equal amounts, had had the foresight to put her camp into a trust for them to share equally, and had put a very substantial amount into a trust fund to cover the taxes for the next couple decades and had made it very clear that the fund was set up in order for them to pass the camp down to the next generation as they aged. She'd asked that they put her home on the market with a dear friend of hers, and had already established its' fair market value and agreed on a listing price, and asked that Joshua oversee its' sale, with 25% of the proceeds to go toward Deidre's soup kitchen to keep them in the black, and allow them to expand when possible, and the remainder to be split three ways amongst themselves. She'd designated $30,000 per child to be used solely toward their respective weddings, and had told her attorney to hush them when they snickered and rebutted that part of the will. All three of them laughed when he read them that part of Elizabeth's will, for she'd known her children would claim that marriage wasn't in the foreseeable future for any of them.

Mr. Phelps continued to read the very detailed instructions regarding who Elizabeth wanted to conduct the estate sale once her children had taken whatever pieces they wanted from her home, along with whom she'd like to "sell" her car to. Her will explained that she worked with a young single mother who took the bus to work every night because her ex took their van when he packed up, maxed up their credit cards and skipped town. Elizabeth wanted her SUV to be given to her friend Brenda, along with a gift card for gas to help her out. Deidre's eyes welled up at the kind act, that even in death her mother was still giving. Everyone silently nodded in agreement, when Mr. Phelps asked if everyone agreed with their mother's decision to donate her SUV. Mr. Phelps read the last remaining paragraphs regarding the distribution of their mother's final assets. Once he concluded reading from his written script, he placed his paperwork on the large oak desk, removed his glasses, and sat back in his chair, waiting for the inevitable questions.

No one spoke for a few moments, but then Josh asked what all three of them were silently thinking.

"Mr. Phelps, I don't mean to sound greedy or like I'm disappointed in what our mother has left each of us. Please understand, that I think that I can speak for both of my sisters in saying, that each of us would give every cent back if it meant we could have our mother back; but we know that's not possible. I guess what I'm beating around the bush to ask, is if our mom had any life insurance policies or any other financial assets because I am pretty certain that both she and dad had both whole life and term life policies and they weren't mentioned here today? Did her disease cause her to have to cash them out? Again, I'm not trying to sound greedy but I'm just very analytical and like covering all bases. Also, he added, I know that our mother had a very sizable 401K through her hospital because she had me assisting her with her bills and paperwork as she became more and more ill. You haven't mentioned that either. If mom donated all of it, that's fine; but we need to know and understand that as well."

Mr. Phelps looked at each of Elizabeth's children and responded slowly, choosing his words.

"You are correct Joshua, your mother does have a very sizable 401K, and a life insurance policy issued by her hospital, along with two insurance plans that she purchased after marrying your father. They are all potentially yours, and I could tell you the stipulations to the disbursement of her policies, but I think it would be easier if you watched the short video that your mom made, and then I'll answer any questions that you have."

Both Maggie and Deidre gasped at the idea of seeing their mother alive again, at least alive on film. Josh, ever grounded, eyed his mother's attorney suspiciously.

"What's going on Mr. Phelps? My sister's and I just lost our mother and I'm not quite sure what this is all about, but I know that I don't want you to present anything that's going to upset them."

"Josh," he responded, "I can't tell you how you're going to feel or how the three of you will respond to the information that your mother wants to tell you herself. The only thing that I ask, as both your mother and father's lifelong friend, is that you listen to what she has to say, listen to what she's asking of you, and then follow your heart. Your parents raised all three of you to be like them. In saying that, I know that your hearts are always open to loving and giving, especially to those who need it the most. Your mother evidenced that by the gestures in her will. She was always trying to help others, and make the world a better place, and I know that once you process what she has told you; you'll do the right thing. Now, I'll start the tape, and give the three of you some privacy. When you've completed watching it and are ready for me to come back in and discuss your mother's request in more detail, then simply open the door and my secretary will notify me in my office.

He hit play, and silently left the room, closing the door behind them. Josh saw Maggie reach across the table to take Deidre's hand. He took her other hand to connect the link between the three of them as the DVD started playing. It took only a second for whomever had been filming the tape to go from a shot of the exterior of their childhood home to inside their family room with their mother sitting in her favorite chair, feet up and relaxed. This was the way her children would always remember her, and she wouldn't want it any other way. She smiled into the camera and spoke. Hearing her voice again after not hearing it so full of life, caught all of them off guard. It was so wonderful to hear her again, but it didn't change the realization that she was still gone.

"Oh boy, if you, my beautiful children are watching this, then I know I'm dead," she chuckled. "Please don't mourn any more for me, because if you're watching this, know that I'm with your dad in heaven and couldn't be happier. I promise you that I'll always watch over you my loves, but if you're watching this video right now, then

God needed me in heaven more than you needed me there on earth so promise me, no more tears; just fond memories."

The DVD zoomed away from their mother and started a slide show that she'd compiled from before they were born, to their childhood when their father had still been alive, to their various concerts, athletic events, and graduations. She'd included slide after slide of happier times, times when all the world had seemed right and perfect and when their family was whole.

After the slide show was completed, their mother appeared back on the screen, but this time, she wasn't filming in their childhood home, but at the lake. Her children smiled, seeing their mother sprawled out on her favorite ADK lounger, with a glass of wine at her side. Each of them thought about how much their mother loved heading to camp for a long weekend, or even for her day off. With their cabin less than an hour drive away, it wasn't uncommon to touch base with her and find that she'd driven to the lake for the day. They watched the screen as their mom took a sip of whatever type of wine that she had in her glass, watched her gaze out at the lake for just a moment, take a deep breath and then square her shoulders, straighten up and look square at the camera.

"Okay guys, obviously Mr. Phelps has read my last will and testament to you. And if I know you Josh, you've already used that analytical mind of yours to realize that all of my money hasn't been accounted for," she smiled.

I know that each of you have worked very hard for everything that you have, whether it's in the form of stocks, bonds, property or equity of some other type, but I want you to fulfill one last wish for me, and in exchange, I want you to have everything that I've worked so hard for all of my life. I've instructed my attorney to keep the actual amount of my investments confidential until you each have decided for yourselves whether or not you are willing to fulfill my last wish. Before I tell you what my wish is, please know that what I'm about to tell you might affect each of you differently, and that being said, one, two or all of you might decide that you aren't interested in pursuing my dream. If you decide against it, you will still be entitled to half your share of my inheritance, with your other half being split between the ones that agree to follow through with my wishes. In the event that none of you choose to pursue my wish, then half of your inheritance will be given to a charity that I've designated." She paused, allowing her children to let what she was asking of them, to sink in. With a few seconds, she continued talking.

"First of all, know that I'm not trying to black mail or bribe you into helping me. Whether you choose to complete my wish or not, you will receive a very nice windfall and I'm happy that I'm able to leave you something more than memories," she smiled. "But what I'm about to tell you means more to me than I could ever convey in words, and I hope that the three of you work together to make my last wish come true. It's something that I should have done during my lifetime, but call me a coward, or whatever, I never got around to it; mainly out of fear of rejection."

Elizabeth's children heard the regret in their mother's voice as she continued talking, with each of them fearing what she was about to tell them. Joshua worried that he might learn that his mother had been in the witness protection program, or that she'd committed some horrendous crime in her youth and had spent time in prison, while Maggie's initial thought had been that maybe she conceived one or several of her children with someone other than the man they'd all known as dad. Deidre, always the dreamer and optimist, simply thought that her mother's wish would be for the three of them to go off on some adventure together and spend their mother's money doing it. Deidre knew that her mother always thought that they'd worked too hard and too much, so in her mind, she thought that maybe her mom's wish was for them to spend more time together.

"Let me start by saying, that as I'm sure Rod has told you by now, I met your father during my first semester in college. I was twenty when I started and had chosen to work a few years after high school in order to save up some money to put towards college tuition. Your father had also worked a couple of years for the same reason so when we met at school, we were both a little more mature than other freshmen students and we hit it off right from the Start. Your father always told everyone that when I said yes when he asked me out on a date, he knew that we'd marry someday; I was the one who took a little longer to convince. You see," she paused for just a second, "I was deeply in love with someone before your dad, and thought I'd marry him. But like life, plans change, and sometimes life throws you curveballs and it certainly did when it came to Danny and I," she laughed.

"I know that some of what I'm about to tell you might be hard to listen to, but if it hadn't happened, then I would have never delayed attending college, never met your father, fallen deeply in love with the man that was the love of my life, and had you three children. Everything that happened up until that fall day that I met your dad, I firmly believe, happened in order for me to get to where I was meant to be in life, and that was with your father."

"Danny and I started dating in our Junior year of high school and we were the "it" couple. We spent every day and most evenings together. We loved the same things, played the same sports, and shared the same friends, values, and beliefs. We were each others' firsts for many things and we lost our virginity together during Christmas break our Senior year. Don't cringe Joshua," his mother instructed. "Just because I'm your mother, doesn't mean I wasn't a teenager like you were once. And yes, I remember when you and Sally would sneak into your room to do "homework" Joshua, so it's no different than that. Just because I'm your mother doesn't mean I didn't have urges just like any other teen. The only difference was the fact that I was head over heels in love with my Danny and I honestly thought that we'd get married right after high school. Out of our love, we created a daughter."

Elizabeth stopped talking, silently smiled still while looking directly at them, wiping one lone tear from her eye. "I became pregnant with our daughter and despite the challenges that being a high school senior and knocked up imposed, I never regretted my decision to give birth instead of abort our baby. Our daughter was born on October 4th 1982, and we named her Michelle Marie. It was a very different world back then and unlike today, where 75% of the births are to unwed mother's; when my daughter was born, only my name was listed on her birth certificate. Most girls in my situation were shipped off until they delivered their babies, whether to a distant aunts, their grandparent's home out of town, or, like in my case, to a home for unwed mothers. They treated us well, but we were alone when we delivered our babies and it was horrifying. When I went into labor, I wanted my Danny by my side, but no one had cell phones back then, and we were only allowed to call home on Sundays. My parents weren't even notified until after Michelle was born. I took care of my daughter 24/7 until it was time for me to return home, without my daughter. Danny came to pick me up, and was allowed to hold his daughter for maybe ten minutes tops. We gave her up because we thought it was her best chance at a good life, one that two 18 year old teens couldn't provide her, and also because our parents basically insisted that we give her up. Danny and I were just kids and our parents kept hounding us, telling us that we couldn't provide our daughter with a good home and that she'd be better off in a home with a married couple. As much as we dreamt of a happily ever after with our little girl, Danny and I let our parents talk us into giving her up. Michelle Marie, my daughter, was adopted about a month after I gave birth to her."

Elizabeth paused, and seemed to be thinking back to that very sad day so many years before. Her children remained silent, each processing what their mother had just told them.

"Danny and I rode back from Buffalo in silence; with both of us forced to acknowledge what we'd both given up. Danny told me that maybe we'd made a mistake and should get married and get our daughter back, but I knew that neither of us was ready to get married, I had just lost my daughter and didn't want to force her father into doing something that he might later regret so I told him no, and basically shut him out of my life, hoping he'd forgive me someday for giving up on our daughter and on him. I loved him so much but didn't want him marrying me out of pity, or falsely placed obligation. I was so confused, so hurt because I'd abandoned my daughter, despite the good intentions associated with my decision, and so lost. I thought that if I gave him space, he'd make his decision and if he came back to me, then I'd know it was out of love, not obligation. He tried to reach out to me in every way possible, through phone calls, daily visits to my parent's home, and through our friends. I refused to see him, ashamed of what I'd done. He begged me to meet with him, and talk to him, but I was literally drowning in sorrow, and the agony brought on by my decision. My heart was completely broken, and I couldn't bear to see the disappointment in Danny's eyes again, so I ignored him and pushed him away. It was the only time in my life that I was consumed with complete misery and despair. It took a few weeks to finally dig myself out of the black hole that I'd fallen in. I knew that Danny wanted to marry me, and despite my parent's opinion, I knew that he could provide for my daughter and I, so when I finally came to that realization, I raced to his house; but it was too late. My Daniel had joined the Air Force and had left just that morning for basic training. Danny's mother yelled at me. As I sit here today telling you my story, I can still hear her voice, blaming me for stealing her granddaughter and taking her son from her. She had always been so kind to me, but through the hurt and sadness of her son leaving, she told me that it was my fault that her only son was gone. She made sure I knew that Danny had contacted an attorney and Catholic Charities, the agency used in my daughter's adoption, to attempt to legally adopt her, but back then, fathers weren't given any rights, and that he was told that Michelle was already in the home of her new parents. The month of October 1982 was the worst month of my life, having lost both my daughter, and her father. My Danny left that fall day and I never heard from him again. I checked the mail every day for months, and I wallowed in self-hate and chastised myself for abandoning my little girl, and pushing Danny away. I worked almost every day of the week, trying to keep my mind occupied, and on anything other than wondering what she was doing, how big she was getting, and if her adoptive parents would ever tell her that she had another father and mother out there in the world who loved her. I can't speak for Danny, but I can tell you that there has never been a day in my life that I haven't thought about my little girl and the woman that she must have grown up to become. You three are my children, and I gave up the right to call her mine, the day I signed away my parental rights; but she will always be my daughter, at least in my heart. I beg you to not think less of me because I was in love with someone before your father. And I hope that you don't judge me for not being perfect. I never proclaimed that I was perfect, only that I was human. And now for my request. What I'm asking for you to do, is something that I should have done at the time of Michelle's birth. I would have pursued it myself, but out of respect for your father, and for the three of you, I never put my plan and dream into action."

Elizabeth took another small swallow from her glass of wine, it was as if she needed to do so to regain her composure.

"I have two requests of you. First, I want you to find Danny and deliver the package to him that's already been discussed. You can deliver it to him either in person or via mail. I would like to think that your curiosity would get the better of you and once you find Daniel, you'll meet him just once in order to deliver the package in person, but that's entirely up to you. I give you my word, what I need you to deliver to him is not in any way a betrayal to your father. I know you'll believe me but I also left the contents that you'll give Daniel, in unsealed envelopes for you to read at your leisure, if you choose to. That is my first request, but my second, and more important request, I implore you to follow through with. I want, actually NEED you to track down and find my daughter. She might only be your half sister, but she is part of me and therefore part of you. I want you to find Michelle Marie, and meet with her, spend time with her, and get to know the daughter that I was never allowed to know. Once you've discovered her new identity, and have made contact, I want you to invite her to our lake house and once there, get to know your sister, and give her something that I've wanted her to have for over thirty years. I know I've left you speechless, and probably confused, and a little disappointed and angry with me; and for that, I'm very sorry. Do not think for a minute

Joshua that you weren't my first born because you were. Your father and I welcomed you as our first child and I can not tell you how much we loved you. You made us a family and there aren't words to describe what a feeling that is. Someday when you and Jena have children, you will understand. Maggie May, if I know you as I do, you're really pissed off right about now, thinking that you're not my first gal. You're wrong. I gave birth to Michelle, but she was never mine. We had decided to give her up for adoption even before she was born, so you need to understand that when your father and I had you, we felt so blessed and complete, having a perfect son and daughter. You have always been my mini-me, and though I wish you didn't have my temper, there isn't a thing that I would change about you. You will always be my oldest daughter. And Deidre, you have the best qualities of both your father and I, and when you were born, you reminded me so much of that little girl that I'd given birth to long before. I'd like to think that my Michelle grew up to be half as beautiful inside and out as you are. If she grew up in a loving home, I would like to think that she grew into the kind of woman who cares about others, much the way you do on a daily basis. Now, I know that I'm asking a lot and there are so many variables in my requests. I honestly have no idea if Daniel is even alive, but if he is, and if you discover Michelle's identity and she is agreeable; my last request is that you reunite Daniel with his daughter. I should have done it back in October 1982, but I can't change time. But you three can change the future.   Please, please give my requests serious consideration, and I pray that you will eventually understand why this is so important to me. I made a mistake, not in having a child out of wedlock, but in letting her go and hurting so many people in the crosshairs. I'd like to make amends now, even though its' too late for me to do it, it's not too late for you. Please help me reunite my daughter with her father."

Elizabeth went silent for a few moments, allowing her three children to catch their breath, and digest what she'd just told them.

"I have instructed Mr. Phelps to assist you in any legal capacity that you may need, and with any expenses that you incur. I know that I'm asking so much of you, and for that, I'm sorry. I wish that I'd have had the courage to find Michelle myself but as I said earlier, I was terrified of her rejecting me, the same way that she might think I did to her. I never rejected her, but she might think of it that way. All I ask of you, is that you try. If she doesn't want to meet with you or learn about her birth father, or spend a few days with you guys, getting to know her half siblings, then that's on her; but I think that she'll be receptive, once you've found her.   Just try, and let whatever happens, happen. Please start by finding Danny and go from there. Don't tell Danny that I've passed, I've explained it all in the letters I'd like you to give him. One last thing that I want to make perfectly clear to you, my children, was that Michelle was conceived in love. I truly loved Danny, her father, but only as much as a teenager has the capacity to love. I never attempted to contact Daniel after I met your father because I would have never done anything behind your dad's back or anything that he might consider some type of betrayal. Over the years, your dad always knew how hard the week leading up to Michelle's birthday was, and being your dad, he always respected my feelings and gave me space until her birthday passed. He asked me on more than one occasion if I wanted to find Danny and Michelle, and told me he'd help find them if I wanted to pursue it; but I always refused. I didn't think I deserved to have either of them in my life ever again, so I never allowed your father to push the topic any further. I never wanted to ever betray your father, in any way, shape or form, and even though he's been gone for a long time, I never once considered dating again after he passed, because in my mind, he was my one and only and no one would have ever matched up to your father. I hope that you always remember that when you take on my request."

"I'm going to say goodbye for now my loves. But don't worry, I'm never far away. Even heaven and your dad can't keep me from coming back and watching over the three of you. I love each of you more than you'll ever know. You are my greatest accomplishments, and I am so proud of all of you. Goodbye for now Joshua, Maggie May and Deidre. Don't cry. I'll always be with you."

The screen went black, and once again, their mother was gone from their lives. Elizabeth's children remained motionless with Deidre trying her best to stifle her sniffles, while Maggie leaned in to hug her tight. Joshua was as shaken as his sisters but knew that he needed to keep it together for them. He squeezed both of their hands and smiled.

"I can't begin to speak for you both, but the way I see it is that our mother might be gone, but she is still worrying about us, and still giving us amazing gifts. We've been blessed with the gift of her love all of our lives, and now she's given us one last gift, and it comes in the form of a sister." He squeezed both of their hands tightly.

" You two might be the only sisters I've ever had, but I think I have room in my heart for one more, and I hope that both of you do as well. She might not want to have anything to do with us, but we won't know that for sure, if we don't at least find her and introduce ourselves. What do you think? Do we find our sister or let mom's secret die with her?"

It was Deidre who spoke immediately. "No!," she responded through tears. "If Michelle came from our mother, then she is part of us and she is family, despite having a different father. We need to find our sister and her father. It's the least we can do for our mother. She deserves to rest in peace, and Michelle needs to know that she was always wanted and loved. We owe that to mom."

Maggie took longer to respond, weighting what her mother had said in the tape, and what her siblings' opinions were, against her own thoughts. She hated change, and hated conflict, but more importantly, she hated the idea that they could track this woman down, and the Michelle woman could resent them for being given away, or worse, not know that she was adopted. She tried to put herself in the woman's shoes, and despite her reluctance, had to acknowledge to herself that if she were Michelle, she'd want to know her heritage as well. So, she looked at her brother, and then into her baby sister's eyes, and through tears of her own, smiled. "I don't know if we'll find her or not, but it appears that we have a sister who's about to gain herself three more siblings," she smiled. "I'm in if you are."

Deidre practically jumped into her sister's arms. "Oh my God Maggie, we've got another sister out there! This is so cool!"

Trying to reign them in, Joshua, ever collected, coughed to attempt to gain their attention. "Before you two are thinking about your next shopping trip with our new sister, I think we've got to take it back a few steps and let all of this digest and think about it a few days, and then go from there." He walked over to the door, opening it as instructed by their mother's attorney, and returned to his chair. His two sisters were talking incessantly as Josh's mind wandered until Mr. Phelps returned into the room.

He was pleased to see that Elizabeth's children had taken the news better than he had anticipated. When she'd first told him about her request of her children, he'd tried to discourage her from pursuing it, but she'd been adamant about locating her daughter and the father of her child. She'd given him every bit of information that she had regarding Daniel's full name, date of birth, the branch he'd served in and his childhood address. Elizabeth had provided her attorney with the agency that had fostered her daughter's adoption, Michelle's date of birth, and anything that she thought might be helpful.

"I assume that your mother's tape has left you with more questions than answers," he smiled. "Let me start by saying, I sincerely hope that you give your mother's request some serious consideration. As I told you earlier, I have known both your mother and father, for a very long time and if her request to you is to help locate her daughter, then you can be certain that she struggled with that decision for a very long time. Elizabeth wouldn't have made a decision like this without weighing all the pros and cons, and I know in my heart that your dad would support you if your decision is to complete your mother's journey."

He already knew their response but needed to hear it from the three of them.

Josh spoke for the family.

"I don't know how we couldn't go forward with the information we now know. Somewhere, out there, we have a sister, who may be looking for us as well, or may not even know of our existence and the fact that she was adopted. Either way, she deserves to know that whether she likes it or not," he smiled, just enough to let his dimples show, "she has three siblings who'd like to get to know her and tell her about her birth mother. We have valuable medical information that we can provide her, and also the name of her birth father, should she want to meet him. If we find her, deliver whatever it is that our mother wants us to give to her, and she then chooses to keep us at arm's length, then at least we've done our due diligence and can move on. The choice will be hers to make."

"Good, I was hoping that your decision was to follow your mother's wishes. I have envelopes for each of you that your mother instructed me to give to you, but only if you agreed to move forward in locating her daughter and her daughter's father. It might not be all that easy as we don't know her adoptive name, and the birth father's name is quite common, but I think between three computer savvy kids such as yourselves, you'll be able to narrow it down fairly quickly," he smiled.

Elizabeth's attorney handed each of her children legal sized envelopes that were sealed, and with their names carefully written, in their mother's hand, on them. Just seeing her mother's handwriting again was enough to trigger a few more tears as Deidre looked at her name, perfectly scribed. Maggie took her envelope, contained any emotion that she might have been feeling, thanking the man standing in front of her. Once Josh was handed the third envelope, the one meant for him, he also thanked Mr. Phelps and ushered his sisters toward the exit. No one spoke until they were out of his office, out of the building and in the parking lot.

"Well holy shit!" Maggie burst out. "Didn't exactly see that one coming," she continued. "Kinda odd that no one mentions that there's another kid out there until both mom and dad are gone and we can't ask them questions. It actually kind of sucks, I think!"

Always the level headed one, Josh was the first to respond to his sister's outburst.

"Mom was always there for us Mags, and she never to my knowledge, ever lied. I think that she and our father didn't tell us about Michelle before this because we didn't have a need to know. Maybe we weren't supposed to know about her until now. Come on, let's get out of here and go have a beer. I know I could use one."

"Okay, but only one since I am heading up to camp for the weekend. Dee's coming with me so why don't you give Jena the weekend to herself and come with us. I have no idea what's in the envelope to mom's first boyfriend and I sure as hell know I'm not wasting my time tracking him down until I know more about this Danny guy. Let's bring all of this shit up to camp with us, have a few beers, wine, or whatever, and talk this through and determine our game plan from there. Will you join us Josh?"

"Oh yes Josh, say you'll come! Please!!!" Deidre added.

"Alright, alright. Let's skip the beer for now. I'll go home and talk to Jena and plan on meeting you up there later tonight, okay?"

"Great. Jena can come if you want. You're going to tell her about our dear sister anyways, so if she wants to join us, it's fine with me," Maggie said, smiling. "She's my favorite future sister in law you know," she laughed, as she said it as she hugged her big brother and held him tightly, still trying to contain her very mixed emotions.

He leaned down and whispered into her ear. "It's going to be okay Mags. I love you." Then straightened himself up and smiled at his two sisters. "I'll bring a couple of extra bottles of wine, most likely Jena, and will grab a pizza and wings on the way up. Let me get home and pack and I'll see you at the lake in a couple of hours."

He started toward his truck, turned and shouted to his sisters.

"Dad always loved a good adventure, and I bet you that he and mom are looking down from heaven, just waiting for us to begin this next chapter. So, no matter how it plays out, let's not let them down and let's give them a great show." He didn't wait to hear a reply, just walked to his truck and drove away.

Maggie still was very unsettled and unsure how she felt about having another sister, one that hadn't been part of her life, ever. Deidre could read her older sister like a book, and didn't attempt to comfort her, knowing she was one to work things out on her own whereas she would prefer reassurance in the form of a hug. She turned toward her car and smiled. "It's going to be an adventure Maggie. And she might fill the hole that mom's leaving has left in our hearts. She's part of mom and we owe her that much. So, I'm going to give Michelle a chance when we meet her, and I hope you will too. See you at the lake."

She waited in her truck until she saw her sister, Miss Optimistic herself, drive off. Looking down at the sealed envelope with her name on it, she felt the emotions finally coming to the surface. There hadn't been a day, hour, or barely a minute that she hadn't thought about her mother since she had passed. She'd see something on TV and would think about calling her mother to remind her that The Voice was coming on, or to remind her that their favorite sitcom was airing a new episode. She and her mother would routinely get together to watch SU basketball games, eating popcorn and laughing through the entire game. As Maggie thought of all the things that no longer were possible or ever going to happen again, she found herself starting to shake. The tears that she'd kept at bay for the last two weeks started to flow, with Maggie making no attempt to hold them in. She was supposed to be the strong one, the one who always kept her composure and here she was, sobbing like a baby in her truck. She always tried to maintain a sense of decorum and never let anyone see that she too was human and vulnerable just like her sister; but found herself unable to will back the tears that poured from her eyes. As she reached into her purse, trying to find a tissue, she didn't notice that she was being watched, nor did she see him until he approached her truck and knocked on her window, causing her to nearly jump out of her seat. She looked up at the man standing beside her truck in what appeared to be a Brunello Cucinelli suit and focused on the face staring down at her. She wasn't sure but she was pretty certain that she knew him from somewhere and didn't feel nervous, sitting in the sanctity of her locked vehicle. It wasn't until he spoke and smiled that his dimples appeared, and she knew who the man behind the Oakley glasses was.

"You look like someone who could use a friend, or at least a tissue and a stiff drink," he spoke in a soft, quiet tone.

"I've had better days. And could use at least two of your three suggestions," she responded, not committing to which two she was most in need of.

"Well, call me an old soul, but I love the band Meatloaf, and you know what they say, "Two out of three ain't bad", he laughed. I'm really hoping that you have a tissue but need a friend and a drink, because I'm offering you both."

She pulled a tissue out of the bottom of her bag and smiled. "Tell you what, I'm definitely a mess right now and actually need to head north to meet up with my sister; but if our paths cross again, you can definitely buy me that drink," she all but purred, not wanting to blow him off, because he definitely intrigued her, but desperately wanting to be alone at the moment. Everything she'd just learned about her mother, and a half-sister that she'd never known about, was still swirling in her head and she needed to process it all before reaching camp and her siblings. But as he removed his sun glasses and looked down at her, she couldn't help but see the kindness in his eyes. They were blue, but not baby blue, more of an azure color like the water she'd snorkeled in, in the Caribbean.

Disappointed but not giving up, he pulled out a card from his briefcase, scribbled something on the back, and handed it to her. Looking down at it, she read what it said and looked back up at the man who was now leaning in, resting his hand on the window frame of her truck.

"Nice," she smiled. "Pretty fancy title for a smelly man from the gym Garrett Brown, attorney at law."

"What can I say, I'm a jack of all trades, master of none; but I clean up pretty well. And Maggie, I'm not sure why you were in our law office today, nor do I expect you to tell me, but I do want to become your friend, and I do want to see you again."

She felt something stir inside her, something that she hadn't felt in a very long time. "You intrigue me Garrett, and I would like to become your friend. It's just that I've, actually my sister, brother and I, have some unfinished business to attend to, and once that's out of the way, I would like to add you to my list of friends. That is, as long as you don't have a wife or girlfriend that would mind," she chuckled, just trying to make sure that he truly was available to pursue, if she desired.

"I'm married, but only to my work. I do have a love that I probably should tell you about though, because if it's a problem, I should probably take my card back right now."

She felt her heart sink and shot daggers at him. "Um, you might want to elaborate a little more."

"Her name is Jazmine and she's been the love of my life for three years now. She's gorgeous and has a habit of taking up way too much of my bed, but I take one look at her face, and can't say no."

She found herself initially getting infuriated that this bozo of a man would have to\he audacity to be hitting on her while he has a woman at home, until he continued talking about his love.

"She's stunning really, and I love that she's darker than the ladies I usually prefer but I thought I'd take a chance and she's never let me down and is always happy to see me walk in the door. I hope you like dogs Maggie, because she comes as part of the package."

Her mind processed quickly that the lady in his life was in fact, a dog and not a woman.

"Actually, I do. Mine love is named Sinjin and he's a handful himself. He's an English Lab, yellow in color and comes with this package," she replied, gesturing to herself.

"I'm very happy to hear that. My Jaz is a Chocolate Lab, also English. I knew when I saw you at the gym that you were a good person, and now that I know you have a lab, I'm 100% convinced."

He stood and stepped away from her truck. "I hope that the issues that you and your siblings have to address are solved quickly and seamlessly for you and your sister and brother. And after they are, I sincerely hope that you call me sometime Maggie. The friendship and drink come without strings or attachments. I'd just like to get to know you, and we can go from there."

"I'd like that too Garrett. Let me get through this little issue, and then let's plan on introducing Sinjin and Jazmine and see what happens," she smiled.

"Great. Have a great weekend Maggie." He smiled, turned, and walked away, leaving her speechless for the second time in one day. Then it dawned on her. She laughed out loud, and looked up at the sky for some time of sign.

"Mom," she laughed. "Enough already," she joked. "I know, I know; I promised that I'd improve my social life, but after the bombshell you just laid on us, I don't think that now is the time to have you trying to play matchmaker, now do you?"

She knew there'd be no response, so she started her truck, threw it into gear and started to exit the parking garage, just as Meatloaf's "Two Out Of Three Ain't Bad" came onto her Sirius radio. She smiled through the tears and headed toward home.

~Chapter 10~

Once home, Maggie threw together an overnight bag even though she and her siblings all kept clothes at camp. Fall nights in the Adirondacks can change like the wind, with one night in the fifties and the following ushering in a snowstorm. Always a minimalist, she packed for warmth and more importantly, for comfort, making sure she remembered extra socks, a pair of slippers and her hiking boots. She packed her camera just in case she and Sinjin decided to go for a hike or simply a walk in the woods. She'd left the packages from the attorney on the seat of her truck, and made a mental note to herself to put them in her computer bag to avoid misplacing them. She'd been tempted to open the letter addressed to her from her mother but didn't know if she was ready to see what it contained yet or not. She packed her laptop in case they wanted to start researching online. And as she thought about the fact that she had another sister, one that an hour ago she didn't know existed, she found herself walking to her wine cooler, and taking out a bottle of Pinot Grigio that she hadn't opened yet. Thinking of her brother, who she knew didn't appreciate wine the way that she and her sister did, she went to her liquor cabinet and pulled out a bottle of Jameson's that she'd been saving for a very special occasion. She figured that now was as good a time as any to have a cocktail or two but wasn't sure if they'd be drinking to celebrate or commiserate. What she did know was that she, Josh and Deidre were in it together, and no matter what, they'd always be her family and whether or not they got to know their mother's other child or not, had no bearing on what they were. They'd always been a unit, especially after their father died; and the addition of another sibling would never impact what they had. She had already made up her mind about the older sister that she'd just learned about. She'd fulfill her mother's wishes and help her sister and brother find her, no matter what it took; but that would be that. She didn't need another sister, nor did she have any interest in forming some type of bond with a woman who only shared her mother's blood, nothing more. If they found her, she'd help reunite her with her biological father, if possible, and then she'd wash her hands of the entire situation and move on with her life. She had everything she needed in her life, and certainly didn't need another sister, or boyfriend despite what her mother had thought; and liked her life exactly as it presently was. As she carried her bag, computer bag, and Sinjin's leash out to her truck, with her dog following, she found herself mad at a sister she'd never met, for messing with her life and her status quo. She went back inside, threw a few essentials into her cooler, and once completed, locked up and headed back toward her truck. Her dog had made himself at home in her front seat she noted as she approached. Remembering that she'd left the envelope on the front seat, she quickened her pace to get inside. In his desire to ride shotgun, he'd pushed the envelope onto the floor of her front seat. She thought about leaving it there but leaned over and picked it up with the intent of putting it into her computer bag for safe keeping. The envelope had been torn partially open, probably from her dog's nails, and holding it in her hand, curiosity got the better of her. She stared at the white business sized envelope with her name neatly inscribed in her mother's hand and couldn't help herself. She found that her hands were shaking, just a little bit, as she reached into the envelope and removed its' contents. In doing so, she found a lone sheet of paper and several pictures, each were of she and her mother. As she stared down at the smiling faces in each of the pictures, memories came flooding back. Elizabeth had put them in chronological order from oldest to most recent. The first one was Maggie as a newborn, cradled gently in her mother's arms. Her heart broke, just a little more, looking down at it, seeing both her mother and father when they were so young, so in love, and so alive. Her brother stood at their father's side, with his arms wrapped around their dad's leg. There was less than two years between she and Josh so she knew that he wouldn't have even been two in the picture. Maggie tucked the first picture behind and found herself staring at herself as a five-year-old on her first day of school. She'd seen this picture a hundred times growing up, but somehow knowing that her mother had included it in her last letter to her hit home and made her smile. She tried to remember back that far but couldn't. The next picture was her making her first communion, along with Deidre. Her parent's had purposely held her back in religion class so that she and Dee could attend communion and later confirmation class together which had irritated her when she was younger but as an adult, she knew that it had been out of convenience and made sense. She burst out laughing at the next picture. Her mother had included a huge closeup of a smiling Maggie, that she remembered was taken the day her braces were finally removed. That day, Maggie remembered well. Laughing to herself, she remembered that night very well also, because it was the first time that she and her then boyfriend Zachary Blackstone had dared French kissing. Up until the day her braces came off, they'd been terrified of kissing and getting their braces locked up like two battling rams. Thinking back now, she realized how silly they'd been, but as 14 year olds, who knew. Their information was only as good as the friends that were forewarning them. She looked at the picture for just a moment more. She could remember her mother picking up their old polaroid and telling her to smile. She had a typical teenager attitude and had been irritated that her mother had wanted to take her picture. All she had wanted to do upon returning home from getting the torture devices removed, was to get on her bike and go hang with her friends before the party later that evening. She saw nothing but a smile and teeth in the picture that she was holding, but remembered well the attitude that could be seen in the other pictures her mother had taken that morning. Thinking about it now, she was embarrassed about how she'd reacted, when her mother had only been trying to capture a happy moment on film. The next picture in the stack showed a seventeen year old Maggie attending her Junior Prom with Paul Hart, her boyfriend of a year at the time the picture was taken. He looked so handsome standing there in his tuxedo, and Maggie had to admit to herself, that she too looked pretty stunning, with her hair in some type of twisted up-do, and make up that Deidre had insisted on helping her apply. They both looked so young and in love with his body leaning in close to her, and his arms around her waist. Thinking about it now, she had a two second moment of regret thinking about how she and Paul had broken up in the beginning of their senior year. She wasn't one to commiserate on the past but sitting there, in her truck looking at the picture, she wondered how her life would have possibly been different if she'd supported Paul's decision to attend St. Lawrence University instead of pushing him away since he'd chosen to attend a college so far away from her own. She took one more moment, wondering what he was doing now and silently wished him well, making a mental note to look him up on Facebook or Instagram. She carefully tucked the picture away and looked at the next one in the stack. It was a picture of she and her mom taken on graduation day. She remembered the day as if it were yesterday. Her mom looked so young, so happy in the picture as she hugged her daughter, standing in her hat and gown. Maggie thought back to the short speech her mom had told her on their way to her graduation about how proud her father would have been and how she just knew that he would be looking down on her during the ceremony. Deidre had started crying, with Maggie just going along with her mother but not believing a word of it. She remembered how irritated she was of her friends who'd balked at the thought of having their pictures taken with their parents after the ceremony and how she'd silently wished that she would have been able to do just that. Sometimes she actually did feel her father's presence, especially when she needed someone to calm her, and keep her grounded. He'd been her rock and they'd been so close that her mother had always said they were "thick as thieves". It hurt to think about the fact that she had lost both of her parents at such early ages. She quickly turned the picture to the last one and didn't know what to think of it. At first she thought the two side by side pictures were of she and her sister Deidre, but in light of the situation, she knew better. With her hand visibly shaking, she turned the photo over and saw her mother's writing.

Michelle Marie *Maggie May*

Age 5 days *Age 5 days*

She turned the picture back over, and there was no denying the resemblance. Even though the lighting was different in the two pictures, anyone would see the similarities. She and her half-sister could almost have passed as twins! From the color of their eyes, to their jawbones, to the slight wave in their auburn colored hair, she and Michelle's profiles and appearance was nearly identical. She wondered, for about 5 seconds, what her sister looked like now, but as quickly as she gave it any consideration, she pushed the thought out of her head again, not interested in acknowledging that she had a half-sister somewhere in the world that might look like her. Wanting to forget the whole day, she started to put the pictures back into the envelope they'd spilled out from. She just wanted her mother back and didn't want another sister. As she started to shove the letter back into the envelope, she stopped. Knowing that she'd be thinking about what the letter contained during her drive north, she made the conscious decision to read whatever it was that her mother wanted to tell her and get it over with. She pulled the letter back out of the envelope and unfolded it gently. As she did, she caught the whiff of her mother's favorite Victoria Secret body lotion. It took her just a moment to regroup and then look down at her mother's writing.

My Dearest Maggie:

Well, I can only guess how pissed off you are at me right about now. Before I say anything else or try to make you understand or accept anything about the situation that I've thrown you and your sister and brother into; let me say just one thing... You are and will always be your father and my first-born daughter. I was merely an incubator for Michelle and I was never her mother.

If I know you as well as I do, you've met with Mr. Phelps, and obviously have seen the pictures I've included and you, my beautiful Maggie, are mad as hell at the world and for being thrust into dealing with something you have no interest in pursuing. I understand, and I'm sorry if I've let you down. I was never perfect, before I married your father, or after; but one constant was my love for you, Josh, Deidre, and your dad. I thought I knew love when I fell for Daniel and had Michelle; but it wasn't until I walked down the aisle to marry your father, and then had the three of you that I became whole.

I loved Daniel, in a different way than I did your father, and I loved the child that I created with him. That is my past and I can't nor won't apologize for it. What I'm asking of you is to go into this with an open mind. You, Josh, and Deidre were raised with two parents who loved you more than words could ever describe. I know that I gave Michelle up in hopes that she'd be raised in the same type environment, but there's no guarantee that she was. I'm asking, begging, that you and your siblings will find her, get to know her, let her know that you're family through blood, and help her find her birth father because she deserves to know that she wasn't a mistake, and that she was loved. I gave her up not because I didn't want her, but because I wanted her to have everything that I couldn't give her. I wanted her to have a family that could provide for her and give her everything that I couldn't. But if nothing else, I want you to tell her that she was loved and the seven days that I took care of her before she was adopted were seven of the happiest days of my life.

I've never asked you to do things that you didn't agree with or that made you uncomfortable, until now. I need Michelle to know that her father loved her and wanted to keep her, but it was me who made the ultimate decision. Let her hate me if she wants to, but she needs to know that he fought to keep her, but back then, fathers of unwed children weren't given any parental rights. She needs to know that her biological father loved her and wanted to legally adopt her. I only found out that he'd gone to an attorney, with his parent's support to attempt to adopt her, after she was in the home of her adoptive parents.

If you choose to help Joshua find her, tell Michelle that there wasn't a day in my entire life that I didn't think about her and wonder if she was okay. I hope that you can find it in your heart to forgive me for not telling you about Michelle until I was gone and forced to tell you this way. I guess after I was diagnosed, I didn't tell you for fear of you rejecting me and not wanting to spend quality time with me before I passed. I know it was selfish of me and for that, I'm also sorry.

I love you so much Maggie May and I pray that you'll someday forgive me for not telling you before...

Love,

Mom

Maggie reread the letter a second time before carefully folding it up and putting it back into the envelope. She kept her tears at bay until she tucked the letter away and looked down at Sinjin, who slept silently in the seat beside her. He was all that she had now. Well, besides a brother, and now it appeared, two sisters. She missed her father so much when he initially passed away. As her mother had indicated in her letter, she and her father had been inseparable, so when he died so suddenly, she was so angry at the world and at God for a long time. Her mother's passing had been different; not because she didn't care about her mother as much as her father, but because she, along with her siblings, had watched their mother waste away as the cancer destroyed her from the inside out. They knew that she was suffering so much more than she let on, so when she passed away, they knew that she was finally free from pain. She and her siblings took solace in knowing that she was once again reunited with their father and that brought them comfort. As she thought about her dad, it hit her that everyone deserves to have a father who loves them unconditionally and if her half-sister's father had taken the initiative to fight for his daughter, despite being a kid himself; then he deserved to at least meet and get to know her. Elizabeth had held the key to their past and Maggie realized that with the assistance of her brother and sister, they could unlock the future for he and his daughter, that is if they were both still alive and agreeable to meet. As Maggie started to back out of her drive, she laughed out loud, startling her dog.

"You clever fox; you knew exactly what you were doing all along didn't you mom?" she laughed. "You knew exactly which buttons to push and what nerves to hit to elicit my help," she chuckled, looking up at the sky. "I'm going to share your letter with Josh and Dee, and we'll compare notes to see how well you did to capture their attention and pull them in to your mystery. Touché momma, you got me." Wiping away one last tear, she smiled. "I'll find her mom, I promise I will. Doesn't mean I'll like her; but I'll find her for you. I just really wish you'd told us about Michelle and about Daniel as well, long before now. Maybe you could have been involved in her life in some way, who's to say. But it was your story to tell and I get that, and if you didn't want it told until now, I get that too. Not sure what we'll find when we track her down, but you know me, I love a good challenge. And yes mom," she continued talking to the air as she headed up Route 12 and towards the mountains, "I'm over my hissy fit, and I'm done being angry with you. You were faced with a dilemma and forced to make some very hard decisions at a young age. I can't imagine what you went through, nor was I judging you when I was so pissed off."

She willed away the tears starting to form again.

"I was just mad that you loved another little girl before me. But I'm over it, and we're good."

She'd made her peace with her mother and cranked up her radio as she turned onto Route 28 North and headed toward her beloved Adirondacks.

~Chapter 11~

"Jena, I really appreciate you wanting to come with me; but I don't want you to feel obligated," Joshua stated, as he threw a few articles of clothing into a backpack. "I honestly have no idea what kind of emotional state my sisters are going to be in and it might be a very emotionally taxing weekend."

She listened as her fiancée attempted to convince her to stay home, but knew that she was going, despite his best argument. They'd been together long enough for her to know the tone and stance, and what they meant; whether he understood how telling his body language was or not. He'd called her on his way home from the attorney's office and before he got home, she had already filled a cooler with a few items to hold them over through the weekend in case they didn't want to go out. She'd packed her overnight bag and packed a few bottles of wine for she and his sisters, and had grabbed an unopened 12 pack of Bud Light Platinum and a half full bottle of Jack, just in case the weekend warranted it. Being an only child, whose parents were both living, she had no clue as to how he and his sisters were feeling about all the information that had been thrown at them earlier in the day. She'd always wanted a sister and hoped that both Maggie and Deidre didn't think of this long-lost sister of theirs as a burden, but as a gift. Jena knew that she couldn't put herself in their shoes, but for just a moment, before Joshua returned home, she'd thought about how she would feel if she had just learned that she had a sister. Jena admitted to herself as she heard the garage door lifting, that she would have been ecstatic to gain a sibling. And she was definitely tagging along for the weekend to see exactly how Deidre and Maggie felt about it as well.

"Honey, unless you tell me that you don't want me to come, and that this is something that just the three of you want to deal with alone; then I'm coming. I've been part of your life for what seems like forever, and your sisters are like my sisters. If Deidre needs a shoulder to cry on, and Mags needs a kick in the ass, then I'm your gal," she kidded. "Seriously Josh, this is a huge deal, and could be life altering, and I want to be there for you and them, and most importantly, as an unbiased opinion, should you need one. Besides, she's part of your family, whether you want her to be or not; and I'm just as curious to learn about her as I know you are."

He wasn't sure how he felt about having a sister named Michelle, and about not being his mother's first born. It was tough enough trying to get back on track after just burying their mother, and now here he was, feeling like his life was being flipped upside down for the second time in less than two weeks. Looking at Jena, with her dirty blonde hair pulled into her usual "weekend braid", he knew that she was right, as usual. The one constant that hadn't changed was family. He still had her, his sisters and as Jena had said, he had a sister somewhere in the world that maybe could use a few more siblings or family right about now. Looking at the woman that he'd chosen to marry, standing beside him in her yoga pants, oversized sweatshirt, minimal makeup, but radiant smile; he felt whole again. He took her into his arms, pulling her in.

"Thank you."

She held on tight, as if he needed the support and reassurance. He truly was the love of her life, but even if he wasn't, she would have supported anyone who was making the right decision to pursue their family, and ultimately, Elizabeth's legacy. She looked up into Josh's eyes and smiled.

"I love you."

"I love you too."

He leaned in to kiss and before either knew it, the emotional roller coaster of the day came crashing in. He thought he had simply wanted a kiss, but feeling her lips and tongue tangle with his, broke the dam and he needed, needed like he'd never needed anyone before. As they tore at each other's clothes, leaving them where they fell, they barely made it onto the bed before he was in her. Stride for stride, they matched each other's pace and finished together. He hadn't known he'd had such emotion bottled up inside himself until that moment. He turned toward his love, who was panting just as hard as he was, and smiled.

"I hope I didn't hurt you. I guess I got a little carried away and I hope I wasn't too rough."

Very comfortable with her nakedness, she rolled over and on top of him, laughing.

"Honey, I think we should find you a new sister each week. You do that and I won't need to go to the gym anymore. Oh, and Joshua, I definitely like this kind of workout far better than sweating at Cross Fit!"

Laughing, he pulled her down toward his lips.

"Let me call Dee and tell her that we're coming but we won't get in until a little later."

"I'm all packed silly, so if you want to head north right away, I won't delay our departure at all."

"Camp can wait," he said, and flipped her onto her back for round two.

~Chapter 12~

Deidre really wasn't too sure how she felt about the whole situation. She knew that Maggie was furious about finding out about Michelle, while Joshua, always the serious one, had remained noncommittal in his comments. As they'd walked out to their respective cars, she couldn't get a read on either of her siblings; but one thing was for certain, their mother had certainly shocked them all. As she started organizing what essentials she needed to bring to camp, she laughed as her cat watched her move from room to room, watching her.

"You're going to have to be on your best behavior or Auntie Maggie will have a fit and tell Sinjin to eat you." Her cat nodded in what appeared to be understanding and agreement.

"I'm serious. Remember the last time you two were together and you thought his tail was a toy. That didn't work out so well for you now did it? Maggie spilled her drink, Josh tripped over Sinjin, and everyone blamed you. I'm warning you my love, you had better behave or you'll be banned from grandma's cabin at the lake."

As she said the words, it finally hit her that camp was no longer her mother's but theirs. There was no longer grandma's this or mom that; and that everything that her mother had always worked for, or cherished seemed unimportant, now that she wasn't around to appreciate them. She's always been her one constant that she could count on. Knowing that it was pointless to rehash the obvious, Deidre headed toward her bedroom to pack, cat in tow. She knew that it would have been easier to leave Sasha at home, but also knew that she might need some four-legged support after she and her siblings rehashed their meeting with the attorney. As she packed, she couldn't help but think how exciting it was going to be to meet a sister that until a few hours before, she hadn't known even existed. She day dreamed, as she threw sweaters, sweatshirts, jeans, leggings, socks and underwear into her oversized bag, about what her sister might be like. She did the math in her head and knew that her sister was approximately ten years her senior but that didn't matter to her. With that said, it suddenly dawned on her that not only was she going to gain a sister, but most likely, she would gain at least a niece or nephew as most of her friends that were in their thirties had a least one kid by the age of thirty-four. Laughing out loud, Deidre smiled at the possibility that she was about to become an auntie for the first time. As she looked across her bed at her cat, she realized that someday she hoped to be more than just a mom to a cat. If she had her way, she thought to herself, she'd like to have a whole houseful of kids, whether biological or adopted. She'd already given some serious consideration to adopting a child from an impoverished country but knew that she didn't have the time that becoming a mother would require, and with no one presently in her life to share the responsibilities of raising a child with, her desire to adopt would have to wait.

"Okay, I'll pack your bed, and your toys and food and you can come. But you had better behave yourself Sasha or else!" she instructed her feline best friend, despite knowing that the cat was going to do whatever she pleased.

She packed the last of her things and set out for camp, but before getting on the highway remembered that no one had probably watered her mother's plants in the time frame since her mother had been gone. She knew that Jena had watered her mother's beloved plants the morning that the four of them went to the house to pick out an outfit for her to be cremated in. Despite the fact that no one would know the difference as she was being cremated, they still wanted their mother dressed in something special. She knew that the plants could probably wait another few days, but something told her to swing by and do it on her way north. Besides, she rationalized that it was right on the way, and she didn't want to be the first to arrive at camp anyways.

Pulling into her mother's drive, she was surprised to see two vehicles in her drive, one very sporty looking Lexus LC Coupe, and one very loved Silverado. She didn't recognize either and for a brief moment thought about calling Josh, but remembered that he'd called and said that he'd be tied up until later in the evening. She thought about calling the cops but upon seeing a smiling face approaching her car, with his hand outstretched, she hung up the phone.

"Hi. Bet you wonder what's going on here?" he said, matter of factly. "I'm Griffin, and I was hired by Coldwell Banker to tidy up some landscape before their agent can list this house," he told her, despite Deidre not uttering a word yet. Before she had a moment to regroup, he spoke again. "Wow, she's a beaut," he said, extending his hand toward her car. Having no clue what he was doing, it wasn't until she remembered that not only was Sasha in her car, but now trying to gain his attention by climbing onto her shoulders and extending her head nearly out of the window. Once she determined that he wasn't reaching into her car to strangle her, she took the card from his hand and read it. "DGO Contracting LLC. Specializing in home repairs & remodeling since 1999." She set the card down on the dash of her car and cut the engine, stepping out to place herself eye level with the man currently invading her mother's house. Just as she was about to give him the third degree, she saw a woman exiting her mother's front entrance, waving, and coming down the stairs to greet her.

"Why hello Deidre," she greeted her, still smiling. "What a pleasant surprise," she added. I thought that you'd be at the lake this gorgeous weekend. Anyway, you've met Griffin? He and his team will be doing just a few last-minute touch ups on your mother's house before I get it ready for the estate sale before I list it. While I have you here, do you have any idea when you and your sister and brother would like to get together here to take whatever items you'd like? I'll obviously want you all to remove the mementos that you're keeping, prior to the estate sale. I know Liz told me that you three have very different tastes than she did, and if I remember, both you and your sister aren't much for collectibles, so to speak."

Still slightly caught off guard that a woman was in her mother's home, peaking through her things, and getting ready to sell everything to strangers for pennies on the dollar, she took a moment to speak. Jacqueline, her mother's friend and Real Estate Broker put two and two together and softened her stance and tone.

"I'm so sorry honey, I take it that your brother Joshua didn't tell you that we were doing some work on your mother's house this week? It must have been quite upsetting, driving into her drive and seeing all of this going on, especially so soon after you lost her. I'm really sorry Deidre." Seeing Elizabeth's youngest start to tear up, she instinctively pulled her into a bear hug and squeezed her, leaving Griffin standing awkwardly beside the two women.

Deidre tried very hard to compose herself as the older woman held her. She pulled herself together and straightened up, using her sleeve to wipe away the last of her tears.

"No, I knew that you were going to be listing the house. I guess I didn't realize that it would be so quickly after her funeral. But, I guess with winter coming and all, it's better to get it on the market, instead of sitting here empty all winter," she conceded.

"I'll get out of you ladies way if you want," Griffin said, looking for a way to escape back inside. "It was really nice meeting you, and I just want you to know that I really like your mother's home and anyone who enters it can tell that not only is it a great house, but a home filled with love. I'm sure it was a great place to grow up in and hopefully will bring the next family much happiness living in it."

She smiled at the slightly scruffy looking contractor standing in front of her. His dockers were currently covered with a little dirt, dust and a few paint splatters, and his work boots showed that they had been used for more than one season. His Carhart jacket also had a few miles on it, but the shirt he wore underneath it was as black as the color of his hair. Deidre couldn't help but stare for just a quick second when he smiled one last time at her. His eyes were the greenest she'd ever seen, even greener than her own sister's. His coloring reminded her of someone of Mediterranean descent or maybe even native American, either way, he was stunning to look at, despite his less than fancy attire.

"It was a great house to grow up in," she replied. "Thank you for fixing it up to the way it used to be. My sister, brother and I, appreciate it."

Looking back at her mother's real estate agent, she asked if she could go inside to water the plants and have a quick look around, to which Jacqueline readily agreed, staying outside to allow her privacy. Once inside, she heard a low Baritone voice emitting from upstairs. She followed the sound , and quickly realized that it was in fact, coming from her old bedroom. Silently she walked toward the source of the singing and stood in the doorway listening. He obviously didn't realize that he had an audience as he painted the wall, swaying just a little bit to the rhythm of the song. He had a nice voice even though he was barely singing louder than a whisper. Much to her surprise, his voice took off to what was obviously the chorus to the song playing in his headphones. She heard the true strength and quality of his voice as he blasted out the Eric Church song, and found that she couldn't help herself, and started singing along, even though she thought he had no clue.

He'd sensed her presence even before he started hearing her voice as it harmonized with his. He'd known that she was standing behind him even before he caught her shadow. As they sang the last line of the chorus, he turned to face her, but kept on singing, prompting her to continue as well.

For two people who'd never met before, and obviously never sang together before, it was shocking to both of them how great they sounded, complimenting each other's tones. He removed his headphones and shut off his phone a moment later and was truly captivated by how beautiful the woman standing in front of him was. For once in his life, he actually felt tongue tied.

"Hi," he managed to squeak out.

"Hi," she replied back. "Never had anyone nearly as cute as you in my bedroom when I was growing up here," she laughed.

Slightly surprised by her honestly and off sided compliment, he blushed. "Wow," he laughed, "should have known that this was your room. Holy crap you're talented. I was noticing all of the awards you received and I'm going to assume that the artwork that your mother has proudly displayed around her home, are all originals created by you?" he asked.

"Guilty," she admitted, blushing at his compliment and also at the fact that this painter, a stranger in her childhood home, had paid enough attention to the pictures on her mother's walls to realize that they were all done by the same person, her. Her opinion of the painter standing in front of her increased exponentially at that moment.

"I wish I was artistic like you though. I have a pretty good eye with a camera, and I love to draw, but lord I wish I had a voice like yours. You sing pretty good Griffin," she admitted. "I love to draw, and mom had always pushed me to go to school for drafting or interior Architecture, but I took the safe route and Majored in Business instead. She always wanted me to pursue my dreams because she said that I had an eye for making things pretty, but I figured that making essential things available to all was more important than making them pretty."

Not quite ready to tell the woman standing in front of him, that he was indeed an Architect, he let her keep believing that he was a painter and handyman so to speak.

"If you don't get offended by me saying it; I'd like to say that you Deidre, your presence makes everything around you pretty. You have a very calming way about you and I don't know what you do to make a living, but I'm going to assume that whatever it is involves people, and I'm betting that you make everyone's' lives a little better, and prettier, just by having you in it. I really hope," he blushed, and smiled, just a little, "that I haven't overstepped my bounds, but I usually tell it the way it is, and I'm sorry if I said more than a stranger should say."

She always was one to shoot from the hip and was usually a very good read of people, so she wasn't at all concerned or offended by the stranger's assessment of her.

"You're very kind Griffin. I do like to help others. And I love to draw because it helps me relax and keep me grounded. Singing is my passion though, but unfortunately, I'm not good enough to do anything serious with it, so I limit my singing to church, my car, and my shower."

"I know I had headphones on, but honey, you have an amazing voice and if you happen to ever venture to 12North and my band is playing there, I want you on stage for at least one or two songs with me," he said, completely matter of factly.

"No shit, you're in a band," she asked, completely surprised. "Oh, sorry, I don't usually swear on a first date," she laughed.

He couldn't help but burst out laughing as well. "As long as you don't say you don't kiss on the first date, I'm okay with you swearing," he retorted back at her, smiling.

"Touché," she responded. "I'll get out of your way after I water my mom's plants. It's really nice meeting you Griffin, and who knows, you might just see my sister and I at one of your performances," she offered sincerely.

"That would be great Deidre. Our band is called Destiny. Come check us out sometime."

"Alright then, I'll get out of your way. Again, nice meeting you Griffin," she said, not quite ready to walk out of her childhood room yet.

"It was very nice meeting you as well. Maybe I'll see you around. Oh, and Deidre," he added sincerely, I'll make sure I take good care of your mom's house for you. I'll treat it like it was my own, alright?" he smiled?

"Thank you," she mouthed and walked away, leaving him wanting more.

She made her way downstairs and found herself in her mother's room first watering the plants that were perched in front of her window, basking in the sunlight. Her mind drifted to the man who was one floor above her and the kind words he'd said. She'd met and talked to him all of five minutes but thought that he'd been genuine and sincere in the things that he'd said to her. When she'd finished in her mother's bedroom, she headed for the living room where the remainder of the plants could be found. She thought about lingering longer, to maybe talk to her new acquaintance a little longer, but knew that not only was her cat waiting for her in her car, but her sister was waiting for her at camp. She took one last look around and then headed outside, said her goodbyes to Jacquelyn and promised that either she or Joshua would get back to her the following week about discussing listing the house, and made her way to her car. Sasha greeted her with a tone that emitted her displeasure in waiting, but Deidre didn't care at the moment. Her mind was still processing the fact that within the next month or so, her childhood home would be listed and probably on the fast track to becoming someone else's home.

"It's okay baby," she reassured her cat, who could have cared less about the house, "I'm sure that the next owners will love it as much as we did growing up in it."

She lifted her cat off her seat, and moved her over to the passenger seat, and climbed in. Always safety conscious, she buckled before even starting the engine, and then took a deep breath, put her Prius in reverse and backed out of the driveway like she'd done hundreds of times before.

It wasn't until she was on Route 12 heading north out of the city that she relaxed enough to turn her radio on and settle into the drive to the lake. Despite her later than expected start, she was pleasantly surprised by the traffic flow and made great time on both Route 12 and 28 as she made her way into the mountains. Slowing, once she hit Thendara, she was surprised, but not shocked to see the first snowflakes of the season. She did a quick inventory of everything that she'd packed for the weekend and was glad that she packed more winter than fall type attire.

"You're going to have a reality check my friend, if you decide to chase Sinjin outside," she kidded her cat. "So remember that your paws will freeze if you venture outside, so be forewarned."

Sasha rolled over in her seat, turning away from Deidre as if dismissing her.

"Be that way you stubborn little thing, but if you go outside and end up frozen in the lake, it'll be on you," she laughed, and she headed through Old Forge and to their camp.

Ten minutes later, Deidre started down the long winding driveway toward her mother's, now her camp. She still hadn't fully processed that the camp was hers, along with her brother and sister. As her mother's will was read, Deidre had listened but not really processed everything, monetarily, that she was about to gain. It wasn't until she pulled up beside Maggie's Jeep and put her car in park, staring at the lake house stretched out in front of her, that it all became real. Her great grandparents had purchased the land, and her grandparents had built the camp themselves, along with the assistance of her grandfather's seven brothers. When her grandparents passed, Elizabeth being an only child, inherited the cabin, such as it was. Over the years, she and Deidre's father replaced what broke, and kept the space livable, but looking at it now, Deidre realized that although they all loved their little cabin in the woods, it definitely needed some long overdue attention. She forced Miss Attitude into the cat carrier that she'd hidden in the back seat, threw her oversized bag over her shoulder and headed toward the door and whatever ciaos lay inside.

Sinjin had alerted Maggie that they had company, even before her sister had shut off her engine, and after locking her dog in the laundry room, rushed out to help her unload. Knowing that her sister had a tendency to overpack, she greeted her at the doorway, removing the overstuffed bag from her shoulder.

"Hi," she greeted her. "I was beginning to think that you weren't coming up."

Deidre walked into the kitchen, setting Sasha and the crate on the floor, before standing up straight and stretching. The warmth from the fireplace that Maggie had blowing full blast felt wonderful compared to the frigid temperature outside.

"I swung by mom's house to make sure everything was okay before I headed up . I figured that her plants needed watering, and I was right," she responded, making her way toward the Hemstrougths jelly buns that she spied on the counter. Taking a huge bite, she spoke as she chewed.

"Yeah, see, I've been swinging by mom's house twice a week since she went into the hospital, and then, well, you know, since she died. I didn't want her mail accumulating in her mailbox and I've been watering her plants, which we're going to have to do something with by the way, since it's going on the market soon."

Processing what her sister had just said, in between bites of donut, she looked at her quizzically.

"Thank you for doing that Dee. I honestly never thought about either. I guess," she said, taking another sip of wine, "that I wrapped myself up in my work after mom died because I didn't want to think about it, think about the finality of it. Have you been dealing with all of her bills and mail and everything," she asked, now ashamed of how she'd dealt with her mother's death.

"No, Josh has been doing most of it. Help me unload the rest of my crap, and we'll talk before Josh and Jena show up, okay?"

As expected, Maggie and Deidre made two more trips out to her pint-sized car before it was unloaded, and everything was inside. Once settled in, she figured they might as well get it over with, letting Sasha out of her crate, who promptly cuffed Sinjin across the nose. Undeterred, the lab proceeded to bark and pounce in front of the feline's face until Sasha raced under the sanctity of the couch. Taking it as their clue that there was finally peace in the kingdom, Deidre and Maggie made themselves comfortable, each in their favorite chairs, ones that they'd claimed as children. Deidre took a few more sips of the delightful tasting wine that her sister had brought, remained silent, just looking around. It was Maggie who spoke first.

"Weird isn't?" she asked. "I did the same thing when I got here today. It's weird looking around now, seeing all of mom's touches everywhere, but knowing that she'll never be here again. It's sad you know. And quite frankly, kind of sucks," she stated, matter of factly.

"I can't believe she's really gone Mags. I keep waiting for my phone to ring or for her to walk through that door, but she won't, and that breaks my heart," she said solemnly. "And no, I won't break down and cry, so no worries. I'm all cried out, and crying won't bring our mother or dad back, so I've decided to buck up and put my energy elsewhere." Taking another couple sips of her half empty glass of wine, she smiled.

"When I was at mom's today, I saw the most gorgeous specimen of a man. And he could sing!" she exclaimed, offering nothing more.

"Um, okay," her sister responded. "And exactly where was this specimen and how did you meet him?" she inquired, knowing that she'd have to pull it out of her little sister.

Sinjin climbed up onto Maggie's lap, forgetting that his 85 pound frame was not lap dog material, curled up and appeared to be listening to Deidre's story.

"Oh, he was in my bedroom," she responded, before getting up to pour them both some more wine, and grab another jelly donut.

"Come again," her sister asked, perplexed by the comment.

"He was singing in my bedroom." Realizing how that statement sounded, she backtracked, explaining the scenario.

"I pulled into mom's drive to water the plants, and the real estate agent was there with a contractor to do some last-minute touch ups to the house before she lists it. She, the agent, said that Josh had been kept abreast of the work they were doing to prep it for listing, and that she'd been in contact with him weekly. So anyways, I meet her and I meet the hunky looking contractor she hired, and he seemed nice enough, and then disappears inside to continue working. So," she dragged out the word so, as if to exaggerate its' importance, and to take another swallow of her wine, "I thank the agent and head inside to water mom's plants, which by the way, she's got a shit ton of them, and what do I hear, but the most incredible voice I've heard in a long time."

Intrigued by her sister's elaborated story, she edged her on, teasingly. "Due tell, so what happened?"

"So I hear this voice, this amazing voice emanating from upstairs, so I follow it to its' source, and there he was, Mr. Hunkman himself, in my bedroom. He was singing and painting, painting and singing. It was so cool. And I told him that I'd never had any guy as cute as he is, in my bedroom when I lived there," she chuckled. "Anyways, he's been hired to neutralize the bedrooms and fix up a few things here and there, and from what I saw, was doing a really good job. He was super nice and said that he's in a band, and that we should come out and see him sometime."

"Sounds like you learned a lot about Mr. Hunky," she kidded. By any chance in your conversation, did you learn his name?" she teased.

"Griffin, his name is Griffin. And you're a smart ass you know!"

"Hey, I think it's awesome that something, other than your soup kitchen got you all fired up. You work too hard, and never do anything for yourself, so I think, if he intrigued you, then you should go check Mr. Painter/contractor/singer out sometime," she smiled. "I'll even go with you when they're playing locally, okay?" she offered, knowing that her sister wouldn't venture out independently, despite how cute she had thought the guy was.

"Deal," she said, reaching in, clanging her glass to her big sisters.

They drank and laughed for the next half hour, reminiscing and telling story after story of the adventures they remembered from spending their summers at camp. Both had nothing but fond memories of playing kick the can, swimming in the lake, learning to waterski, bear sightings and so many more things. When their stories were finished, both went silent for a moment of reflection, each caught in their own thoughts. It was Deidre who spoke first.

"Have you read mom's letter yet?" she asked cautiously.

"Actually, yes I have," her sister answered, in a monotone voice.

"I wanted to, and actually pulled over twice on the way up here but Mags, I'm afraid of what might be in it," she responded honestly. "Would it be okay if I read it with you here with me? I kind of want to do it before Josh gets here."

"I'm sure there's nothing in it that you couldn't read with Josh and Jena present, but sure, if you want to read it now, it's fine. She loved us Dee, always remember that. There's nothing in her letter that's going to say anything otherwise," she reassured her sister.

Hearing her sister's words, and knowing that despite whatever it contained, her sister was there for her and would always be, she moved the sleeping cat off her lap and walked over to her purse, pulling out the envelope that she'd tucked in there after their meeting with the attorney. She returned to the couch, asking her sister to join her there, and with shaking hands pulled out the enclosed pictures and letter. Unlike her sister, she chose to read her mother's letter before viewing the pictures. She gasped, looking down at her mother's distinctive penmanship, and started reading out loud.

My Dearest Deidre:

Wipe your tears my love, there's no need wasting another tear on me. If you're reading this, then be reassured my beautiful girl, that I'm with your dad and couldn't be happier. If I know you as well as I do, you're with Maggie May right now, and hopefully you gals have had a glass of wine for me as well!

First and foremost, I want you to know how incredibly proud I am of all of my children, and it always tickled my heart that you were the one who followed in my footsteps. Granted, you didn't choose Nursing as your profession of choice, but you are still helping the people who need you the most, and I couldn't be prouder of your soup kitchen and your business. As I made you promise before I died, you need to take more time for yourself and only then, will you be able to continue to give to others. Your business is about to grown in leaps and bounds, I just know it, and I'm honored to be a small part of it, at least in spirit.

As things start to change in front of your eyes, as I know they already have, you have always been the one of my three children to "go with the flow" so to speak. My request of you is that you keep Joshua and Maggie on board and keep them grounded when they start to buck the changes. The sale of my home is the first change. Deidre, I want each of you to take what you want out of my home, and I have identified one particular piece of furniture that I want each of you to have. When you meet with Jacquelyn, she has the list. Dee, I want you to take some of the money that I've given you to expand your business, and I want you to give yourself evenings off. I've already spoken with Amanda, your business partner who confirmed that you work 12 hour days, and eventually it's going to affect your health. Amanda and I both agree that you need another part time employee to oversee the supper hour, and she will work with you in hiring someone. Non-negotiable Deidre. I know how short life is, and it's about time you start living it.

The next thing that I want to talk to you about is Michelle. If I'm right, I predict that Joshua absorbed the news but didn't comment; with his analytical mind already formulating the ramifications of finding her. My Maggie May is still slightly pissed off about having to deal with the potential drama that finding your long-lost sister might create, and you, my beautiful girl, you think it's very cool that you're gaining another sister. Deidre, even though I know that your heart is in the right place, I want you to consider that Michelle might not be as receptive to meet you and you are to meet her. When you find her, and I know that you guys will find her, be sensitive to the fact that one, you've had time to digest the information, and two, she might not even know that she's adopted. If she doesn't know that she was adopted, then it might be an emotional blow that she'll need time to absorb. Be there for her Deidre, if she needs you. Answer any questions she has Dee, but don't make me out to be a saint. The hardest thing that I ever did in my life was give up my daughter, she needs to understand that. It's easy to put it in writing that I made my decision solely for what was best for my daughter, but the truth of the matter is, I was terrified of letting her down. Please tell her that I'm so sorry for letting her down anyways.

Get to know her Deidre. Something tells me that you two will have a lot in common. And be there for her if you find her father. She deserves to meet the man who helped create her. He's a kind man, a gentle soul and if he's still alive, should get to know his daughter.

I love you with all of my heart.

Love,

Mom

Elizabeth's Legacy

Deidre has promised herself that she wouldn't cry, and she kept her promise, that is, until she looked over at her sister sitting beside her.

"She really loved us Mags, didn't she?" she asked.

Maggie pulled her sister into a hug. "Yeah she did Dee. I think that she had to make a really horrible decision when she was so young, and I think that it probably haunted her nearly every day of her life. I think that if times and circumstances had been different back then, that she would probably have kept Michelle, married her high school flame Daniel, and we wouldn't exist. There's a reason for everything in life Dee; it just takes a while to figure out what it is sometimes. I honestly don't think she was meant to keep her, otherwise, you know how stubborn and determined mom always was, she would have fought harder to keep her baby, and the man who fathered her. Everything happens for a reason."

Maggie took another sip of her nearly empty glass, quietly contemplating what she'd just told her sister.

Starting to feel the effects of the wine slightly, Deidre turned toward her sister and smiled.

"What" Maggie asked, as she saw a giddy type smile form on her sister's face.

"I was just wondering what the reason is that we're still both single and our only love life is with our four-legged

139

friends loving us?" she chuckled, leaning in towards her big sister.

"Dee, my love life is presently nonexistent, and that's exactly the way that I like it. Work is insane, and I'm doing overtime every week, we're about to spend a lot of time tracking down a sister and her father; so I definitely don't need a man in my life interfering with it."

"But if you did, what kind of man would you want in your life?" she continued, knowing she'd get under her sister's skin but also get an honest answer.

"Again, I don't want a man, but if I did, I'd want someone who makes me laugh. Not stupid kind of goofy, but someone with a good sense of humor, who doesn't take themself too seriously. I'm always serious and never seem to relax, so I'd like someone who could sort of counterbalance me." Thinking for just a quick second about the guy at the gym with the long legs, she added quickly, "and he'd have to be tall. I might be short, but I like tall guys, I think," she laughed, starting to feel the effects of a lot of wine on an empty stomach.

Catching the change in her sister's tone, even though it was subtle, Deidre picked up on something. "Okay, spill. Who'd you meet and what's his name?"

Nearly choking on her wine, Maggie snorted, while laughing at the same time. The noise was so strange that even her dog woke from his nap at her feet.

"I have no idea what you're taking about Dee. It's just me and Sinjin, as always. Remember I swore men off after that last fiasco with Patrick?"

Knowing her sister the way she did, she let her ramble on about excluding any and all men, but Deidre could tell by her continued insistence that she'd written off all men, that there in fact was one that had, at least caught her attention.

"Maggie, remember who you're talking too. I know you too well. If someone has entered your life and he's good to you and for you, then I'm happy. You shouldn't work so much and like mom said, you should at least consider, having a man in your life. So, if and when, you want to at least tell me his name, I'd love to hear about him."

She knew that she shouldn't even mention his name, because she'd met him twice in her life, and had spoken to him for a grand total of less than fifteen minutes, but there was something in Garrett's eyes that made her feel some type of connection. Trust had never come easy for Maggie, despite being raised in a loving home void of any anger, fighting or reasons not to trust people. Her first impression of the man that she'd met at the gym was that he was not only kind, but also trustworthy. She could read people well and knew that she wasn't wrong in believing his sincerity.

After another sip of her wine, she put her glass down and simply stated, "His name is Garrett, and all I know is that he belongs to the gym I just joined, is gorgeous and is an attorney. Oh, and has the most beautiful eyes, kind eyes. He's asked me out twice and I think that maybe, once this crap with our long-lost sister is resolved, I might actually take him up on his offer," she admitted, surprising even herself.

"It's time Mags. I know that Patrick did a number on you; but it's time. I also think," Deidre stopped mid-sentence seeing Maggie's dog spring to attention and head toward the front door. "That we must have company. Josh must have finally made it," she finished, setting down her glass, standing, and attempting to regain her balance. Maggie was already two steps ahead of her, heading towards the door and whoever was on the other side.

Just as Sinjin barked in anticipation of their company, Josh, followed by Jenna came through the doors, loaded down with shopping bags, and an enormous cooler. Deidre and Maggie quickly took bags from Jenna's arms, with Maggie grabbing the case of beer off of the top of the cooler for her brother. Making eye contact with him, she smirked, "You are planning on staying one or two weeks?" she joked.

"Yeah I know, but I figured that once we start delving into the Michelle and Daniel mystery, we might be surprised to find out how much we go through this weekend." Stepping in, he looked around and smiled. "Thanks for getting the fire going, it smells and feels great in here."

"I did it for Jena," she teased. "Hey, hi honey. Let me see that rock on your finger one more time," she said, pulling her future sister in law into a hug once they'd set the bags down in the kitchen.

"Me too," Deidre squealed. "I'll never have one like that so at least let me drool over yours Jen. I never realized that our big brother would have such great taste in rings," she said, punching her brother who was standing next to her, in the arm.

"Of course I have great taste. And the jeweler assured me that this one would knock her socks off, so there you have it!" he admitted.

"It did," Jena responded, sending her fiancée a look that depicted nothing but pure love. "Let's get settled and eat, shall we?" she asked, looking from one to the other of her soon to be sisters?

"Judging from the nearly empty bottle on the counters, you two have been here awhile."

Laughing at their brother's keen observation, they helped them free their arms and put the pizza and wings into the oven to warm. After the hugging and jokes were completed, they filled their plates with the antipasto that Maggie had prepared, and with the pizza and wings that Josh had picked up in town and sat at the dining room table where they'd share countless meals together growing up. Deidre, always the sentimental one, filled her mother's favorite wine glass with wine and set it at the head of the table where her mother had sat ever since their father had passed away ten years earlier. Maggie thought that now that their mother was gone, Joshua, being the oldest would assume the role of head of the household and take over the spot, but that could wait. For now, they would enjoy what they had together, and the future could wait just a little bit longer.

They ate in relative silence, each caught up in their own feelings and emotions. It felt almost surreal to be at the lake and know that their mother wouldn't be stopping by or invading their party, as she'd been known to do in the past. There had been plenty of weekends that each of them had spent the weekend at the camp independently, but none of them needed a reminder that it was their mother's choice back then not to venture up. Now it wasn't.

Once dinner was finished and the dishwasher was stacked, the empty pizza box was discarded, and everyone refilled their glasses, or in Josh's case, grabbed another beer; they all made their way into the living room where the fire's warmth could be felt upon entering. Deidre's cat and Maggie's pooch had called a truce, and both were sleeping in front of the hearth, soaking up the warmth from the fireplace blower. Josh knew that putting off talking about it wasn't going to change the outcome, so he started the conversation that no one wanted to have.

"Okay, it's just the four of us now, no attorney's or pretenses needed. I'm sure that you both have been thinking about the information that mom's attorney gave us, nearly nonstop since we met with him earlier this afternoon. I'd like to know your honest opinion now that it's just the four of us here. I know what mine is but I think we all have to be on the same page to either go forward with this or forget we ever learned about her."

Deidre was the first to speak. "Her name is Michelle Marie. She has a name and since we won't know what her new name is, if it was changed when she was adopted, we will refer to her as Michelle, not her, the baby or it. I might be the youngest and maybe that's why I feel less threatened, but I for one, am 100% in favor of finding Michelle, finding Daniel, and introducing father to daughter. I know it's what our mother's dying wish was, and I for one will not let her down. Come on guys, Michelle is of no threat to us. She's thirty something years old, probably has a husband and couple of kids by now, and most likely was raised with other sisters or brothers. I'm sure she's not some nut job out there looking for a ready-made family in us, and since mom is dead, it's not like she can play the sympathy card and hit her up for love, affection or money. Besides," she laughed, winking at Jena, "we've got our own built in council and if she's a scum bag, we can get a restraining order easily enough."

It was Maggie, who surprisingly joined in alliance with her sister. Even though she was always the skeptical one, Maggie couldn't deny that she was at least a little curious about her recently discovered half-sister. During the drive to camp, she'd thought about Arnold Gesell's Nature vs Nurture theory that she'd studied in one of her many psychology classes in college. With that theory in mind, she pondered on whether or not she or Deidre would have any commonalities with their biological sister or whether her upbringing would trump any genetics that she'd inherited from their mother. Yes, the need to fulfill her mother's dying wish might have been the catalyst; but her curiosity was now the driving factor in her decision to go forward in searching for and meeting their sibling.

"I agree with Dee, and think that we should find her."

Both Deidre and her brother looked at her with expressions of pure shock. Always the skeptical one, and the one who tended to look for the bad in people, both were surprised that she'd made up her mind so quickly to go forward.

"As I've already stated, I have no interest in gaining another sister. The reason I'm agreeing is two-fold. One, mom asked us to do this and out of respect for our mother, whether I agree with it or not, I'm willing to track this woman and her father down; and two, I think she deserves to know her medical history, especially if she has children because the information could be invaluable as she ages, and they grow up. And mostly because I'm curious to see if she looks like either of us, especially since the picture that mom gave me of Michelle looks identical to the one of me as a baby."

"Oh my God Mags, you have a picture of our sister," Deidre nearly shouted. What does she look like?"

"Relax. It was taken when she was five days old and looks like every other five day old baby!"

Jena, who'd been relatively silent since dinner spoke up, "Maggie, how did you obtain a picture of your sister?" she asked gently.

"It was in my letter from mom," she answered bluntly.

"Mom gave me a half dozen photos as well," Deidre added. "Didn't she give you any in your letter?"

"I don't know. I didn't open it yet," he answered truthfully.

"Why not?"

"Um, because Jena and I were a little busy, packing, before we came up here."

Maggie laughed. "Is that what they call it nowadays? Guess I wish I could be doing some packing sometime soon!"

With everyone laughing, and Jena blushing, Deidre had only one comment to her sister's self-pity. "Hook up with Mr. Gorgeous from the gym and maybe you'll be "packing" before you know it!"

"Wait, what?" Jenna piped up. "What's this about meeting someone from the gym," she teased. "Have you been holding out on us Maggie? Have you met someone that I need to hear about?"

"Finishing off her glass of wine, she smiled slyly. "Let's just say I've met someone who intrigues me and after all of this is over, I might consider getting to know him a little better, because he definitely intrigues me. Oh, and he's a lawyer like you," she added.

"What's his name? Utica is a very small town and I know most of the attorneys in the area."

She hadn't thought of that when she'd offered the information. Realizing now that she'd opened a can of worms, Maggie tried to divert the conversation away from her non-existent love life and to the topic at hand. "I don't remember, Garrett something. Anyways, didn't mom leave you a letter as well Joshua? I thought we each got one. Didn't you open yours yet?" she asked, desperately trying to change the subject.

"I have one. I just haven't opened it yet. And to be quite honest, I'm not sure if and when I will open it and read it. I don't know if I can fulfill more of mom's wishes if she asks more of me. It's just so hard," he broke off.

Seeing their big brother in a weak moment sobered them up faster than any pot of Joe, and had them rushing to his side to embrace him. Jena stood next to her man, watching the exchange between brother and sister with pure admiration.

"Honey," she coaxed gently, "Why don't you open the letter here with your sisters and read it with them? I can go out for a walk and give the three of you some privacy," she offered.

"No," Maggie spoke up immediately. "If Josh decides to read mom's letter, you should be here. You're already part of this family and the four of us are in this together," she added. Looking back at her brother, she added, "But obviously the choice is up to you whether or not you'd like to read it now or not."

"Did you read yours?" he asked.

"Yes, and it made me feel loved, made me feel that our mother was even better of a person than I thought she was, and made me realize that her first biological child will never take our place, and that she loved us independently of whatever feelings she may have had for Daniel and Michelle. They were her past and we, the three of us are her family. So, long answer to your question, but yes, I read it and I will cherish it forever as mom's last gift to me."

He looked from one sister to the other and smiled. "Do you think I should read it now?" he asked and before he could finish the sentence, he heard three YES's screamed back at him. He said nothing, but stood, walked over to where his duffel bag still sat on the stairwell leading up to his childhood bedroom, reached in, and withdrew the white envelope with his name scrolled on it. Staring down at mother's cursive for just a moment, made him think back to all of the letters he'd received while he was in college. Despite both of them owning cell phones and computers, Elizabeth had always insisted on sending him a letter or two each month, usually with a little spending money, articles of interest from back home, or something inspirational to get him through his long weeks of studying nearly 24/7. When he gently pulled the folded paper out, pictures fell out and onto the kitchen island. There, the very first one he saw was a hit to the gut. He picked it up and stared. Looking back at him, and taken years ago was a picture of he and his father, fishing on their boat. They both were beaming ear to ear, with their silly baseball caps on backwards, holding up their catches of the day, with his father being the better, more successful fisherman on that particular day. Josh closed his eyes, bringing himself back to the day as if it were yesterday. He could smell the fresh Adirondack air, the Coppertan lotion that their mother had insisted they practically slather on any exposed skin and could hear his father's laughter when they posed for the shot and bragging rights at the dinner table that evening. His stomach had just been turned into knots, and knew that he'd never be able to keep it together to read his mom's letter at that moment, so he took a deep breath and made the conscious decision to continue weeding through the pictures to compose himself before he read her words to everyone. The next picture had been taken years before their fishing expedition. It showed Joshua with his back to the camera, waiting hand in hand with his mother for the school bus on the first day of school. Knowing that his sisters weren't old enough to use a camera, he surmised that either his father or grandmother must have taken the shot. Their faces weren't exposed, but their body language told anyone who viewed the picture, how innocent and pure the love between mother and child were. Though it was a very foggy memory, Joshua remembered back to the day he waited to climb onto that enormous yellow bus for the first time. He'd been terrified, actually sick to his stomach and remembered that he had told his mother that he had a tummy ache and shouldn't go to school. He remembered her soothing voice and she reassured him that all five year olds were expected to have tummy aches and that once he climbed the three steps onto the bus and sat down in one of the big black seats, his stomach ache would magically disappear. He remembered that even though he hadn't completely believed her at the time, once he sat down next to another five year old, his mother had been right, and his stomach ache was a distant memory.

Jena watched her fiancée as he struggled through the emotional roller coaster that each picture brought. Her parents were still alive but her family dynamics were far different than the loving environment that Joshua and his sisters were raised in. She leaned in and kissed him in reassurance and to encourage him to keep going. With her support, he picked up the next picture and laughed. It was he and his mother doing the Limbo together at his graduation party. Be it unconventional or not, but Joshua had insisted on having his graduation party at the lake, so half his class and many of their parents invaded Old Forge for the weekend. Elizabeth used to love to brag that she made the best Belgian Waffles in town, and that Sunday morning, after a very late night of partying, swimming, and laughing, she was up bright and early, cooking up pound after pound of Canadian bacon, Sausage, and waffles by the dozens. Majority of the adults had returned back to the city, but all of the kids had spent the night at the lake with Josh and his family. Thinking about it now, he honestly had no idea, as he looked around the cabin, how her mother had done it. Over sixty teenagers spent the night, in sleeping bags on the floor, the privileged first arrivals got the beds, some brought their own tents, and some slept in the garage under the beer pong table. Despite the ciaos that a group that size should have created, looking back now, he realized that his mother had made it look easy. That was one of her many amazing traits, and yet another thing that he'd miss about her. She was organized to a fault but never made anything in their lives feel rigid. Looking at the picture and her look of determination, Jena spoke.

"So who won?"

Laughing, he responded honestly. "Mom of course! Everything she did, she excelled at and she credited her Yoga for her flexibility."

"What the hell?" He gasped when he saw the last photo, with Jena grabbing his arm. "Oh my God!"

"What?" both Deidre and Maggie said in unison.

Joshua held up a picture of he and Jena. Both Maggie and Deidre looked at the picture of his profile and a radiantly smiling Jenna out to dinner, but saw nothing else, and certainly not anything special about it. When they looked at their brother for answers, they saw that he was trying to wipe tears from his eyes without being noticed.

"How did she do that Josh? She was in the hospital and then she , well, you know. How did she manage to get a picture of us on the night you proposed?" Jena asked, somewhat confused.

"Carlo. I bet she had Carlo in on it and knew that when I made the reservations, that it was the night. That sneaky woman!" he laughed. "Good job mom. You definitely were and still are full of surprises. I love you mom," he whispered, as he turned the picture over and saw the note on the back, in what he surmised was Carlo's chicken scratch.

"Your mom wasn't with you in person when you asked for Jena's hand in marriage, but I assure you, she was here in spirit. And she said to tell you that she's very proud of you and so happy for both you and Jena. She loves Jena like a daughter."

Deidre shared the box of tissues with Jena as Joshua finished reading. Everyone still was in awe as to how their mother had pulled off such a wonderful gift.

It was Jena who prompted him to finish. "Honey, why don't you see what her note says."

"I don't know if I can handle it now Jen."

"I think the pictures are to coincide with the letter from your mom. Do what you want, but I'd read it now, and I think your mom would want you to read it when you're with your sisters."

Knowing she was right, as usual; Joshua pulled out the neatly folded white piece of paper and stared down at his mother's precise penmanship. From the neatness of the writing, he realized that she'd written it long before the Cancer started winning its' battle.

He took a breath to steady himself and started reading aloud:

My Dearest Joshua:

Look at you, all grown up. As I've watched you grow from an adorable little boy, to your father's helper, I've been in awe of you. I didn't know your father until we were young adults but everything in my heart tells me that he would have been just like you growing up. You have a kind, gentle heart but a strong will and solid work ethic and every good quality that your father had, you inherited from him.

You were such a blessing to your father and I. Jarod knew that once we were married, I wanted to start a family right away. First and foremost, let me stress, you were NEVER a substitute for the child I'd given away. Your dad and I wanted to start a family together because when I was with your father, I was so overjoyed and happy, that I thought we should share it with the product of our love. Your father and I seldom argued, but like all couples, we disagreed from time to time. Once he figured out that I was right, everything worked out! LOL!!!

Once you and Jena set a date, know that I'll be there to see your beautiful Jena walk down the aisle and I'll be there when you two share your first dance as husband and wife. And with a little luck, I'll convince your dad to waltz me around a cloud or two up in heaven.

This journey that I've set you and your sisters on will be taxing and emotional. But I wouldn't have asked the three of you to do it if it didn't mean everything to me. I owe it to my daughter. She deserves to know the truth that she wasn't some fling in the back seat of a car and then given away like yesterdays' trash. She was loved Joshua. You are so very level headed that I know when you guys hit some roadblocks; you'll keep everyone on track. And Jena will be at your side for any legal issues that you might run into.

Promise me, that when its' done, and you've found her, you will give her a chance. The news might come as a shock to her and well, if she's got my blood in her, which we know she does, she might be a little stubborn, and not very receptive to all of you. Just don't give up on her and the possibility of gaining a sister. I can't be certain, but something tells me that she needs the three of you and its' destiny that you're brought together at this time in your lives.

I love you so much Joshua Michael, and I'm so proud of the man you've become. You are so much like your father and that is the highest compliment I could ever pay you.

Be strong for our family and always protect my girls.

Love,

Mom

Josh set down the letter and looked at his sisters and at the love of his life. It only took him a moment to regroup.

"Mom was usually right, so I guess this means we're supposed to find her."

Maggie was the first one to broach the subject. She'd carried the large envelope from the attorney's office up to camp but hadn't opened it, hadn't wanted to know its' contents until now.

"Now that we're all in agreement that we need to finish the road that mom has sent us down, does anyone have any ideas as to where to start? Also, do we brainstorm first, or should we review whatever surprise mom has for us in the Manilla envelope that Mr. Phelps gave us?"

"Mags, I'm mentally and emotionally exhausted so my vote is that we brainstorm a little bit more tonight, and then sleep on it, and open the envelope tomorrow. Is that okay?" she asked, yawning.

"I agree with Dee. This has been a pretty intense day for all of us, and I think a good night's sleep in this slightly frigid mountain air will do us all good. And we can formulate our plan in the morning. Jena, have you given it any thought as to where or how we should start our search?" he asked, knowing she was well versed in New York state law.

"Actually I have. New York is one of a few states in our nation that still has what are called sealed records, meaning that it takes a court order to have the adoption records unsealed. That being said, there are all sorts of adoption registries, and networks that you can log onto to see if Michelle is registered."

"That's all well and good, but if Michelle, or whatever her current name is, doesn't know what her birth name is, then what good does it do to throw mom or our names in the registry?" Maggie countered.

"From the little bit of research I did this afternoon, you put whatever information you have, whether you're the birth parent, sibling of an adoptee, or the adoptee him or herself in and the data base matches the hits, based on that information. It can be as simple as matching birthdates, place of birth, and adoption agency. Obviously, the more information, the better; but according to one of the sites I googled, they've had success with just the date of birth of a child. There is also what is called non-identifying information that was provided to the adoptee when she was adopted through Catholic Charities, and it can be obtained in reverse, meaning, that if "Elizabeth, ie. One of you," were to request information from Catholic Charities, there's a possibility that they'd send you some generalized information regarding the home that Michelle was adopted in to. I've seen people put posts on Facebook seeking their birth parents, there are many social networking groups, and there are ways to get the records unsealed, but as an attorney, if you go that route, I need to look the other way. All in all, I think that we have to bank on the fact that Michelle probably grew up knowing that she was adopted, and therefore, when we find her, it shouldn't be a devastating shock to her. That said, my recommendation would be for one of your sisters to send a sample to Ancestry DNA and the other one to one of the other DNA sites such as My Heritage or 23 and me. The reason I said that Deidre or Maggie should do it is because of the similar chromosomal features that they might have more in common with another female than you would. That's what I'm thinking. It's only a start, so let me give it a little more thought and I can probably come up with a few more angles to explore."

"Oh my god you are brilliant!" Deidre exclaimed. "Here I thought that my brother was the smart one for picking you to marry, but you're the brains in the relationship all along," she kidded. "Seriously, those are all excellent ideas, and I agree with you that it should be either Maggie or myself who send our blood or spit or whatever it is into Ancestry. I'll volunteer as long as it's not blood," she laughed. "And now Sasha and I are going to bed because I'm slightly drunk and very tired." She stood, tittered for just a moment, walked over to her sleeping cat, lifted her into her arms, and headed toward the stairs.

"Good night. I love the three of you very much."

"Night," they all said in unison. Taking Deidre's cue, Joshua stood and started picking up the dirty dishes, with Maggie and Jenna coming in behind him to pick up the remaining glasses, bottles and plates. Sinjin must have realized that it was bedtime because he finally moved from his post in front of the fireplace, and was situated by the rear door. After Maggie let him out and back in again, the kitchen was cleaned up and everyone headed for bed.

Elizabeth's camp was tiny compared to many of the mansions that had sprung up over the years. Gone were many of the original camps that had dotted the shoreline for decades, replaced with mega-mansions, some monstrosities that belonged in Vail or Miami. Elizabeth and her family had updated their camp where needed but had stayed true to themselves and the idea of camp living. Despite its' modest size, their camp had four small, but adequate sized bedrooms, and a full bath on both levels, along with a washer and dryer tucked into the lower level bathroom's closet. The true value was not in the size of their camp but in the dirt on which it was constructed. Elizabeth's grandparents had had the foresight, and financial means to purchase a large tract of land when the state starting selling off waterfront lots. Though, at the time, it was what they'd considered a vast amount of money, they knew that waterfront real estate was a commodity that would only increase in value. That said, they purchased the equivalent of four waterfront lots, giving them over four hundred feet of lake front on Fourth Lake, the largest of the Fulton Chain of lakes, and purchased it on the north shore in order to enjoy the gorgeous Adirondack sunrise. Though her great grandparents purchased the land, they never got to enjoy it. It wasn't until her grandparents were adults that the camp was finally constructed. Now, all these years later, it remained essentially the same as when it was built, with updates completed here and there, but the structural integrity remained the same.

Maggie washed up and made her way to her childhood bedroom. Tongue and groove pine covered majority of the walls, always giving the rooms a fresh smell, despite being closed up for weeks on end. As she entered the room, she found her dog already curled up on the rug beside her bed. Though Sinjin usually snuggled next to her at night, he never jumped on her bed, whether home or at camp, until given the command to. She'd taken him to obedience training as a pup, graduating with top honors. The trainers at the doggie school had told her that Sinjin would be an excellent candidate for becoming a service dog, an idea that Maggie put on the back burner. Looking at her snoring pup, she fully understood what unconditional love was. She'd found him, but he'd saved her in more than one way, and her love for her dog was beyond description. He was her best friend, confidant and support system. And if she spoiled him sometimes, so what; it was her prerogative.

She changed into flannel lounge pants and a tank top and climbed into bed, signaling for Sinjin to join her. The response was immediate and very welcome as she'd forgotten to turn on the electric blanket and felt the chill instantly. As she shivered momentarily, trying to warm up, her mind remained in overload. She knew that sleep should come easily as she was exhausted but doubted it would. As she lay in the dark, her mind kept jumping back to the fact that she now had another sister, whether she wanted to deal with it or not. She knew that between the four of them, and with Jena's legal expertise, they'd find their mother's daughter, and with a little luck, be able to reunite her with her birth father. Maggie's biggest reservation about the whole scenario was that her younger sister Deidre would get hurt, if they discovered that their half-sister wasn't like them, or didn't want anything to do with them. Unlike herself, Deidre had always looked for the good in people and the fairy book ending; and if the outcome of finding their sister wasn't a Hallmark made for TV moment, she worried about how it would affect her. From her own perspective, she could care less if she met her sibling or not. In her mindset, her mother was an incubator for the child that she gave up; whether she wanted to give her child up or not. She wasn't being cruel or cold, but honestly felt no tie or bond to a woman who for 25 years hadn't been part of her life. Doing the math in her head, she realized that Michelle would be 34 by now, and most likely had a family of her own. As she started to drift off, she realized that she could very likely be an aunt to nieces or nephews or both, and though she didn't realize it, she fell asleep smiling.

~Chapter 13~

Deidre and Maggie made their way downstairs shortly after the sun came up and were greeted by Jena humming away in the kitchen. Sinjin sat at her side, as if observing, but hoping that she'd drop a piece or two of the bacon she was currently cooking. Looking up at her two future sisters, she smiled.

"You two don't look any worse for wear, despite the empty bottles I've picked up this morning. How are your heads," she laughed.

"I'm fine," Maggie answered, bending over to receive kisses from her dog.

"I'll be fine once the drums pounding in my head cease," Deidre offered, rubbing her eyes for the tenth time that morning, trying to clear her head. "I'm not quite sure how much wine I drank last night but I know it was more than a glass or two because my head is vibrating."

"It was definitely more than a glass or two Dee. Go take a couple Aspirins and you'll be better within the hour," Maggie offered. "Hey Jena, what can I help you with?" she offered, making her way over to the coffee pot that smelled like heaven to her now. Pouring herself a cup of what smelled like Caramel flavored coffee, she waited to hear what her future sister in law wanted to cook next. Sipping her coffee, she looked around for her brother, and from the already lit fire, she assumed that he was up already.

"How'd you sleep Jenna? Once I got done freezing, I slept like a log and didn't hear a thing until Sinjin rolled over on top of me. Where's Josh?"

"Oh, you know him. He said that it wasn't cold outside, so he went for a run. I think he's nuts, but he seems to love running so I'm not going to stop him."

As Deidre made it back into the room, she handed her a mug of coffee, after having added plenty of cream and just enough sugar to satisfy her palate. Now that she had both Deidre and Maggie together and alone, she seized the moment. "I wanted to be the first to tell you that Josh and I have picked a date," she all but shouted. "He said that since he'd made me wait so long to propose to, that we should have a short engagement. And you know us, we're not very fancy and don't need some over the top wedding."

"Oh my God Jena, spit it out," Maggie commanded, though half kidding. "When is the big day and where? I've never done the whole wedding thing, but I assume that it takes a while for a dress to be made once its' ordered, so how quickly do you plan on having this wedding? And have you already secured a location for the reception, because I've heard that some places book two years in advance, which granted, sounds ridiculous to me, but then again, what do I know," she laughed.

"Shut up will you," she kidded, "and I'll tell you!" She took a deep breath and told them, their plans. "We've picked July 8th to get married, and if it's okay with you, we want to get married right here at camp, and have the reception here as well!"

She waited for Josh's sisters to respond and after neither spoke for a moment or two, unable to contain herself, she blurted out, "And I pray that the two of you will be my bridesmaids because you're already like sisters to me!"

Still processing the first part, Maggie watched as her younger sister flew into Jena's arms.

"Oh my God, yes! Yes, I'd love to be in your wedding. I love you like a sister already and I can't wait to be in your wedding," she exclaimed.

"Count me in too Jena. I'm just surprised that you want to have it here," Maggie commented as she looked over at Jena, still in a bear hug with Dee.

After his run, Joshua made his way into the kitchen to find his sisters and fiancée in some type of talking marathon, with his presence going unnoticed until Sinjin moved to join him in the hallway. As soon as Deidre saw her big brother, she raced over to him to embrace him as well. Looking at his fiancée for support, he smiled.

"I guess this means you told them about our plans?"

"Yes, she did, and I think it's awesome that you'll honor mom's family by having it here. I just hope we can help you pull it off," Maggie offered, cautiously.

Laughing, he left his little sister, making his way over to Jena, and hugging her from behind.

"You know my Jena. She makes even you look unorganized compared to her. She's already got spreadsheets made, caterers lined up, tent people for those huge tents that you rent in case of inclement weather, has already contacted DJ's and photographers. And luckily for me, all I had to do was sit back and write checks," he smiled. "But in all seriousness, after breakfast, I'd like to sit down with both of you and discuss just a few updates I'd like to see happen before we host the wedding and reception here. They're updates that we should have done when mom was alive, but never got around to them. And if you're in agreement, don't worry about the cost because Jena and I will cover it."

"Bull shit to that," Maggie countered. "You are right, there are numerous things that we should have updated here, and now is definitely the time to get them accomplished. But it is all of our responsibility and I will pay my fair share of the updates as well. It doesn't have to come solely out of your pocket, and I won't agree to the work unless you let us help cover our share of the cost."

"Agreed," Deidre offered. "Up until now, I've always invested everything I've made back into the business and never done anything for me. This camp is partly mine as well, and I will contribute my third of the cost, just like you are. Call it my wedding gift to you and Jena. Besides, after we've made some long overdue improvements, it'll only increase its' value, and make it more comfortable for us when we're here."

"So we're all in agreement then?" Joshua asked. "A summer wedding at camp it is," he laughed. "I think mom would be so happy if she knew," he added, somberly.

"She knows Josh," Maggie stated matter of factly, but sincerely. "She knows."

All three joined in helping Jena finish preparing breakfast. Sitting down at the table where they had shared pizza just twelve hours before, they filled their plates with bacon, scrambled eggs and massive sized pancakes. Deidre fired off question after question to both Jenna and Joshua, while Maggie listened and enjoyed overindulging in a meal that she'd never go through the effort to make for just herself. Once Deidre's questions seemed to all be answered, at least for the time being, Maggie changed the subject to something more pressing, at least in her eye.

"I know we were just hit with the information just yesterday, but have either of you given any thought as to how we start this process of finding mom's daughter? I mean, other than what you said last night? I guess what I'm getting at, is, can you run some type of check on her once we know who she is. I'd sort of like to know what kind of person we're dealing with before we go making contact. And Deidre, don't go and get all sappy on me. There are all sorts of people out there in the world and I have no intention of opening the door and letting one walk into my life if I know they're trouble."

"I know that you can get a little paranoid on me from time to time and you never give people the benefit of the doubt, but in this instance, I agree with you Mags," her sister responded, shocking both she and their brother. "I've taken Jena's advice and ordered the Ancestry DNA kit last night and it'll be here next week sometime. I'll send my sample in and see if I get any hits on it once it's processed, but I have no intention of contacting anyone who it links me with, unless all three of us are in agreement. We don't know if she's registered with Ancestry or not, and for all we know, she could be, and has already found her father and then we're off the hook."

"In answer to your question Deidre, yes, I can have a background check run on her. I won't invade her privacy, because it would be unethical for me to do that, but I can check the system to make sure she's not a felon or worse," she offered.

"Which avenue should I pursue?" Maggie volunteered. "I'm still not enthused about gaining a sister, especially since we know nothing about her upbringing or what type person she is, but if you are going to check her out before we make contact, then I can do something to help us locate her."

"Jena is going to contact Catholic Charities and try and determine who the attorney was for the organization at the time of the adoption and go the legal route. I think that since you're so computer savvy, and you have all sorts of Federal clearances, maybe you can search for Michelle's father, that Daniel O'Malley guy through your connections with the military. I mean, mom knew he joined the Air Force and knew what year he joined, so how hard could it be to access their archieved records?"

"Oh yeah," she repeated back to her brother snidely, "How hard could it be? I'll just tap into the Air Force's records and search for O'Malley, you know, since it's such an unusual name and all," she laughed. "I'm sure the United States Government won't mind if I do a little snooping," she added. "In all seriousness, I can search public records and come up with a birth date for him and then do some cyber digging. I'm sure I can come up with something," she offered. "And like Dee, I have no intention of contacting our mother's former lover, until we've done a back ground check on him as well."

"Ew, Mags, don't be so crude. My vote is that we refer to Daniel as Michelle's father, nothing else," Deidre offered, as she sipped on her second cup of coffee. "I know they were intimate and everything, but that doesn't mean I have to think about it all the time. I like living in my bubble world, where it was just mom and dad forever. Okay?"

"Okay Dee. Okay. We'll let you live in that bubble world of yours," Maggie laughed.

The rest of the day flew by for the four of them. Jena decided that they all needed some fresh air, so with Sinjin in tow, they layered up and headed a few miles up the road towards Roxdane Lake. Once in the parking lot, they grabbed their daypacks and started up the trail for Bald Mountain, which would soon be closed for hunting season. The sky remained slightly overcast with the clouds overhead hinting of more snow to come. The air was brisk, but not frigid; that would come soon enough to the north country. Sinjin led the way, with his blaze orange vest easily visible, despite the distance between them. Though he was technically supposed to be on a leash, Maggie let him run free because there had been no other cars in the parking lot except for one that looked like it'd been there overnight, and also because she knew one whistle and he'd be back heeling at her side, and she could leash him if she needed to. Her dog was only two years old, but not only was he smart, but very obedient to his master.

They made their way up the worn trail quickly and within a half hour, they were walking the narrow rock ridge toward the firetower. With occasional wind gusts, the summit was chillier than their fast paced walk up the mountain, but as usual, the view made it worthwhile. The mountain, compared to most in the Adirondacks was hardly worth mentioning to a 46er, but the view could compete with any high peak out there. As they started climbing the firetower, an obligatory must, Josh stopped to take a few pictures with his phone. They'd climbed the mountain as children, scrambling over the rocks, and jumping off boulders along the way, just so they could hear their mother gasp and pretend to scold them. They'd climbed it with teenage friends, and snuck a few beers from camp into their backpacks to drink at the summit. Each of the siblings had climbed Bald more times than they could remember, but each time the view unfolded of the Fulton Chain of lakes, with McCauley Mountain to their south, followed by Old Forge, 1st, 2nd, 3rd, the channel, and finally 4th Lake to the north, they were in awe. Though not completely a 360 panoramic view, the landscape in front of them was always spectacular, despite the season. They climbed the tower to its' watch tower while Sinjin sat beside their packs. Once the photos were done, they headed back down the mountain and into Maggie's truck, which she'd started while they were on the last leg of the trail. The warmth greeted them like a long lost friend. Only mildly tired, Deidre realized that her headache/hangover was gone, while Maggie felt nothing but rejuvenated. Josh and Jenna rode in the back seat, while Sinjin curled up in the rear as they made their way back to Route 28 and camp. Once back at camp, their brother and Jenna packed up first and headed home, while Deidre and Maggie lingered behind. They both nibbled on left over pizza, but deliberately avoided the half full bottle of wine that sat on the counter beside them. As they ate in relative silence, with Maggie on her computer, and Deidre her phone, they both were starting the search for their sister, each going at it in their own way. While Maggie was emailing a letter to Mr. Phelps, their mother's attorney, Deidre was on Ancestry plugging in names, without success.

After the pizza was gone, and they started hitting roadblock after roadblock, both decided to pack up and head for their respective homes, knowing that Monday and the start of another work week was just around the corner.

Once home, Maggie unpacked her truck, let Sinjin out the slider in her living room, and promptly put everything in its' place, she fired up her computer again, and went back to searching. In her mind, if she could find her sister, and her sister's father, and reunite them, then everything in her life could get back to normal. Well, as normal as it could be now that they were parentless. She thought about her friends, and none of them were without both parents. Sure, many were products of divorced families, but between her co-workers, and her friends outside of work, she couldn't think of anyone who'd lost both their father and mother at their age. Sitting there, she realized that twenty-five was way too young to be without her mom. She didn't know how or why it happened, but the tears started flowing, and with Sinjin by her side, she wept for her mother for the second time that weekend.

~Chapter 14~

The week flew by as they returned to their respective jobs, with each agreeing they'd get together the following Friday night to discuss their progress, if any. They'd agreed upon where to start in upgrading their mom's camp and both Deidre and Maggie had insisted that their brother should tackle that project since Jena was pursuing finding Michelle via the legal route. He'd let his fiancée do her thing while he lined up contractors to take a look at camp. Deidre had suggested that he contact the contractor that his mother's real estate agent was using since they were a local, family based business. He made contact with them, and scheduled an appointment with them for the following Sunday.

Deidre called Maggie the moment her DNA kit arrived in the mail and was so excited that she provided the saliva sample and drove to the post office to put it back in the mail. While on the phone, Maggie informed her that while she was hitting snags along the way, she was making progress in locating their mother's former boyfriend. She'd been able to access former military records of servicemen, which anyone with a little computer savvy could do, and she assured her little sister, that she wasn't doing anything illegal, well, at least not anything too illegal. Okay, so maybe she was using her extensive knowledge of computers to her advantage, but it wasn't like she was tapping into security systems or sending encrypted messages to a communist country, she was simply trying to locate a former serviceman. She'd also downloaded three applications from various adoption registries to complete and send in, in hopes that their sister might be on one of them.

With the evenings getting shorter and darker so much earlier, Maggie decided to head to the gym after work since she hadn't been in a week. She had meant to go after work both Monday and Tuesday, but hadn't paid attention to the time and before she knew it, it was after five both nights and she had a dog anxiously waiting for her at home.

She pulled into the parking lot and again, was relieved to see that it wasn't overly crowded. She wanted to just get in, work out for an hour and get home. She scanned the room as she made her way toward the woman's locker room, chastising herself for looking for him. Odds were that he wouldn't be there, but she'd found herself searching anyway. Exiting the locker room, water bottle in hand, she made her way towards an empty treadmill and climbed on. With her headphones on and music already playing, she didn't hear the whistle.

He'd seen her the second she'd entered the gym and headed straight toward the changing room. All business as usual, he noted. Glad that she didn't look as sad as she had during their last encounter, he kept climbing higher and higher on his stationary stair climber. She was beautiful was his first reaction, but once he'd spoken with her, he knew that she was not only beautiful but intelligent, and definitely someone he'd like to get to know. He'd spoken briefly with Rodney in the office and had learned that she and her siblings had recently lost their mother and that they had no other living relatives beside themselves. He hadn't pried, nor had his partner in the firm offered anything else about their meeting, including the contents of the will. He had asked only in order to learn why her eyes spoke of such sadness, and now he knew. He'd lost his own father a few years ago, not to death, but to divorce, and then his disappearance. He and his sister learned, less than a year after he'd walked out on their mother, that he'd remarried and was living in Mexico with his new bride, a woman younger than he and his sister. He didn't really care, but his older sister had taken it hard, and their mother, even harder. Garrett felt blessed that he still had his mother in his life and when his sister's marriage imploded, leaving her with two small children, he'd stepped in to help both of the women in his life.

He watched her attack the treadmill like she was on a quest. She'd jacked the incline as high as it would go, and was climbing her stationary mountain faster than most people could walk. He knew he shouldn't, but he watched her muscles flex as she pushed them to their limit and took note of just how toned and ripped she truly was. For such a short little thing, her tiny 5'2" package delivered a wallop and Garrett knew that if he didn't divert his eyes someplace else, he'd be in an embarrassing situation right there on the stair climber.

She could feel his eyes burning into her back, even though she hadn't noticed him when she'd walked through the gym. She knew that he was watching her. It wasn't just her practice in the Martial Arts that kept her sense of her surrounding sharp; Maggie had always been one to be aware of her surroundings. Deidre on the other hand set herself up to become a victim without even realizing it.

Her heart saw nothing but the good in people, whereas Maggie saw them for what they really were and did not give anyone the benefit of the doubt. Yes, she and Deidre were sisters, barely a year apart in age, and polar opposites of one another.

She kept climbing, enjoying the burn and adrenaline rush. She finished her time on the treadmill before she'd acknowledge Garrett, she thought to herself, knowing that he was still looking her way. Not one to play games, she wasn't ignoring him intentionally, but rather, didn't want to resent him for interrupting her workout. Her best laid plan took an unscheduled detour when she opened her eyes that had been closed in concentration, and into his piercing blue ones, that were attached to his very appealing looking physique.

"Hi."

"Hi yourself."

"Sorry to interrupt your climb up Everest," he smiled, "I just wanted to say that you look much happier than when I saw you last, and I'm glad."

"Thanks. It was a pretty rough weekend, but we got through it."

"Remember what I said about Meatloaf," he offered.

Panting and nearly out of breath from talking while climbing, she looked at him strangely, not sure what he meant.

Seeing the look of confusion come across her face, he smiled, just enough to allow his dimples to pop. "Remember, I love the band Meatloaf, and I've already told you, Two Out OF Three Ain't Bad. Remember that Maggie, and hopefully the next time we run into each other, it's because we're heading out for coffee together, and something more relaxing than dying here at this gym," he laughed.

She almost asked him if he'd like to go for coffee right then, but as quickly as the impulse came to her, she suppressed it, thinking of her dog waiting for her at home. She'd use Sinjin as her excuse, but in reality, she knew that she needed to proceed slowly with Garrett. He reminded her of gasoline, with her being a match; and while she knew if she allowed herself the pleasure, they'd burn hot and out of control, but then smolder out. Garrett Brown was the first man that had appealed to her intellect, and she didn't want to have a quick fling with him and then move on. He intrigued her and kept her guessing, and she wasn't quite sure what to do with him yet, so she'd stall until she had it all figured out

She believed in brutal honesty, and although it had gotten her into trouble more than once in the past, she wasn't about to change her personality.

"I would like to get to know you Garrett, really I would. It's just a very complicated time in my life right now, and there's a lot going on that my sister and I have to deal with, with the loss of our mother, and all. Our mom was a wonderful lady, a very kind and gracious woman and would do anything for anyone. It's just, she threw my sister, brother and I a huge curve ball and we need to take care of some of her unfinished business before I can tackle anything else in my life," she answered honestly.

He heard every word she'd said, and knew that she wasn't just blowing him off, but also knew that he wasn't giving up.

"Do you like hockey?" he asked, throwing her off.

"Yes, love it. Why?"

"Great. I have two tickets to the Zetlin's lounge suite for Sunday afternoon's game. Join me. It's not a date, just two people who enjoy hockey going to a game. It's several days away so you can work on the project that you're doing with your siblings, and I won't even kiss you if you don't want me to," he added, chuckling.

She smiled and turned red simultaneously. She definitely didn't need to become involved with him, yet shocked herself when she simply said. "Okay, I'd love to go with you to the game." Catching herself, she added, "But it's not a date. Just two people who love hockey, attending the game together, that's all."

"Yup, that's all. But I'm still secretly hoping for that kiss," he added, turning to leave. "Call me on Saturday Maggie, and we'll finalize all the details. Oh, and have a great week. I'll see you Sunday," he smiled, whistling to himself as he strolled away like a proud peacock.

She'd been set up she realized, and she'd walked right into it. He'd been smooth, sweet, and very calculating. If he'd convinced her to go out with him without her even realizing it, she could only wonder what type of lawyer he was. Yes, Garrett Brown was definitely one she'd like to get to know, and as she finished up on her stationary climb, she realized that she'd soon find out more about the man behind the smile.

~Chapter 15~

Maggie found herself hitting stumbling block after stumbling block trying to locate Michelle's father. The military allowed civilians onto generic sites, and despite her Federal clearance levels, she found herself hitting several dead ends going the military route. She'd scoured various search engines and came up empty with the exception of one lead that she'd discovered on a 2000 census. As of that year, there had been a Daniel O'Malley who would have been the approximate age of the man she was looking for, living in Rome, New York, less than twenty miles from her mother's home. She found it ironic that her mother's first love, was living essentially around the corner from her and she didn't even know it. Not sure how she would have felt if in fact her mother had known and met up with him, despite being a widow and single, Maggie realized that she was glad that she hadn't known.

Jena and Josh were hitting a few roadblocks of their own but remained as determined as Maggie to fulfill their mother's wishes, get it over with, and then move on. With Jena pursuing the search from a legal standpoint, Joshua, at both of his sister's insistence, had contacted the contractors that their mother and her real estate agent recommended and upon viewing the work they'd completed on their mother's house, hired him during a phone interview. Joshua explained what they were hoping to accomplish at camp and gave the contractor their deadline. He, in turn, explained that winters were slower in the mountains, and since it was all interior work, that he guaranteed that it could and would be completed long before their July deadline. They agreed to meet at the camp Sunday morning to look at the area and walk through exactly what Joshua and his sisters were envisioning.

Deidre checked in with her siblings every day while she waited for the result of her Ancestry DNA to arrive via computer. She found herself checking her email two or three times a day, despite knowing that the pamphlet provided when she'd received her kit, clearly stated two to three weeks. She'd literally just sent it back less than a week prior and knew that there was no way that they'd even received her sample yet, but she couldn't help herself. She'd joined a support group, comprised mainly of birth mothers searching for their long-surrendered children, and upon speaking over the phone with one older woman, whom she suspected was approximately her grandmother's age, she learned a great deal about what it was like to be an unwed mother in the sixties. She told of being sent off to Our Lady Of Victory, a home for unwed mothers outside of Buffalo. She told Deidre how her parents put her on a bus, told her how much disgrace she'd brought to their family, despite the fact that only her parents had known about her pregnancy. The woman, Maria, told Deidre that her mother's last words to her were, "Have your bastard child, and don't come home until you've given him away, and when you return, this issue will never be spoken of again." Maria went on to tell Deidre that despite being nuns, therefore an extension of the church, they were brutal, to say the least. Upon arrival, each woman was assigned a new fictitious name that they were to use among the other women at the home. They were told in no uncertain terms, that they were to never reveal their real name, family or hometown and that if they ever gave any thought to keeping their baby, the headmaster, a very tall and mean nun named Sister Martha, promised them that their child would be taken away and placed in an orphanage and left there to rot, and never be adopted into a loving home. Deidre shuttered listening to this woman's recollection of how cruel the atmosphere must have been and how sad that women were forced out of their home, away from their families, in a time when they probably needed their families love and support more than ever. Maria told her that when her child was born, she, like all the other new mothers, was forced to take care of her child 24/7 for the first week. She had to feed, bathe, and try not to love the infant that she'd just delivered, and then, one week from the day she'd given birth, she was told that she was discharged and being sent home, on the very bus that had brought her there four months earlier; except this time, there would be no child making the trip. Given just moments to say good bye to the daughter she'd grown to love with every ounce of her heart, she gave her one last kiss before the nun picked her child up and carried her out of the room like yesterday's leftovers. Maria went on to say that watching that woman take her daughter, changed her for life and until the day that she was reunited with her only child, she'd never be whole. Deidre found herself crying on the other end of the line, as Maria told her story, and prayed that when her own mother was there in the early eighties, that things had improved for the young women over the course of twenty years. She knew that her mom had only spent less than two months there, and she silently prayed that it wasn't such a horrible and cold environment. She tried to imagine what it must have been like to be young, pregnant, alone and scared, but couldn't. After hanging up with the elderly woman that evening, she felt drained, and emotionally exhausted. Packing up to head for home, she shut down her work computer, and started shutting off the lights. Looking around, she noticed her one lone spider plant looked wilted, and then it dawned on her that she'd forgotten again that week to water the plant. Chastising herself, she took the water bottle from her pack and quickly poured it on the plant that looked moments away from dying.

"I forgot you again. I'm so sorry. I'm a horrible plant mom." She gently touched some of the plants leaves and made a mental note to swing by their mother's home to water her plants before they ended up in the same condition as her own. She called Maggie on her way across town and was disappointed when it went to voicemail. She left her sister a message just as she pulled into her mother's drive behind a big gray Silverado. Recognizing it from the other day, she realized that the contractors must still be working on her mother's place. As she made her way inside, she could tell that it was in fact

Griffin who was there working once she opened the door and heard him singing. His voice echoed through the rooms, catching Deidre by surprise when she recognized the tune. It wasn't necessarily the words, but the intonation in his voice that mesmerized her. He sang from his soul and had a way of bringing the listener into the story of the song. She followed the voice and found him in her mother's room, painting the last wall of the room, indicating that he'd been there for some time. He sensed her presence and turned to face her.

"Oh hey Deidre. I'm just finishing up in here. What do you think?" he asked.

She found herself smiling at the thought that he'd remembered her name. "Hi Griffin, it really looks great in here! The light grey really makes the room look a lot larger."

She noticed that he'd moved all of the furniture into the center of the room and had neatly covered everything in plastic.

"Hey, I'm just here to water all of my mom's plants and then I'll get out of your way."

"You're fine. I'll be done in about two minutes anyways, and then just have to put everything back into place and we'll be all set for the home to go on the market."

"Then I had better remember to water these more often or better yet, take some of them home with me so they aren't dead looking when people come to preview the house," she kidded. She finished watering the ones in her mother's room, excusing herself to go get more water and take some of the plants in the living room to her car. When she was ready to leave, she wandered back towards her mother's room, to say goodbye. Finding him attempting to move the bulky furniture on his own, she quickly set down the watering pot and reentered the room.

"Typical man, trying to do everything on his own, without asking for help," she teased, and she grabbed a side of the triple dresser he was pushing. With her help, it slid back into place against the wall.

"Typical woman," he teased back, "always thinking they know how to do things better than us men!" he laughed. "Seriously Dee, I don't want you to hurt yourself. I can do this on my own."

"Or I can help you and it'll go even faster," she countered, not dissuaded easily. It was her mother's house and she was going to help him put it back in order. Besides, she liked looking at him. He was generic looking, not ugly, not gorgeous; but the way he carried himself, and sang from his heart had captivated her attention and she wanted to discover more about the man with the amazing voice and jade green eyes.

They talked about anything and everything that came to mind as they rearranged Elizabeth's room and put everything back in order. She told him a little bit about growing up in the home, and he'd told her a little bit about the places he'd worked on in the past. Once they had the bed, dresser and night stands back in place, the last piece left was her mother's enormous solid cherry armoire. Looking at the piece, Deidre thought that there was no way that they could move it in its' present state, and as if reading her mind, Griffin walked over to the massive piece of furniture, and pulled out the top drawer, setting it on the bed.

"When I moved it earlier today, I took out all four of the drawers to make it easier to slide. Maybe with your brute strength to help me, I'll only have to remove two," he winked.

"Ha ha," she teased back. "I think we need to remove those drawers regardless she stated, trying to sound insulted, but failing miserably. There was something about him that she found comfortable. She hadn't had more than twenty minutes of conversation with the guy, yet, being alone in the room with him didn't alarm or concern her, and she knew from those few moments of laughing and talking, that he was a good man, one that you could shoot a game of pool with, innocently flirt with, or simply have as a good friend. Since she didn't play pool, she had already decided that if their paths crossed again, and at a different time in her life, she'd like to get to know the painter a little better.

They pulled the drawers out of the armoire and once all four were removed and lying on the bed, they easily slid the piece back to its' rightful spot. Once in the exact spot where it had been before the room was painted, Griffin instructed Deidre to remove the plastic sliders out from underneath each corner as he lifted the monstrosity from one side to the other. Deidre had wondered how he'd managed to get them underneath the unit by himself but didn't ask for fear of sounding silly. Once he'd tucked the sliders away, she followed his lead in grabbing a drawer to put back into the armoire, being careful to line up the tracks, sliding them back in place. Glancing down at her mother's sweaters carefully folded in the drawer that she was carrying was like a punch in the gut. Her mind went back to their last Christmas together when her mom had worn the sweater she was presently looking at. Only ten months ago her mother had been the picture of health. They'd decided to have a Christmas get together at the lake, and each of them promised to wear an ugly sweater, with the winner getting to choose the theme for the following year. Looking at the obnoxious holiday sweater so neatly folded in her mother's drawer, she laughed, remembering how shocked everyone had been when Elizabeth paraded around in her Walmart sweater, showing Santa's reindeer humping. She'd won, hands down!

Griffin knew that Deidre was thinking about her mother and didn't interrupt as he stood beside her holding the next drawer. Once she had put the first drawer in its' place, she turned and took the one that he was holding, quickly sliding it into its' allotted slot. She didn't speak as she took hold of the third, but smiled as he handed it to her. It slid in almost as easily as the first two. Griffin knew that somehow it was a task that she needed to complete although he couldn't possibly fathom what she was presently going through, he knew that Deidre needed to help him until the job was done. He handed her the last drawer and she started to slide it into place and stopped. He watched her try to force it into place, after pulling the drawer out and making sure the tracks were lined up. It still wouldn't go all the way in. Hearing her swear under her breath, he stepped in to take the drawer from her. Once Griffin was holding the drawer, Deidre stepped up on her tippy toes to see what the problem was. When she didn't initially see anything blocking the track on either side, she turned the light on her phone and shined it into the slot to have a better look. She still didn't initially see any reason why the drawer was getting hung up. It wasn't until she reached in and did a blind sweep that she felt something. Not sure what she felt, she gave a hard tug and felt something that felt like paper give way in her hand. Once loose, she pulled her arm out and looked down at what she was holding. Griffin said nothing and wasn't sure what to make of what appeared to be, a crumpled up envelope in her hand. He stepped forward, and slid the drawer into place. Not sure what to do, whether he should stay or give her space, he silently stepped back and started to exit the room.

"Please don't leave." She looked at the man standing less than five feet away from her and smiled. He'd stopped in his tracks with her three words.

"Please stay with me Griffin. Please be here with me. I know I don't know you, but I think I'd like to become your friend, and I'm not sure what is inside this envelope I'm holding. If it's okay with you, I'd really like to open it right now and see what's inside, and see," she added sincerely, "I've learned so much about my mother this week that I didn't know, that I'm scared of what is inside this," she gestured, holding up the faded envelope.

Not quite sure how he should react, he did the only thing that came to mind. He stepped forward and rubbed her arm solidarity.

"I'm sure it's just some old newspaper clippings about one of your achievements or your siblings," he offered.

"I hope you're right. Let's find out, shall we?" she said, gently opening the envelope.

He noted that her hands were shaking as she opened the very weathered looking envelope and removed its' contents. He gave her as much space as he could, while remaining in close proximity to catch her, should she faint on him. He didn't have much experience with fainting women but then again, he didn't know enough about Deidre to determine if she were the swooning type or not. He watched her silently remove a yellowed piece of paper from the envelope that appeared to be from a newpaper. As Deidre unfolded what was in fact a clipping from the local gazette in Utica, he couldn't see the article, just the heading that read. "Local Boy Injured in Air Strike". He saw her hands start to shake even more, and the color start to drain from her face as she started to read the article and then quickly fold it in quarters and stuff it back into the envelope.

She turned toward him, and he saw that her color was finally returning, and he took a breath, not realizing that he'd been holding it. "Everything okay," he offered nonchalantly.

"Yup. Thought the clipping might be about my family or relatives of ours but it was just a clip about one of mom's grade school friends, nothing important," she offered, not elaborating. He could tell that she wasn't telling him the truth, or most likely telling him that she recognized the name, but he'd let it go for now. He'd barely met her and knew that she had just buried her mother and despite the fact that he was attracted to the sad looking woman standing beside him, he had no right to pry. Instead he just accepted what she'd offered.

"Deidre, I'm sure you're used to dating executive type people, and people with fancier cars, clothes and degrees than I have; but I was wondering," he stammered. "Would you possibly like to grab a pizza together sometime? I mean, after the dust settles and you've got more time and possibly are free some evening?" he asked sincerely, knowing that she'd probably politely decline his offer. Standing there, looking at Elizabeth's daughter, he thought she looked like some type of Bohemian goddess, with her slightly wrinkled clothing, messy hair, and no makeup, not that she needed any. He thought that she was simply beautiful sans any plastered on makeup, which he always thought made woman look make believe.

She laughed, not at him, but at his convoluted way of asking her on a date. She found it endearing and cute that he'd think that she would be attracted to someone

190

based on their social status or net worth; nothing could be farther from the truth.

"I'd love to go out with you Griffin. And it just so happens that I'm starving," she smiled. "So how about right now?" she offered, catching him completely off guard.

"Now?" he nearly choked on the word. "Like in now, now?"

"Yes, like in now, now," she countered, finding him adorable with his shocked expression.

"You need to eat. I need to eat, and it's Friday night; so, if you don't have plans, why don't we go out right now and grab a pizza, wings, and a couple beers?" she offered. As soon as the words came out of her mouth, she remembered that she'd promised to get together with her siblings and found herself backpaddling. He picked up on her change in posture and didn't need to hear the words to know that she'd changed her mind. Just as he was about to give her an out, she simply told him that she'd be all set once she made one quick call. He didn't want her to feel pressured and offered her more than one opportunity to walk away. Deidre walked towards the front of her mother's home as she put the phone to her ear. He tried not to eavesdrop as he heard her start to speak. It took her less than thirty seconds to return to her mother's bedroom with a large smile on her face.

"All set," she exclaimed. "I was supposed to meet my sister this evening but when I told her that I had a hot date, she told me to go for it," she laughed. "So, Mr. Hot date, are you ready?"

Still flabbergasted, he picked up his keys and smiled. "Mr. Hot Date is ready, willing and thrilled to head out for pizza with you. You definitely keep me guessing Deidre; and I think I like it."

"You ain't seen nothing yet Grif."

~Chapter 16~

Maggie hung up the phone with her sister, who'd just backed out of their plans. Slightly pissed, and slightly jealous that her kid sister had a hot date and she was home alone on a Friday evening, Maggie looked around her house, saw her dog looking at her questioningly and gave a two second thought to dialing Garrett's number to see if he was free. But then, she laughed out loud as Sinjin rolled over, seeking attention.

"You're right baby. I'll just pour myself a glass of wine and we will curl up on the couch and watch something on Netflix, okay?" she asked her pooch, not expecting an answer. Walking back into her kitchen, she threw her dog a treat, poured herself a glass of Pinot Noir, picked her phone up off the counter, and made her way to her couch. Once settled in, with her dog already curled up beside her, she went about surfing her television channels to find something entertaining on. It only took her fifteen minutes and a half a glass of wine to realize that she was about to be bored silly watching ridiculous reality TV or watching a movie that she'd already seen once or twice. She looked at her phone, again thought about calling him, and chastised herself for not being content in her own home, alone.

While Maggie was sulking at home, Deidre found herself becoming slightly nervous as she pulled in beside Griffin. He came to her car, opening the door for her. With all of the pizza joints in Utica, she was relieved that he'd picked one of her favorites. One that she knew offered a quiet, casual environment, that would afford them privacy and a place to talk and get to know one another.

"I love Rosarios, so I hope this place is okay with you?" he asked, extending out his hand to help her out of her little car. She took it, despite the fact that she certainly didn't need assistance getting out of her own car. They walked in together, and were both greeted by name by Natalie, one of the employees. She took their beverage orders and then Natalie asked both Deidre and Griffin if they'd like their usual toppings. They looked at each other, and simultaneously said, "Pepperoni, Mushrooms, Sausage and double cheese."

Natalie laughed and turned without saying another word. They left the counter and found a table away from the other patrons. Once seated, they felt the awkwardness that comes with first dates settling in. Griffin spoke first.

"Let me guess, this is your favorite pizza joint too?" he asked, taking a sip of his beer and smiling.

"Guilty," Deidre responded, already feeling her nerves starting to settle down.

They made small talk while waiting for their pizza to arrive, and both dug in once it was placed in front of them. As usual, it didn't disappoint, and both ate in silence for a few moments.

"Thanks for inviting me out for pizza Griffin; this was a great idea," Deidre commented. "So you know a little bit about me through my mom and her real estate agent, tell me about yourself," she asked, trying to sound generic and only semi-interested in her request.

"Well, let's see," he said, leaning back in the booth. "I'm twenty four, have a wife and five kids, two dogs and seven cats" he started, smiling as the words left his mouth. "No seriously, I'm twenty eight, single, no pets, have been working with my father since I got out of college, love my job and the flexibility it allows me for traveling, and I think you are a very beautiful person, both inside and out," he added, blushing slightly as he took a large swig of his half empty beer. "What about you Deidre, what moves you?"

Recovering from the shock of his honest compliment, she thought about his question for just a second and answered from the heart.

"I love helping people. That's what moves me. I'm relatively shy, quiet and I guess what you'd call an introvert, despite being a people person. I love traveling as well, but time and financial resources, or lack thereof, have me resorting to traveling only through books I've read or through pictures I see or paint from my imagination. I, along with my business partner and friend, run a soup kitchen down on James Street, and have a little business on the side that employs a dozen or so veterans, most of whom are homeless. Oh, and I think you're quite beautiful as well."

"Thanks."

"You're welcome. So tell me Griffin, tell me about your travels and what places you liked, loathed, and everything in between. Paint visual pictures for me Grif, so I can imagine them in my mind."

"Sure, would you like me to start with Europe, Asia or South America? And tell me where you've traveled first, so that I don't overlap on the places that you've already seen," he smiled.

"Okay. The only place I've traveled outside of the US was to Europe between my Junior and Senior year in college. Against my mother's wishes, I went with two other friends, and we flew into London, and drove all over England before traveling to France and finally Germany. We did all the touristy things and flew home from Berlin to totally pissed off parents. We were broke, exhausted, and grounded for the rest of the summer, well at least as grounded as a 21 year old can be; but we had a blast, and if given the opportunity, I would do it again in a heartbeat," she added for good measure.

"Cool. What did you enjoy most in each country?" he asked, not telling her that he knew England very well, as he had spent nearly two years living there as a teenager.

"Well, in England, of course I loved Buckingham Palace, the changing of the guard and all the pomp and circumstance that surrounds royalty; but in all honesty, I loved visiting Stonehenge the most. I loved the mystery behind it, loved riding the Tube out of the city, catching a train, and then finally a bus to the site, and I especially loved the way the air changes once you're walking toward the sacred ground. In France, I loved touring the Louvre, and viewing the centuries of history displayed there. Yes, of course I did the whole Eifel Tower tourist thing, but it was the Louvre that really moved me. And," she said, closing her eyes for just a moment as if picturing the places, she'd visited in Germany, "I believe that I enjoyed the people of Germany more than I did the sites. I loved our boat tour on the Rhine River and seeing the Berlin Wall, or at least what was left of it; but I think that it was talking to and meeting people of our generation that I enjoyed the most. They've been through such changes over the years and I found it fascinating to simply talk with them and hear their stories."

"Very cool.   I've toured Germany also, and I believe I understand exactly what you're talking about," he offered.   "From what I remember, everyone spoke excellent English and they wanted to talk about their struggles, accomplishments and achievements.   I remember leaving Germany with a sense of pride for the people our age who lived there.   Regardless of the adversity, they were standing up for democracy and for change, despite the risks associated with going up against the government."

He took another drink, finishing off his bottle of beer. Deidre did the same and noted that Natalie walked over with refills, without being asked. If she had planned on eating her pizza quickly and making a run for it, Natalie wasn't helping by giving her another bottle of beer, that she now was obligated to drink. Luckily for her, she was enjoying the food and the company, and she really had no desire to escape quite yet. She found Griffin interesting, and definitely easy on the eyes and wanted to get to know him a little better.

"So, tell me about your travels Griffin. I'd love to hear where you've traveled."

He had always kept his private life private and had never divulged to the women he'd dated much about his personal life or his family. He'd never stayed with a woman long enough or invested enough of himself to let them in. But sitting there, across from a woman he hardly knew, he found himself talking and opening up as if she were a long-lost friend.

"I had the luxury of studying abroad in Florence Italy during my Junior year of college and found that I fell in love with not only the country, landscape and architecture, but also the people. I spent nearly five months there and would love to go back again someday. While there, we traveled to Germany, Switzerland, and Austria. Of course we hiked every chance we could and while the Alps were stunning and amazing to see, I think I truly loved Italy more. I took four years of Spanish back in High School and though it was a slightly different dialect, I was able to converse with the locals, at least to a certain degree," he smiled. "I also found that as long as you were trying, they appreciated the effort and opened up to us, despite our age and the fact that we were American students."

She stared at him as if she were trying to see the country through his eyes. Italy was on her bucket list and listening to him speak so affectionately about the people made her want to see it even more. He continued describing what Florence, Milan, Naples, Rome and the Amalfi Coast were like, and she found herself mesmerized as he described touring the ancient Island of Pompeii.

They both were nearly finished with their beers as he finished speaking of the other countries that he'd visited in Europe and Asia. She'd asked generic questions and he'd answered them. Despite the fact that he'd told her more about himself than he'd ever offered to the past women in his life, he still found himself holding back.

They'd spoke about growing up, their siblings and where they'd attended college, but neither had divulged their actual degrees or provided intimate details regarding their families. Having lost both of her parents at such an early age, Deidre found herself very territorial about her family, while Griffin simply didn't like to give strangers any ammunition to be used against him. Maybe it was his strict upbringing or maybe it was a protective measure, but he never liked to open up about his childhood. He did reveal during their conversation that he had an older brother who was an Aeronautical Engineer for NASA. He didn't elaborate except to say that he lived in Florida and that they tried to get together at least twice a year to go camping, backpacking or hiking together. He didn't know what there was about the woman sitting across the table from him that intrigued him so; but as the evening came to a close, he realized that he'd told her more about his family and his life than he ever had told anyone.

After fighting over the tab, with Griffin paying, but only after promising that if they went out for pizza again, it would be on Deidre's nickel; they walked toward their cars. He desperately wanted to kiss her goodnight but didn't want to press his luck. She seemed so sweet, and for whatever reason reminded him of a baby fawn, who would spook easily if he made the wrong move. The evening had flown by and he knew that he wanted to see her again but wasn't quite sure how she'd feel about it. As Deidre reached into her purse for her keys, she turned back at him and smiled.

"Griffin, thank you. I had a really nice time tonight and I'd like to see you again, if that's alright with you," she added, blushing slightly. Before he could answer, she harnessed her courage, and stepped forward, bringing her lips to his. She only allowed them to brush over his, and only for a brief second; but it was enough to ignite his entire system.

When she stepped back, she looked into his eyes for any sign of approval. It took him a second to allow his heart to stop racing from the shock and delight of yet another one of Deidre's surprise moves. As she waited for a response, Deidre found herself growing increasingly embarrassed at her brazen actions. Just when she opened her mouth to apologize, he reached for her and pulled her into an embrace that she never saw coming. In one quick move, he pulled her to him and took her mouth, gently at first, trying very hard to suppress the desire he felt growing inside him. His kiss lasted for just a moment, leaving her wanting so much more. When he stepped back, neither said a word but their smiles spoke volumes.

"Yes, I want to see you again Deidre, and again, and probably again. I knew that you were beautiful and had a kind soul; anyone would know that by simply speaking with you. But I had no idea how smart and talented you are, and I'd really like to get to know you more," he added sincerely.

Deidre took what he'd just said and despite her insecurities, jumped on the idea that had been swirling in her head.

"Didn't you say that you're heading up to my mom's camp to meet my brother Sunday?"

"Yes, why? Will you be there," he asked, hoping for an affirmative response.

"I hadn't planned on it, but if you'd like, possibly if you don't have plans after the meeting, would you like to go hiking somewhere up there afterwards? That is, as long as we don't get a heavy snow in the next forty-eight hours," she added.

"I'd love too, and even if it snows, that's what crampons are for," he winked. "I was planning on meeting Josh at 9am at your cabin, so I'd say anytime after 10 works for me."

"Great, then I'll head up to camp tomorrow night and see you there Sunday morning, ready to climb."

"Great, see you then Deidre. Oh, and Dee, thank you. This was a wonderful first date and I look forward to many more."

"It wasn't a date," she kidded. "Just two hungry people eating pizza together," she countered, not quite ready to admit that she had enjoyed herself far more than she thought possible.

As he opened his truck door, he shouted back. "Oh yes it was, and Sunday will be our second date. Have a good night Deidre, and I'll see you Sunday."

She watched him back up and drive away and realized that she was smiling.

~Chapter 17~

Despite her libido, Maggie had decided against calling Garrett and had stayed in, watching reruns and drinking wine. She woke early and hit the gym as soon as she was up, changing her routine in hopes of avoiding the man she'd contemplated calling and inviting over the night before. She'd been in a mood and knew that if she'd seen him, she'd probably have jumped him, and not one for one-night stands, despite how cute they were, she'd avoided the temptation by drinking wine and pouting.

She pulled in and noted that either everyone else was in the same type mood that she was, or that 7am was simply a popular time on a Saturday morning. She found herself searching the parking lot for his car and felt relieved that it wasn't there. He'd have had no clue what had been on her mind the evening before, but she had known, and for that reason alone, she was thankful that she wouldn't have to face him so early in the morning. She grabbed her gym bag and made her way inside.

He spotted her Jeep the second he pulled in and smiled. He'd hoped but hadn't expected to find her there and upon seeing her truck, took it as a sign. Whistling, he quickly made his way inside the crowded gym, changed his sneakers and went in search of her.

He found her, ear buds in, cursing softly to herself as she climbed her imaginary mountain. From the sheen on her skin, he could tell that she'd been at it for a while. He couldn't help but admire the way her compact body filled out the spandex that she was wearing. He made a mental note to thank LuLa Roe for inventing such lovely attire for a physically fit woman to wear. He didn't want to disturb her, nor startle her so he simply climbed on the closest available stair stepper and started working out.

She'd known that he'd walked in long before she'd seen him out of the corner of her eye. Never one to play games, she knew that she'd acknowledge him once she completed the circuit she was presently on. Her mind played mental ping pong as she once again thought about inviting him over for a quick round of horizontal limbo. She had no interest on settling down and getting serious with anyone, despite their looks and credentials, and since Garrett didn't appear to be the one-night stand type of guy, she tabled the thought and tried to focus on something else. When her calves were sufficiently on fire and her time was up, she sprayed down her stair stepper, drank heartedly and proceeded to walk toward the man who was miserably failing in his attempt to ignore her.

"Hi."

"Oh, hi Maggie. Didn't see you come in," he offered, as he continued to hyperventilate on his machine.

"That's because I was already here when you came in Garrett," she laughed. "And don't tell me you didn't see me when you walked in," she added, trying to sound accusatory, but only half serious.

"Who me? All you women in your cute little outfits look the same to us guys. No, I hardly noticed you at all," he retorted.

"Uh huh, is that so?" she laughed out loud. "Same goes with all you muscle men. We women don't pay any attention to your kind. We're just here to work out."

"Go out with me tonight Maggie." The words just blurted out. "I know that we have the hockey game tomorrow, but that'll be crowded, noisy and with the game going on, we won't really have time to talk. So, I know that it's short notice, but would you like to go out to dinner with me this evening?" he asked, catching her completely off guard.

It took her a second to respond but when she did, she tried to sound as sincere as possible.

"Garrett, I almost called you last night and invited you over. What stopped me is that it would have been for all the wrong reasons and you seem like too nice of a guy to do that to. I told you before that I'd really like to know you better, and I meant that. It's just that we, my siblings and I have some kind of heavy stuff going on right now with my mother's passing, and her dying request, which I'll tell you about someday, once we get to know one another a little better," she smiled.

"I get it Mags, I honestly do. I'm not quite sure how I'd feel if I'd just lost my sole parent. My parents are very much alive, and I cannot begin to understand what you and your siblings must be going through. But regarding last night," he smiled, allowing his dimples to pop out, "I'm okay with being invited over for all of the wrong reasons; really, I am. But since that didn't happen, and I'm assuming tonight isn't an opportune time either, then I'll just wait patiently until the timing is better. I'm a very patient man Maggie, and I believe you're worth waiting for."

"What about brunch before the game tomorrow?" she offered.

Jumping on the opportunity she presented, he responded almost immediately. "Sure, where?"

"How about Raspberries on Genesee Street? They have a great Sunday brunch until late afternoon, and if we time it right, we'll avoid the church crowd and have time to talk before the game. I have to head up to my mother's camp tonight to meet with a contractor early tomorrow morning, but should be back in town before noon."

"Great, how does 1:30 sound? It'll give us plenty of time before the game and also not force you to race home from your camp."

"That sounds wonderful. Oh Garrett, just so you know, if I didn't have to be at camp so early tomorrow morning, I would have taken you up on your offer for this evening."

"And I would have taken you up on yours last night Mags," he winked. "See you tomorrow at Raspberries at 1:30pm. Unless you'll let me pick you up and make it a real date?" he asked sincerely.

"You can pick me up Garrett. I'll text you my home address later this afternoon," she offered, turned and walked toward the door. Turning back quickly, she added, "but it's not a date Garrett. It just doesn't make sense to have two vehicles going to the same places and dealing with parking." She turned back and headed towards the door before he could respond.

He started working out again and spoke softly as he started climbing on his stepper. "Oh, it's definitely a date Maggie; definitely a date."

~Chapter 18~

The day flew by for Joshua, and his sisters. They each drove separately and met up at camp before supper. Over dinner, Jena told everyone about the hurdles that she had encountered and conceded that she hadn't learned anything from her correspondence and calls to the various agencies and attorneys that had handled Elizabeth's daughter's adoption. The only thing that she was able to learn, that they didn't know before was that Michelle Marie had been adopted into a childless home and that the family had adopted another child a few years later. Other than that, and the fact that the family resided in Oneida County; she'd come up dry. They ate at their mother's dining room table and just as Jena was about to start clearing the table, Deidre spoke up.

"I have some news that you all might want to hear," she said, gaining everyone in the room's attention. "I think that our mother's Daniel is dead. Or at least, quite possibly he's dead," she added.

"What?" Maggie exclaimed! "You mean we've been going through all of this emotional turmoil shit for nothing?"

"Stop Mags!" Josh cut her off before she started on any kind of tirade. Always the calm and practical one, Joshua addressed his youngest sister. "Dee, what makes you think that Daniel, Michelle's father is deceased? Did you get something back from ancestry?"

"No, but Griffin and I found a newspaper article in mom's dresser that told about a helicopter crash. I only glanced at it quickly because Griffin, mom's contractor was standing right there, and I didn't want to freak out with him present. I brought the article with me so we could all read it together," she offered.

"You have it with you now Deidre," Jena coaxed, curious as to what the article said. "You said that you found it at your mother's home?"

As she reached into her purse, she answered her future sister in law.

"Yes, from the looks of it, I think mom saw the article in the paper, cut it out, put it in her dresser drawer and must have forgotten about it because it was jammed behind the drawer. We only discovered it because I couldn't get the drawer back into place when I was helping Griffin put mom's furniture back where it belonged."

"Would the contractor, Griffin, be the hot date that you blew me off for?" Maggie asked, half kidding.

"One and the same. And it was a wonderful date, I might add. And one that you will NOT mention when he and his father show up here tomorrow to give us an estimate."

"Okay, okay. Relax. Read what it says. Maybe it'll answer our questions and make it easier to find Michelle Marie whatever her name is now and close this chapter once and for all."

"Maggie, she's our sister whether her biological father is still alive or not, and I intend to welcome her into my life if, and when, we find her. She is not a threat to what you, Josh and I have. I look at her as an unexpected bonus," Deidre said matter of factly.

"I tend to agree with Deidre. I have no idea how I would feel if it were me, but I would like to think that I'd be curious, somewhat interested, and definitely a little intrigued to speak with someone who knew my mother before my father did. So for that reason alone, I sincerely hope that Daniel isn't dead. Michelle may or may not even know that she was adopted, and she might want to take baby steps getting to know the three of you, or there's the possibility that she might have no interest in meeting you. If that's the case, and her birth father is deceased, then you've done your due diligence on your mother's behalf and case closed. But curiosity, if nothing else, would force me to follow it through and get to know someone who shares my blood. On the most basic level, you all share your genetics with the woman and that alone binds you to her. What you do once you make the connection I would think, is an independent decision on each of your parts," Jena finished, looking at the three siblings sitting next to her.

"You make me so hot with all your fancy legal mumbo jumbo," Josh kidded. "No seriously, I am interested in at least meeting her once."

"Um, do you think I can read the article now and then we go from there?" Deidre asked, becoming slightly impatient.

Once she gained her siblings attention, she read the faded news clipping word for word. It told of a military helicopter crashing during a training exercise, killing two of the soldiers and critically injuring the rest on board. The article did not give the names of the soldiers who died, simply stated that one of the servicemen, Daniel O'Malley, was on board at the time of the crash. The article went on to say where the men were airlifted to, and that there was no word on their condition or prognosis. When she finished reading the newspaper article, she neatly folded it up and put it back in the same faded envelope that she'd found it in. Looking at her sister and brother, their expressions mirrored hers. All sat silently for a moment, absorbing the information and concluding that the man they wanted to locate could very well be dead.

Still frustrated that they'd been thrust into this unwanted predicament, Maggie was the first to speak.

"Mom's diaries."

"What?" Deidre asked, not following her sister's comment.

"Mom's diaries. If her Daniel perished in that helicopter crash, then mom would have mentioned it in her diary, whether she was already involved with our father or not."

"You're right Mags," Josh exclaimed. "Mom wrote in her diary every day since she was a kid. I always thought it was kind of hooky because I guess I never wanted to know what an asshole I was during puberty, so I never had an interest in reading them.   But I think you're onto something Mags. If the guy died in the crash, she would have at least mentioned it. Is there a date on that article Dee?"

"Yes, August 1st, 1984. Oh, and Josh, you were an asshole growing up, not just during puberty, but Maggie was worse" she kidded.

"Bite me," Maggie offered. "I would think it would be easy to find, now that we have his name, hometown and date of the crash. Mom's diary will probably provide us with a lot more information about him, and possibly about the adoption. I, like Josh, have never wanted to read mom's diaries, but if they help us get this over with quicker, then I'm all for it."

Jena, who'd sat silently until now, spoke up. "I'll read them if you'd like. I mean, I love each of you dearly, and you three are my world; but I am not blood related to you, nor did I know you growing up, so from an objective perspective, I'm the most logical choice. If you'd like me to scour over your mom's diaries from around the time Michelle was born, to the time of the accident, I'd be more than happy to."

"Great," Maggie offered, "You've got the job. I'll go to mom's house tomorrow and get them for you. That is, if that's okay with Deidre and Josh," she added.

"Works for me," Deidre said, smiling.

"Me too," Josh added. Besides, I know where you live and if there's anything juicy in them, I know you'll tell me right?" he chuckled.

"Wrong. Consider your mother and her property, my client and I won't breach attorney-client privilege. But I will read them and let you know if you truly were an asshole growing up!" she kidded.

"He was," left both Deidre and Maggie's mouth's simultaneously, causing everyone to laugh.

They made small talk, exchanging stories about their childhood growing up in Elizabeth and Jared's home, with each sibling recalling different stories as they went. They laughed a lot, shed a few tears, and each retired for the evening knowing that they couldn't possibly have had a better home to grow up in, despite losing both of their parents at such early ages. They said their good nights with each of them retreating to their childhood bedrooms. Joshua remembered to text the contractor before it got too late, to confirm their appointment for the morning, and found it odd that it took the contractor nearly thirty minutes to respond. What he didn't realize was that his kid sister in the adjacent room was the reason for the slower than average response time. As Joshua became frustrated, Deidre found herself becoming more and more comfortable "talking" with the man on the other end of her phone. She and Griffin texted back and forth for nearly two hours before they both agreed it was getting late, with each saying they were looking forward to seeing each other in the morning. Deidre called him to review the driving directions one last time. Despite knowing exactly how to get to her mother's camp, he listened to her rattle off the directions, just so that he could keep her on the phone a little longer. Before hanging up, he asked her if she was still interested in a short hike after he'd met with she and her siblings, to which she readily agreed. They hung up, with each of them smiling ear to ear at the prospect of spending another day together, doing something they both loved.

As Maggie lay in her bedroom at the end of the hall, she knew that she was tired but found herself restless and unable to sleep. Staring at her phone, and realizing that despite it being late, she wanted to text Garrett. After a thirty second internal debate, she used the rationale that it was only 9:30 on a Saturday night and that made it okay to send him a quick message, to hopefully make him smile when she saw it.

She took a deep breath, debated on what to say and then simply texted, "Looking forward to brunch and the game tomorrow, and of course your company. See you at 1:30pm. And it's not a date."

She hit send, and then quickly shut her phone off, afraid of the response or lack thereof, which, in her mind, meant that he was out on the town for the night. Little did she know that she'd fall asleep thinking about the goofy looking attorney, and that fact would cause her to dream of him throughout the night.

~Chapter 19~

Griffin got on the road early enough to swing by his favorite bakery to pick up a dozen jelly donuts. He didn't typically bring treats to a prospective client, but since he'd already met with Joshua at his mother's home, and had taken Deidre out on a date, he felt as if he wasn't a stranger who was walking in blind to a prospective job site. Josh had already explained what they were looking to accomplish at their mother's camp, so Griffin had taken the information provided, along with the rough sketch and room dimensions and put it into his computer and came up with different layouts to propose. As he headed out of the city, and towards Holland Patent on Route 365, he found himself singing along to Chris Stappleton's latest hit. He typically was a very easy going individual and generally was good natured, but found himself in an especially good mood today as he made his way north. The sketches he'd done offered four different options for each of the rooms that Josh and his sisters had mentioned they'd like to renovate. He'd saved his renderings in his CAD system and didn't know if they had internet service or not, but had packed his computer just in case they wanted to tweek some of his drawings. To be safe, he'd printed out the blueprints as well.

He'd packed a small backpack that he'd need for latter in the day if he and Deidre did decide to go for a hike. Having no clue how much snow he'd find in Old Forge, he'd had the foresight to not only pack his crampons, but also his snowshoes just in case. He felt bad that his father had come down with bronchitis and wasn't able to join him, but also took pleasure in the way it had all worked out. With his father home, pushing fluids, resting and taking his antibiotics as prescribed, Josh would be the spokesperson for their company and hopefully, the one to seal the deal. His father had always taught him to come up with a quote, and then knock 10% off, that way the homeowner felt that they were winning, and getting a fair deal. Griffin's father had explained to him when he first got out of college, that building a good business wasn't always about making money, it was about customer loyalty and creating a good name for themselves. And because of that model, their business thrived, thanks in part to their referrals. Thinking about his career path, Griffin had never expected to end up remodeling homes when he'd attended college to become an architect, but here he was, working side by side with his old man, and loving every minute of it.

He really wished that his father could have come along with him, not only to help sell their proposal, but he had also wanted him to meet Deidre. Even though he'd spoken with her only a few times, and had been on one date with her, he found himself drawn to her and felt some kind of connection, on many levels. Though he wasn't interested in settling down per say, he admitted to himself that he was definitely interested in getting to know the shy, gypsy artist a little better.

As Griffin was driving north, Elizabeth's camp was filled with commotion. Four sleepy adults were fighting over prime kitchen space, while trying to step around and over one very large dog and one lazy cat. Jena had made a pot of coffee that was presently brewing, but not dripping fast enough to satisfy Maggie's impatience, while Josh was swearing at the bacon that was spitting grease at him as he tried to flip the pieces over. Deidre had already showered when she'd joined her family downstairs, with Jena noticing her very subtle application of just enough makeup to draw attention to her eyes. Never one to wear makeup, Jena looked at her future sister in law quizzically.

Once everything was ready, they dug in and ate in virtual silence. It wasn't until they had full stomachs and enough caffeine flowing in their veins that they spoke of the changes they wished to see happen at camp. Always the pessimist, Maggie was the first to say that she hoped the contractor was as good as his reviews implied. Refusing to be drawn into an argument, and having no interest in defending, so to speak, a man she'd barely met, and only had one date with; Deidre listened to her older sister spew her comments but remained silent. It was Josh who took the role of defending not only their work, and reputation; but also reminded his sister, that if their mother felt the company was good enough, then they were good enough and the right company for the job.

As soon as they finished a very hearty and fulfilling breakfast, it was Deidre who practically jumped up from the table to start clearing the dishes. While her siblings continued to talk about the changes to their mother's camp, only Jena noticed Deidre's nervous energy. Always the calm and mellow one of the three, Deidre seemed jittery and Jena surmised that the anticipated arrival of the contractors was the cause. Smiling to herself, she quickly got up and helped her future sister in law clear the table and start loading the dishes.

"He must be something Dee," Jena stated matter of factly.

"Come again?"

"I said, this guy must be pretty impressive if he's got you this worked up after only one date," Jenna chuckled.

"How do you know?" Deidre started to ask, feeling herself blushing.

"It's written all over your face Dee. You're the calm, controlled one of the three of you; and this guy must really be something if he's got you this worked up, anxious to see him, and got you wearing makeup," she kidded.

"Oh my God," she looked at Jena in terror, "Is it too much? Can you tell I have it layered on? I mean, I don't usually wear this shit but thought I'd try and look like, you know, other women. But did I put on too much?" she asked, panicking.

Jena tried her best to stifle her laugh, but it slipped out anyways.

"Tell me about him Dee, what's this contractor like?" she asked sincerely. "He's obviously already very important to you or you wouldn't be in the state you're in," she remarked, as gently as she could.

"I don't know Jena. There's something uniquely special about him. Average looking, average build, generic job, but so incredibly interesting to talk to. There's just something about him that's genuine, you know. He's down to earth, no pretenses, no bullshit come on lines or anything like that. And when he asks me a question, he actually listened to my response, and was interested in hearing it. Weird huh? I just felt some kind of amazing connection to him, almost like a   de-cha-vo   type thing, from the moment I met him. Almost like I knew him before I met him. I know how silly that sounds, but I swear it's as if I knew him in another life. Yeah, yeah, that sounds weird, even to me," Deidre laughed, "But honestly, I felt as if I really had met him before. And his eyes, it's as if he could look into my soul," she remarked, not realizing that she was still speaking aloud.

"Yup, you've got it bad my friend," Jena said, putting her arm around Deidre, who was still thinking about Griffin. "Welcome to the being in love club," she kidded.

Hearing her remark, Deidre snapped out of her trance almost immediately. "I'm not," she broke off her rebuttal hearing a door slam outside, and then the doorbell ringing moments later.

"Oh my God, he's here" she jumped, finding herself checking her reflection to make sure she looked presentable. Jena squelched a chuckle as she reiterated her earlier statement and gave a quick pep talk.

"Dee, you look beautiful. Just be yourself. That's what our contractor fell for in the first place. Now go and invite our guests in," she said, gently nudging Deidre toward the door.

Joshua beat his sisters to it and by the time Deidre made her way to the entranceway, Griffin was already inside and unzipping his jacket. He looked up and saw her, and at that moment, it was just the two of them in the room.

"Hey," he smiled.

"Hey."

For a brief second, he'd forgotten that they weren't alone. Everyone in the room took notice of the interaction between their sister and the man now standing in their entranceway but remained silent.

It took a moment or two for Deidre to realize that all eyes were on her.

"Griffin, where's your father?" she asked, breaking the silence.

Suddenly feeling slightly awkward, he quickly answered as everyone's gaze had shifted and was now clearly on him.

"My dad came down with what we thought was a simple cold earlier in the week. Turns out he had bronchitis, bordering on pneumonia so I told him to stay home," he smiled. "But don't worry, I've reviewed the plans and estimate with him and he's available via teleconference if you'll feel more comfortable discussing everything with him," he offered.

It was Josh who spoke first. "That won't be necessary. I think I speak for everyone when I say we can't wait to see what you've come up with for our mother's cabin."

Immediately feeling at ease, Joshua followed their lead and walked into the kitchen, taking in the room as he did so. Jena brought up the rear and once everyone was in the kitchen, Griffin lifted the satchel that doubled as a briefcase onto the island. He pulled out several renderings that he'd drawn up, starting with the kitchen. As he spread them out, he had everyone's attention.

He started with the most straightforward, explaining what he envisioned. As he moved from one sketch to the next, each showed more detail and different options for the same space. Joshua, Maggie and Deidre all remained silent, as they watched their childhood camp transform in front of their eyes.

"Oh Griffin, these are amazing," Deidre spoke first. "Your eye for detail is outstanding."

"Thank you, but much of the credit goes to my father. I'm just the guy with the computer who puts his ideas on paper," he laughed. "Oh, and I'm the skilled labor of course, as well," he chuckled. "I showed my father the pictures that you'd emailed me, and he incorporated the current floorplan and added his ideas to it. You already have a great home and the layout works, so it was quite easy to draw inspiration from it."

He went back to the drawings and continued to explain what added features they had incorporated into each sketch. Josh, Maggie and Deidre commented and added their opinions as Griffin reviewed each blueprint. Jena remained in the kitchen listening, but stayed back, allowing the three owners of their mother's home to have the contractors' undivided attention. She'd offer her opinion if asked, but truly wanted it to be the three of them who wrote the next chapter for their family camp. Besides, she was enjoying the silent interaction between Deidre and the man that had obviously stirred something inside her. She'd known their family for years now, and up until that moment, she'd never seen her fiancé's kid sister so enthralled with anyone. From the way he spoke, Jena could tell that there was significantly more to the down to earth looking contractor who was presently talking about his ideas for the new bath. He was obviously well educated and knew how to remodel a room but was more than simply a home remodeler. When he finished explaining his ideas about the bath, she spoke up.

"Coffee's ready for whoever needs a refill," she offered, holding up the pot of freshly brewed coffee. He looked up and smiled.

"You've read my mind, and if I'm not mistaken, that heavenly aroma is compliments of Tug Hill Coffee?" he asked, as he accepted a cup.

"Good sense of smell," Jena commented. "How did you discover Tug Hill?" she asked, trying to learn more about the man in front of her. "And where did you get your Architecture degree from?" she asked, going out on a limb with her hunch.

"Well, that's a loaded question," he chuckled. "I discovered Tug Hill Coffee at a farmer's market in Syracuse and fell in love with not only the flavor, but the aroma. They sell it at Brenda's Health Food store in Rome, and since I like to purchase local and from small businesses, it was a win-win when she started carrying their line. Your other question isn't as straight forward to answer." Despite never revealing much about his personal life, he found himself opening up when he realized that he had Deidre's full attention. I graduated from Syracuse University, but also completed my DPhil in Architectural History from Oxford. When I studied in Florence during my Junior year, I knew that to be a successful architect, I needed to understand the history of how Architecture has developed over the centuries. Besides, I'm a nerdy overachiever who likes to learn, so I wasn't satisfied with just one degree."

"Impressive," Josh commented. "But what made you choose Oxford when there are amazing schools in this country that probably offered the same degree?"

"Easy. My mother is British, and we lived there for a few years when I was a kid, and I loved the fact that European history is centuries in the making, not just a couple hundred years, like here in the states. Besides, it pleased my mum immensely that her little boy has a degree from there," he laughed. "She lives in Alfriston now, which is a really tiny village outside of London, and she loves to boast about her boys having fancy degrees. Not a big deal to me," he conceded, "But it makes her happy that I did it, and that's really all that matters," he answered sincerely.

And at that moment, Deidre reaffirmed what she already knew. Griffin was it; he was the person she'd been waiting for all of her life.

They drank coffee, talked about the different options for the three rooms that Griffin and his father had designed, and unbelievably, all three siblings agreed on the same design for each room. Griffin tweaked a few very small details in the sunroom, but overall, his designs had been spot on, with each of the siblings signing off on the three designs. When they were finished, Maggie asked how quickly they would be starting and if he'd like a deposit check. Deidre spoke up and informed everyone in the room that she and Griffin would be staying a little longer, hiking and then would lock up camp when they returned. Maggie refused to read anything into it and took the opportunity to say her goodbyes and make her retreat for home. She grabbed her overnight bag, her travel mug, and her dog and made her exit, wanting to get home in time to get ready for her "not a date" with Garrett. Josh and Jenna said that they too would most likely be gone by the time they returned, with Josh shaking Griffin's hand in agreement to the plans he'd presented and thanking him for his time. Griffin promised to make the few desired changes and would email the contract and new plans to everyone for their electronic signature in the morning.

Deidre grabbed her backpack, coat and hiking poles, indicating that she was ready to hit the trail. Jena stood by her man as they watched his kid sister exit the camp. Once out of earshot, she pulled Joshua into a hug and smiled.

"Call me a romantic, but I'm betting that will be the next wedding we attend, after our own."

"What? You my love, are crazy! They've just met and barely know each other," he exclaimed.

"They are kindred spirits and anyone who believes, would see that. The energy when they're both in the same room is electric, and I know that they are meant to be together, just like you and I are," she whispered, bringing her lips to his.

He kissed her back, and once their tongues touched, he could care less whether his kid sister had found her soulmate or not. Knowing what his kiss implied, she quietly walked over to the door, turned the deadbolt, took her fiancé's hand and led him back to the room they'd exited just a few hours before.

~Chapter 20~

Deidre had offered to drive but graciously accepted Griffin's invitation to ride shotgun and be the navigator. The once blue sky had turned gray with a few flakes of snow starting to fall. Griffin had left it up to Deidre to choose the hike and despite the possibility of impending snow, they both agreed that Blue Mountain was not only an easy day hike, but a short drive and quick climb. As they started their journey north, Griffin found himself much more relaxed than he envisioned he'd be. Their conversation bounced around from one topic to another and before either of them realized it, they were driving past the Blue Mountain Museum and pulling into the parking lot for their hike.

They geared up as a few more flakes started falling. With the temperature hovering right around 32, both agreed that they should bring their crampons just to be on the safe side. Neither had discussed attire, but Griffin took note that Deidre was appropriately layered and from the looks of her hiking boots and scuffed up poles, she was an experienced climber, a fact that suited him just fine.

They started their climb laughing and talking practically non-stop, with Deidre now talking his ear off with questions about the time he'd spent living in England. He wasn't quite ready to tell her that his parent's divorced when his mother refused to continue to live in the states, or that she broke his heart when she left. He laughed at her rapid-fire questions, asking him about topics from British food and nightclubs to whether he dated while there. Despite the increased incline, her pace and questions never slowed, indicating that she was probably in better shape than he'd given her credit for.

He answered her questions, and then changed the subject to hiking as they climbed side by side. She was not one to talk about herself, or her accomplishments and it took a lot of coaxing to pull it out of her that she was in fact, not only a 46er, but had also completed two-thirds of the AP Trail before her senior year in college. She admitted to Griffin that she felt as if she'd failed because she hadn't completed the journey to Maine. He countered by telling her that he'd never met or known anyone who'd not only attempted the 1300 mile journey but had completed as much of it as she had and that he was truly in awe of her willpower, stamina and dedication. He could tell that his compliments and praise made her uncomfortable and that she was not one who liked to talk about herself so he changed the topic to something they both could relate to and be passionate about. As they crested the summit, the topic of conversation centered on her tiny house village concept. Afraid of spooking her, he wasn't ready to tell her that he'd designed some tiny home blueprints that he wanted to share with her; but knew they could wait until she was more comfortable with him. They stopped once they reached the fire tower, with each dropping their backpacks and drinking heartedly. Once they quenched their thirst, Deidre turned toward Griffin and smiled.

"Race you up the fire tower!" she teased and took off running up the steps of the tower.

"Hey, you got a head start cheater!" he laughed as he chased after her. They ran up the circular steps as fast as each could go, with Griffin right on her heels as she entered the cab of the tower. Slightly dizzy from the climb, she swayed, ever so slightly once her momentum stopped. He pulled her close, to catch her balance and brought her mouth to his. The dizziness she'd initially felt paled in comparison to the way her head was spinning when his tongue danced with hers. The embrace lasted longer than either had anticipated. Finally separating and stepping back, only slightly, he looked directly at her and smiled.

"You move me in ways I never thought possible Deidre, and I feel very blessed to have had you enter my life. It's weird, but being around you sometimes feels so comfortable and familiar and even though we're only getting to know one another now, it feels like we've known each other forever and that whatever this is that's starting between us, has been in place for an eternity." Blushing, he laughed. "And now that I've sounded like some kind of pathetic creeper, I'll shut up now."

She said nothing at first, simply removed her snow-covered glove and brought her bare hand to his face. Touching his cheek, he felt her warmth, and something else. "This is all really new to me as well Grif; but I honestly believe that it was meant to be. Something brought us together and not only does it feel right, but it feels like it has always been meant to be. I don't necessarily believe in fate per say, but there's something in the universe that pushed us together, and I am very glad that it did."

"Me too."

She put her glove back on her now freezing hand and looked out from the cab of the tower at the steady stream of snow that had started falling. Both were thinking the same thought as Griffin exited the cab and started the descent down the winding stairs with Deidre right behind him. Once on solid ground, they grabbed their packs and poles and started down the now snow-covered trail, not stopping until they reached his truck a little over an hour later.

~Chapter 21~

While Deidre was descending a mountain, her older sister was in a race of her own, trying to figure out what to wear for her afternoon with Garrett. She knew she'd be inside an ice rink, but assumed that since they'd be in one of the VIP boxes, they'd be far enough removed from the ice that she shouldn't be cold. She wanted to dress casually but didn't want to underdress if he introduced him to some of his colleagues who may or may not be present. Her mind played ping pong back and forth with what would be suitable for the event that was NOT a date. She settled on a cream colored cashmere V-neck, black jeans, and ankle boots. Next came her dilemma over makeup. She wanted a casual look, something that made her look like she wasn't wearing makeup, but not so little that she looked like she'd just rolled out of bed. After toying with a few applications, she settled for simple eye liner and mascara, with just a touch of green shadow to accentuate her eyes. She kept her jewelry simply, a sterling chain from her mother, and hoop earrings. She always wore the same three rings on her fingers so that decision was already predetermined. When she was finished, she stepped back and gave herself a once over in the mirror. She hadn't been sure what look she was going for but the reflection looking back at her was pleasing and would suffice. She checked the time on her phone and only then did she notice the missed texts from both her sister and Garrett.

Her sister's two lines were straight to the point. "We're off the mountain, safe and sound. Have a great time on your date!"

Garret's two lines made her laugh out loud. "Can't wait for our Not-a-date. See you soon☐"

She grabbed her purse, gave Sinjin a cookie, and headed out the door for her Not-a-date with Griffin.

~Chapter 22~

He texted her when he was pulling into her drive at precisely 12:58 and noted that she was already outside. Always one to be punctual, she made a mental note to give him credit for not only being on time, but a little early. She had deliberately headed outside to keep a little separation between her home which was her sanctity, and the man picking her up for their first outing together, other than meeting up at the gym. She waved as he put his car in park and got out. Not sure what he was doing at first, she found it sweet that he'd gotten out to not only greet her but also open the door for her. Seated on the passenger seat was a bag that he leaned in and picked up. He gestured for her to sit, and upon doing so, he handed it to her. She took it, looking at him questioningly.

He waited until he got back into his car to answer her. "Hey, I'm taking you away from your pooch for the day so I thought I might want to suck up to him a little bit. Go ahead, open it. I wasn't sure how big your dog was, so I bought a couple different sizes," he admitted.

She lifted the tissue paper and saw several dog bones and treats staring back at her. Completely impressed, she laughed. "Wow! Definitely trying to score points with me through my dog!"

"Yup!" he agreed. "Keep digging, you might find a little something in there for you as well," he blushed.

She lifted treat after doggie treat out of the bag, setting them on her lap and she searched for whatever was earmarked for her. Finally at the bottom of the bag she found a neatly wrapped box. Now she had no clue why Garrett would be giving someone new in his life a gift, she found herself second guessing his invitation. Her ever skeptical mind started racing, worrying that maybe he was a nutjob and she'd just gotten into his car and was temporarily at his mercy. As if reading her mind, he put the car into reverse and started backing out of her driveway.

"Just open it Mags, it's not a wedding ring," he laughed.

Slowly and tentatively she removed the neatly formed bow and ribbon, loosened up the wrapping paper and opened the lid. And proceeded to burst out laughing. Inside, he'd tucked, hand warmers, earplugs, lifesavers and Tylenol. When she stopped laughing, she commented about her goodie bag.

"Guess you covered all of your bases. Well aren't you the boy scout!" she chuckled.

"That would be Eagle Scout mam, and yes, I'm always prepared!" He waited just a brief second and offered one more comment. "And you can take that any way you'd like."

"I just might..."

And with that, they headed toward Raspberries, as their date officially began.

~Chapter 23~

Maggie had no idea that she'd enjoy the competitive game of hockey as much as she had. She had seen several high school games and watched the Stanley Cup Final every year; but she was pleasantly surprised to find that the energy emitted during a live game, was not only captivating but enthralling.

Garrett had insisted on paying for their pre-game brunch, introduced her to some of his colleagues and their spouses whom he was sharing the box with. He'd explained the basic rules of the game, with Maggie listening intently. She hadn't had the heart to tell him that she knew what off sides and icing meant; she just let him think he was educating her on the finer points of the game. Her only slip up had been in stating that she couldn't wait for the shoot out with the game and overtime ended in a 1-1 tie. It was then that Garrett realized that Maggie was familiar with the game and its' idiosyncrasies all along. He didn't get angry or embarrassed when he realized he'd been had; he simply laughed and chalked it up to another one of Maggie's amazing qualities. The shoot out had ended with the Comets winning, and everyone ecstatic as they made their way to their respective vehicles. He'd asked her if she'd like to grab a bite to eat but she'd politely declined. It wasn't that she wasn't enjoying his company, because she certainly was; it's just that she had other things racing through her mind.

They made small talk as they left the rink and approached her home. As he pulled into her driveway, he put his car in park and appeared to be getting out to open the door for him. Before he could exit, she let impulse take over.

"Hey, would you like to come in for a cup of coffee or a drink," she asked, already knowing the answer.

"You sure?" he asked, implying what she already knew.

"Yes, I'm sure Garrett. I'm inviting you in, not asking you to marry me. And I never say or do anything unless I'm completely sure, and I want you to join me, be with me, and most likely, be in me," she purred.

He knew that the evening might very well turn into a round of casual sex, but there was nothing casual about the way that she was drawing him in with her eyes. Not one to have one-night stands either, he shut his engine off and joined her as she led him into her home, knowing that it would be more, much more, than a quick roll in the hay. After spending the day with her, he'd already made up his mind that he'd have many more dates with Maggie, whether she was ready to believe that or not.

~Chapter 24~

The next two weeks flew by for everyone. Joshua, Maggie and Deidre had signed off on the final designs for not only their kitchen, but bathroom and sunroom. Josh had met with Griffin and his father to give them a deposit check, pick up the building permit and review their timeline. Griffin had made a few sets of keys from the originals that Deidre had provided, with his father promising them that work would commence the following Monday. Josh texted his sisters, updating them on what he'd learned, with everyone agreeing that they should meet at camp Saturday morning to move everything out of the way for the contractors.

Deidre and Griffin were still trying to figure out how the dating dance worked. Their schedules never seemed to coincide with one another, but both took solace in speaking on the phone late after most of their friends were fast asleep. Deidre was a romantic at heart, although she hadn't actually realized it until she'd met Griffin, and found it endearing that despite talking sometimes for over an hour; he still sent her a quick text afterwards wishing her "Good night & pleasant dreams". They would talk about their travels, their hope and dreams, and often the conversation circled back to Deidre's fantasy of developing a tiny home village for the homeless veteran's in her area. Unbeknownst to her, Griffin had taken her idea and ran with it. He could see it in his mind, how it could be, with each homeless person or family having their own home, their own little parcel that was theirs. He'd designed common areas for their gardens, along with an area that could serve as a laundry mat for the residents that was pass key accessible only, along with the possibility of little storage units for things that didn't quite fit within the confines of their pint-sized homes.

Friday finally rolled around, with Deidre finding herself physically exhausted from the fifty plus hour week she'd put in. As she'd promised her mother, she had hired a part time employee to cover for her one or two evenings a week, but it didn't negate the fact that she still worked longer than everyone else involved in her food pantry. It was her baby and something she took great pride in, but at the moment she wanted nothing more than to curl up with her cat, a glass of wine and a good book. She pulled into her carport and jumped out, remembering to grab the two bags of groceries that she'd picked up at Price Chopper on the way home, and her mail. She juggled everything on her hip as she struggled to unlock her door and enter her condo. Greeted by a very lonely cat, she set everything on the table and squatted down to give Sasha some much needed loving.

After a few minutes of pampering, she put her cat back on the ground and set about the task of unloading her groceries, thinking the bills could wait until after supper. Once she'd changed into her traditional evening attire of an oversized t-shirt and yoga pants, she heated up some leftovers, poured herself a glass of wine and decided it was time to stop postponing the inevitable. Taking a sip, she picked up the stack of bills and started opening them, one by one, to see how bad the damage would be to her checking account. When she got to the third envelope, she quickly realized that the legal size envelope with a return address of Oneida wasn't a bill. Not recognizing the return address, she almost tore it in half and tossed it, assuming it was just another scam. Instead of discarding it, her curiosity got the better of her and after taking another sip of her wine, she tore open the envelope to review the contents before throwing it out. She opened the neatly folded pieces of paper, picking up two pictures that were tucked inside. Sitting down on her barstool, she placed the pictures on her island and started to read what appeared to be a handwritten letter to her.

Dear Deidre:

I'm not quite sure where to start so I'm just going to jump right in. My name is Samantha Bowing, and it appears, at least according to

Ancestry DNA, that we share a common parent, and well, are sisters. I certainly hope that my bluntness doesn't come as a complete shock to you and as you participated in DNA testing, I hope that my news isn't more than what you'd bargained for when you submitted your saliva sample.

First and foremost, let me assure you and any of your family members, I am not psychotic, crazy or mentally defunct in any way, or at least that I know of, LOL. You see, I have always known that I was adopted, along with my sibling. We were raised by kind and loving parents and while they weren't my biological parents, they were, in fact, better parents than I could have ever asked for or prayed for. So when I received the email that I had another hit (when you must have submitted your test), I wasn't shocked to learn that I had a half sibling out there.

I am 34, a divorced mother of two beautiful children, am an elementary school teacher with a passion for kayaking, mountain climbing and repelling. I love to travel and take my kids on family camping trips. We have one dog, two cats and a very spoiled rabbit. If there's anything I could ask of you, it would be to learn if there are any hereditary medical conditions that I should be aware of. I'm in great health and to date, have no preexisting conditions, but as a mother, I know how imperative it is to know your family history. I ask this on behalf of my children, as they deserve the best medical care, I can provide them, and knowledge is power.

If I can ask one more thing, it would be to have you tell me if I have any resemblance to either your mother or father as I have no clue which one I'm related to. I've enclosed a couple of photos (and no, I'm not photogenic but at least I clean up okay). The other photo is one I took of my kids this summer when we hiked up Mount Marcy near Lake Placid. My kids share my passion for nature and being outside, and hiking is something we all enjoy very much.

Deidre, I am very financially stable, and have a wonderful family; but by shear genetics alone, we too are family. If you're agreeable, I would like to talk, or text with you sometime and get to know you. If not, I completely understand and want you to know that my request is open ended. As I said earlier, I've known since childhood, but if this is all news to you, then take as long as you need to digest the information.

Thank you for taking the time to read my letter. I really hope that you'll give serious consideration to my request. I've enclosed my return address and email address, SammyB1982@gmail.com. If nothing else, would you please respond regarding any hereditary medical conditions that I should be aware of. I will not contact you ever again unless I hear from you first; you have my word on that.

Sincerely,

Samantha

Deidre read and reread the letter for the second time, standing in her tiny kitchen, afraid to move, for fear that she would find it all a dream. Was it possible, she thought to herself, that her sister had found her instead of the other way around? She looked at the envelope that the letter had come in, and there, sure as shit was her mailing address which indicated that her half sister lived less than twenty miles from she and her siblings, and sadly, she thought now, had been less than a thirty minute drive from their mom all along. She looked back at the letter and at the way her sister had signed her name, simply Samantha, as if they were already friends. She set the letter down again, and instead of pouring herself a glass of wine or making herself a cup of Chamomile tea to soothe her nerves, she found herself pouring a shot of Jack and downing it in one swallow. The burn always caught her by surprise, despite anticipating it before the shot glass ever touched her lips. She poured herself another and felt the same burn the second time as well.

She knew that any more Jack and she'd be asleep on the couch within minutes, so she put the cap on the bottle, placed the shot glass in the sink and paced. She had so many emotions swirling in her head that she felt like she would explode. She knew that she would have to tell her sister and brother the amazing news, but found herself hesitant to tell them over the phone. She'd want to tell them as soon as possible but wanted to do it in person. Knowing that their camp was torn apart and in construction mode, she realized that their mother's request to spend time up at camp would have to wait. Her heart continued to race as she thought about so many things she'd like to ask Samantha. She wondered if her half sister was as excited and nervous about gaining family members as she was. As she continued thinking of questions, she didn't hear her phone bing indicating she had a text message, until it binged for a second time.

Snapping her back to reality, she quickly dug into her pocketbook and found her phone. Seeing Griffin's name on the ID, she found herself smiling, even before she opened the texts.

"Hi. I just ordered a large pizza from Rosario's and was wondering if you had plans and if not, would you like to share it? I told them take out, but if you're free and want to meet me there, we can enjoy it there."

"Oh hey. Guess you're busy or didn't get my second message. I was kinda hoping to share my pizza with you but you must have other plans. Have a great night Dee. Hope to catch up with you soon..."

She read the text, checked the time on them, and chastised herself for not hearing the first text come through. Not usually one to act on impulse, she dialed his number before she thought it through. He answered on the second ring.

"Oh hi ya stranger," he answered, finding himself thrilled that she was calling him.

"Hi. Sorry I missed your first text." Working on impulse and an adrenaline rush from the letter from her sister, she just blurted out what she was thinking.

"Where are you?"

"Um, I'm on 12 heading out of the city toward 49, why?" he asked, thinking her voice sounded slightly funny but refusing to read anything into it.

"Quick," she nearly shouted, get off 12 and come over to my place and spend the evening with me!" she exclaimed. "I have some amazing news that I'd like to bounce off you. Oh, and I'm starved and would love some pizza," she giggled. She rattled off her address, hung up and raced around her tiny home, throwing things in closets, and tidying up as quickly as she could. Sasha looked at her quizzically, wondering what was going on but caring less, now that she had Fancy Feast in her dish, and warm milk in the other. Maggie practically ran into her bathroom to brush her teeth, comb her matted hair, apply a little mascara and blush to her lips, and then looked down at her attire. When she'd left in the morning, fashion had not entered her mind. As she viewed herself in her bedroom mirror, she realized how frumpy she'd looked all day at work. Whipping open her closet, she grabbed a weathered but comfortable, and clean, pair of jeans, and a sweater to thrown on. She didn't know what possessed her, but as she changed, she caught a glimpse of herself in the mirror again, and realized that if the evening progressed past pizza, she should probably have on a cute matching bra and panty set. Nearly laughing out loud at how ridiculous that sounded, she nearly kept on her present well-loved undies, but decided that she'd feel more self-assured if she knew she wore something sexy under her clothing. She knew that he'd never know the difference, but she would, and that was all that mattered. She finished dressing, and then ran to the kitchen to make sure she had cold beer in the frig. She saw the bottle of

Jack still sitting on her counter, and took one more shot of liquid courage, just as her doorbell rang. She glanced at her Fitbit and realized that he must have drove like the wind to have gotten to her place as fast as he did, but as she opened the door, she was thrilled that he had. Standing there, on her porch, she smiled as he simply said "Hi."

She stepped back, inviting him inside and out of the frigid air. The wind had picked up considerably in the short time since she'd gotten home, and from the feel of it, they were bound to get more snow again that evening. Once he was inside, she quickly closed the door, and deadbolted it out of habit, a gesture that didn't go unnoticed by Griffin. She took the pizza and bouquet of flowers out of his hands and gestured where he could hang his coat. She told him to leave his work boots on, to which he politely declined, removing them before he followed her into her tiny kitchen. She didn't ask, simply reached in and pulled out two beers from her refrigerator, popped the tops off and handed one over to her guest. He carried the plates and pizza over to her table, setting it down on the hot pad she'd provided before taking a sip of his beer. He'd been dying of thirst but didn't want to start drinking until they were ready to eat. He'd noticed the bottle of Jack Daniels and shot glass on her counter but didn't want to assume anything or ask so he made small talk with her, noting that she appeared jittery or nervous. The last thing he wanted to do was make her second guess her invite, but at that very moment, he didn't want to leave either.

"I don't know about you Dee, but I'm starving," he offered, trying to corral her into sitting down and eating.

Taking the hint, she ushered him to the table and sat down across from him. "Oh my God, me too," she exclaimed as she bit into her favorite style of pizza. "Thinking about it now, I just realized that I haven't eaten since my bowl of oatmeal this morning at 6!"

Filling his mouth with another bite, he wanted until he swallowed to respond. "That's not good Deidre. It's not healthy to skip meals. You're athletic enough to know what breaks down when your body is lacking in nutrients," he offered, trying not to scold or reprimand her, simply state the facts.

She nodded, savoring the wonderful flavors of the cheese and sausage as they practically melted in her mouth.

"You're right Griffin. I know better, but I got so busy at work today that I completely forgot." Then she remembered the reason she'd been so excited to see him in person.

"Grif, can I tell you about something? It's something I haven't even told Maggie or Josh about yet but I wanted to share the information with a neutral party first. Once I tell you, that is if you're willing to listen to me; then I'll ask you to please give me your unbiased opinion and response. I know we've just become friends and all, but I really need to tell someone, or I'll explode!" she exclaimed.

Realizing that whatever it was that she wanted to reveal to him must be pretty important to her, he immediately agreed and promised her that he would keep the information to himself, but also, would give her his honest opinion of whatever it was she wanted to tell him. She listened to his reassuring response, then poured both she and Griffin a shot of Jack, clanged their shot glasses together, and downing their respective shots. Once the burn ended, she reached across the table, taking his hand, and told him everything. She told him about their mother's deathbed wishes, the reading of her will and what she was asking her three children to do, and lastly about the letter she received in the mail. He listened intently as she read the letter from her newly discovered half sister and how she felt about gaining a sibling. He found that he was intrigued by her story and couldn't help but wonder how she was keeping all of her emotions in check. Her mother had obviously shocked them, but also had enough faith in her children to follow through with her request. He tried to put himself in their shoes but couldn't. When she was all finished talking, he could tell that she was waiting for him to comment, say something about what she'd just divulged to him. Never one for being articulate, he spoke from his heart.

"Deidre, I'm not sure how you feel about this Samantha woman, but I would like to think that you've been given a gift from God. Every star aligned up at the right time and brought you two together for a reason. There are so many variables that could have changed in both her and your life that could have altered the outcome and made it so you never would connect. I would like to believe that your momma up in heaven played a role in nudging Samantha to reach out to you. How far you take it is entirely up to you. But even if you never are able to help her find her birth father, isn't it cool that you can meet someone who shares your genetics and your blood? From a curiosity standpoint, I would have to meet her, at least once. I don't want to say that you owe her that much, but I think that maybe it's the right thing to do, don't you?" he asked, not wanting to overstep any lines.

She didn't say a word, but jumped up from the table, walked over to where he was sitting and grabbed him, pulling him into a bear hug. With tears starting to flow, she smiled up at him. "Thank you! Thank you so much for reaffirming what I already knew in my heart was the right thing to do. Can you believe it Griff, I just gained a sister!" she exclaimed, taking his mouth before he had a chance to answer. Her kiss was warm, inviting him in. Passionate in everything she did, her kiss was no different and when her tongue continued to dance with his, he couldn't help but feel something long dormant spring to life.

Deidre knew that she was impulsive and usually acted on whims if they pleased her. But nothing had prepared her for the thoughts swirling in her head as she continued kissing the man who's lap she was practically sitting on. She had had boyfriends over the years, but no one had stirred her the way this gruffy looking contractor did. She knew that she probably shouldn't, and maybe it was the alcohol talking, but at that moment, she knew what she wanted, and she knew that she wanted him right then and there. Sensing the intensity increasing between them, she withdrew back, just far enough to face him, and smiled.

"I swear I've never invited someone over before and jumped them in my kitchen," she giggled, still feeling her heart racing.

"Um," he stammered, "I don't recall complaining or stopping you. I really like you Deidre, and have told you on more than one occasion, you intrigue me, and I really would like to get to know you a lot better," he answered honestly.

"How well would you like to get to know me?" Deidre asked, leaning in to kiss him.

His mind started racing faster than his heart already was. He knew that he wanted her and wanted her right then and there; but thought that there was probably no correct way to answer her suggestive question. So, he went with the truth. "I've wanted you since the first time we met at your mother's home. I wanted to strip you out of that bohemian styled dress of yours, loosen the clip in your hair and watch it fall around your shoulders, and make love to you like we were the only two people on the planet. I felt a connection to you like I've never felt, and I want to get to know everything there is about you. You turn me on like no one else has ever stirred me and I plan on asking you out over and over again until you're mine. If I were one to believe in fate, I would say that something brought us into each other's lives at this moment in time, and I will be forever thankful that it did."

She appreciated his honesty. She stood, extended out her hand, took his and led him up the stairs leading to her 2nd story and bedroom. Always straightforward and extremely comfortable in her skin, she sat him on her bed, and stepped back away from him, just far enough to be out of arm's reach.

Standing in front of him, as if a sacrificial offer, she asked him just one question. "Do you want me Griffin?"

He felt his groin nearly catch on fire. "More than anything in this world Deidre."

"Then no pretenses, no promises, no falsities, just you and me tonight; with tomorrow being a new day. I want you too Griffin," she said, as she pulled the tie from her hair, and ran her fingers through it, loosening her braid. She said nothing as she stood in front of him, unzipping the long zipper on the back of her dress, allowing it to fall off her shoulders and to the floor. She stood in front of the man sitting on her bed in a mismatched bra and underwear, never having a clue that when her day had started out hours earlier, she'd be stripping in front of someone. But to Deidre, it didn't matter. What mattered to her, in that moment, was the fact that she was openly giving herself to the man that she wanted, and somehow needed. Watching her, he felt his throat go dry. He'd never seen a more beautiful, more wholesome, perfect specimen of a woman in his entire life. Sure, he'd been with his fair share of women in his time, but no one had captivated him the way the woman standing in front of him had. Before he could say anything, she approached him. She pulled him to his feet and leaned in to kiss him. Still saying nothing, she reached in to assist him in removing his cotton flannel shirt, one button at a time. He wanted to just tear it off, in order to have his skin touch hers, but she methodically removed each button, kissing his chest as she did. Thinking he would burst, he tried desperately to think of anything except the fact that the most gorgeous women he'd ever met was standing there, half naked, undressing him. Once she'd stripped him down, not stopping until he was standing in front of her au natural, did she smile. She released her bra, then slid off the last of the cotton touching her skin and stood in front of him. Neither felt embarrassed or uncomfortable. Then took in every crease, curve, muscle and angle of each other as if reuniting with a long-lost friend. Neither spoke but their actions spoke volumes with both simply savoring the moment. They kissed, with their tongues dancing to the familiarity of each other's mouths. Knowing what the intensity of their touch was leading up to, Deidre pulled the sheets down and welcomed him into her bed, and into her soul.

"Are you sure?" was all he asked before entering her.

"More sure than I've ever been of anything in my life," was her only response before he plunged and took them both over the edge.

~Chapter 25~

Deidre woke rested, smiling as she looked over at the man sleeping next to her. Never one to do anything out of impulse or on a whim, she'd known with every ounce of her being that what had transpired last night had been preordained long before she'd met Griffin. Looking at him as he started to stir, she would make him a nice breakfast, thank him for a magical night, and tell him he owed her nothing. They had both been consenting adults, each filling a need that the other had, and just because he helped her fill her "need" multiple times during the night didn't mean that he was obligated to ask her out on another date or continue to see her. She exited out of her side of the bed, grabbed his shirt where it had dropped to the ground the night before, slid it on, and silently left him sleeping.

He woke to the distinct smell of bacon. It only took a few seconds for his mind to acclimate to the fact that he wasn't in his own bed. The fact that there was a very irritated looking Siamese cat sitting inches from him staring him down was his first clue, second being the aroma of bacon. Memories of the night before came flooding back to him, and as he looked around her room, he realized that it was in fact real, and not just some fantasy he'd dreamt up in his sleep. He quickly slid out of bed, found his jeans and got dressed from the waist down. Unable to locate his shirt, he quickly used her master bathroom, and brushed his teeth with his finger, ran his fingers and a touch of water through his hair and went in search of his Bohemian goddess. He found her, and his shirt in the kitchen, singing softly to an old Janis Joplin song, joining in for the chorus. Turning, she smiled.

Forcing himself to ignore the fact that she'd put on his oversized shirt, but hadn't bother to button it, exposed herself when she turned. Thinking there was no sense in being embarrassed since he'd seen, kissed and caressed every inch of her now exposed skin already, she greeted him warmly.

"Well good morning Griffin. I hope you're hungry because I'm ravenous! I've made corn muffins, and blue berry pancakes, and am almost done with the bacon. Help yourself to some coffee over there," she gestured. "I'm not much of a coffee drinker, but I have several kinds of coffee you can choose from and I just used my Keurig so it should be ready for you." She turned back to attend to the bacon on the stove.

"You are amazing Dee, simply amazing. And I could definitely get used to this kind of spoiling," he said, walking up behind her, putting his arms around her waist and kissing her neck.

"You my love, rocked my world last night and that was definitely the most enjoyable sex I've ever had," she responded. I could definitely get used to that and if cooking for you is all that it takes, then game on!" she laughed, wiggling as he kissed her neck again. Knowing that would happen if he continued to hold her, he loosened his grip and moved to her side. "What can I do to help you?" he asked as he waited for his coffee to brew.

"You can grab two plates in the cupboard over there," she gestured with her head. "And grab some silverware in the drawer by the dishwasher. This is just about done," she said, as she removed the lid off the bacon to have another look. As she did, some of the bacon grease popped, splattering up at her, catching her exposed abdomen. "Shit," she screamed, as the hot oil scorched her skin. Diving into action, he grabbed the frying pan lid that she still held, while simultaneously moving the pan off the burner and shutting down the gas. Next, he turned her to see the damage, noticing the three red areas on her abdomen already starting to increase in size. He said nothing, but raced over to her freezer, grabbed a handful of ice and asked her where she had zip lock bags. In less than a minute, he had her sitting down, examined the burns, and applied ice.

"Do you have any aloe?"

"What?" she asked, with her thoughts still jumbled from the stinging from the burns.

"Do you have any aloe cream, or Silvadene burn ointment, or even an Aloe plant?" he asked again, with a voice showing nothing but concern.

"I've got Triple antibiotic ointment I think," she answered, trying to visualize what was lurking in her overstuffed and messy medicine cabinet. "Oh wait! I think one of the plants I took from moms might be an aloe plant. Or is it a jade plant?" she asked herself, as he left her pondering. Knowing he hadn't seen it in her bedroom, he made his way to her living room and spied three of her mother's plants on a corner table. Sure enough, one of them was in fact an Aloe tree. He gently snapped off one of the leaves and quickly walked back to Deidre where he'd left her sitting, holding the ice against her burns. She pulled the ice away, and although she wasn't exactly sure what he was planning on doing with the Aloe leaf, she put her full trust in the man kneeling down next to her. Gently he brought the leaf up to her biggest burn, and squeezed the end of the leaf farthest away from her. She could feel the liquid as it touched her raw skin, and almost simultaneously, she could feel the burn starting to fade, almost instantly. He searched her face for any type of reaction but could tell from her eyes, that it was working.

"Aloe will calm the heat, relieve the pain, and is a natural antibiotic," he offered, as he applied more balm to the remaining, smaller burns. Once done, he sat back and evaluated the burns closer.

"I think that only the largest one might blister, the other two should absorb by this evening. But do not pop it if it blisters up. Let your body naturally absorb the interstitial fluid itself, okay?" he instructed.

She leaned in and kissed him gently on the lips. "Thank you Griffin."

Those simple three words and the way she looked at him was all it took; he'd fallen and fallen hard.

"Um, I probably should get some clothes on," she said, realizing that the present state of her abdomen had just crushed any chance of going another round after breakfast. Knowing she was right, he smiled.

"Despite you looking absolutely beautiful in my shirt, you probably should cover those burns with some type of bandage, preferably non-adhesive gauze if you have some. If you don't, I have a first aid kit in the truck I can run out and get."

"I don't have anything other than possibly a bandaid," she admitted. "I'd always run over to mom's if I got hurt. She was the nurse in the family," she lamented.

He stood, grabbed his jacket before heading toward the door. "Go get some clothes on Dee; I'll go grab some gauze and be right back in. Make sure you wear something loose fitting, so it doesn't rub against those burns," he instructed, walking out the door.

By the time he found the size dressing that he wanted, and returned inside, he found her filling their plates and carrying them over to her tiny table. He rushed over to help, lifting both plates from her arms. "Give me those Dee. Don't do anything that might pull your abdominal muscles and irritate the burns."

He set the plates on the table, motioned for her to sit down, then washed his hands, knelt beside her, and gently lifted her blouse. She held it up as he expertly dressed her wounds, applying just enough tape to hold them securely in place. Satisfied with how they looked, he set the extra non-stick pads, and tape on her table. He walked over to the sink and washed his hands again, then joined her at the table.

"You should put either aloe or Silvadene cream on those burns twice a day and cover them until they're dried up or healed. They should heal up fine and hopefully not scar that amazing abdomen of yours," he smiled. "Now let's eat, I'm starving!" he laughed.

The dug in and devoured everything that Deidre had prepared before her little incident. He insisted on picking up and doing dishes, despite the fact that she had a perfectly fine dishwasher. After everything was in order, he knew that he had to get going as he had two job proposals to present later in the afternoon and knew that Deidre had some very incredible news to share with her siblings. He thanked her for an amazing breakfast, her company and for sharing with him such a personal moment. Not knowing if he meant the news of discovering a new sibling, or what they'd shared in bed, she simply accepted his gratitude. She never looked to the future, she simply accepted the here and now. And at the moment, she was grateful for the time she'd spent with an amazing man, both in and out of bed. He intrigued her, captivated her, and seemed to be very grounded and likeminded; but she wasn't looking for someone to finish her sentences for her, so enjoying his company and uncommitted sex was more than enough for her. He kissed her goodbye and made his way to the door.

"Thank you for fixing me up Grif," she offered as he opened it to leave. "Where'd you learn to treat burns?" she asked sincerely. "You're not a doctor on the side are you?" she kidded.

"Nope, just a contractor. I've taken a couple first aid courses, and survival training courses and have a pretty good memory," he smiled. "Glad I was able to help."

"Grif," she offered, with a hint of sexy in her voice, "You helped more than you'll ever know. And I might need your help again, in the very near future."

"Glad to oblige a pretty woman such as yourself. Anytime Deidre; anytime." With that he quietly closed the door and walked toward his truck, with the biggest smile he'd had in years.

Deidre took a few more minutes to enjoy her second cup of tea, reread the letter from Samantha, their sister, and relived the night she'd spent with Griffin. He'd been a very gracious lover, gentle and sweet when she wanted it, aggressive and assertive when she'd asked him to be, and everything else in between. She couldn't recall the last time someone had rocked her world the way he just had, and not just in the sack. She knew that there was significantly more to the soft spoken guy who professed to be a contractor, and she had full intentions of finding out exactly what. As she reread her sister's letter, she wondered what she was like, what her personality would be like, and if they'd have anything in common. She'd heard of cases where siblings were raised in completely opposite living environments, yet when they met, they found many unexplained similarities, opening the debate of nature versus nurture. She had her number, email and home address, but knew that any correspondence had to be mutually agreed upon with both Joshua and Maggie taking part in the conversation. Despite desperately wanting to simply dial her number, she neatly folded up the letter, put it in her purse and dialed her sister Maggie instead.

~Chapter 26~

Even though she'd wanted to get to the gym early, get her work out over with and be back home by ten, Maggie cursed to herself as she pulled into the very crowded gym at 9:15am. She'd gotten sidetracked with a couple work related emails that needed addressing despite the fact that it was Saturday, and by the time she'd finished them, played with her dog, and made her way across town, it was after nine. Just as she was about to exit her Jeep, her cell rang. Initially willing to ignore it, she chose to answer when she saw her kid sister's name on the caller ID.

"Good morning," she answered, trying her best to not sound irritated.

"Hey good morning Mags. I'll only keep you a second. Just wanted to share some really amazing news with you!" she offered, practically shouting. "I got a letter from our sister!"

"What? What the hell are you talking about Dee?" she nearly shrieked in disbelief. "What do you mean you got a letter from her? How is that possible?" she asked, now that Deidre had her full attention.

"Ancestry. She got the hit on her profile that she had a sister! Must be when my sample was analyzed, it disseminated down to her profile as a positive close family match."

"What the fuck Dee? Why didn't you tell Josh and me that you got your results back?" she nearly shouted into the phone, furious at her sister for not telling her.

"Relax Maggie," she answered calmly. "I would have told you BUT I haven't received my results yet. I called you first, and will call Josh second with the same information, and then I will contact Ancestry to find out when I should expect the analysis in my email. I would never have withheld that kind of information from you Mags and you should know better than to insinuate that I would or did." Deidre chose not to tell her sister that she'd had the information since last evening, but had been otherwise occupied and not available to tell her then.

Maggie took but a moment to process the information that her sister had just told them. "Could it really be this easy that their sister found them instead of them searching endless leads to find her?" she thought to herself before responding.

"I'm not sure how Josh will feel about this discovery, but I think we shouldn't do anything until you've received your information back from Ancestry. Make sure yours says the same as what she's professing. I'm sure she's legit, but let's not take any chances okay? I know you're always willing to give someone the benefit of the doubt, but please don't respond to her, and open your heart to her, until we know she's really related to us through DNA. I just don't want you to get hurt, okay?" She softened her tone, trying to make her kid sister understand that not everyone in the world was who and what they professed to being. The world was filled with all kinds of scumbags and she didn't want her little sister becoming friends with an impostor and getting hurt, or worse, getting scammed.

"Dee, what did she say her name was anyways? I can run it in my system and I know Jena will do the same."

Slightly put off that her sister was already challenging the authenticity of the letter, she responded curtly. "Her name is Samantha Bowing, and she is our sister Dee," she stated matter of factly. "She enclosed a picture of herself, and one of she and her children, and she is the spitting image of mom at that age. Her daughter could pass as your kid Mags. That's right," she answered, not allowing her sister a second to respond, "You're an auntie to a niece and nephew."

"I guess that makes me the Cool Aunt," Maggie responded, not sure why she felt a huge lump in her throat but liking the sound of being called auntie. "I think that maybe we should all get together this afternoon and brainstorm. I'd say we could go to camp, but I know Lee sent a picture to Joshua yesterday and the kitchen is pretty torn apart. You guys can swing by my place if everyone's free. I could grab a pizza or something," she offered.

"Your place sounds great, but do you think we could make it Chinese or something other than pizza? Grif and I ate way too much of it last night," she said, realizing that she hadn't meant to divulge that much information.

"So our contractor took you out on a date for pizza last night huh?" Maggie teased.

"No, actually I invited him over and he brought the pizza. I enjoyed it and his company very much," she added, just to tweak her older sister a little.

"Oh great, now my kid sister is getting some; everyone's getting some but me. My life completely and thoroughly sucks," she teased.

"What about Mr. Hockey game man from a few weeks ago?" her sister countered.

"What about him? We went out for brunch, had a few drinks and watched hockey. Not a big deal. I see him at the gym every once in a while, but he's a lawyer, and definitely not my type," she stated, trying to convince both she and her sister.

"Why not Mags? Life's too short, mom said so herself. If he interests you, or intrigues you, why not give him a chance? You have nothing to lose and potentially, everything to gain. Besides, it's time you release some of that pent-up energy that you have," she teased.

"Bite me Dee," she teased back, knowing that her kid sister wasn't too far off. "I'm heading into the gym for my workout but call Josh and let me know if you want to get together later this afternoon."

"Will do. Oh, and Maggie, if Mr. Attorney is there, ask him out..." Deidre hung up the phone before her sister could say another word.

Knowing that her sister was probably right, Maggie walked into the gym in search of a man and possibly a date. It didn't take long for her to find just who she was looking for.

Garrett was just finishing his last circuit and ready to head out when he saw her walk in and walk right towards him. He'd barely opened his mouth to greet her when she stopped right in front of him and asked him one simple question.

"If you are free tonight, would you like to spend it with me?"

"Are you asking me out Maggie?" he teased, already knowing that the answer was most definitely yes, yes he would spend any amount of time she offered, with her.

"I believe I am," she smiled. "My life hasn't settled down much, and there is still a lot of unsettled business that I need to attend to, but my kid sister just reminded me that mom stressed to us that life's too short, so I was thinking that if you're free this evening, that maybe we could hang out at my place, watch a movie on Netflix, have a few beers and get to know one another better. Nothing fancy, nothing formal, just you and me, oh, and bring Jazmine with you. Whatever this is that we have starting, isn't going anywhere if our dogs don't get along," she laughed.

"Besides, if you have your dog with you, it makes it much more difficult for me to seduce you on my couch," she kidded, watching his reaction.

"Honey, you want to seduce me on your couch, you can bet Jazmine and your Sinjin will get locked up somewhere fast!" he teased back.

Both laughed, finalized a time, with Garrett insisting on picking up take out dinner for them, and agreeing to arrive around 7. Garrett excused himself and left the gym, leaving Maggie alone in her thoughts. She put her ear plugs in, cranked the music and started her treadmill, smiling to herself.

While Maggie was thinking of her upcoming date, Deidre was trying to answer Joshua's rapid fire questions about their newly discovered sister. He, like Maggie, had some skepticism, but was more enthusiastic than his sister about the possibility that she found them and their search could now be focused on finding her father. Both Josh and Jena said that they were able to meet up with she and Deidre at Deidre's home at 1pm, and for her to bring the letter with her. Once she finally hung up with him, she thought about Griffin and the night they'd spent together. Just as she was about to text him, a message appeared on her phone.

"You are so beautiful Deidre. Thank you for inviting me into your life. May you have a wonderful day."

She looked at the simple text and despite herself, she found her heart swelling, just a little. She had no time in her life for romance, dating or whatever the trendy term was; but knew that she'd make time for Griffin. She sat at her tiny table that she had shared breakfast with him just hours before and thought about her response. Deciding to just say what she felt, her reply was simple. "If you are free, be one with me again tonight Griffin."

Her response blew him away. Of course he wanted to be with her and inside her again, but she wasn't a one night stand kind of woman. If he returned to her home and her bed tonight, it would be making love, not screwing; and despite her insistence that she wasn't looking for anything serious, he knew in his heart that it already was. He just needed her to come around to that realization.

"I'd love to spend the evening with you Deidre, but only if you let me pick you up and take you on a date."

"I don't do dating Griffin. I've already told you that. If you want to be with me, then say yes and come over."

"I want to show you something Dee. I will pick you up at 7pm sharp. Wear something very comfortable and layer your clothing as it's going to be chilly tonight. It's not a date Deidre, but it is a surprise so don't bother asking details. You let me show you this one thing, and then we can head back to your place and you can show me anything you'd like. I'm yours for the rest of the evening."
?

"I'll be ready at 7 Griffin, but if I play along with this, then you're mine the rest of the night. Deal?"

"Deal!"

~Chapter 27~

Joshua, Jena and Deidre all converged on Maggie's condo at 1pm. Josh and Jena had picked up Chinese, while Deidre had baked a half dozen Apple Turnovers before she arrived. She'd made a full dozen but because she was meeting Griffin later in the evening for some kind of adventure, she thought she might as well save a few for him. Maggie and Sinjin met them at the door and welcomed them. Her condo suited her just fine; clean lines, minimalist furnishings, neutral throughout, and everything in precise locations to add to their efficiency and usefulness. Unlike her sister's home that frequently caused her sensory overload with its' vibrant colors, overstuffed furniture and typically cluttered counters; Maggie's was clean beyond a fault. Both sisters were amazing cooks, or at least Joshua thought they were, with each specializing in completely opposite types of cuisine. Maggie was known for throwing together seven course meals, and making it look simple; while Deidre was the master of desserts. Everyone's eyes were on the beat-up wicker basket that Deidre carried in, knowing that whatever was inside would probably taste as good as it smelled as she set it down on Maggie's slate black granite counter top.

Maggie set about grabbing plates from her cupboard, silverware and napkins, with Jena pulling out a pitcher of sweet tea and filling everyone's' glasses. Once everyone had their orders, they sat down at Maggie's table and waited for Deidre to get the letter from Samantha out and read it. She read it slowly, articulating clearly what she wanted to stress, that the woman was mainly interested in medical information for her children. After she finished reading, she held up the picture and heard Jena audible gasp as she looked at the woman staring back at them.

"Oh my God Joshua, it's your mom. Or at least looks like she could be her twin. Maggie had felt a quick jolt as well the second she looked into the eyes of the woman in the picture. There was no doubt, this woman shared the same blood as their mother, and therefore them. She remained quiet, picking up the picture of Samantha and her children. She looked at the picture, of the children standing together with their mother in what appeared to be a first day of school type picture. She studied their faces and thought the boy looked a lot like Josh had at that age, but more importantly, she studied the picture the way she would any investigation that she was involved in. She looked at their attire, noted that they were dressed in clean, non-label attire, though she did note that the girl's blouse was Aéropostale. The boy's sneakers weren't the most popular trending sneak ers available, but they were newer, with the girl's crocs looking like what every young girl her age was wearing. The woman who went by the name Samantha was wearing pleated slacks, a simple black sleeveless pullover, and shoes that from the angle of the picture, Deidre couldn't tell if they were Sperry's or not. There was nothing ostentatious about them, and the homes in the background looked to be in a middle to upper-middle class neighborhood. She made a mental note to google the address when she was alone.

"I'm not sure how I feel about being an Aunt," was her only comment, handing the pictures back to her sister.

"Well, I don't know about you Mags, but I know I'm going to be one very cool aunt to those kids!"

Joshua finally spoke. "I think we are all in agreement, that from the pictures alone, we can safely say that Miss Bowers is definitely related to us, and in all likelihood, is our half-sister. But before we hold a family reunion with her, I think it's imperative that we dig a little and learn more about her just to make sure her intentions are what she professes they are. If Jena and Maggie check her out and she is exactly who she says she is, then by all means, will we move forward and meet her, and fulfill mom's wish."

"Agreed. But dealing with her is only part of mom's deathbed confession, and dying wish Josh. We still need to track down her father."

"Don't you dare talk about mother with disdain in your voice Maggie," Deidre warned. "She wasn't perfect, but pretty damn close, and a hell of a better person than I'll ever be."

"Chill out Dee, I never implied she wasn't a wonderful person. It just pisses me off that she didn't tell us about all of this before she died." She couldn't help herself as she felt the tears welling up in her eyes. "We could have tracked Samantha down, and reunited them before mom passed away. Now, she'll have to settle for us three."

"Aw, see Maggie," Deidre exclaimed, hugging her sister, "You do have a heart after all!"

"You're such an ass Dee."

"Yup, but I'm your kid sister and your favorite! Well at least until we meet Samantha! Who knows, then I might be your second favorite!" she kidded, with just a hint of truth in her jesting.

"You're a pain in my ass Dee, but you will always be my favorite sister!" she exclaimed, punching her sister gently in the arm.

"So Jena, will you be able to look our sister up and make sure she doesn't have a rap sheet a mile long? I can do some digging on my end also, but figure you have easier access to that sort of info."

"Already on it," Jena offered. I shot a text to one of my best friends at the police station, explained that for personal reasons, I needed a background check on an individual. She didn't ask details and I didn't provide them. She said that she'd have our information within a day or so."

"That's great," Josh offered. I think for the interim, we can at least send Samantha an email and tell her generic information about ourselves. Obviously, nothing revealing. She's googled where you live Deidre, which is public record, and I appreciate that she sent you a letter as opposed to showing up on your doorstep. I think, if everyone is in agreement, we email her and let her know that you did, in fact, receive her letter, and that we would be happy to provide her with what medical information we have that runs in mom's side of the family, not that there's much of anything to tell her. "

Maggie thought about what his brother was proposing and interjected her opinion. "I agree with Josh. We respond that it's not just you Deidre, that there are three of us. We give her the information that she requested and stated is the most important reason for reaching out to you. It appeases her, and bides us time to make sure she's legit, and not someone with an ulterior motive."

"Great," Deidre exclaimed. "Can we use your computer Mags and while we're all here, send her a note right now?" she asked, wanting to capitalize on the fact that they all were together and in agreement of how to proceed with their newly discovered sister.

Getting up from her chair, Maggie walked over to her desk and grabbed her laptop. Once seated again, she turned it on and pulled up her email.

"Okay, shoot. You guys dictate and I'll type." And for the next twenty minutes, the four of them collaborated on their first correspondence to their sister.

Once the letter was typed, changed several times, tweaked some more, and then finally agreed upon by everyone, Maggie took a deep breath and hit the send button. Still slightly leery of taking Samantha at face value, Maggie used the excuse that she had work to do and politely kicked everyone out, insisting that she'd cleanup and do the dishes. Deidre readily agreed, wanting to get back home in order to figure out what she should wear for her evening adventure with Griffin. Joshua and Jena took the opportunity to cut out early as well and decided to take a trip north to check on the progress at their mom's camp.

The second she was alone, Maggie cleaned up quickly and then sat down with her computer, armed with her sister's name, date of birth, and present address and started digging. She already knew what dessert she planned on cooking for her evening with Garrett, and knew that she could throw it together in a matter of minutes. Looking at the time, she allotted herself one hour, 90 minutes tops to see what she could uncover on her big sister.

~Chapter 28~

She'd give him credit for being punctual. She watched him pull into her drive with two minutes to spare. She didn't want to seem anxious or excited, so she waited inside until he came to her door and rang the bell. Thinking it was taking him far too long to grab a bag of take out and make his way to her door, she found herself slightly irritated as she opened the door to find him standing there, about to knock. Take out, flowers and some type of package in one hand, and his dog's leash in the other, he smiled just enough to allow his dimples to show.

"Hi. Nice leash. Isn't there supposed to be a dog attached to it?" she teased, opening the door wider. "Sinjin, sit" she commanded with her dog stopping in his tracks as he approached the door, and sat immediately. "Stay," she spoke sternly. "Down." Her dog didn't want to listen, but did so anyways, staring at the new face that had just entered his home, smelling of some other dog. Maggie took the flowers he extended towards her, and set their dinner on the side of her table. "I have Jazzy in the car and if you still want our kids to meet, I can go get her; but I thought that maybe I should get approval from your boy before I add in another variable."

"Smart move counselor. Sinjin, come; friend." Her dog was at her side in one second flat, sticking his nose to Garrett's pantleg for a better sniff. With his tail starting to wag, Garrett reached down to pet the yellow lab at his feet.

"Well I take it I've passed?" he asked, already knowing the answer as he crouched down to pet the dog presently in his face, giving him doggy kisses.

"Yeah, I'd say so. How'd you win him over so quickly? Do you have dog treats in your pockets?"

He reached in and pulled one out. "Guilty as charged. Momma didn't raise no fool!" he laughed.

"I guess not. Got get your dog Garrett and I'll put our supper on the table. What'd you bring any ways," she asked as he slipped out the door, choosing not to answer her.

As he was outside grabbing his dog and allowing her to mark her territory outside before entering Maggie's condo, he hoped that his diner choices would surprise and appeal to her. Having no clue what her culinary palate was like, he brought a wide variety.

She first pulled out a lovely looking antipasto and some fantastic smelling bread. The next container, which was still quite warm to touch contained asparagus with some type of white sauce and what she thought were tiny red pepper accents. The next container she removed were her favorite restaurant's signature potatoes and she knew then where their meal had come from. She chuckled to herself as she thought about all of the restaurants in Utica and the surrounding area, that he had chosen her favorite one to order their meal from. Wondering what the main course was, she removed the last container just as Garrett reentered her condo, with dog in tow. His dog stayed at his side, with Sinjin smelling the new addition immediately. "Sinjin, SENTAR, permanecer!" she barked the order to her dog, who didn't move from the spot where he'd stopped, mid step.

His stare was directly on their company, with his front paw shaking in anticipation of meeting the new four legged friend who'd just entered his domain, but he knew enough to wait for her command.

With his dog still healing at his side, he looked at her and laughed. "Le ensenaste a tu perro commandos en espanol?"

"Por supuesto. Aleman se hubiera esperado!"

"Of course German would have been expected IF your dog were a German Shepherd Mags, but it's an English lab, therefore should know English silly!" he laughed.

"So you habla Espanol," she asked, impressed that he was fluent in Spanish.

"Yes, and German, and passible French as well; but Spanish is the only one that really comes in handy in my line of work."

"I'm impressed counselor. You think we should just let them go and see if they become friends?" she asked, looking down at her quivering dog.

"Sure, Jazmine won't hurt your Sinjin."

"I think my Sinjin can handle your pup," she countered, releasing him with one single world. Sinjin waited until Garrett's dog was unleashed and then the two of them darted toward one another, circling, sniffing and getting to know one another, in a way that only dog's could.

"Don't expect me to circle you and sniff you the way my dog just did," Maggie said, as she opened her refrigerator, pulling out the bottle of wine that she'd had chilling in her refrigerator.

"Nah, I have many other ideas of how we can get more familiar with one another," he winked. "But dinner is hot so let's start with that shall we?"

"Sound's good. Out of curiosity, why'd you choose to order our food from there?"

"Because it's the best in town, and you deserve the best," he offered matter of factly. "I'm starved woman, so let's eat!"

While Maggie and Garrett dug into the gourmet meal that he'd brought for them, Deidre, opened her door to Griffin and the start of their date. She had no idea what he had up his sleeve but was ready to see. He greeted him at her door with two tiny decorative bags.

"What are these?" she asked. "Nothing much, just a little something for you and Sasha."

"You remembered my cat's name," she asked, affectionately.

"Of course, Dee, I remember everything you've told me."

Deidre opened the first package and pulled out a couple metal tins with different herbal teas in it. She smelled the first container and nodded in approval. "It smells divine, thank you Grif."

"Wait until you sniff what I got Sasha," he kidded.

She sniffed the remaining bag and burst out laughing as she redrew a large stuffed mouse. The tag attached to the mouse's ear indicated that it was stuffed with Catnip. "Perfect," she laughed. "Thank you for being so thoughtful Griffin."

"Are you ready for my surprise?" he asked, reaching for her hand. "And do you have a few layers on? It's starting to get a little brisk out."

"I'm good."

"Great, then let's get this party started. I would like to show you something." And with that, they started their evening, with Deidre having no clue where they were going, but excited just the same.

They made small talk with Deidre not giving details but simply stating that her meeting with her sister and brother had gone far better than she'd anticipated it going. She said that they'd sent an email back to the woman professing to be their half sister and had provided her with the medical information that she'd sought. He listened intently, trying to put himself in their shoes but couldn't. He thought about how hard it must have been to accept this woman into their life and gave each of them credit for following their mother's request and not shutting her out completely. She didn't ask where they were going but paid attention to each turn. Always one to trust people, she knew that she was in no danger where he was taking her, but also, knew that she needed to be aware of her surroundings as well. When he drove past Metropolitan Life Insurance Co and into Oneida County Airport, she looked at him suspiciously.

"Um, Grif, why are we at the airport?"

"Because that's where my plan is located silly," he responded, and kept moving toward a hangar at the far end of the tarmac.

"Your what?" she repeated, positive that she'd misunderstood what he'd said.

"My plane Deidre. I've been a licensed pilot since I was eighteen and my father, brother and I store our plane here. Of course, my brother rarely gets a chance to fly her, but Dad and I enjoy taking her for a spin whenever we have a little free time. You're not afraid of heights, now are you?" he teased, as he put this truck in park outside a massive metal building that Deidre assumed housed said plane.

"No, I'm not afraid of heights but I am of dying. You actually do know how to fly it right?" she asked hesitantly.

"Yup, that's what the instructor told me when he passed me several years ago. Look Dee," he said as they stopped in front of the plane they'd affectionately named Esther, "If you don't want to take a ride, it's okay; but if you do, I give you my word, I'm an accomplished pilot and would never let anything happen to you. I just really would like to show you something that is only visible from the air."

"Then time's wasting, let's go!" she exclaimed, grinning ear to ear. "I trust you Griffin, so let's go see my surprise."

"Great! You'll love it Dee." He opened the passenger side door after finishing his pre-flight check list and once he climbed in, handed her a headset, started the engine and taxied out for take-off. As they wheeled down the runway, she sent Maggie a quick text, said a quick hail Mary, and swallowed quickly as he hit the thrust and accelerated. Before she had time to panic, she felt the wheels lift off the runway and they were air bound.

"Oh my God, we're flying!"

"Yes mam; sure beats the alternative," he chuckled.

It took him less than fifteen minutes to reach his destination. Just before he reached it, he instructed

Deidre to trust him, and close her eyes. She did as instructed and waited patiently to open them again. Once they were almost there and the lights started to come into view, he told her to open her eyes. When she did, she gasped.

"I've never seen anything so beautiful Griffin. Where are we?" she asked.

"Onondaga Lake. Everyone can see the Lights On The Lake from their cars, but I thought you might like to see them from a different perspective," he added, watching her facial expression. "My dad showed them to my brother and I when we were kids and I've come back to see them every year since I've had my license. And in case you were wondering, I always come alone. You are the first person I've ever shown them to, from the air. Do you like my surprise?" he asked sincerely.

She took just a moment to formulate her response. "I have never met anyone like you before Griffin, and I have never had anyone give me such an amazing gift and it's something I will never forget. I couldn't have asked for a better sight, and I am enjoying the company more than you know," she added.

At that moment, everything in the universe felt right. He was in the air, doing something he absolutely loved. The woman he'd shared the night with was sitting beside him and with a little luck, would want to spend the rest of the evening with him, the sky was filled with stars, and the

Christmas show was as visually stunning as it had been in years past. He was a very lucky man, he thought to himself. As they turned to fly back over the lightshow on their way back towards Oriskany, he reached over for her hand.

"Thank you for spending your Saturday evening with me Deidre."

"Will you spend your Saturday night with me Griffin," she asked, already knowing the answer.

"Of course. I would spend all of my nights with you if I could. I know it sounds cliché or ridiculous, but I've waited for you all of my life Dee, and on some level, I've known you all of my life, and it's as if we're simply continuing something that was already started. I can't explain it, but when I'm with you, everything seems natural and normal and the way it's supposed to be. And no, I'm not some fruitcake or weirdo," he laughed, knowing how preposterous he sounded. "It's just comforting to have you around, and just seems like it was always supposed to be this way. Again, let me iterate; I'm not some crazed serial killer or lunatic, just someone who believes in fate."

She said nothing, absorbing what he'd said. Afraid to tell him that she understood exactly what he was saying, because she'd experienced some sense of de ja vu from the first moment that she'd met him; she remained quiet, simply holding his hand and enjoying the view. Everything looked different from this vantage point and Deidre knew that it was an experience that she'd never forget. Never one to mince words, nor say something she didn't mean, when she finally spoke, the words were spoken from the heart.

"I wasn't looking for you Griffin, yet you found me. I thought we might have a few fun filled nights together and that would be enough to satisfy me; but I was wrong. I had no idea that something was missing in my life until you entered it and for that I'll be forever grateful. I know this is really quick, but something has drawn me to you, and I would like to discover more. That is if you feel the same way," she added quickly.

"Deidre, no one has intrigued me the way you do. And I'm not going anywhere," he offered, as he released her hand in preparation for landing. He guided his twin piper down the way he'd done countless times before, gently touching the pavement without so much as a jolt or bump. She watched the way he maneuvered the controls and realized that not only was he an accomplished pilot, but also loved flying. Once they'd taxied back to the hangar where he stored his plane, he helped her out of the cockpit and pointed her in the direction of the lavatory. When she returned, they made their way towards his truck.

"Thank you so much Griffin. I will never forget this experience." And with that, they walked hand in hand towards his truck, and her home.

~Chapter 29~

While her kid sister and her date were high above taking in the sights, Maggie was enjoying an enjoyable bottle of Pinot Grigio, and excellent meal and even better company. When they actually started talking about their hobbies, and travels, they were shocked to realize how much their interests and tastes mirrored one another's. Both admitted they hated going to the gym, but it was a necessary evil to keep them in shape for the things they actually loved doing. Both were accomplished mountaineers and ironically were part of the same climbing club. When they started talking sports, they both admitted to being huge Giants fans, and when he spoke about enjoying hockey, she let it slip that she knew significantly more about the game than she'd let on when they went to see the Comets play. When Maggie asked Garrett where he'd attended college, she was shocked to learn that they'd both attended college in Albany at the same time. Once their favorite bars became the topic of conversation, they both realized that their paths could have very likely crossed throughout the time they had spent there. Maggie was surprised how well behaved the two dogs were, basically entertaining themselves while she and Jazmine's owner talked. Garrett was obviously very well educated, yet he was as down to earth as she was. When she got off the couch to grab another bottle of wine, she was shocked to see the time. Following her eyes, he stood, realizing that it was his clue to grab his dog and head out.

"Wow. I had no idea it was getting to be so late Mags. My girl and I had better get going," he offered, allowing her a way out.

As if working on impulse, Maggie set the bottle of wine down and walked over to where he was standing and standing on her tip toes, brought her lips to his, just brushing them.

"I know you're right Garrett. And I also know that if you didn't have your dog with you, I'd ask you to stay here with me tonight," she purred. "I like you, and I never play games. But there is something about you that fascinates me and if you're willing, I'll invite you over again in the very near future; and ask you to leave your dog at home. That is if that's alright with you."

"I can run her home right now Mags," he kidded. "And I can drive very very fast and come right back," he winked.

Bursting out laughing because she knew he would if she let him, she simply handed him his dog's leash. "Not tonight Garrett. When I invite you over again, it will be for the entire evening, and night. I don't like to rush things, and some things are definitely worth waiting for."

"That they are," he offered, clipping the leash on his impatiently waiting dog. He leaned in to kiss her goodnight and felt the room spin when she opened her mouth to allow him in. In that moment, they both knew that they'd started something, something that they'd both refused to look for but were both lacking. Sex was easy, and both could have fulfilled that need, if and when they'd wanted to. This was completely different, and both of them knew it. She melted into his kiss, soft at first, and growing with intensity and need. She knew that if she didn't stop it right then, that he'd never make it to his car. Lingering in the kiss for just a brief moment longer, she felt everything around her freeze in that moment. Finally breaking from their embrace, she stepped back and smiled.

"Good night Garrett. Thank you for a wonderful evening."

"Good night Maggie. Want to do something tomorrow afternoon?"

"Like what?" she asked, slightly intrigued, and definitely interested.

"Meet me at Clinton Arena at 1 and we'll go ice skating. I promised my sister and her family that I'd go with them tomorrow. I'm their favorite Uncle, and the only one who knows how to skate," he kidded. "Come on, it'll be fun. We'll go skating for an hour or so, and then grab a late lunch. Deal?"

"Alright. Deal," she agreed, knowing that if it were awkward meeting his sister and her family, that she could politely excuse herself if she had her own vehicle. She hadn't skated in a couple of years, but figured it couldn't be much different from riding a bike.

"I'm already looking forward to our date tomorrow Mags. Goodnight," he said turning towards his car.

"It's not a date," she shouted back, smiling. Watching him load his dog, and then get in and drive away, she noted that he was smiling just as much as she was.

"Oh boy, what have I gotten myself into?" she wondered, knowing that she was definitely getting into something that she hadn't planned for, looked for or wanted. But also realized that she wasn't shutting him down either.

~Chapter 40~

"I'm really sorry Garrett, but we can't join you this afternoon. Yeah, Mikala's been vomiting all morning and I have no clue if it's a stomach bug or not, but I'm going to lay low with her today."

"It's alright sis. I'm bringing a date and I really wanted her to meet you but it can wait," he offered, understandingly. Having never had children, he didn't fully understand what it was like to be a parent, let alone the sole parent in a child's life, but he understood sacrifice was an aspect of it. His sister was both mother and father to her children and after coming from a divorced family themselves, he knew that she made every effort to be as good a parent to her children as she could be. She lived modestly and refused any financial help from him. Occasionally she did allow him to help run the kids places when they both had to be somewhere at the same time. He loved his big sister and couldn't imagine his life without his niece and nephew, so he looked forward to helping in any capacity that he could.

"Oh my God, is it the chick from the gym you were telling me about," she teased. "So you finally conned her into going out with you? That's awesome Gar. What's she like?" she asked, sincerely interested. "I have some news of my own, but it can wait," she said.

"What sis? Are you back into the dating game? I hope so because it's been too long, and you need to meet someone and start living again."

"Something like that," she offered, but nothing more. "I'll tell you all about it when we get together. Let's plan on next weekend. I'll have you come over for pizza and wings, okay?"

"That would be great. I'll talk to you later."

"Bye Garrett. Oh, let me go, I hear Mikala calling my name.

~Chapter 41~

The weekend had flown by and it was nearly ten Sunday night before Samantha finally caught her breath. She read and reread the email that she'd received back from newly discovered sister. Deidre had explained to her in the email, that yes, it appeared that their mother Elizabeth was in fact her mother as well. She and her siblings had answered so many of her questions in her email, including telling her that not only did she have Deidre as a half-sister, but also another half sister named Maggie, and a brother, closest in age to her, named Joshua. Deidre had seemed genuinely nice, sincere and brutally honest in her email response, explaining that while she might have always known of her adoption, she and her siblings had just learned of Samantha's existence. She'd explained that they would help her learn more about her birthmother and provide her with what little information they knew about the man Elizabeth had conceived her with. She felt a light tug at her heart when she read the words she dreaded; that her birthmother had recently passed away. Deidre had stressed that they would have sought her out sooner if they'd known about her, but it wasn't until after their mother had passed, that they discovered that they had an older sister. As Samantha reread the paragraph again, she could tell from the heartfelt words, that her siblings really wanted to help her in whatever way they could. Armed with their names, she knew that she'd "stalk" them on social media, and any other legal way possible, to ensure that she hadn't opened a can of worms. If she found that they weren't good people or had any unscrupulous past, she'd sever all ties with them as soon as she gained whatever medical history they'd offer her. In her heart, she knew that she wasn't looking for any kind of new family, but also deep down, knew that she wouldn't turn them away if they ever wanted to meet someday, even if it were only once. With her parents still living, her sibling and her own children, she had all the family that she'd ever need. But reading her half sibling's email for the third time, she found herself intrigued.

Deidre, along with her siblings, told her all of the medical information that they knew, which wasn't much. She'd explained her in the email that their mother had just passed away from cancer, but other than their maternal grandmother having hypertension, and their grandfather being borderline diabetic, there really weren't any other potentially hereditary condition that they knew of.

As she shut down her computer, Samantha processed the information that her siblings had just conveyed. She felt relieved to learn that on her mother's side, there were no hereditary issues of concern, and that her mother had led a healthy life, up until the time cancer took over. Her siblings had also told her that they had no predetermined medical issues and that all three were healthy. As she got ready for bed, she now had 50% of the answers that she sought. Slightly saddened that they hadn't mentioned anything about who her birth father was, she accepted the fact that at least she had some closure on her birthmother's side. She'd never really thought about what she would have wanted or done, had her mother still been alive; would she have wanted to meet her or simply obtain the medical information, she thought to herself. Now a mute point, she realized that she felt a little robbed and a little pissed off that the woman who'd given birth to her had lived less than a half hour's drive all along, and had never sought her out until after her death! Finding herself getting angry at the woman who'd carried her for nine months, and then given her up without so much as an inquiry into her whereabouts for over thirty four years. She now realized, that despite never verbalizing it out loud to anyone, she'd always thought that someday she'd be able to meet her birth mother in person. As she crawled into bed, for what was most likely going to be a sleepless night, she felt the tears starting to form. Her dream of getting to know her birthmother would never come to fruition. As she cried herself to sleep, the only comfort she felt was in the fact that her mother's other children were willing to get to know her, and that would have to be good enough.

~Chapter 42~

Less than one month after Griffin and Lee had started remodeling Elizabeth's home, they found themselves finishing the last few details required to wrap up the job. It was a few days before Christmas, that Griffin and his father inspected their work one last time and then as

Griffin was putting the last of his tools in his truck, he heard his father placing the call to Joshua, who'd been their main point of contact, giving him the good news.

Returning inside, he saw his father smiling as he made his way towards the door to join his son for their journey home.

"Another satisfied customer son. It has always done my heart good to know that we've done right by our customers. And I think that with your designs, you outdid yourself this time Griff," he exclaimed, sincerely and from his heart. "Your talent is wasted on doing the grunt work son. You really should take a job at an architecture firm that would showcase your talent more."

"Dad, we've been over this a thousand times. I'm not a suit and tie kind of guy, and I truly enjoy the grunt work as you call it. Besides, who else would be able to keep you in line if I wasn't working side by side with you every day?" he teased. "And I enjoy what I'm doing, but if it makes you feel a little better, I'd like to show you a project that I've been developing and hoping to start in the spring; that is if the brainstorm behind it will let me."

"Now I'm intrigued. Let's pack this stuff up and head for home and you can tell me all about it. Does it have something to do with a young lady that you've been seeing, and not telling me about? I know she must be pretty special since I heard through the grapevine that you took her up in old Esther."

"I'm still learning how to dance with her dad, but yes, she is pretty special. Her name is Deidre, and she is an amazing person, gentle soul and someone who always thinks of everyone else. She runs a soup kitchen dad, and as if that's not enough, she employs a dozen or so veterans in the shop." He started his truck and started backing out of the driveway. "You won't freaking believe what her business is?" Before his father had a chance to respond, Griffin kept right on talking. "She keeps her soup kitchen open seven days a week, but in the back of her building, she has a business making coats that turn into sleeping bags for the homeless. I think her business is expanding more than she can keep up with, but when I try to talk to her about it, she says it's all good. So, I have been thinking about it a lot and I'd like to help her expand her business even more," Griffin said sincerely.

Lee took a moment to digest what his son had just told him. It wasn't so much the words, but the intonation in his voice that had surprised him. As he listened to his son speaking so affectionately about the young woman that he'd yet to meet, he remembered a time long ago when he too, had felt that way about a woman. But one divorce later, he didn't hold much credence in love anymore. Maybe love was just for the young, he thought to himself. He thought it was about time that his son found something other than work to stimulate him. And if a young lady running a not for profit soup kitchen was what it took to make his son happy, then he'd encourage their friendship until it blossomed and flourished. But in listening to his son speak, he knew that it wouldn't take much for their relationship to grow.

"So, tell me about your idea that was Deidre's brainchild?" he asked as they made their way south.

"She wants to build a tiny home village for her veteran's dad," he responded proudly. "She's got the basic fundamentals all worked out already and once we get through the holidays, which I'm sure will be heard having lost both of her parents, I'm going to discuss the possibility of us going in together as partners and fulfilling both she and her mother's wishes, to build tiny homes to help others in need."

"Your Deidre sounds like an amazing woman. She reminds me so much of a woman I knew a long time who was always trying to save the world," he chuckled. "Hold on to her tight son, but never smother her. Treat her like a precious, irreplaceable gift and always let her know how much she means to you, even if the words terrify you to say them. True love only comes around once in a lifetime."

Taken back by his father's solemn words, he looked at him questioningly.

"I've never heard you talk like that dad. Who was the love of your life that you're talking about?" he asked, honestly interested in hearing about the woman who'd obviously broken his father's heart.

Lee took a few moments to answer, as if having an internal battle as to whether or not he wanted to rehash distant memories; but decided that his son had a right to know.

"Your mother son. She took my breath away from the moment I met her. Everything happened so quickly, we met, had less than a dozen dates and before I knew it, I was getting shipped back to the states and she wanted to be with me so next thing I know, I'm in my uniform standing before a Justice getting hitched. Yes, when your mother left me to return to London, it broke my heart. But I also know that everything happens for a reason and if we hadn't met, I wouldn't have you and your brother, and you two are my biggest accomplishments in life."

"I miss her too dad." The next twenty miles down Route 28 were driven in silence, with Griffin's father thinking about the past, and Grif thinking about his future with his Bohemian goddess. They'd gotten into a comfortable routine and had started spending more evenings together as the weeks had progressed. Despite their work schedules, both he and Deidre kept Sundays open for hiking. They'd chased fire towers, high peaks and waterfalls, alternating each week who got to choose their destination. They shared meals together several times a week if their schedules allowed it, and many times, he'd bring take out for her staff to enjoy as they all ate together. Even on the days that they couldn't get together, both he and Deidre looked forward to their nightly texting marathons just before they retired for the night. It had become a ritual that both of them not only enjoyed but counted on as a way to end their day. Of course, he enjoyed the nights she'd invited him to share her bed even more. He never pushed or asked for anything more than she offered, and despite whatever he had going on with his schedule, he never refused her invites. He still really had no idea what Deidre was looking to get out of their relationship as she would never discuss it, but he knew that he wanted her in his life long term and somehow, someway, he was going to make her come around and realize that she was in love with him.

Josh hung up the phone with the contractor, and then placed a conference call to his sisters. He explained to them that the work was complete and that they had told him to head north and inspect their work prior to making their final payment, to which he agreed, but knew that the finished product would not only be high quality but exceed their expectations. When he and his sisters had saw what they did with the kitchen and bath, they were blown away and knew that whatever Lee and Griffin had done to the sunroom would be just as magnificent. While they were on the phone together, Deidre came up with an idea.

"Hey guys, you know how much mom loved the holidays? I just really don't think that I want to be here in town this year, so I was thinking that maybe, now that camp is complete, why don't we spend Christmas Day in Old Forge at camp?" she asked, trying to contain her enthusiasm. "And with Christmas being on a Thursday, and now that both you and Jena have investigated our sister thoroughly and realize that she's what she said she is, I was thinking that maybe we could fulfill mom's request and invite her to camp for the weekend."

She nearly held her breath waiting to hear their response. It was Maggie who spoke first.

"You're right Dee, there is absolutely nothing criminal or suspicious in her history, and obviously we all have been corresponding with her to a degree. I'm okay with her coming up, maybe for the day on Saturday and then we can play it by ear if we have her spend the night or not. I'm mean, yes she's biologically our sister, but how much time do we really need to spend with her getting to know her?" she asked sincerely. "She has her own family and parents and none of us have ever expected our families to blend together. But in answer to your question, I'm okay with her coming up after Christmas. We have to meet with mom's attorney tomorrow so why don't we talk about it after the meeting and if you want, you can call her tomorrow evening and extend the invitation," she offered.

"Oh my God," Deidre nearly shouted. "I'd completely forgotten about that meeting. Thank God you reminded me! What exactly do you think Mr. Phelps is going to surprise up with this time," she kidded.

"He's just the puppet Dee. It's our momma that is still pulling the strings, and after her first surprise, God only knows," she laughed.

They concluded the call with everyone agreeing that they'd head up to camp Christmas Eve morning and stay through the weekend, whether their sister chose to join them or not. Jena had mentioned while they were on the conference call, that maybe her future sister in laws would like to invite the men in their lives to spend the day with them, or even come up for the weekend, and offer that was quickly rejected by both Deidre and Maggie. Maggie explained that while she was still seeing Garrett, meeting their new sister was family business and outsiders shouldn't be part of what could be an emotional weekend, a notion seconded by Deidre. While Jena respectfully disagreed, she let it slide for the moment, and figured she'd work on the two of them after the meeting with the attorney. After everyone hung up, and continued with their day, Deidre kept thinking about possibly inviting Griffin and his father up for Christmas Day. She tabled the idea and went back to work, trying to finish up her workday.

As evening rolled around, and she'd settled in to her bed for the night, she picked up the phone to call Griffin just as it rang, with her caller ID showing it was in fact Griffin on the other end. She laughed to herself because it wasn't the first time that he'd done that to her. She no sooner start thinking about him and decide to give him a call and her cell phone screen would light up with his name appearing.

"Hi."

"Hi yourself gorgeous. How was your day? Did you have a big dinner crowd?" he asked, knowing that each night varied, and Monday's were typically slow.

"Actually yes, we were pretty busy. Sometimes as we near a holiday, I think people come in to gorge themselves so to speak. Many of my regulars know that I am not open on Christmas Day, and despite it being a day that they probably need me even more, I promised my mother a long time ago, that I would always be closed on Christ's Birthday, and spend it with family. That being said," she started, took a deep breath, and tried to formulate exactly what and how she wanted to ask him, "I was wondering if you would possibly like to spend Christmas with me and my family up at camp? It'll only be Joshua and his fiancée Jena, Maggie and me so nothing formal or anything," she stammered.

He found it endearing listening to her try to make it sound like no big deal. In his heart, he knew how hard it must have been for her to even ask him, and despite her words, he also knew that it was a very big deal. He found himself suddenly very saddened by what he had to tell her.

"Deidre, thank you so much for the invite, and nothing would have made me happier than to spend Christmas Day with you, but I can't this year. You've stirred feelings in me that I can not even begin to describe to you, and I have never believed in love at first sight, but it was from the second I laid eyes on you Dee. I'm half in love with you Dee, and it breaks my heart to tell you that I can not join you and your family for the holidays. You see," he went on, "my brother is flying in to surprise my dad for the holidays and weekend, and I am picking him up at the airport Christmas Eve. I know my dad's been bragging about how incredible your place turned out and my brother mentioned that he would love to see some of our work sometime. Maybe the three of us can take a drive up on Saturday or possibly Sunday morning so you can meet my brother, I can give you your gifts, and we can show off our handywork? That is if that's not an inconvenience," he added quickly.

Still focused on his statement about being "half in love" with her, she completely forgot about the possibility of her half sister joining them for the day on Saturday. Never one to reveal her feelings, but also one to always speak honestly, she responded quickly, before she lost her nerve.

"I'm not half, I'm completely in love with you Grif!" she nearly shouted into her phone. "You complete me and make me a better person. There's no one else I want to go through this journey called life with, and as long as you want me around, I'm not going anywhere. I don't need rings, or wedding cakes, or picket fences Grif; I just need you."

He heard her words but couldn't believe what he'd just heard. Remaining silent on the other end, Deidre spoke again.

"I hope I didn't scare you Griffin but as you know, I'm one who shoots from the hip so to speak. I told you that from day one. You don't have to tell me that you love me; but I wanted you to now, that I Love You Griffin. And if you, your dad and your brother would like to visit us at camp, that would be awesome; but only if you promise to stay and have dinner with us. Nothing fancy, just a homecooked meal to show our gratitude for the amazing job you did fixing our mom's place up. Agreed?"

"Let me speak with my brother, but at this time, I'd say, yes, you have a deal! Oh Dee, he's going to love you," he exclaimed. "But he's way better looking than me and cleans up way better so promise me you won't decide you want him instead of me," he kidded.

"Not a snowball's chance in hell Grif. I'll see my brother and sister tomorrow afternoon and let them know that you guys will be joining us. If your father gives you any argument, tell him I said that he has to come so that we can settle up with you guys financially, and that we won't take no for an answer." They finished their nightly conversation shortly afterward, with each calling it a night. Just before they hung up, Griffin put in the last word. "Deidre, I love you too. Sweet dreams."

She hung up allowing his words to sink in and fell asleep smiling. He had told her that he loved her and wished her sweet dreams, and they were.

~Chapter 43~

They met at their mother's attorney's office at 3:55 for their 4pm meeting. Each had thought about what the meeting's agenda would be this time. The last time they'd sat in Mr. Phelp's office, they'd been given the shock of a lifetime. As they waited to be ushered into the conference room, each silently prayed that today's meeting wouldn't be quite as dramatic as the previous one.

With Jena and Josh on one couch and Maggie with Deidre on the other, they waited patiently for the secretary to bring them into the conference room. She heard him before she saw him, and found herself smiling as he rounded the corner, talking on his cell.

He saw her and took a second to recover from the shock of seeing her not only in his office, but looking amazing in her long wool skirt that accentuated every curve that she had. Sure, he knew what was lurking under her form-fitting dress, but seeing her dressed up so nicely, with her just a hint of make up on took his breath away.

"Look sis, I've go to go. Yes, of course I'll be over for Christmas. I've really go to go. I'll call you later. Bye," he said, hanging up on his sister before she had a chance to say another word.

Maggie stood to address him face to face.

"Hi."

"Maggie, what a wonderful surprise," he said, taking her into a hug, whispering in her ear. "Keep that dress on until tonight." He quickly released her and smiled.

"You never mentioned that you had a meeting in my office today," he added, approached what he assumed was her brother, with his arm outstretched. "Hi, I'm Garrett Brown, Rodney's partner, and you must be Maggie's brother Joshua," he said extending his hand in greeting.

Josh stood, eyeing the man standing in front of him. "So, this was the man who'd finally settled his kid sister down," he thought. "Nice to meet you Garrett, Maggie's told us very little about you but what she has revealed has all been good."

"She's told me all about you guys and shame on her for not doing the same about me to you both. Looking over, he saw Josh's fiancée staring at him. It took a second for him to recognize her, but when he did, he laughed out loud. "Oh my God, Jena is that you? Holy crap, I have the toughest, most beautiful defense attorney in Utica gracing my office?" he teased.

"None other Garrett, but you forgot to mention, one of the smartest," she laughed. "How do you think I have such a high success rate? I might be tough, but I'm smarter and definitely know how to read people both in and outside of the courtroom," she added, a comment that she knew Maggie picked up on. "So you're the guy that's been taking up so much of Maggie's time? Small world."

Up until that point, Maggie had remained silent. "Um guys, said Maggie is standing right here beside you. Since you two have obviously already met," she said, gently touching his arm, she steered him toward her sister. "Garrett, this is my little sister Deidre. Deidre, Garrett."

It didn't take a rocket scientist for Deidre to realize that her sister hadn't told her nearly enough about the very tall, very handsome blue-eyed man standing in front of her. She'd seen the way her sister's eyes lit up when he'd walked into the room, and from the way he'd abruptly ended his call and made his way over to her, the feeling was mutual.

"It's very nice to meet you Garrett. I hope we get to see each other again, in a less formal atmosphere."

"That would be very nice Deidre and I look forward to your sister inviting me over sometime when all of you are at her home visiting. She's a pretty good cook you know," he added, partly to tease her but also partly to stake his territory and get the point across that he wasn't just some fling she was having.

"Um again, I'm right here in the room," Maggie added. "And yes, I'd say it's time that we get the six of us together for dinner soon." Garrett didn't know who the sixth person would be but assumed it was someone that her little sister was involved with and smiled. "That would be great. If you'll excuse me, I believe Rodney is ready for you now and I've taken up enough of your time. He leaned in and kissed Maggie gently on the cheek before she could stop him. "See you tonight Mags, and it was very nice meeting you both, and seeing you again Jena."

He left the room, as Brittany, their secretary directed everyone into the conference room. Everyone took a seat, and remained silent until the door was shut. Maggie barked out an order, "Do not say a word, not a single word!" Everyone was laughing as their mother's attorney entered the room.

Once the preliminary introductions were completed, Mr. Phelps thanked them all for coming in on such short notice and so close to the holidays. Through email correspondence with Maggie, he'd been kept abreast of their communication with their half sister, and knew it was now time for the second part of his client's request.

"Your mother would be very pleased to learn that you have not only found her daughter but have been communicating with her. As you know, part of your mother's wish was that you would meet Michelle Marie, or Samantha as she now goes by, in person, at least once to give her the package that I provided to you during our last meeting. Before we go any further, I would like to play you another tape that your mother made before she passed. I want to give you fair warning that your mother mentally was still completely lucid, but as you will see in the tape, her physical condition was starting to deteriorate. You mother was beautiful no matter what, and I'm only mentioning her appearance so that it won't upset you when you see her." He put the take in, and handed Josh the control, exiting the room silently.

Josh looked at his sisters and fiancée and asked, "Okay, are we ready for this?"

"As ready as we'll ever be Josh. Just hit the play button and let's get it over with."

Deidre seconded the sentiment and, reaching over for her sister's hand, they connected just as Josh hit the play button.

It just a moment or two for their mother to appear once again, on the screen. This time, she looked pale and tired, but still just as beautiful as she ever was. She smiled into the camera and started to speak.

"Hello Joshua, Maggie and Deidre. It pleases me more than words can convey that you're sitting here today watching this tape because that means you've found my Michelle! Rodney was given very specific instructions and

I'm so incredibly happy that you persevered and following through with my quest. I hope that it wasn't too difficult of a task and most importantly, I hope that you found her not only alive, but well, and happy that you made contact with her. I have no way of knowing if she knew that she was adopted, and pray that it wasn't an unpleasant conversation or meeting for anyone involved." Elizabeth took a brief moment to reflect and gather her thoughts and emotions before she continued.

"Oh how I wish you could tell me what she's like, what she looks like, and if I have grandchildren. Now I know that you and Jena will give me grandchildren soon Joshua, and I'm not giving up hope that you girls won't be too far behind your brother in starting families, but with Michelle being that much older than the three of you, I can only hope and dream that she's been blessed with children. I know that Rodney gave you an envelope to give to Michelle Marie if you ever found her. In it, is sort of an abridged version of everything I have ever wanted to tell her. Now that you've found her and hopefully you will meet her, if you haven't done so already, my attorney will give you something else that I'd like you to give her. As I said with my first envelope, everything is unsealed and you are free to read any or all of the letters, should you choose to. The only secret I ever kept from you kids was about my daughter Michelle, but your father was aware, and actually encouraged me to write letters to her. He offered to help me find her, and encouraged me to not only express my feelings in letters, but also was the first one to buy her a gift for her first birthday, even though she wasn't with me. Your father knew everything and I was an open book with him, from nearly our first date, so again, if you choose to complete this journey for me, know that you are NOT, in any way, betraying your dad!"

Elizabeth looked directly into the camera, and again started to speak. "When your journey comes full circle, and you reunite Michelle with her father, I want you to give Danny a letter for me. I never got a chance to apologize to him for how I acted after we'd given up our daughter, and I want, actually need, him to know that I blame myself for destroying our relationship. While I know now that everything happens for a reason, and without us breaking up, you three wouldn't be here today, I still want him to know how very sorry I am for hurting him and disappointing him. My Danny was a very good man, a man that deserved so much more than what I could offer him. Please tell him, that there hasn't been a day that's gone by that I don't remember and regret what I did to him. Please tell him Deidre, that I sincerely hope that he found love and marriage and was blessed with beautiful children. I want nothing less for him as he deserved all of it. When he joined the service, I never had a chance to speak to him again, and if there is one other thing that I'd like you to tell him, it would be to tell him how very proud of him I am for joining the Air Force and serving our wonderful country. With that said, I honestly don't even know if my Danny is still alive. You see, not long after he joined, there was a helicopter crash and he was on it. Two enlisted died and by then, I had severed all ties with my hometown, and everyone who lived there. I never asked my parents if he'd survived the crash, and they never offered. I always assumed that he'd lived, because I'd never heard otherwise, but part of me thought that I didn't have a right to know, so I never asked. We truly were just kids. I know that now. But despite being kids ourselves, I took the coward's way out and allowed everything in my path to crash and burn so to speak. I hope that Michelle and Danny are able to connect and form a bond that is long overdue. That's enough on that topic. The past needs to stay in the past. Now on to you three."

Despite the chronic pain that Elizabeth couldn't shake, she took another sip of her tea and continued to speak.

"Joshua, I hope by now there's a big old rock of a ring on Jena's finger. And you two better have picked a date too. I have to believe that when I'm up in heaven, I'll still be able to look down at you two and enjoy the day your beautiful Jena becomes your bride. If you don't do it soon, I assure you, I'll come down and kick your ass. I want grandchildren!" she exclaimed, laughing. "All kidding aside Josh, please set a date, and use what I've given you toward your wedding. Money is replaceable but memories are not. Make sure you do it right and however you want because with a little luck, you will only get married once, and Lord knows you'll never do better than our Jena. Jena, if your there and I presume you are, I want you to know that I know you will be a stunning bride, and I couldn't envision anyone more suited to marry my only son. I've loved you as a daughter for as long as I've known you and I wish that I could be there in person when you walk down the aisle. Know that somehow, someway, Josh's dad and I will be right there with you on your big day. And promise me that you'll always love my boy."

Next, she turned her viewpoint as if she knew where her daughter was sitting. Elizabeth looked into the camera again and started to address her second daughter.

"Maggie May, I hope that you've been doing what I asked of you. I know that you probably gave yourself carpal tunnel on that damn computer of yours researching your sister, making sure that she wasn't some convicted felon or worse. I admire your drive and know that you will always protect your little sister and big brother, but I pray that you heeded my advice, and joined a gym or some clubs or anything that will get you out of your office and into the world. You need to start living Maggie and having fun. Loosen up my love and if you've met a man, don't you dare blow him off or keep him at arm's length. I know you guard your heart Mags, have faith in him, and take people for face value. If he's the right one, he won't let you down and with a little luck, you'll be planning a wedding shortly after Joshua." She stopped talking long enough to let her words sink in, knowing that her daughter would be reacting to her proclamation as soon as she heard it.

Not wanting any of her children to feel left out, she addressed her youngest next. "Deidre, I know that you are very busy with your soup kitchen and your other business, but if can ask something of you, it would be to let someone help you. I hope that you also heeded my advice and aren't working as many crazy hours as you were when I was alive. I pray that someone has entered your life that makes you smile and makes you laugh and introduces you to many new experiences. I guess I always expected you to be the one of the three of you, who had a houseful of kids running around. I hope that whoever has captured your heart is the one, and he helps you achieve my dream for you. I know Dee, you don't need anyone to complete you, but honey, sometimes it's not a matter of need but want. I also know Deidre LeeAnn that you don't believe in the conventional sense of the word love, but honey let me tell you, it's the greatest gift anyone can give you. So, if and when someone enters your life and he tells you that he loves you, genuinely loves you just the way you are, flaws and imperfections and all, embrace it and him because he's offering you the world. I know because that's what your daddy did for me. I loved Danny, I truly did; but your father was the one and only one for me. I think that you've found your one and only Dee, and I pray that you realize it before it's too late."

"Now, after this clip ends, Mr. Phelps will be there to answer any questions that you might have. Remember, I want Michelle to meet you all, and spend time with you and I hope that she's receptive to my request. Maybe invite her up to camp as it's a neutral location? I wish I had more to offer you to help you find her father and reunite them, but I don't. I know that his parents are dead and he was an only child. I tried to locate a couple of his friends before I made this tape, but even with Rodney and his partner's assistance, a wonderful young attorney by the name of Garrett, which by the way Maggie, would be perfect for you; I wasn't able to locate them."

Hearing her mother mention Garrett by name caught Maggie off guard. Wanting to disagree and tell her mother that her relationship with Garrett was no big deal, she caught herself starting to argue, and then stopping, remembering that her mother was no longer able to hear her rebuttal. When Elizabeth starting to speak again, she snapped out of it and again focused her attention on the TV monitor.

"In a perfect world, I would be there in person to tell Danny and Michelle exactly what them entering my life meant to me and how it impacted the rest of my days on earth, but we know that I'm not able to be there with you when you meet them both and hopefully bring Danny and his daughter together. When that day arrives, there is a tape I would really like for you to play for them. Again, in a perfect world, you would invite them both to our camp and have them meet there for the first time. You all know how much our family camp meant to me and all of the wonderful memories that we've created there. I don't know why I think it, but I do; I just have a feeling that Danny and Michelle would appreciate the coziness that our lake home offers. And I can't think of a better place for you three to meet your sister," she smiled, as if thinking about the infant she'd loved so long ago.

"Anyways," she continued, after collecting her thoughts, "if the opportunity presents itself, I've already given you the envelopes to give to Michelle, and Rodney has two other items that I've instructed him to hand over to you once you've accomplished your mission. The main thing that I want you to take away from this meeting with Mr. Phelps today, is that I'm not trying to gain another child, for Michelle will never be mine again. I lost the privledge the day I signed the damn papers giving her up. And I'm not trying to rekindle a long-lost love; I'm simply trying to make up for the past and the poor decisions I made back then. They most likely mean nothing to the two people most affected but I won't rest up here in heaven until I know that they both realize how sorry I am for my rash decisions. I know I've said it before, but I'll say it again; I wasn't given a choice really. Everyone involved said that it was the best thing for the baby, and that is why I gave her up. But truth be told, I gave her up because I was terrified of being a mother at eighteen and that selfishness and guilt is something that has haunted me every day of my life since."

Elizabeth looked down at her folded hands, trying to keep her composure. It took her a moment, but then she looked into the camera lenses one last time.

"I think that's enough of me wallowing in my self-pity. Make sure you give them both a chance guys. And tell them I never stopped loving either one of them and I'm so incredibly happy that they've found one another. Joshua, Maggie, Deidre; you three are my world, and I've never been prouder of you. I love you more than you'll ever realize. Good bye for now my loves."

And with that, the TV screen went black and their mother was gone, yet again.

"Jesus I hate it when she does that!" Maggie exclaimed, frustrated, and slightly pissed off.

"I know Mags," Deidre said, leaning in and grabbing her hand, "I miss her too. But she asked us to find her daughter, and we did. And now we're going to finish mom's journey for her. I agree with mom, we meet our half sister on neutral territory and I can't think of a better place than camp, can you?" she asked, already knowing the answer.

"I agree with Dee," Josh interjected. Why don't you shoot Samantha a text, email or give her a call when you get home and invite her up to camp for the weekend or even just for the day on Saturday? It's after the holidays and since she's a teacher, it won't interfere with her job at all."

"Absolutely," Deidre agreed, all over the idea of finally meeting her sister in person. "I'll ask her what type of food she likes and make sure we have everything to make her feel comfortable. I'll be in charge of the dessert, and Mags, you can plan the dinner, and Josh, I'll have you pick up whatever she drinks, be it beer, wine, or whatever, okay?"

"Well aren't you little miss party planner?" her sister teased. "Yeah, I'll whip something up but find out if our half sis has any allergies or not please. I'd hate to kill her the first day we meet her," she laughed.

"Very funny Mags! Oh my God, I hope she can make it! We will actually get to meet our sister in less than a week, this is so cool!" Deidre exclaimed as their mother's attorney reentered the room.

"It looks like you finished the tape," he smiled. "Your mother was always full of surprises and I'm sure this whole thing has been quite a shock to you. She and I spoke at length about her daughter and the possibility of you someday finding her and meeting her. Let me tell you how proud I am of the three of you. Not only did you tackle what I'm sure was no easy task, with dignity and grace, but you set any personal feelings aside in order to fulfill your mother's dying wish. Jarod and Liz would be very proud of you." He made his way to the table and sat down next to Elizabeth's children. He didn't want to stand above them, but be eye level with them.

"Now that you've found Michelle Marie, have you given any thought as to how you're going to approach meeting her for the first time? I assume that you're going to do it as a group," he offered.

Joshua spoke for his sisters. "Yes, actually, we're going to invite her up to camp for the day or possibly weekend. We'll ask her tonight and if she's interested, we'll have her come up this coming weekend and go from there. It's after Christmas and if she's free, we'll complete our mother's request."

"Well I think that's absolutely terrific news," he exclaimed! "Please touch base with me after the holidays and after you've met with Michelle. I have another packet to give you that your mother had me hold until the time that you connected with her. It comes with instructions and is very self-explanatory. I know with the holidays around the corner, you must be very busy so I won't keep you any longer."

He stood and extended his hand. Josh, Maggie and Deidre stood and shook his hand, thanking him for everything. Just as they turned to leave, they were greeted by an older woman carrying three large manila envelopes. Maggie stepped forward, taking the envelopes out of the woman's arms, surprised at the weight of them.

They made their way outside, and stopped next to Maggie Jeep.

"Okay, so we're all in agreement, I'll call Samantha as soon as I get home and invite her up to camp this weekend?" she asked, excitedly?

"Sounds good," Joshua offered, taking his fiancée's hand. "Call us afterwards and let us know how it went and if she will be joining us."

"Will do."

"Give me a head's up Dee so that I can run to the store this evening."

"Sounds good! Oh, and Maggie, lets bring our snowshoes and get some snowshoeing in before she arrives," she said, as she approached her car.

"Alright, call me later," Maggie said, as she opened her Jeep door and got in.

Everyone left in different directions, with Deidre racing to get home in order to start the next chapter with her new sister.

~Chapter 44~

Deidre read her sister's letter one more time, staring at the cell number, took a couple breaths to relax, and dialed her sister's number for the first time. She listened as it rang three times and just when she thought it would go to voicemail, she heard someone answer.

"Hello."

Shocked by the voice emitting from her cell phone, she nearly dropped it from her hand. It took her a second to realize that the voice on the other end wasn't coming from her mother, but from her sister, her mother's first born.

Hearing no one respond, Samantha spoke again, exaggerating the syllables. "Hello?"

Deidre snapped back to the here and now. "Um, is this Samantha? This is Deidre."

Controlling the tears that had welled up in her eyes, and forcing the lump from her throat, Samantha took a second to respond.

"Hi."

Knowing she was speaking with her sister, Deidre felt her heart nearly burst. "Hi."

"Before I say anything to hooky or ridiculous sounding," Samantha started, can I simply tell you, that you picking up the phone and calling me has just made my Christmas!" She paused just a second and added, "Oh boy, even that sounded hooky! I swear I'm not a nut job! I guess I've just always dreamed of this moment and I can't believe that I'm actually speaking with someone who shares my blood!"

Deidre couldn't control her emotions any longer. "Sam, you sound exactly like our mother. If someone didn't know she was dead, and you spoke to them, they'd mistake you for our mom," she responded, in between sobs.

Shocked at what her sister was saying, she wasn't sure how she felt. "Really?"

"Yes REALLY! It's like hearing mom's voice, and my heart saying it's mom, but my brain reminding me that she's gone. Anyways, hi," she repeated again. "It's really nice to hear your voice and put it with the face from your picture. You look a lot like our mom as well, and I'm, actually all three of us are really glad that you reached out to us, and as we've said via email, we're really excited to get to know you."

"Thank you. The feeling is likewise. I have to admit, I didn't know what to think or how I felt until it actually happened. I guess I've always known that I was adopted and I love my brother and my parents to pieces, so I never allowed myself to speculate what it would be like if and when I ever discovered who my biological parents were. And then bam, I got the hit on Ancestry and here we are, talking on the phone. It's sort of surreal you know?"

"Oh, trust me, I know," Deidre responded. "We stalked you on Facebook and other social media you know. I just feel that we need to confess that. With mom and dad gone, and now it's just the three of us, I guess you could say that we are all very territorial of one another and always looking out for each other. So, I have to admit, we checked you out and that's what took a little time before we responded to your email."

Laughing on the other end, Samantha responded. "I had my brother put me in contact with a buddy of his to check you out too! He works with a police department locally, so I had him run you guys as well! Guess it's a good thing that we're all upstanding citizens," she laughed.

"Good thing!" Deidre agreed, laughing as well. "That leads me to the reason I'm calling Sam, I mean Samantha. We realize that Christmas is just a few days away and with you having children, we're sure that it's a hectic time; but quite frankly, we're dying to meet you as soon as possible, and well, we were wondering if you would like to possibly get together next weekend sometime so we could all meet? We could meet you anywhere neutral, or, we were hoping that maybe you'd be interested in meeting us at our mother's camp in Old Forge? If that's too far from your home, we could meet you anywhere, we just thought that maybe you'd like to see where she spent a lot of her time growing up, and we could show you pictures of what she looked like, and it's a place where we could talk without interruptions. But if you'd rather meet in a public place, that's fine too," she quickly added.

"No, Old Forge would be fun," Samantha replied, almost immediately without thinking it through. "I've brought my kids to Enchanted Forest every summer since they were old enough to walk, but have never ventured up that way in the wintertime and I think it would be fun. If my mom will watch my kids, which I'm sure she will, I would definitely like to meet all of you at your mom's camp on Saturday. What can I bring?" she offered.

"Bring yourself, and any questions that you have," Deidre said, excitedly.

They talked for another half hour, asking each other all sorts of questions, laughing, occasionally crying and joking as if long lost friends. Deidre gave her the address and promised to email her directions. They wished each other Merry Christmas, with both knowing they would be speaking to each other on the 25th, with neither wanting to conclude the call but both knowing they had to. They said their good byes and as they hung up, each was again on the phone, with Deidre phoning Maggie, and Samantha phoning her brother.

Answering on the first ring, her brother picked up.

"Hi Sam."

"Hey. You free on Saturday?"

"Yeah probably. Why? What's up?" He could tell by her tone, that something was wrong or going on.

"I want you to come on a road trip with me Saturday. I really need you with me for moral support in case it doesn't go well," she added, nearly pleading.

"You know I will. What's going on Saturday Sam and what are we doing?" he asked, starting to get concerned.

"Well, it seems, I was just invited up to my sister's camp in Old Forge to meet my two half sisters and brother this coming Saturday. Can you believe it G, I'm finally going to meet my biological family for the first time? I'm shocked, thrilled, and terrified all at the same time. What if they don't like me?" she asked in a near whisper.

Wishing he could go through his phone and give his sister a hug, he answered honestly.

"Sam, what is there not to love? You're a good person, a kind soul and have a heart of gold. You're a great mother to your kids and work hard for everything you've got. You have a Master's degree, speak three languages and volunteer for more places than I can count. Anyone who doesn't meet you and love you instantly, is an idiot!"

"Thanks G, but you're my brother so you have to say that," she kidded, but admitted to herself that she felt better already. "It'll just be awkward you know, entering their territory so to speak. I'm definitely outnumbered if you don't come along and even the odds a little bit."

"Sure, I'll tag along and with a little luck, maybe we'll have time to swing by a friend of mine's place afterwards. I'd really like you to meet her Sam. She's pretty amazing."

"You've got it bad little brother," she teased. "And I'm glad. It's about time you opened yourself up to loving someone again. I know how badly that bitch Nicole hurt you and I'm really glad that you've found love again."

"Wow, hold on there a minute sis. I never said anything about falling in love, so cool your jets a minute. Better yet, let's change the subject off of my love life and tell me more about your sisters and brother."

"Deal. But I'm going to grill you after I meet her Saturday!" They changed the subject from his love life to her newly found siblings and spent the next half hour talking about everything she'd learned in their conversations so far. When she finally hung up with him, she felt less anxious, and more excited than ever to meet her sisters and brother in person. She poured herself a glass of wine and as she started a quick text to Deidre to confirm that she'd definitely join them on Saturday, baring any child related disasters, her children came barreling in from their indoor soccer practice, followed by her mother.

"Hi guys," she greeted her children warmly. "Anyone ready for taco's?" she asked, already knowing the answer. She saw their faces light up immediately and cut them off before they could make their way toward the table.

"Don't even think about it, guys. Go wash up so I can speak with grandma a minute. Go on, hurry up because everything is still warm!"

She turned toward her mother and smiled. "Thanks mom. As always, I really appreciate you helping me out." When she stalled, just a little, her mother spoke up.

"What happened Sam? What is it?"

She took a deep breath and told her mother the truth. "Mom, I spoke on the phone with my biological half sister just a few minutes ago. I actually heard her voice and we talked like we were long lost friends. How can that be possible?" she asked, feeling herself tear up again.

"Oh honey, you and she share blood, so of course you're going to be connected. Just because you and your sisters weren't raised in the same house doesn't change the fact that you will always have a bond that time nor circumstance couldn't change. So, tell me all about your conversation with her? Which sister were you on the phone with, Deidre or Maggie?" she asked, genuinely happy for her daughter. When she'd originally heard that they'd connected through Ancestry, she was a little envious and worried that somehow finding her blood relatives would negate their relationship, but her daughter very quickly squashed any fears that she'd been having. Samantha had told her about every email and text that she'd sent or received from her siblings and because of it, felt that she somehow was forming a bond with them as well.

Samantha told her quickly about their invitation to meet them in person on Saturday after the holiday and before she could even ask the question, her mother was already completing her thoughts.

"I'll come over here and stay with the kids. Pack an overnight bag because my guess is, you're all going to get along so fabulously that they'll want you to spend the night. Did you tell your brother about your great news yet?" she asked.

"Actually yes. I got nervous and asked G to come with me."

As soon as Samantha had started telling her about the invite, somehow, she'd known that her son would tag along with his only sister.

"Oh, that's a splendid idea Sam!" she acknowledged. Then he can hopefully surprise that young lady he's so hooked on, and stop in and see her as well. I think your brother's in love with her, despite denying it each and every time I try to pry," she laughed. Just as she was about to elaborate, two very loud and hungry kids raced into the room, making their way towards the chips and tacos that were waiting for them.

After helping them fill their plates, she left her kids inhaling their dinner while sitting at the breakfast bar, and signaled her mother into the living room.

She waited until they were out of earshot of her children, and then reached for her mother's hand. Turning to face her directly, she smiled.

"I'm so nervous mom. I'm excited as hell, but terrified as well. What if I'm not what they expect or they're not what I expect? I mean I know they're good people, and not scumbags, because we stalked them online and had G's friend run a background check on Joshua and his sisters, and everything came back spotless. They're upstanding citizens, and while I know I'm totally safe heading up there alone, Garrett said he'd come with me."

"Great. So, what time would you like me to come over to your house on Christmas Eve? Are we still planning on attending 7 o'clock mass?"

"Yes, G said that he invited his girlfriend over but that she will be up north with her family so he'll join us for mass as well." She didn't want to ask, but knew that she needed to.

"Have you heard from Daddy? Are he and Gianna still living in Cancun? I know that he's been gone a long-time mom, but the kids still ask if grandpa is ever going to come and see them again. They sometime ask if dad is living down in Mexico with their dad, and I try really hard not to tell them that their dad's hopefully living in hell right about now."

Her mother stifled a laugh. "Samantha Marie, that's a terrible thing to say," she laughed. "Hopefully they're there together, both getting a permanent sunburn," she added, no longer resentful or bitter, simply noncaring.

She hugged her mom before they rejoined her children and the ciaos at her dinner table. When they joined her children, they were practically inhaling their tacos, while telling their grandmother about their upcoming soccer tournament. The four of them ate, and laughed as Samantha's children told their grandmother about all of their Christmas wishes, and their plans for the holiday break. Their grandmother told them that she would be spending Christmas eve staying up all night to catch Santa Claus when he arrived, which was received with skepticism and laughter. Grandma Brown also went on to tell her grandchildren that if it was alright with them, she wanted to sent their mom and uncle on a mission after Christmas which might require them to stay overnight, but that she would be staying with them and had all sorts of exciting adventures planned. She told them of a new snowtubing park that had just opened and that she'd like to bring them to and go tubing with them. Her grandson laughed and told his grandmother she was "too old" to go snowtubing to which she informed him "game on." Everyone laughed and continued eating the rest of the tacos.

Samantha's mother left shortly after lunch was completed and her grandkids took off to the basement to play video games.

"Alright then, I'll get going. Christmas is right around the corner and I have a few last-minute things to do. And Samantha, they're going to love you and I'm so very happy that you are going to discover more about your heritage. I know that I can't speak for your father, but as your mother I want and need you to know that I'm sorry that your birthmother has passed away and that you'll never get a chance to meet her in person. If she were still alive, I would have wanted the opportunity to thank her in person for giving me the most precious gift I have ever received. You and G have no idea how much you were wanted and how happy we were the day that we brought you home. You made our house a home and becoming your mother was one of the happiest days of my life. I don't know your birth mom's circumstances, and maybe your sisters and brother will be able to enlighten you; but I know that I will be forever in her debt for her selfless act." She smiled and added, "I'll see you and the kids at the house before mass. And before I forget, when you meet the young lady who's captured your brother's heart, you must fill me in on what she's like. He's extremely secretive and closed mouthed about her; hasn't even provided me with her name," she laughed. "Talk to you tomorrow Sam; love you." And with that, her mother breezed out the door in her usual hurried manner.

Samantha took just a moment to think about what her mother had said. She'd been right as always; she was a good person and there would be no reason for her siblings to dislike her. Besides, if it didn't go well, then she and her brother could thank them for meeting her, say their goodbyes and then visit one of the many pubs in the area and drink away her sorrows, she chuckled.

Now feeling better about the entire situation, she set about picking up the remnants of their meal, and continue on with the day.

~Chapter 45~

Deidre called her siblings as soon as she hung up with Samantha and told them about her conversation, and that she'd accepted their invitation to come up on the Saturday following Christmas, for the day. She told them that their newly discovered sister sounded exactly like their mother on the phone and that it had kind of freaked her out initially and then she found it comforting to listen to her sister talk. She went on to say that Samantha had agreed to join them at their mom's camp and that she'd drink and eat anything they had and didn't have any allergies. Deidre explained that Samantha wasn't familiar with town and that she said that she'd email her the directions. Before they hung up, all three had finalized who was bringing what and that they'd meet up at camp sometime during the day on the 24th. After she'd answered all of Maggie's and Josh's questions about their sister, she hung up, grabbed her purse, and took off for the mall, to find a Christmas present for her new family member. Unbeknownst to her, while she was driving, her sister and her future sister-in-law were shopping online, doing the same thing. None of them knew her style, but each of them wanted to give her some sort of gift, welcoming her into their family.

Samantha called her brother as soon as she'd hung up with Deidre, to update him. After that, she went downstairs to join her children who were focused on nothing other than beating one another on the game they were presently playing. She studied them silently, wondering how she'd been lucky enough to be blessed with two amazing kids. They were her rocks, the thing that kept her grounded when life seemed to get too overwhelming. Since her husband had skipped out on she and her children's lives, she'd been forced to become both their mother and father, mentor and disciplinarian, and their main role model. Without ever asking, both her brother and mother had stepped up and ingratiated themselves into helping her raise her children. She could have probably managed on her own, but knew that with their support, she would always have someone to count on to help her out in a pinch if she ever needed it. As she watched her children silently, she hoped that her brother would someday have a family of his own, and with a little luck, be blessed with children as wonderful as hers.

Her mind drifted from her children to her own childhood, and wondered what her sibling's lives had been like. She added that to the list of questions she had already thought of and though she didn't want to pry, knew that once she was face to face with them, she'd probably have more questions. She wondered what that first moment would be like, what they'd be like and how she and they would react upon first meeting. Though she certainly wasn't an emotional type person, she secretly hoped that she would be able to keep her emotions in check when the moment came that they were reunited. Oh well, she thought to herself, it is what it is and in less than five days, all of her answers would be answered. Satisfied with that idea, she squeezed in between her children and watched them battle it out in their video game. With her arms around both of her kids, she settled in and thought that her life couldn't possibly get any better.

~Chapter 46~

Joshua, Maggie and Deidre, along with their pets, all arrived at camp within minutes of one another. While his sisters were putting all of the groceries for their holiday week in the pantry and refrigerator, Joshua asked Jena to come back outside with him. She wasn't quite sure what was going on, but followed him anyway. He handed her a huge tote bag and plastic bin, and originally thought that she wouldn't be able to carry them until she took them into her arms and realized they had virtually no weight to them at all.

"What's in them Josh? Feels like I'm carrying empty containers."

"You'll see," he said as he lifted a huge plastic bin from the back of his SUV. She followed him in, and as they passed the kitchen, caught both of his sister's attention.

"What've got there Josh?" Deidre asked, as she took a sip of wine.

"Just something to make it a little more festive in here. Once we get everything put away, I'll show you."

"Probably all of our Christmas presents that he didn't get around to wrapping Dee. Let's finish putting all of this crap away and then we'll find out."

"You wish Mags! I didn't realize we were exchanging presents this year since we did all the work up here at camp, I thought that that was our gift to one another," he said so sincerely that he sounded totally believable. He saw the immediate frown come over his kid sister's face and quickly added, "Just kidding Deidre. Of course, I bought you a thing or two."

She put down the bottled water in her hands and raced over to her brother, pulling him into a bear hug. "Thanks Josh! I've been having a really hard time with getting into the holiday spirit this year because, well, you know. And the thought of not exchanging presents would have kind of put me over the edge. I got you something too big brother. Love you."

"Love you more Dee," he said, as Maggie approached and was pulled into a family group hug. Jena grabbed her phone and took a couple candid shots before she too, was pulled into the bear hug.

They finished unpacking and after everyone was settled with their respective drinks, Josh addressed Jena and his sisters.

"Now before I tell you what I have in those bins, I need you three to promise me that you'll keep it together and not ball on me," he teased. "It kind of sucks that mom's not with us this year and I for one, have been dreading this holiday the most since we all know how much mom loved Christmas. With that said, we can't have mom here, but," he said, as he lifted the lid off the first tote bag, "I thought that we could have her memory come alive if we decorated with her tree and ornaments."

Jena gasped at the thoughtfulness, and as requested, held back the tears threatening to form. Deidre and Maggie remained silent, absorbing the fact that their brother had taken the initiative and time to sort through their mother's ornaments and haul them all the way up to Inlet. They knew that it wouldn't be the same as it was in years past, when the four of them had spent the holiday nestled in the mountains. Nothing would ever be the same again now that their mother was no longer there, but thanks to

Josh's thoughtfulness, she would be there in spirit. Each had their favorite ornaments and as they gazed into the open container, each had memories of Christmas past come flooding back. Maggie was the first to speak.

"No time like the present. Let's put the tree up and decorate it right now!" she said. "Grab Josh a beer Dee, and let's get this tree up and decorated for mom."

"Absolutely!" Deidre seconded, as she opened the frig, and pulled out one of her brother's favorite beers. "Jena, you need more wine," she asked, as she closed the door and turned toward her brother.

"Nope, I'm good Dee but thanks."

Once everyone joined him in the living room, he started to lift the pieces of the tree out from the bin. Their mother had always loved the smell of a real tree, but since she was deathly allergic to most species of trees, they'd always had artificial ones, and her children had followed suit. Each sibling took part in putting the tree together, almost as if they each needed to do it together. Once it was completely assembled, they started with the lights, and then the honorary silver tinsel that their mother had always insisted needed to be on the tree. While they were starting the decoration process, Jena had turned the stereo on and found a Christmas station, which further put everyone in the holiday spirit. They shared their favorite holiday stories as they put ornament after ornament on the huge blue spruce tree, and when nearly finished, Joshua lifted the angel from the bottom of the tote bag. As he turned to hand it to Maggie to top the tree, their mother's favorite holiday song, Silver Bells started to play on the radio. Each froze for just a moment, waiting to hear their mother start singing her favorite song. Maggie was the first to start, followed by Deidre, with Joshua and Jena joining in. They lifted their mother's angel, placing her on top of the tree, as they sang along with the chorus, knowing that their mother was singing along with them up in heaven.

Once it was lit, everyone stood back, admiring their handywork. There would be no sad tears tonight, only warm, fond memories. Their mother would never have wanted them to dwell in sadness, but embrace the season with love and excitement, the way she did each year, even after losing their father suddenly. If she'd been able to find joy in the season, even that first Christmas without their dad, then they would to.

"Oh guys," Deidre started. "It looks just like mom had hers decorated every year. She would be so excited to see her tree here, decorated like this. I love it!"

"I'd like to believe that she can see it up in heaven and I think dad is right there with her smiling down at us. I honestly believe that."

"You think so Mags?"

"Yeah Dee, I do. And I think that mom is going to be right here with us on Saturday when we meet Michelle for the first time. If I know our mother as well as I do, then there is nothing in heaven or here on earth, that will prevent her for participating in our reunion with her daughter."

"I agree Mags. Why don't we light a fire and relax a little bit. I for one, could use another drink," Josh said, already heading towards the kitchen. While he refilled his sister's glasses, Maggie and Jena set about starting the fire, which was already set up with paper and kindling. It only took a moment or two for it to ignite and spring to life. They each settled into their favorite spots on the couch and chairs next to it and reminisced. The music played softly in the background, and with the fireplace crackling and its' flames seeming to dance to the rhythm, they sat silently, each caught up in their own thoughts.

"I think I'm going to go to midnight mass," Deidre stated. "Anyone want to join me?"

Their mother had always loved to attend midnight mass, and had dragged her children out on more than one occasion during their teenage years to attend it with her. They'd always given her a hard time, but each had actually enjoyed bundling up and heading out in the black of night to attend services. They'd always see many of their friends at the same mass, and despite being a religious requirement, to them, it was about seeing their friends and celebrating the start of the holiday with their best friends present. After the conclusion of the service, their parents would always allow the kids to sit together while the adults enjoyed the refreshments that the parish provided. It had become tradition and although they wouldn't be attending their childhood parish, Josh knew that Deidre was on to something.

"I'll come with you Dee. I think mom would like that."

"Oh shit, you guilted me into it. I'll come," Maggie added. "But just because we're going to church doesn't mean that I'm not going to have another glass or two of this amazing wine you brought up Jena."

"God won't care Mags," Jena offered. "It's from a new winery in the Finger Lakes, and we love it, and if you approve, then it's the wine we'll serve at our wedding reception."

"Yes, Jena, definitely have this wine. It's fabulous!" Deidre offered. "Oh, do tell us what plans you've come up with so far for the wedding."

Jena, took her fiancée's hand and smiled. "Well, you already know you're both in it, and you know the date and location is right here at your lake house, but, what we haven't told you yet, is that we just booked our honeymoon!" Jena exclaimed, unable to hold her enthusiasm any longer.

"Oh my God Jena! Where did you guys decide to go? I know you were tossing around several places. Which destination did you finally choose?" Maggie asked, genuinely curious to know.

"Well, in honor of mom and her heritage, we chose Ireland!" Josh exclaimed.

"Oh, that's so awesome guys," Deidre responded. "I'm so happy for you, and Ireland in the summertime should be lovely! I'm so jealous and envious of you both, but so incredibly happy for you as well," she added, taking her hand and blowing a kiss to her brother from the chair she was curled up in.

"Thanks. Dee, where would you go, if given the opportunity to see any part of the world. If you were picking a honeymoon destination, where would you want to go?" he asked his sister. "Where would you go Mags?" he asked his other sister so she would feel left out.

Deidre spoke first. "A good friend of mine told me about his travels in Italy, and I think I'd like to experience it with my own eyes. His description made me visualize it in my mind and I think I'd like to see the places that he made come alive in my mind."

"And would this friend go by the name of Griffin by any chance?" Joshua asked, already knowing the answer.

"Possibly," she admitted, feeling herself blush. "He described the cities of Italy and with each description, I swore that I was right there walking the cobblestone streets with him."

"Well Deidre, maybe that's where he'll bring you someday. And if my hunch is correct, and he feels the same way about you that you feel about him, then I bet you two will be planning your honeymoon before you know it," Jena offered, smiling.

"What?" Deidre responded, genuinely confused. "Oh no, Griff and I aren't a couple. We're just two people enjoying each other's company, without any formal type of commitment."

Before her brother or sister could respond, Jena spoke up. "Answer me this, are you seeing anyone else?" she asked. "Is Griffin seeing anyone else besides you? Do you speak to him everyday and spend majority of your evenings or nights with him? And when he's not with you, do you find yourself thinking about him? Do you find yourself thinking about what you and he are going to be doing a day from now, a week from now or sometime in the future?" she asked gently.

Deidre remained silent, taking another sip of her wine, pretending she was pondering the questions, when she already knew the answer was yes to each and every one of them.

"Guilty," she replied, looking down at her wine glass. "But that doesn't mean anything. We're just two people enjoying spending time together, that's all. He wasn't looking for anything, and neither was I," she said, trying to convince both her siblings and herself.

"Deidre," Jena replied. "It means that somewhere along the way, when you weren't looking for it, you found love.

You and Griffin are perfect for one another and that's what's so wonderful about love; it happened when neither of you were looking for it, or expecting it."

"I'm not sure what it is Jena, but I know that he's an amazing man and one I would like to keep in my life. As to how he feels about me, I don't know. We've never talked about the future; we're just enjoying the here and now. And when we're all together in the same room, please don't mention this conversation because I'd die of humiliation if he isn't thinking along the same lines that you are."

Maggie remained silent. She'd taken the questions that their future sister in law had thrown at Deidre and answered them herself, shocked to realize that her answers were all Yes as well. How had it happened, she thought to herself? At what point had she stepped over the edge and fallen for Garrett? Sure, they'd spent several fun evenings and occasional nights together, but they hadn't been on more than two dozen actual dates. She felt herself growing angry because she'd never seen it coming, and here she was, head over heels in love with a goofy blonde attorney!

"Son of a bitch," she heard herself say under her breath. Her comment didn't go unheard by her future sister in law, who said nothing but smiled to herself.

"I'm sorry Maggie, I didn't hear you," she said innocently. "Where would you go if given the opportunity to travel anywhere?"

Still in shock over the revelation that she might very well be in love with Garrett, despite promising herself that she'd never fall again, she snapped at Jena.

"I have no damn clue! Besides, marriage and honeymoons aren't part of my grand plan. It's for people like you and Josh, and dreamers like Dee, but not something I've ever wasted my time thinking about." Standing, she excused herself, stating that she wanted to head upstairs to make her bed before mass and figure out something warm to wear, that would presentable for the church services, they'd be attending later that night. Everyone knew that her bed was still made from the last time they'd been up, but no one stopped her from leaving, knowing she needed to walk off her mad.

Deidre, Josh and Jena talked about the reality of meeting their sister in just a few days, with everyone offering differing opinions as to what they hoped to accomplish with the meeting. Deidre was the most open about wanting to get to know her new sister, while Joshua admitted that he was curious to learn about her upbringing and what her childhood was like. Despite the fact that Maggie was still sulking up in her room, they all were very well aware of how she felt about meeting their mother's first born. She had stated from day one that she was willing to meet Samantha, out of duty, but really had no interest in establishing any type of relationship with her. Joshua and Deidre respected her opinion of the situation and her decision, but secretly knew that once they met Samantha, their sister might change her mind and welcome her into their family.

~Chapter 47~

"Holy crap! When did you get here and how did you manage to get time off when you were knee deep in that huge project for NASA?" Lee exclaimed, as he embraced his eldest son. "I can't believe it!" Turning toward Griffin, he smiled, "And you jackass you; you knew all about this didn't you?" he accused, grinning ear to ear. "Should have known only you two could pull off a surprise like this! I can not believe that the three of us are going to be able to spend the holidays together! This is the best Christmas ever," he said, tears forming in his eyes. "Now if you could somehow get your mother to appear, it would be a Christmas miracle," he said, jesting with a little bit of truth mixed in.

"Dad, you know that's not going to happen," Logan replied. "Mom's doing her thing back in England. Just because she's not here with us physically, you and I know that emotionally, she'll always be connected to us. She just couldn't continue living here in the states.," he added. "Do you still speak with her often," he asked gently. It took Lee just a brief moment to answer. "Yes, your mother and I speak at least every other day. She always ends our conversations with the fact that she's so incredibly proud of the two of you. She still loves us you know," he said, trying to reassure both his sons, and himself. "It's unconventional to say the least, but we're still more of a family than many people who live under the same roof. And your mother knows that if ever she needs us, we'd all jump over the pond to her rescue in a heartbeat."

"That she does dad," Logan answered. "That she does." Changing gears, he stood back, looking at his father and brother. "You two both look awesome. And if I didn't know better, I'd swear there was something different in you Grif. Spill it!"

"He's in love," their father answered, nonchalantly. "Let's grab a few beers and I'll let him tell you all about the young lady."

"Really now? Well this trip just got interesting," he teased, punching his younger brother in the arm.

"Um, excuse me… Anyone notice I'm still in the room and can speak for myself!"

"He took her flying Logan; twice," was their father's only response, as he stuck his head in the refrigerator, coming up with beers in hand.

"Holy shit, baby brother is in love!"

"Shut the hell up, both of you," Griffin replied, laughing, as the three O'Malley's made their way into their father's living room and caught up.

~Chapter 48~

Christmas Day proved to be the warmest day of December, with temperatures unseasonably warm in the mountains. Joshua, Jena, Maggie and Deidre spent the day at camp, opening presents, reminiscing, laughing and crying as they remembered Christmas's from years past, spent in their grandparents, which was now their cabin. Their mother had always loved the holidays and each knew, in their own way, that they'd made their mother proud by enjoying the day with each other, in the home that her family had built and cherished. They'd feasted on another one of Maggie's over the top meals, with each heading to bed early partly due to their food comas. In the days following the holiday, each of Elizabeth's children had allowed themselves to unwind, enjoy the snow and each other's company.

While Joshua, Maggie and Deidre were nestled in at camp, Lee, Logan and Griffin were busy catching up, and sharing a long overdue Christmas together. Despite having several jobs lined up and in progress, both Lee and Griffin allowed their crew to work without them for the few days that Logan was in town. He'd explained to his father that he couldn't manage to get away for an entire week and needed to catch the redeye out of Syracuse Sunday night, but that they'd make the most the five days that they had. Christmas Day came and went, with the three of them traveling to Oneida Lake to do a little ice fishing on the 26th, followed by a quick trip to Lake Placid on the 27th to climb a few high peaks. Knowing that Logan needed to fly out on Sunday, all had agreed that they'd return to Rome sometime on Saturday following their hiking adventure, in order for Logan to spend his last day in town relaxing on Sunday. The weather proved to be cooperative with each day brighter and warmer than the next. Logan commented on how built up Lake Placid had become, with his brother agreeing. They enjoyed burgers and beers at Big Slide Brewery before retiring for the night. It had been a whirlwind five days but worth every moment. Logan missed his family, and wished that he lived in New York or at least closer to his father and brother, but with his job, it just wasn't a possibility. For now, they made it work, and for that, he was forever grateful.

His brother eventually opened up about the young woman who he'd been seeing. Still not convinced that what he felt for Deidre would constitute love, Griffin scoffed at the idea when his brother told him that he had it bad. Griffin tried to divert the topic of conversation from his love life to his brother's life in Florida, to no avail. They retired for the night in their hotel room in Lake Placid, with Lee grateful for the time he'd spent with his two sons. Lee heard Logan softly snoring and Griffin's breathing slow as he lay awake in his bed next to theirs. He reflected on the last few days that they'd spent together, laughing, having a few beers, hiking and sightseeing together, and realized that he'd missed this type of family time. When their family had been whole, the four of them were always off on some type of adventure, whether while living here in the states or when they'd lived abroad. His wife had always been one of the guys, able to keep up with them, despite the grueling conditions that they sometimes inadvertently got into. He'd truly loved her and the family that they'd made, and though bitter and angry when she'd first returned to London, he'd moved past the pain and disappointment, understanding that she'd never adjusted to life not only here in the states, but also as a mom. He didn't begrudge her, nor condemn her, for he knew that she'd truly tried; but neither life had been what she'd wanted and knew that everyone involved was ultimately better off with her physically out of the picture. As he glanced over at his two sleeping sons, he knew that he'd done the best he could raising them alone, and when he thought of their accomplishments, realized that he'd done something right along the way. Both had great degrees and were using those degrees doing something they both loved. As he drifted off, his mind relaxed and went back to another time, when everything in life felt right.

~Chapter 49~

Deidre was the first to wake Saturday morning. In her anticipation of meeting her new sister for the first time, she got up and showered before turning her phone over and seeing the text from Griffin. Her heart swelled seeing his simple note wishing her luck meeting her sister, and giving her reassurance that Samantha was bound to "love" her like anyone who met her would. She re-read the simple text another time and thought about calling him but knew that he was still in Lake Placid with his father and brother, and didn't want to disturb him. And then it hit her, and she responded as fast as her fingers could type. She desperately wanted to meet his brother, and since he had told her the evening before that Logan was only in town until Sunday, she knew that it would have to be today or never. She also deep down knew that she wanted to introduce Griffin and his family to the rest of her family and with a little luck, to her half sister as well, so she texted quickly and hit send before she could change her mind.

"Good Morning Grif. Please stop with your father and brother on your way back through Old Forge. I would like to show off your amazing handiwork to your brother, and also have you meet my sister. It would mean a lot to me and somehow, though I can't explain it, I really need you to be here with me today, even if only for a brief visit. Please don't let me down; I need you. Thank you. Love Dee."

As soon as she'd hit the send button, it dawned on her that she'd signed it "love". She'd never done that before and felt herself starting to shake, ever so slightly at the thought that she might really, actually, be in love with the man. She was terrified of his response, so she tucked her phone in her back pocket, and went about her morning, making a huge breakfast for her family.

Griffin saw her message as soon as his phone pinged. He read it and didn't know what to make of it until he read her last two words, Love Dee. She had just basically told him in print that not only did she love him, but that it was important to her that he meet her sister, and she his brother; and he wasn't sure how, but knew that he'd make it happen later that afternoon. And since they'd come up in his truck, he'd be driving and would take a little detour to her cabin in the woods on their way home.

While Deidre was knee deep in making a massive omelet for her family, Samantha was pacing around her own kitchen, doubting her decision to drive to Old Forge. While her mother was frantically trying to reassure her and keep her calm, it wasn't until her brother showed up, that she completely panicked.

"G, I'm sorry for dragging you out on a Saturday. I've been thinking about it, and it wasn't fair that I sort of steamrolled you into joining me in the mountains. I know that your free time is precious so you don't have to come if you don't want to."

"We're going Sam, period. You've got an opportunity to meet your blood sisters and brother, and that's a gift and you're not backing out. You're going and I'm going with you, so end of discussion," he said smiling.

She'd needed the kick in the pants. Smiling, she walked up to her brother, hugging him tightly. "It's going to be alright, right?" she whispered.

"Sam, they're going to love you. I promise."

"Thanks."

Marla stood silently watching the exchange between her son and daughter. Even though his job required him to be hardnosed, bordering on cutthroat, the boy she'd raised had always been one to provide comfort when she or his sister had needed it. Today was no exception. She'd tried to reassure her only daughter that her siblings were not only going to like her and accept her, but most likely fall in love with her wit and personality upon meeting her. But it had taken her son's matter of fact statement to convince her that she was doing the right thing, and that no matter how their meeting turned out, he'd be there by her side. That alone was what Samantha had needed to hear to calm her fears.

They ate breakfast together, with Marla's grandchildren joining them at the tail end of the meal. Both looked still half asleep but waking quickly to the smell permeating from their tiny kitchen.

"Why are you going up north mom?" Makala asked her mother, in between bites of French toast.

Never one to lie to her children, she answered as honestly as she could. "You both know that grandma will always be my mom, but that I was born to another woman named Elizabeth. Well, Elizabeth is in heaven so I'll never get to meet her, but she had another son and two daughters after giving me to your grandma, and they would like to meet me. So, as long as you promise to behave for your grandmother, Uncle G and I are going to take a quick drive up to Old Forge and meet them. Is that okay with you guys?"

Both of her kids thought about it for a brief moment, with her son speaking first. "So, this means, that if you meet them and then we meet them, we get a new Uncle and two more Aunts, right?"

Not sure where her son was heading with his line of reasoning, she answered anyways. "Yes, that's correct. Why?"

"Cool, do you think that's three more Christmas presents for us next year?" he asked, completely serious.

"Maybe they'll have presents for us this year when mom meets them today?" Makala offered.

"Guys, I'm going to meet them today, not hoping for presents, but simply to meet them for the first time. We have a lot to talk about and I'm sure that if we all get

347

along, then there will be a time that you'll get to meet them. This is all sort of new territory for me, so hang tight with all of the questions that I know you must have. But I promise you guys, that if there are presents, I'll make sure to put in a good word for you two and let them know that you've been on Santa's good list this year," she kidded.

"That's so lame mom," Michael added, with everyone bursting into laughter.

Everyone at the Brown household finished their breakfast with Marla insisting that she'd take care of the dishes in order for her daughter to finish packing her overnight bag, just in case it was needed. Samantha informed her mother that she had no intention of spending the night at their camp, but just to appease her, went upstairs to pack anyway. She took that opportunity to confide in her son.

"Your sister is wound tighter than a drum this morning. She's literally a basket case because she's so worried that her biological siblings won't approve of her and accept her," she confided.

"Mom that's utterly ridiculous and Sam should know that! Anyone who meets her and doesn't like her instantly, in my book, is an idiot, and not worth associating with," he responded, quick to defend his only sister.

As she stood back, listening to her son immediately come to his sister's defense, she couldn't help but feel proud. Despite her husband leaving her high and dry, she'd been able to raise two remarkable, kind children. Not only did they both have advanced degrees, great jobs and nice things to show for all of their hard work; but both her son and her daughter were the kind of individuals who would stop and help a stranger, or give their last nickel to someone in need. Samantha, Marla thought, was possibly too nice, and that's why her ex had been able to run off with his girlfriend, draining her entire bank account. But that was water under the bridge. Looking at her now, and the home that she'd made for her two children, Marla knew that Samantha could do anything she set her mind to. And if meeting her biological siblings and having them accept her was on the agenda for today, Marla knew that it would not only happen, but be a piece of cake. She took the brief moment that just she and her son were alone in the kitchen to make one request.

"G, I know that they're going to love your sister, and I'm sure the meeting will go off without a hitch; but please, if for any reason, it's not going as planned, or they're not what they professed to be, please get Samantha out of there and bring her home. I don't want my girl to be disappointed or see her get hurt."

"Mom, I promise you, they will not hurt her. No one will ever hurt Sam again if I can help it."

Knowing her son meant every word, she turned her back toward the sink once again, in order to avoid him seeing the tears forming in her eyes. He didn't have to see her face to know, and simply walked up behind her and put his hands on her shoulders.

"Mom, nothing changes today. We are still her family. They share the same blood but we are her family. That simple. So, let's be happy for Samantha okay," he asked, reassuringly.

Knowing he was right, she sniffled and responded. "I know. They are her sisters and brother, but we are her family and Sam meeting them today is a good thing, and hopefully some type of closure for all of them. I guess I just had a little panic attack, worrying that she wouldn't need us anymore," she confided.

"Mom, there will never be a time that I don't need you and my idiot brother," Samantha said, as she entered the kitchen after hearing the tail end of their conversation. And they will NEVER replace you guys; you have to believe that."

Her children entered the kitchen to find their mother, uncle and grandmother is a group hug. Grabbing a Gatorade, Makala turned to her brother and stated, "Grown ups are so weird."

With everyone bursting into laughter, despite the tears shared by all, they smiled, knowing that it was time to move forward with the day. Marla wished them well, and gave her daughter one more hug for reassurance and then watched her children walk away and toward potential new beginnings for her daughter. She refused to dwell in self-doubt about her relationship with her daughter, nor would she worry about how their meeting would go.

Instead, she squared her shoulders and took off in search of her grandchildren. "Anyone around here still interested in going tubing today," she asked, knowing what the answer would be.

~Chapter 49~

Just about the time that Sam and her brother were pulling out of her driveway in Oneida and starting their journey toward the mountains, Deidre was pulling plates out from underneath her sibling's forks and clearing the table. Her nervous energy was apparent, but no one teased her about it as they were all a little on edge as well. Good, bad, or indifferent, they were going to meet their mother's daughter in a few short hours and everyone involved wanted the day to go off without a hitch.

Taking her que, they each got up and helped her clear the table, and clean up the kitchen. Since Deidre had already showered, she offered to sweep and mop the floor so that Maggie should shower, with Jena insisting that she'd vacuum, instructing her fiancée to start a fire to get the chill out of the room. Everyone worked together, knowing that they'd only get one opportunity to make a good first impression. It wasn't that they were trying to show off for their sister, they just wanted to make sure everything looked welcoming.

Maggie shut the door to the bathroom and turned on the shower. Knowing that it always took a minute or two for the pipes to warm up and provide something other than ice water, she took the opportunity to shoot Garrett a quick text.

"Hey. Good morning. I'll be home from camp later this evening if you'd like to get together..."

Garrett heard his phone ding but didn't look at it as he was driving at the time it pinged. Figuring it was just the office or one of his many clients who thought it was alright to ask his advice, despite it being a Saturday, and a holiday week, he kept on driving, reminding himself to check his phone when he stopped.

When he didn't respond right away, Maggie found herself slightly irritated as she stripped and jumped into the shower that remained tepid, bordering on warm. She showered quickly, and pushed any thought of him out of her mind.

As Samantha and her brother turned off Route 12 and onto Route 28, the reality started to hit. Out of the corner of his eye, he saw his sister's facial expression change, though she remained silent. He continued driving, focusing on the road ahead, but reached over, squeezing her hand.

"It's going to be okay; I promise. I'm here Sam, and I've got your back."

"I know. Thanks."

They rode in silence until they hit the outskirts of town, slowing as they entered Thendara.

"I brought a bottle of white wine," she said, breaking the silence. "Do you think I should stop for a bottle of red, just to be safe?"

Knowing it wasn't about the alcohol that she bringing to meet her siblings, for the first time, he answered her noncommittally. "Sure Sam, we can stop at the liquor store and grab a bottle of red just to be safe." He parked in front of the first liquor store he spotted, and turned toward his sister. "I think you're fine with what you brought, but we can go in if you'd like. Or we can just sit here in my car until any signs of a panic attack pass," he offered, smiling.

He knew her so well, she thought to herself. And he was right. Stopping wasn't about the wine. She just needed another minute to conquer her self-doubt. He let the car idle, in order to keep the temperature up as the current outdoor temperature was a balmy 28. It only took her less than thirty seconds to regroup. She relaxed, and addressed her brother.

"Alright I'm good. Like me or not, let's do this!"

"Yup," was all he said, putting his car back into drive. With minimal traffic, they made their way quickly through the heart of Old Forge and toward Inlet. Less than fifteen minutes later, the GPS was announcing that there had arrived at their destination. Pulling in behind a Lexus,

Prius, and Jeep, both sister and brother took in the view in front of them. There, nestled in a very wooded lot, was a quaint looking cabin, complete with metal roof and stone accents. Large wooden columns that had once been massive trees held up the front porch, welcoming its' guest. Though they couldn't see the water from where they stood, they knew it was there, and both were curious to see what other surprises their visit had in store for them.

Inside, Sinjin alerted Maggie immediately that they had company. She called for her dog to heel, but for the first time since he was a pup, he ignored her, which completely pissed her off. Grabbing her dog to lock him in the laundry room, she told Joshua that their guest had arrived. Joshua and Deidre made their way toward the door to welcome Samantha as they heard Maggie scolding her dog, dragging him away.

Though her brother had anticipated greeting his sister's siblings with her, once he shut his car off, she turned to him, asking him to let her do it on her own. She said that she wanted meet them alone initially. She asked him to give her five minutes and then he could join her, to which he reluctantly agreed. He started his car again, wished her luck and watched her walk toward the next chapter in her life.

Before Samantha could chicken out, Deidre whipped open the door, smiling.

"Oh my God, you're really here!" she said, pulling Samantha and the wine bottle she was carrying, into a bear hug. The moment that Josh looked into his sister's eyes, he knew with 100% certainty that the woman presently being engulfed by his sister, was in fact, their mother's daughter. The resemblance was uncanny and unnerving, all at the same time.

"Dee, you're smothering our sister, let the woman breathe," he laughed. When she finally released Samantha, she wiped the tears from her eyes, and greeted her.

"Hi. Guess you figured out by now, I'm Deidre, and I'm really happy to meet you. Oh my gosh Josh, she's really beautiful, isn't she," she added, as if Samantha couldn't hear her, despite standing two feet away.

"Yes she is, and looks like she could be mom's twin, well at least when she was her age," he added, stepping forward, hand outstretched. "Welcome Samantha, I'm Joshua, your brother. And it's really a pleasure to meet you."

Front his vantage point in his car, her brother saw the door open, but not much more. He could tell that she'd been greeted and welcomed there on the front step, but couldn't make out their faces. Though he was dying to be at her side, should she need him, he remained seated in his car as promised. He'd give her another couple minutes and then he'd join her inside.

Jena opened the door, summoning everyone inside and out of the cold. As they entered the foyer, Maggie came around the corner and stopped in her tracks. Seeing this woman, her sister, standing in their mother's cabin was like a punch in the gut. There was no denying that the woman presently sizing her up was in fact, biologically related to not only their mother, but them. It was like looking at a ghost. Her posture was exactly the same as their moms had been, but it was her eyes that solidified everything. Samantha had their mother's eyes, expressive and all knowing; the kind of eyes that seem to pierce ones' soul when they looked at someone, which was exactly what she was doing to her at the moment.

Snapping out of it, she spoke. "You must be Samantha. Glad to see you found your way up okay. Welcome."

"Thank you. You must be Maggie."

"Yup, the one and only. Come on in and make yourself comfortable."

"Thanks. Um, this is kinda crazy isn't it? And am I the only one who's really, really nervous right now?" Samantha asked sincerely.

Jena answered for everyone. "I'm Jena, Joshua's fiancée, and let me also welcome you to the family. Samantha, I might not be blood related to you, but even as just a bystander, I've been wound and nervous all morning so I can't imagine what the four of you are feeling. I just know that Elizabeth would be so incredibly proud of you guys right about now, and not to sound silly, but I think that she's up there in heaven just smiling away at this very moment."

Everyone let what Jena had said sink in, hoping that somehow it was true. They made their way toward their family room, with Samantha following their lead.

Just as they were seated, their doorbell rang, startling everyone. Samantha quickly spoke up, explaining that her brother had come up with her for moral support, and in case she needed a quick escape. Everyone laughed, with Maggie jumping up to get the door.

She heard her dog barking in the laundry room and made a mental note to let him free once everyone was settled back in the living room. Distracted by her dog's incessant barking, she whipped open the door to let her sister's brother in, and found herself face to face with the man who had invaded her dreams on more than one occasion.

"What the hell?" she said out loud, staring up at the man with piercing blue eyes staring down at her, dumbfounded.

"What are you doing here?"

"Hi Mags, I was about to ask you the same question."

"I live here Garrett, but that doesn't explain what you're doing here!" she said, rather flippantly, starting to put the pieces together in her head, and not liking the answer.

"Huh, well this certainly just got interesting," he said, looking past Maggie to see Josh approaching.

Maggie felt the room start to spin, but kept herself together long enough to spit out the words "You're Samantha's brother?"

"Yes mam, the one and only. And from the look on your face, you look like you'd better sit down or have a stiff drink Mags," he said, touching her arm.

Recognition shown in Joshua's face as he made eye contact with the man presently standing in their foyer. He knew his sister's temper and wasn't quite sure why she was sounding so pissy to the guy who obviously was Samantha's brother, until it clicked with him where he knew him from. "Aren't you the guy from our mother's attorney's office?" he asked, questioningly.

"Yes I am, and it's nice to see you again Josh. And I think I really could use a drink if you've got any more of that beer that's in your hand," he said, as the pieces of the puzzle started falling into place."

Samantha and Deidre remained in the living room talking as Jena excused herself, making her way to the kitchen to see where everyone was. The second she entered and saw the three of them together, she laughed at the craziness of the situation. "Garrett Brown, is that you?" she asked, already knowing the answer.

"Wow, this whole day is definitely turning out differently than I'd expected. Yes, Jena, it's me, and it's very nice to see you again, despite these really strange circumstances. I'm not quite sure what's going on, but I think it's all starting to come together." Josh handed him a beer as they made their way into the living room to join Samantha and Deidre. Samantha smiled seeing her brother, and motioned for him to join her on the couch.

"I see you've met my brother. G, this is Deidre, Joshua and his fiancée Jena, and my sister Maggie. Guys, this is my brother Garrett," she said proudly. Upon speaking she realized that the air had almost immediately changed in the room, but wasn't sure why. It took a moment for anyone to speak, with Garrett finally cluing his sister in.

"Sam, you know how mom always says that everything happens for a reason? Well, you're going to get a kick out of this one, and so will she when we tell her someday. You know that young woman that I've told you about, that I'm pretty hooked on?" he started, speaking to his sister, but looking across the room at another woman, still standing, and obviously still fuming. "Well, funny thing about that is that her name is Maggie, and from what I'm gathering here, she happens to be your biological sister."

"Oh my God G, you've been sleeping with my sister?" she blurted out unexpectedly. Quick to defend himself, he started his rebuttal. "Sam, I've been seeing someone who's not only smart, but beautiful, and someone who makes me look forward to the next time that I can spend time with her. Our dogs love one another, and I think she's rather sweet on me as well," he kidded. "And remember Sam, it appears that you're definitely blood related to her, but I am not, so I know this might take a little bit of getting used to, but I plan on continuing to see her."

Maggie listened to what he had to say, and then finally spoke for herself. "Garrett, this really is way too weird for me. I mean, I love our time together, but you're my newly found sister's brother, and this whole thing just became really f'd up." She stood, and excused herself, escaping to the kitchen, with Garrett on her heels.

The second they were alone, he reached to touch her sleeve. She turned on him and blew up.

"You knew! This whole damn time, you knew!" she accused. "When you knew I was spending time up here with my family, and you knew that I was going through some really intense things, you sat back knowing that I was sleeping with you and that my biological sister is your sister too! Oh my God, it's so disgusting!" she nearly screamed, running her hands through her hair. "I can't do this Garrett, I can't! I know we're not blood related, but oh my God!"

Feeling his temper rise, he switched from lover to attorney in a New York minute. "First of all, Maggie, I DID NOT know about you, nor did I know that my sister was your sister. If you recall, you kept your reasons for meeting with my business partner, tight lipped. You never once told me anything about you having a half-sister, let alone it being Samantha. And even if you had, I would have had no clue that it was my sister! She, like you, is close mouthed about everything, and I had no idea until I was sitting outside in my car, wondering if I was going to have to pick up the pieces if my sister's new family hurt her in any way. It was then, and only then that I saw your damn Jeep, and realized whose camp this was. That's when I raced to the front door and rang the god damn doorbell. So, if you think that this hasn't shaken me a bit too, then you're more thick headed than I thought you were!"

She took a moment to let what he'd said, sink in. Despite his attitude and obvious anger with her at the moment, she could tell from his sincerity, that he wasn't lying, and that maybe she should consider how he might be feeling about the situation as well. "Back."

"What?" he asked, having no clue what back meant."

"Back," she said again, allowing a slight smile to cross her lips. "Lake side of a home is the front. You came in the back counselor," she responded, this time breaking into a full-blown smile. "Give me a second to refill my glass, and I think we can go rejoin the rest of them. They're probably taking bets on whether or not we've killed each other yet," she laughed. He waited long enough for her to fill her glass, then pulled her into an embrace. "It's going to be okay Mags. No matter what, this is not going to affect you and me. Promise me you won't let it."

"I'm not going anywhere Garrett," she replied. "But you have to admit, this is really weird."

"Yup," he said, allowing his lips to crash down on hers.

"Hey, when you two are done swapping spit, you think you both can join us back in the living room so we can all get acquainted?" Josh teased, exiting the kitchen as quickly as he entered it.

Samantha, Deidre, Jena and Josh continued talking while Garrett and Maggie worked out what they needed to in the kitchen. When they rejoined the others, they were hand in hand, causing everyone in the room to smile.

"We're better now," he offered. "So, give us a minute to get situated, and let's get this party started," he offered, bringing Maggie's hand up to his lips and kissing it.

They sat down, and for the next two hours, they talked incessantly, as Garrett and Samantha told them about growing up in the Brown household. They told Joshua, Maggie and Deidre everything they could think of, and answered every and all questions asked of them; with everyone realizing that they'd all been raised in relatively similar surroundings and with the same type of values. When it was Elizabeth's children's turn to talk about their upbringing, Samantha listened intently, trying to visualize what life must have been like before and after they lost their father, forcing their mother to become a single parent. She listened as they described their mom, and told story after story about growing up in their home. When the stories slowed, Deidre excused herself, running up the stairs toward her bedroom and back down again, cradling something in her arms. She walked over toward Samantha, and handed her a picture.

"This is our mom. She was about your age when this was taken. I want you to have it Sam. You look so much like her; you are as beautiful as she was, both inside and out. Our mother was one of the kindest, warmest, most nurturing women I've ever known; and in the two or so hours since we've met, I can tell that you're just like her, and I'm so incredibly glad that you've entered our lives."

Completely floored by her newly found sibling's proclamation, Samantha didn't really know what to say. So instead of answering, she stood, and stepped forward, embracing Deidre, whispering "thank you."

Jena took the opportunity to stand, grab a couple more beers for Garrett and Joshua, and top off everyone else's wine glasses. She also brought out the cheese and cracker platter that they'd made up earlier in the morning. When everyone was once again settled, relaxed and making small talk, Joshua remembered their attorney's instructions. He waited until the timing seemed right, and then chose his words, and spoke.

"Samantha, I know that this is all really new to you, as it is for us as well. I know that Deidre explained to you during her initial correspondence, that we didn't know of your existence until after our mother passed away, and we met with her attorney to review her estate and will. She made herself very clear about the circumstances behind your conception, birth, and subsequent adoption. We could tell you what she told us, but I think it would be better coming directly from her."

Slightly confused, she addressed Joshua, making eye contact with him, and then Maggie and Deidre. "I don't understand. Your mom is gone so I'm not quite following how she can explain anything to me."

Maggie spoke up. "Sam, our mom made several tapes prior to her passing. Her attorney played them for us during our meetings with him shortly after she died. When she asked us to find you, she told us that if and when we located you, to play you a tape, if we ever got to the point where we met you. None of us have viewed the tape, so I honestly have no idea what will be on it; but if you're up to it, we can play it for you now. It may or may not answer some of your lingering questions."

Samantha thought about what they were offering her. Her biological siblings had been nothing but gracious in opening their home to her, honest in their answers to her questions, and overall kind. They owed her nothing but were offering her something she'd stopped dreaming about once she learned that her mother had passed.

Unsure whether she was psychologically really to see and listen to her mother, her brother spoke up.

"Sam, this is so amazing! What an opportunity. Your mother had the foresight to make you a tape that may or may not explain everything that anyone who was adopted, asks. She must have cared about you very much, even after she surrendered you; and you have been very blessed to have been born to someone that caring. I envy you and hope that you understand what an opportunity this is. Please let them play the tape that your mother wanted you to see," he coaxed.

She took a deep breath, and addressed everyone in the room. "I'm not sure I can handle this, but I also realize that this truly is a dream come true. What you three have given me today is beyond anything I could have ever hoped for and for that I'll be forever grateful. And despite the fact that I know I'll probably use up your entire box of Kleenex, yes, yes I'm ready and would very much like to see whatever tape your mother left for me."

"Alrighty then, let's see what mother has to say this time," Maggie said, turning the TV on and putting the DVD into the Blue Ray player. "She certainly has surprised us with her other tapes, and I bet this one won't be any different," she laughed, hitting the play button.

It took a few seconds for the tape to start playing and when it did, the scenes were snapshots of the very cabin that they were presently in. There were shots of the water, mountains in the distance, loons floating just beyond their deck, shots from Christmas's past and then their mother came onto the screen, saying nothing initially, but smiling and looking directly into the camera lense, and into Samantha's eyes and heart. They watched their mother silently wipe a tear from her eye, and then speak, in a near whisper.

"Oh Joshua, Maggie, and Deidre; if you're watching this, it means you've found my daughter and she's there with you. You will never know the gratitude and love I'm feeling right now. You have made me so happy and I will forever be in your debt for reaching out to Michelle, when I was too much of a coward to do it. Thank you, my loves; thank you."

"I'm so sorry, I don't know your name so please excuse me ineptness for not calling you by your correct name. I'm Elizabeth, and to me, you will forever be my Michelle, my first-born child. I wish that I could be there to apologize and explain everything to you in person. But if you're watching this DVD with my other three beautiful children, I know that my being there in person is not possible. First and foremost, if you take nothing else away from this tape, know that you were never a mistake, and that you were loved. I hope that someday you are reunited with your birth father, and when that happens, I want you to know that he fought, fought like hell, to keep you, and even after we'd relinquished you, I found out after it was too late, that he had hired an attorney to try and get you back. Your father is an amazing man, a wonderful man, and I hope that if fate is kind, you will get an opportunity to not only meet him, but form a relationship with him. His name is Danny, Daniel O'Malley, and he was my first love. You were conceived out of love Michelle, know that. Danny and I lost our virginity together, were high school sweethearts and if circumstances back then hadn't interrupted our plans, we would have gotten married. But the past is the past, and I guess everything happens for a reason. I carried you for nine months, but it was never destined in the stars for me to be your mother. I pray that the woman who you know as your mother provided you with more than I ever could. I gave you up Michelle, in hopes that the ones who adopted you could provide you with what I couldn't. I was eighteen years old, and terrified of becoming a mother. I could barely take care of myself, and maybe I took the coward's way out, but you need to know, that I held you and took care of you for the first seven days of your life and those seven days were seven of the most wonderful days of my life. When the time came, I didn't want to surrender you, but knew that I had to, to give you the kind of life that you deserved. Please understand," she said, again looking directly into the television screen and directly at Samantha, "there has never been a day since I surrendered you, that I haven't thought about you and wondered where you were, how you were, and hoping that you were okay. I never stopped loving you Michelle, never. And although I married Joshua, Deidre and Maggie's father, whom I loved dearly; I never stopped loving your father for giving me, you."

Everyone continued watching the DVD that Elizabeth had made, listening to her tell not only Samantha, but her other children as well, the circumstances surrounding her pregnancy and birth. As the tape continued, it took everyone a moment to realize that the doorbell had rang. Joshua hit the pause button, freezing his mother mid-sentence, in order to get up and answer the door. Having no idea who was ringing their doorbell, Deidre followed her brother to the door, leaving everyone else in the living room.

With four vehicles in the driveway, Griffin found it odd that no one was answering the door, despite the fact that he could hear a dog barking inside. He thought that maybe they'd all gone out for a walk, but knew that if they had, Deidre's sister would have taken her dog. He stood on the landing realizing that maybe he should have texted her to let Deidre know what time they would be passing through Old Forge, but since he had been the designated driver, he wasn't going to text and drive. Pulling out his phone, he started to send her a quick note, just as the door opened beside him. It took Josh a minute to realize who it was, but not Deidre. She flung herself into his arms, welcoming him in. When finally out of her embrace, Grif explained that he, his brother and father were on their way back from Lake Placid and just wanted to show off their work to Logan who was up from Florida for the holidays. Already considering Samantha family and no longer simply a guest of their home, Josh insisted that Griffin invite his father and brother in, out of the cold. Deidre followed him back to his truck, smiling. Seeing her approach, it took Logan less than a second to understand why his little brother had fallen and fallen hard for the woman walking by his side. She was beautiful, not in a classic sense, but all natural and no pretenses kind of way. When she approached the passenger side window leaning in, despite not knowing him, she smiled addressing both he and his father like they were long lost friends. She explained that they must come inside, and that both she and her brother, who was still standing on the landing, would not take no for an answer. Quickly realizing that it was futile to argue with the woman, they exited the vehicle and made their way inside, with introductions made once they embraced the warmth permeating from the wood stove.

Garrett wasn't sure why, but found himself instantly territorial when he watched the three men enter the room, each better looking than the one they'd followed. He quickly surmised that the older gentleman must be the younger men's father. As he stared at them, and at Maggie who was studying them, he knew that they needed to keep their visit to a minimum and move on.

Joshua made the introductions, explaining that the stranger was in fact Griffin's brother who was up from Florida for the holidays. When it came time to introduce their guests to Griffin's family, Joshua simply introduced them as Samantha and her brother Garrett. They stood as the introductions were being made, with Joshua noting how Garrett had positioned himself in between his sister and Maggie. When Griffin's father Lee shook his hand, he could tell from the firm handshake and gentle smile that he was a good man. When he smiled, he watched his face soften and dimples pop out. Samantha too was studying the men in front of her, thinking that they all were very handsome men, both father and sons. Logan, followed by Griffin introduced themselves, but when she turned to face their father, he stopped, frozen in place. His face changed in front of her, and seemed to take on a totally different expression, as if suddenly in pain. She might not be a nurse, but from working with children for years, she recognized someone who looked as though they might get sick. His coloring had gone from rosy cheeks to chalk white in a matter of seconds, and his eyes had glossed over.

"Sir, are you alright," she asked, touching his arm gently. "Do you need a glass of water or something?"

The jolt of electricity that went through his arm from her touch jostled him back to the here and now. He closed off the memories of his youth as quickly as he'd opened the floodgate. Even though his brain and heart were still in a deadlock, he allowed common sense to rule and settle him down. Maggie quickly handed him a bottle of water, which he accepted and drank heartedly. All eyes were on him, with his own sons looking at him with genuine concern.

"Thank you miss; I'm fine. I just got a little rattled because you are the spitting image of someone I knew years ago. And even though I knew that you aren't her, it just shook me up quite a lot. I'm fine now," he smiled, feeling the color return to his face. "I sure didn't mean to make an entrance quite like that," he chuckled.

Jena, who had remained detached from the introductions, continued to study the men presently standing next to their father in the living room. Always one to read a crowd, and usually do it quite well, she couldn't help herself, and acted on a hunch.

"Excuse me Lee," who was the person that Samantha reminded you of?" she asked innocently. "Her name didn't happen to be Elizabeth was it?"

Her fiancée, and two future sister in laws spun around, facing her. Deidre's look was one of confusion, Maggie's was one of pure anger, while Josh stared at her in what appeared to be disbelief. She knew that she was teetering on shaky ground, but continued anyway.

"I know that is a long shot, but I couldn't help but see the resemblance also. Samantha's mother's name was Elizabeth; and I thought maybe we're talking about the same person."

He stared at the woman standing just a few feet away and knew. Every ounce of his heart and soul knew. Afraid to touch her, or say anything to scare her away, he responded as openly and honestly as he could.

"Yes, the woman that this young lady reminds me of went by the name of Liz when I knew her and loved her, but her legal birth name was Elizabeth. My turn to go out on a very long limb," he said, squaring his shoulders and looking directly into Samantha's eyes. "Please don't think I'm crazy, please don't. But the second I looked at you, it was like I stepped back in time thirty-five years. You see, you are the spitting image of someone I knew and loved with every ounce of my being back then, and her name was Elizabeth, or Liz for short."

Samantha found herself starting to shake, while her heart was racing faster than any racehorse could. She didn't have to hear the words because she already knew where the conversation was going so she spoke up. "Elizabeth was my birth mother."

Tears filled his eyes, as he stated, not asked, one more statement. "Elizabeth and I conceived a child, a beautiful little girl, who was born October 4th, 1982; and if by chance, that is your birthday, then I believe I am your father."

Through tears, and a radiate smile, Samantha responded. "My birthday is October 4th, 1982." Though not a touchy, feely kind of person, she couldn't help herself; throwing her arms around the man standing in front of her. When his arms wrapped around her, she knew for certain that she'd found her birth father, and come home.

There wasn't a dry eye in the room as the two embraced, father and daughter for the first time. Always skeptical, Maggie was the first to speak up.

"I think it's wonderful that you've found your daughter but I'm a little confused. Mom said on the tapes that she'd left us that Michelle's birth father's name was Daniel, and your name is Lee."

"My legal name is Daniel Lee O'Malley. I started going by Lee when I joined the service. I needed a clean break from everything that reminded me of my Lizzie, so I left the name Daniel behind and started using my middle name and it just sort of stuck," he confessed.

Still holding the hands of the woman in front of him, he continued to look into her eyes. "I hope that all of this isn't as overwhelming to you as it is to me right now. I pray that you knew that you were adopted, and I pray that you were raised by parents who loved you and took good care of you. I can't speak for Liz, but I will anyway since she's not here with us to say it; giving you up was the hardest thing that I've ever had to do in my life and it shattered both your mother and I. I've never gone a day since October 4th, 1982 that I didn't think of you and say a prayer that you were alive and well. We gave you up not because we didn't want you or love you, but because we wanted you to have the world, and as two teenagers with no money and no jobs, we couldn't give it to you," he confessed.

Samantha absorbed what he was saying and saw the sincerity in his eyes. She reached over, grabbing her brother's hand and responded. "Garrett and I had a wonderful upbringing, with two loving parents and a very stable home. We weren't spoiled but we were very well taken care of and I couldn't have asked for a better family to be raised in," she replied. "Because of you and Elizabeth's selfless act, I was raised in a home full of love, discipline and respect; and I owe you my thanks for giving me up and allowing me to flourish and grow. What you and Elizabeth did must have been very hard, and I'm sorry for any pain I have caused you," she said, breaking down.

Seeing his sister cry, Garrett became very territorial. "Lee," he spoke quietly, using his attorney voice, "I think that we all will agree, that this is a lot for everyone to take in, and I'm sure that my sister is going to want to get to know you, but I think it's in the best interest of everyone, that all of this is absorbed and digested, and then we can go from there."

Griffin who had remained by his father's side, but up until this point had been silent, spoke up. "I agree with Michelle, I mean Samantha's brother; this is a lot for everyone to process, and while I can't speak for my brother, I for one, am excited about gaining a sister, so to speak, but really think we should slow down just a little, and not start planning holiday get togethers quite yet."

Deidre, who had been standing next to Griffin was shocked to hear the words leave Griffin's mouth; not because she didn't agree with the excitement part, but because she was thinking just the opposite, and was already planning weekends with her newly found sister. And then it dawned on her, and as the color drained from her, she felt like she was going to be sick, and quickly sat down, with Griffin kneeling beside her in an instant.

Now the center of attention, Deidre tried to ignore the others in the room, as she tried pursed lip breathing to calm herself. She could feel her heartbeat pounding in her head and felt dizzy and nauseous all at the same time. Griffin took both of her hands, instructing her to open her eyes and look at him, as he dictated to his brother to grab a cool cloth and a glass of water. It took a moment for her to come around, and when she did, and opened her eyes, she felt better. Taking a sip from the glass she was handed, she spoke.

"Our mother did all of this Griffin. She put us together, she put Maggie and Garrett together, and she is the one responsible for reuniting Samantha with your father. Our mom knew exactly what she was doing as she lay there dying from cancer; I know it as sure as I'm sitting here," she exclaimed!

"That's bullshit!" Maggie burst out. "If she knew where to find her daughter and her daughter's father, she would have reunited them herself and been with them."

Josh followed his little sister's line of thinking and realized that it all made sense. Speaking up, he agreed with Deidre. "I think Dee is correct. Maybe mom knew where Daniel was all along, maybe she didn't. But one thing is for certain, she loved you Daniel, with all of her heart. With that said, despite the fact that our father has been gone for years, our mother never wanted to date anyone else, and told me years ago that she'd been in love twice and had no interest in looking for a third love. I think out of respect for him, she never dated again, nor would have sought you out and interfered in your life. Whether she knew you were alive or not, I don't know. Deidre found a newspaper article that told of you being in a helicopter crash so we didn't know if you were alive either."

Daniel took in everything that Josh was saying, wondering also if his Liz had known all along where he lived. It took him a moment to respond, but when he did, he responded honestly and sincerely.

"I was in that helicopter, and one of the guys who perished was my best friend," he spoke quietly. "I was one of the lucky ones with just a few broken bones, and a wicked concussion. Regarding your mother, I don't think she knew that I'd returned to the states. I haven't attended a high school class reunion, all of our mutual friends no longer live in the area, and my parents moved away years ago. Besides, the Liz I knew was fiercely loyal, and she wouldn't have sought me out after all these years, whether your father was living or deceased."

Having an epiphany, Deidre spoke up. "Oh my God Griffin, it just dawned on me, my sister, is YOUR sister! God that sounds gross, you know, since we're, well, you know," she said, feeling herself blush.

Wanting to stop her line of thinking immediately, Griffin spoke up quickly. "There is nothing wrong with us being together Deidre! She is your sister on your mother's side, and my sister on my father's side. And I think that Josh might be right; your mother couldn't be with her soulmate, so she tried to help guide her children towards theirs. It was meant for us to meet one another and be together, you complete me and if your mother somehow had a hand in aligning our stars so that we crossed paths, then I'll forever be in her debt Deidre. I'm so madly in love with you that I don't care how it happened, I'm just so thankful that it did."

Maggie listened and heard every word spoken in the room, while she was replaying the tape they'd listened to in her attorney's office, in her head. Then it all clicked.

"Son of a bitch," she said more to herself, but drawing the attention of the room.

"What it is Mags," Joshua asked, but somehow knew the answer.

"That first f-ing tape Josh. What was it mom was insistent on me doing? Going a gym and "meeting" new people. She practically insisted that I join a certain gym and take certain classes, probably knowing full well that her daughter's brother, ie: you Garrett, would be in the class and the gym when I was there. Son of a bitch, she conned me!"

Laughing, he replied, "Maggie, I never had the pleasure of meeting your mother, nor have I been privy to any of the tapes that she made with Bradford before she passed away; but I can assure you, that she wasn't the reason we met. I've belonged to that gym for years, and up until the day that you walked in, no one nor nothing has caught my attention. Your mother might have encouraged you to join a gym, but you made the conscious decision to follow through, so us getting together is not some preordained fate, it's destiny. But I'll give your mom credit, like Griffin, I'll be forever in her debt as well," he said, smiling just enough to let his dimples show.

Samantha couldn't help but envy her two recently discovered sisters. Both had men in their lives, that adored them, whether they realized it or not. Still hurt and disillusioned with men after her bitter divorce, it was refreshing to see that true love really did exist. She looked at her brother and then at Maggie, and knew that what they had would last, despite the hurdle that her relationship to both, imposed. As she stared at her half sister, it didn't take a rocket scientist to see that she was still reeling over the fact that the man she was involved with was her brother, through adoption. Just as she was about to speak, Maggie spoke first.

"Daniel, Lee or whatever you prefer to call yourself today," she started. "How is it that you were hired for the projects at our mother's house?" she asked, almost accusatorially. "Did our mother contact you directly?"

He took a moment to formulate his words before responding.

"Maggie," he said sincerely, "The last correspondence I had with your mother was 34 years ago, on our way home from Buffalo, after she'd signed the adoption papers. I tried for weeks to speak to her following that day, and she wouldn't see me, speak with me or return my calls. You see, neither one of us wanted to give away our daughter," he said, looking directly into Samantha's eyes, "but we really weren't given a choice. Tearing apart our newly formed family ultimately destroyed our relationship, and it took years for me to come to grips with the fact that it wasn't Liz's fault, nor my fault; it just wasn't meant to be if we couldn't all be together as a family. Times were different back then and we weren't allowed to keep our daughter, despite the fact that we both wanted to. But as God as my witness, I loved your mother with all of my heart and would have done anything for her, if given the chance. Logan and Griffin's mother is a good woman, and a great mother, and I will forever be grateful to her for giving me my son's; but Elizabeth was my soulmate. She was, is, and will forever be. But in answer to your question, I was hired by your mother's real estate agent, not your mother. And until now, I had no idea that it was Liz's house, nor this camp was Lizzie's either. As he spoke, he glanced over at the TV screen that Joshua had paused when he answered the door, and gasped, seeing her face on the screen.

It was Jena who took over the situation before anyone else could say another word.

"Daniel, Elizabeth was very specific in her wishes prior to her death, and since her attorney isn't present to represent her, and while Garrett is from that office, but obviously has a vented personal interest, I'd like to be Elizabeth's voice, if you'll allow me. The tape that presently is in the DVD player was earmarked for Samantha, and while I'm sure you would love to see her face and hear her voice again, it's a very personal tape meant for her daughter. With that said, if everyone is in agreement, Elizabeth made a tape, that she wanted us to give to you, should we find you. If it's okay with everyone present, I suggest that maybe we play it here and now. I have no way of knowing how personal it is, but if you're comfortable with it, I think that maybe there's no time like the present to let Elizabeth speak," she gently coaxed.

Before his sister could interject, Joshua stepped up in alliance with his fiancée. "I agree with Jena, and think mom needs to speak her mind in order for all of us to have closure and move forward. I think we should play it, but only if everyone else is in agreement." He looked at his sisters, hoping for their support.

Maggie spoke first. "Yeah sure, what the hell. What more could she possibly surprise us with?" she laughed. "Besides, I'd really like to know if she orchestrated all of this, and knew all along. Maybe her last tape with give us answers and not more questions."

"Agreed," both Griffin and Deidre said simultaneously.

Daniel looked at Samantha and then his sons. "Yes?" he asked.

"Yes. It's time that Elizabeth tells us what she needs to tell us," Samantha spoke up, with Logan nodding in agreement.

As Jena looked around the room, as saw all of the people who'd been affected by Elizabeth in one way or another, she couldn't help but feel the love. With the exception of Logan, Daniel's eldest son, her future mother-in-law had touched so many lives, and was still doing so. As he excused herself to get the tape, even though she'd never previewed it, Jena knew in her heart that the last and final tape that Elizabeth had produced prior to her passing, would be full of hope, promise, and love. Once they viewed it, her only wish was that Elizabeth would finally be at peace.

By the time she returned back into the room, everyone had crowded together in front of the TV, waiting patiently. She noted the positioning of everyone, and smiled to herself. Whether anyone wanted to acknowledge it or not, their families had formed a subconscious alliance with one another. She put the tape it, hit play, and proceeded to take her position between Joshua and Maggie. It took just a moment for the screen to come alive, with a view of 4th Lake, and then Elizabeth appearing on the screen, looking not only alive but healthy and well.

"Well hello everyone," she said, tears spilling down her cheeks. "It's hard for me to imagine the possibility that you're actually watching this tape but if you are, then all of my hopes and dreams have come true, and you have not only found my daughter, but also found Danny as well," she exclaimed, smiling through the tears. "Danny, I'm sorry. I'm so sorry for never believing enough in us, and I'm sorry for being childish enough to ignore your calls, letters, and visits, all those years ago. Before I go on and on about how much better our daughter's life hopefully was, in a stable home that I didn't think we could provide her; let me say, that I'm so incredibly proud of you for trying to get our little girl back. It wasn't until the day you left for boot camp that I came to my senses, raced over to your house to tell you that we'd made a horrible mistake and that yes, yes I wanted to marry you and get our Michelle back. Only then did I find out that not only were you gone, but that you'd hired an attorney and tried to get custody of our little girl. Had I not been so damn terrified of raising a child, and if I hadn't listened to what everyone was telling me I had to do, then I would have come around sooner. I'm so sorry that I didn't believe in us more."

She paused, as if still contemplating her past decisions, took a sip of whatever was in her glass, and continued. "I want you to know that I wanted to contact you from the day you left for basic training, but didn't think I had the right to reach out to you. Besides, you were gone, our daughter was gone, and I was still broken from losing both of you. I wrote you letters every day, but was too scared to mail them. You need to know that I thought about you everyday of my life from the day you left. With that said, I met a wonderful man who gave me three beautiful children and a very good life. From the moment I met him, I never once compared him to you as each of you had a different spot in my heart. Jared was a good man and he loved me and I loved him. I hope with every ounce of my being that you too found someone to love Danny. I hope that your life has given you more blessings than hardships, more joy than pain, and children as beautiful as the one we created together," she added sincerely.

"If by chance, you all are together watching this tape, then I'm sure my Maggie May has been analyzing the entire situation, thinking that I might have known your whereabouts all along. Let me be the first to say, that no, no I never tried to locate you again Danny, and I didn't for many reasons, one being out of respect for my husband.

The way I look at it," she said, slightly smiling but with a look of profound sadness in her eyes, "we had our chance and I blew it. I destroyed what we had and could have had, in so many ways. I never meant to hurt you or Michelle or anyone and every decision I made way back then, was made out of my love for you both. I now realize how wrong I was. I hope that you've had a good life Danny, and that somehow, someday you'll be able to forgive me. I truly am sorry for any and all the hurt that I've caused not only you, but my children and our daughter. There's one request I have for you, and it's for you to get to know our daughter, and love her for the two of us. I know that you will, and that makes my heart smile. There's so much more that I could say to each and everyone of you, but there aren't enough hours in the day for me to do so. When this tape concludes, don't be sad for what might have been; rejoice in what can be now that you've found our daughter. I can't be there with you, but know that I'm never far away and will never stop loving either one of you. My children are my world, always were and always will be. My final words to all of you are simple, don't take anything for granted. If you've found someone who makes you laugh, makes you smile and makes your heart sing; then love them with everything you've got and never let them go. I know that my Joshua has found that in his Jena, and I hope that you both, Maggie and Deidre, have found that by now as well. Michelle, if you haven't, know that he's out there and it's just a matter of time until you find love again. I firmly believe that with all of my heart. And lastly, Danny, know that even though we couldn't complete what we started, you were my soulmate; and I will forever love you."

The TV screen went blank. No one moved or spoke for a moment, absorbing everything that they'd just heard. Not two of them had the same feelings after listening to Elizabeth's words. It was Daniel's son Logan who finally spoke.

"Wow, I'm the only one detached from all of this, but with that said, I feel as if I've missed out somehow." He turned his body to look directly at Joshua, Maggie and Deidre, and smiled. "You were raised by a very strong woman, and what she just gave everyone in this room is probably just a fraction of the love that she most likely showered on you all of your youth, and probably until her dying day. The sincerity in her voice was apparent in every word that she spoke and I can't believe that making that tape for my father, and for all of you to view, was easy for her. That makes me wish that I'd had the opportunity to meet your mother; and that affirms why my father never quite got over her. Our father and mother had a good marriage, a great marriage by many people's standards, but even as kids, both Grif and I knew that there was something missing in it. We never saw our parents fight, and when our mother decided that she couldn't live in the states any longer, all of us were okay in letting her leave. So, in a way, I guess we grew up similar to your family, with one parent being both mother and father, and that's okay.

Like your mother, even after dad was single again, he never chose to date and to my knowledge, never tried to find your mother. In hindsight, and after listening to that tape, I'm sorry that neither my father nor your mother pursued looking for each other. It's rather sad that they both spent all this time alone for their own reasons." He turned back toward his father. "I now understand why you always told Grif and I to hold on tightly and never give up on the one you love. From what Elizabeth told you on that tape dad, she never wanted to give up on your love; it sounds like fate intervened and from where I'm sitting, made you both go in opposite directions in order for all of us to be here today."

Deidre spoke up, "Logan, you hit the nail on the head. It wasn't our parent's time back then, and despite how much they loved one another, it wasn't enough. I believe that they were soulmates, and I would like to think that the love that they shared despite being so young, was genuine. It wasn't until recently," she said, reaching over to take Griffin's hand, "that I discovered what real love is. And until I met your brother, I hadn't found my soulmate," she smiled. "I still am not convinced that our mother might not have had something to do with sort of pushing Griffin and me together, and I'll never know for certain if she did; but the one thing I know is that I'm going to heed her advice and as long as Griffin is agreeable, I've never going to let go. Maybe our parents weren't meant to be, but we are, and I know that my mother wouldn't want it any other way."

Samantha remained quiet, absorbing everything that had transpired in the last few hours that had transformed her life in ways she'd never thought possible. She had gained three siblings, found her birth father and been accepted by not only him but his two sons, her other half siblings, and had been able to not only see pictures of her birth mom but actually listen to her voice and see her "live" on TV. Every lingering question that every adoptee has, had been answered from crucial medical information that would prove invaluable for she and her children, to simply who she looked like when she looked in the mirror. Both her adoptive and birth parents had given her so much to be thankful for and despite some of the obstacles she'd faced in her life, she truly felt blessed. Garrett remained by her side, looking at her, and trying to get a read on her thoughts and feelings. When the room quieted and she felt several eyes shifting towards her, she formulated her words carefully.

"As a little girl who was raised in a pretty strict Catholic family, I was taught to say my prayers every night before I went to sleep. Daniel," she said, turning to look directly into her father's eyes, "you need to know that I always thanked God for giving me two mothers and two fathers. Our parents were always very open with Garrett and I regarding the fact that we were adopted so even as a little girl, I knew that there was someone out there who'd given me life. And I can say with complete certainty that I couldn't have asked for better birthparents than you and Elizabeth. Thanks to Elizabeth, I now understand the circumstances surrounding how I came to be, and if you're willing, I'd really like to continue to get to know you and your sons. I am a divorced mother of two great kids, whom I know will want to get to know you, that is, if you're willing to continue getting to know one another. I'm a school teacher, and have a stable job, a nice home and don't need anything from you or your sons; but if you're willing, I sure would like to get to know you better," she offered, reaching over, squeezing his hand.

"Samantha, you were my daughter from the time that you were conceived. I promised your mother way back then that I'd take care of you. I meant it then and I mean it today. There is nothing I'd like more than to get to know you, your brother, and your children. And if given the opportunity, I'd really like to shake your parent's hands someday, and thank them for raising you and loving you the way I would have, if things had turned out differently back then."

Listening to everyone speak, Deidre knew what needed to be done, and refusing to allow the day to end and everyone go their separate ways, she spoke up.

"I can't speak for my brother and sister, but I for one don't want this day to end; and I certainly know that there's so much more that we need to learn about one another. I have no idea who has what plans for New

Year's Eve, but how about we all spend it here, at mom's cabin, celebrating not only the start of a new year, new friendships and relationships, and also Elizabeth's legacy. I know that I have so much to be thankful for this year and would really like to spend the holiday here, with each and everyone of you," she said, smiling. "Our cabin isn't fancy Samantha and Garrett, but it's big enough to accommodate all of us, and your parent's too if they'd like to join us. And my invite includes you too Logan; that is, if you could make it back up again from Florida and your gorgeous weather," she laughed.

Surprising her siblings, Maggie spoke up, agreeing with her sister. "You're right Deidre, I don't like unfinished business and I think that we all could benefit from spending a little more time together. We certainly aren't fancy by any means but we would love to have you all join us for a low-key New Year's celebration here at our cabin. And Samantha, please say you'll come and bring your children. I've never given any thought to having any of my own, at least I hadn't up until this point in my life. But I really think I'll be a good aunt and I'd like to meet my niece and nephew, though it's still really weird for my analytical brain to wrap around the concept that my niece and nephew are Garrett's niece and nephew," she laughed. "Guess I'll just have to stop overanalyzing everything and let things be. Our very wise mother recently taught me that," she smiled. "It won't be a party without you Daniel, so please say you'll join us as well.

That invite goes for your sons too," she said, making direct eye contact with Griffin and Logan. "From where I'm sitting, we're all connected in one way or another, so we might as well go with it, and become better acquainted."

"I'm in," Griffin said, smiling. "And to save on space, I can bunk with Deidre," he winked.

"Thank you," Daniel said sincerely. "Thank you for all of this. My life has always been fulfilling and I've been very blessed with a good life, and a great family. I never thought that it could get any richer, but thanks to everyone in this room, I realize that I was wrong. Of course, I'd love to spend New Year's with all of you. I can't think of any other place I'd rather be, than with family."

Samantha spoke next. "I second what Daniel just said. If you're sure you're ready for my kids, then yes, yes I'd absolutely to ring in the new year with all of you. And if you meant it, then I'd really love to bring our mother with me to meet all of you. Garrett's and my adoptive father is out of the picture and has been for many years, so I'd hate to leave mom at home alone. Besides, I know she'd love to meet all of you; and while you're thanking her Daniel, don't be surprised if she's thanking you right back," she added, smiling.

As everyone in the room committed to returning to the mountains the following week to ring in the New Year, Logan finally spoke up.

"Joshua, Maggie, and Deidre; I realize that I'm definitely the lone man out here, as I have no connection to any of this, but it seems that we're all interconnected in one way or another, and if you were sincere in what you said earlier, I think I'd really like to take you up on your offer and fly back up next week to spend more time with all of you. If there's no room, I can grab a hotel room in town, that's not a problem. But Dad," he said, turning towards his father, "There's someone I'd really like you to meet. Ironically, her name is Beth, short for Elizabeth. She's pretty special and well," he grinned, "I was going to tell you another time, and not quite like this, but, well, she's going to make you a grandpa this spring." Before his father could respond, Logan added, "I was planning on asking her to marry me on New Year's Eve, and if it's okay with all of you, I can't think of a better place to pop the question than surrounded by family and friends...."

~Epilogue~

"Well my love, you always loved a happy ending," Jared smiled, holding hands with Elizabeth as they looked down from heaven. From where they were sitting, it appeared that many things had come full circle for their families, and in the end, fate and destiny had prevailed. Elizabeth looked at her four children, together in one room, laughing, smiling and forming an inseparable bond. She looked at the man who'd given her a daughter, and felt joy and love, not sadness over what could have been. In the end, everything had worked out the way it was meant to, and for that, she would be forever grateful, though she wasn't quite finished yet. With a little luck, and hopefully, heavenly persuasion, maybe Samantha's adoptive mom and her birth father would find love again, and if she could have anything to do with it, Elizabeth knew they would...

Made in the USA
Middletown, DE
16 June 2023

32152221R00234